A Heart of
Devotion

A Heart of
Devotion

A NOVEL BY TIA McCOLLORS

MOODY PUBLISHERS
CHICAGO

All Scripture quotations, unless otherwise indicated, are taken from the *New King James Version.* Copyright © 1979, 1980, 1982 by Thomas Nelson, Inc. Used by permission. All rights reserved.

Scripture cited on 306–307 is from the *Holy Bible New International Version*®. NIV®. Copyright © 1973, 1978, 1984 by International Bible Society. Used by permission of Zondervan. All rights reserved.

ISBN: 0-8024-5913-7
EAN/ISBN-13: 978-0-8024-5913-8

Library of Congress Cataloging-in-Publication Data

McCollors, Tia.
    A heart of devotion / Tia McCollors.
       p. cm.
    ISBN 0-8024-5913-7
      1. African American women—Fiction. 2. Single women—Fiction. I. Title.

PS3613.C365H43 2005
813'.6—dc22

                           2004018876

1 3 5 7 9 10 8 6 4 2

Printed in the United States of America

To my heavenly Father,
who gave me the faith to believe I can fly.

To my mother, LaVerne Carter, and all of my family,
who, if I said I wanted to fly, would help me build wings.

And to my husband, Wayne McCollors,
the wind beneath my wings.

Acknowledgments

I would be remiss if I didn't honor God first. Before I was formed in my mother's womb, He knew me and sanctified me (Jeremiah 1:5), and for that I am grateful. Lord, I pray that I will always accurately transcribe the stories You've whispered in my ear, so that my works may bring glory to Your name. I trust that You will put this book in the hands of all whom it will minister to. You are my greatest editor, agent, distributor, marketing representative, publicist, and bookseller.

I won't attempt to try and list the names of all of my family members—biological and spiritual—for fear of leaving someone out. You all should know that each of you holds a special place in my heart. Thank you for believing I can do anything. I especially want to thank my mother, LaVerne Carter; my father, Woodrow Webster; my grandmothers Ruth Carter and Maggie Webster; my little bro and sis, Trey and Jamie; Uncle Aaron, Aunt Angie, and my godparents, Douglas and Carolyn Gilmer.

I am thankful to Moody Publishers and my acquisitions editor, Cynthia Ballenger (Lift Every Voice). Thank you for believing in my work and my vision. You have been a joy to work with, and I appreciate your openness to my opinions and suggestions. You've also chosen a wonderful copy editor in Tanya Harper, who is concerned not just about the words but the message. Thanks for your eagle-eye skills, Tanya.

I honor the shepherd of my spiritual house, Bishop Eddie L. Long and First Lady Vanessa Long of New Birth Cathedral in Lithonia, Georgia. Thank you for being a mouthpiece that boldly declares the unadulterated Word of God—a Word to "conquer and possess." And to the congregation of New Birth, as Bishop would say, "Walk in your be-ness!"

There is a mighty army of trailblazers for the Christian and inspirational fiction genres who exemplify the difference between Christian fiction and "church" fiction. From one soldier for Christ to another, I salute Jacquelin Thomas (my adorable and anointed mentor), Victoria Christopher Murray, Patricia Haley, Angela Benson, Linda Hudson-Smith, Kendra Norman-Bellamy, Maurice Gray, Terrance Johnson, and others. You all have offered a word of encouragement to me. You were never selfish with information, because we all have the same goal—to glorify God. I'm glad God placed me among a group of like-minded individuals who have a passion to creatively spread the gospel through the power of the pen.

In Atlanta there is a group of talented writers who will be joining the rank of author in due season. My writing and critique group is full of aspiring and growing talent whose books will be on the shelves soon (right, ladies?). We've all become more than critique partners. Sherri, Ashea, Dee, LaMonica, Rhonda, Sharrunn, Trina, Vanessa, and Veronica have also become my friends. Keep pen to paper!

To my agent, Sha-Shana Crichton of Crichton & Associates— thank you for your literary contract expertise.

One of my first massive literary experiences was made a lot easier by Robin Green and Felicia Polk. Thank you for showing me the ropes and giving me the inside scoop at BEA 2003. And I can't forget Danita, who gave me a place to bunk!

The saying is true: "Friends are like angels who lift you up when your wings have trouble remembering how to fly." My girlfriends have stuck by me through the good, bad, ugly, thick, thin, in-between, tears, and laughter. We've done it all—some things that we'll tell and some things that we won't! But don't worry. You're bound to find some of it dropped in a book every now and then. As we always say Waverly, "You know how we do."

To the readers—without you, this book would gather dust on the shelves. Thank you for your support and encouragement. It is my prayer that after you close these pages, you will walk away with more than a good read.

Finally to my husband and best friend, Wayne. At the release of this novel, we will have entered our third month of marital bliss. I'm sure it has been one of the most exciting—and definitely interesting—times of our lives. No doubt I'm still basking in the newlywed glow. You inspire me, and I pray I'll bring honor to the McCollors name. The best is yet to come.

Dear Reader:

God coexists as a Trinity (Father, Son, and Holy Spirit). God is one in essence, but with three distinct and separate functions. The Holy Spirit is the third "person" of the Trinity. (See 1 John 5:7–8).

When a person accepts the Lord Jesus Christ as Savior, they are born again by the Holy Spirit. The Holy Spirit dwells within, convicts people of sin, instructs, and empowers (see John 14:17, 26; Romans 8:9; 1 Corinthians 12:13). In *A Heart of Devotion,* the italicized bold print is used to indicate the internal prompting of the Holy Spirit.

*A*nisha Blake had a love-hate relationship with Fridays. They symbolized the end of a hectic week at work but ushered in yet another dateless weekend. Seventy-eight weekends to be exact—not that she was counting.

Anisha tossed her briefcase on the bed and her keys on the night-stand. The blinking red light on the phone cradle caught her attention, and she picked up the cordless phone to enter the code and retrieve her voice messages.

"Hello. Sorry we missed you. We have an exciting offer . . ."

Anisha hit the delete button, stopping the automated voice before it could finish its spiel. *Stupid telemarketers.* She peeled off her suit jacket, plopped down on the edge of the bed, and kicked off her two-inch heels so she could massage the balls of her feet. She slowly worked her way up her body, kneading the sides of her thighs and twist-ing her waist, before rolling the knotted tension from her shoulders. She closed her eyes and wished for the luxury of a massage to release the stress from her body and mind.

Out of habit, Anisha picked up the phone to call her best friend,

Sherri Dawson. Her fingers found the numbers on the dial pad without having to look.

"Girl, if I'm cooped up in this apartment one more Friday night, I'll die," Anisha said when her friend answered the phone. "Another Friday night in the house, and your girl might keel over."

"Girl, don't say that," Sherri said. "The way things are going for you, you'll be at the pearly gates next Friday begging for Saint Peter to let you in."

"Very funny," Anisha said.

"What's your tally on dateless weekends now?" Sherri asked.

"Wouldn't know," Anisha said, stretching out on her bed.

"Whatever," Sherri said. "You know you can spit it out faster than your checking account balance."

They laughed easily together, and shared more than the same sense of humor. After five years of friendship, they were like salt and pepper. One was rarely seen without the other.

Anisha turned over on her stomach and propped herself up on her pointy elbows. "If your social life was any better than mine, I wouldn't have somebody to talk to every weekend, now would I?"

Anisha knew her quick-witted friend was gearing up for a comeback, so she armed herself with one of her own.

"Hey, if it wasn't for my stint with Orlando—" Sherri started.

"Live-at-home-with-his-mama-but-still-never-had-any-money Orlando?"

"Well, at least I'm not tied with your record," Sherri teased. "You're the reigning queen, and you can keep the title."

"Oh, I can see you've got jokes tonight. Keep on. I'll remember that." Anisha pushed herself off the bed and dumped her work clothes into her dry cleaning hamper.

"Well, you can always come over here if you want," Sherri offered. "I'm in for the night, so we can order some pizza and watch a couple of movies. You know, the usual stuff."

"That's the problem," Anisha said, pulling a tank top and a pair of gym shorts from her dresser drawer. "It's the usual stuff. No offense, but it's becoming a little too routine. You're my girl and all, but not tonight," she said, pulling the tank over her head. "Anyway, if I was going somewhere, I'd probably be too sleepy to move by the time I got dressed. Dudley & Associates made sure I earned every dime in my check this week."

Anisha pushed her hair back with a headband and scrubbed the remains of the day's makeup from her face while Sherri rattled on about her latest workplace drama. Anisha had never met Sherri's coworkers, but if she ever had the chance, she was sure she'd be able to point each of them out. Given Sherri's weekly updates, her office was a daily soap opera.

Anisha strolled into the living room and looked out the front window to the parking lot. A group of neighborhood kids were huddled together at the curb, their bicycles and scooters entangled in a metal heap beside them. Even their Friday nights were exciting, Anisha thought. She felt even more pathetic.

"Uhhh . . . hello? Are you even listening to me?" Sherri's voice popped back into Anisha's head. Anisha sensed her friend's annoyance.

"My bad, girl. I was in those little kids' business outside. What did you say?"

"Never mind," Sherri said. "Anyway—so your mind's made up? You're staying at home tonight?"

"Yep. It's just me and Jesus tonight,"Anisha said, yawning.

"That sounds like a plan, girl. See ya later," Sherri said.

"Okay, see ya."

Anisha shook her head and smiled at the thought of her friend. "That girl, I tell you," she murmured softly. "What would I do without her?"

Anisha's and Sherri's paths first crossed at the church's Singles Ministry picnic when they both took refuge under the same shelter to escape the pelting from a summer storm. Before the storm clouds rolled on, they'd already established a connection like lifelong friends.

Anisha went into the kitchen and scanned the spotless apartment as if a source of excitement would jump out and reveal itself. Though it was barely six o'clock, exhaustion had taken over her body. The thought of going to bed so early on a Friday evening was too depressing, so she grabbed the growing stack of mail threatening to spill from the basket on the kitchen counter. She slid the glass patio door open. The thickness of the humid air met her as soon as she walked outside.

Anisha slid the single chaise lounge closer to the small patio table and sorted through a week's worth of bills, junk mail, and magazines. She sighed as she flipped through each piece. She had grown weary of her mundane routine of life. She slaved all week and was so tired at the end of each day that she could barely function for the rest of the night. Much like tonight. She wasn't living life—life was living her.

Anisha enjoyed relaxation in the shade over the next hour and a half, watching as the setting sun cast a picturesque backdrop for the children still crowded at the curbside. She thumbed through the last mail-order catalog, then gathered the stacks of mail and went back inside. Like always, she resorted to watching a movie.

"Okay, what's on for tonight?" Anisha asked, searching the rows of movies lined on the shelves of the entertainment center against the wall. She rested her hands on her hips and stared at the massive collection of neatly arranged VHS tapes and DVDs lining the shelves.

You couldn't have forgotten about Me already. I thought it was our night together. You can spend time with Me tonight and experience love no man can duplicate.

Anisha slid a DVD into the player, sank into the plush pillows on the couch, and propped her feet on the glass coffee table. Barely thirty minutes into the movie, her eyelids grew heavy and begged to close.

Quiet time. Intimate time. We need to spend some quality time together so I can show you what your life really holds. You promised Me tonight. I've been anticipating our time together.

The shrill ring of the telephone startled Anisha out of her sleep. She jolted forward, banging the back of her ankle on the edge of the coffee table. "Shoot." Anisha winced from the pain and grabbed her throbbing ankle.

Focusing her blurry vision on the clock situated on the fireplace mantle, she wondered how long she'd been asleep. To her surprise, the clock's hands were nearing eight thirty. She didn't even remember closing her eyes, and already an hour had crept by.

The phone's ring startled her again, and Anisha fumbled to answer it before it rang for the third time.

"Hel—" She paused to clear the frog caught in her throat. "Hello?" she said again, forcing herself to sound more alert.

"Did I catch you at a bad time? Were you asleep?" the deep, mellow voice asked.

"No," she lied. "Just watching a movie." Anisha sat up straight on the couch as if she could be seen by the person on the other end. Even in her half-comatose state she knew the voice belonged to Tyson Randall.

Tyson and Anisha had first become acquainted with each other while serving as chaperones for the church youth field trips. Since then, he'd visited her apartment at least twice when she'd had some of the youth ministry leaders over for a board game party night. To Anisha's pleasure, their paths were crossing more frequently lately. And though Tyson had given Anisha the impression that he might have been interested, he'd never pursued anything in the year since they'd met. It wasn't until recently that he finally asked for her number. She gave it to him without hesitation and wondered what had taken him so long to ask in the first place.

"I can't believe you're home on a Friday night," Tyson said. "Most beautiful women have men beating down their doors."

Knows how to pour on the charm, Anisha thought. "I had plans for tonight but decided to chill out." She looked at the television where her so-called plans would soon have credits rolling down the television screen.

"So is it too late for a lady to have company?" Tyson asked.

Anisha glanced at the clock again. Any other time she would have turned down the offer for a man to come to her house on the first date. *But then again, this wasn't a date. Was it?* She convinced herself further. *It's still a decent hour.* She needed Sherri's advice and searched for a subtle way of escape but found none. "I think that's my other line. Can you hold for a second?" Anisha asked. *Bump it.* She didn't have time for subtlety.

"Sure."

Tyson's voice sent chills up her spine, and she could have sworn she felt the feeling travel to the end of her fingertips as she clicked over and called Sherri.

"Hello?" Sherri answered on the first ring.

"It's not a man," Anisha said, laughing. "You could at least let the phone ring a couple of times so a brotha won't think you're desperate."

"Whatever, girl. What's up?"

"Tyson is on the other line and wants to know if he can come over. It's not even nine o'clock yet. What do you think?"

"Looks like somebody's dateless weekends are coming to an end."

"It's not a date, Sherri. Hurry up, girl—he's on the other line."

"Tyson? I think if he wants to see you, he can pick you up and take you out. Maybe you can let him slide this one time, but only if—" Sherri started to list her acceptable conditions before Anisha interrupted her.

"That's what I thought you'd say," Anisha said. "I'll tell him it's all right."

"Whaddya call me for in the first place if you were going to do what you wanted to anyway?"

"Who knows? Bye."

"And for the record," Sherri defended herself, "I didn't think you were a man calling. I happened to be picking up the phone to make a call when it rang."

"Yeah, and I won the lottery this morning. Look at your caller ID next time, girl. You'll break your neck trying to get to the phone. Bye!"

Anisha clicked over before Sherri had a chance to respond. "Hello, Tyson? Sorry to keep you holding. So when are you leaving?" Anisha was shocked by her own boldness, but it was too late to retrieve her words. *Bump it.* That was her motto for the night.

"I take it that means it's okay."

Anisha's face grew warm, and she was thankful he couldn't see her blushing. "Yes, it's fine."

"Cool. Give me a few minutes, and I'll be on my way."

"All right."

"And could you do something for me?" Tyson asked.

"Sure. What is it?"

"Tell your girl I said thanks for the approval."

Anisha couldn't help but laugh. "You busted me on that one," she said, then made sure Tyson remembered directions to her house.

Anisha started to question her decision to let Tyson come over but pushed it out of her mind before she had a chance to think twice. Shouldn't two adults be able to enjoy a good time together?

Anisha lounged on the couch for a few minutes before a wave of frenzy suddenly rushed her into the bedroom to find a change of clothes. The last thing she'd expected was company, especially not Tyson.

Anisha tugged at the stretched elastic in her gym shorts while rummaging in her closet for something that didn't need ironing. Based on Tyson's explanation, she calculated that he lived less than twenty minutes away. Give and take a few minutes for him to get ready, she only had a short time to freshen up and get her act together.

Anisha slipped on a pair of jeans and a soft pink cotton shirt and walked into the bathroom to inspect her impromptu outfit.

"Voila." Anisha admired herself in the mirror, turning to examine herself from every angle. She tucked the shirt in her jeans and ran her hands down the sides of her thighs. The jeans were a little snug, but still modest, she decided. Anisha leaned forward to study her bare face in the mirror then opened one of the drawers to find her cosmetic case. "What am I doing?" She put the cap back on her lipstick tube. "It's Tyson, and we're just watching a movie." She settled for a little lip balm and stuffed her cosmetic case back in the drawer. "Good enough," she said, staring at herself in the mirror.

Anisha shook her head and laughed.

"Who am I fooling?" She reached for her compact again and

dusted a light layer of powder across her nose and forehead. She dabbed on a neutral lip gloss, brushed her eyelashes with a coat of mascara ,and slid the headband from her hair. She ran a comb through her freshly layered bob cut and framed her face with her tresses.

When Anisha was finally satisfied with the woman looking back at her, she made a quick run-through of her apartment for any misplaced items and, of course, found none. The handles and surfaces of the black appliances in the kitchen gleamed with impeccable cleanliness. As always, the rest of the house would pass any scrutinizer's white-glove test.

Anisha nestled on her couch. According to her watch, she still had five minutes to spare. The second hand on her watch seemed to lap slowly, making those five minutes seem more like five hours.

Outside, Tyson sat in his car, now watching the fourth minute pass on his dashboard clock while he built up the nerve to go to Anisha's door. He'd decided to take a chance and call her. It would be their first time getting together outside of a group setting, and he wondered if it was a good idea. He knew it wasn't the proper thing to do, but his lips had moved faster than his mind. He usually didn't operate like this—practically inviting himself over to a lady's house. Maybe it was fear. Something a little less formal than a date to break the ice.

Tyson sensed a sort of sweet mystery about her and was attracted to it. He'd promised God he wouldn't pursue a relationship with a woman for at least a year, but when he first met Anisha last year, he wished he could've taken the promise back. But now with his period of consecration over, he determined to know more about this woman.

Tyson ran his hand over his hair and looked at the clock to see the fifth minute pass. He'd delayed long enough.

The doorbell sent Anisha's heart racing, and she fought the urge to run to the door. An old college roommate of hers used to make her male company wait an obligatory ten seconds before she opened the door. As foolish as it had sounded then, Anisha started the count in her head. She didn't want Tyson to think the only thing she had to do was sit around and wait for him to arrive. Even if it was true.

Seven, eight . . . That's long enough. Anisha opened the door.

"Hi." They greeted each other with a friendly embrace, and Anisha felt the weight of nervousness lift from her shoulders. "Come in," she said. "Did you have any trouble getting here?"

"No. Everything looked pretty familiar," Tyson said.

"Good," Anisha said, easing the door closed behind him. "Make yourself comfortable."

When Tyson walked in, Anisha couldn't help but notice how his biceps pushed against the sleeves of his shirt. Funny how she'd never noticed them before. Before she could continue her personal inventory, Tyson turned and handed her a Styrofoam container.

"On the way over, my stomach reminded me I hadn't eaten, so I stopped for some hot wings—mild ones for you, though. I remembered from the time we had the youth lock-in that you don't like spicy foods."

Anisha was impressed he'd noticed and flashed him an approving smile. "Thanks. These will definitely hit the spot. Let me grab some plates and napkins," she said, setting the container on the coffee table.

Tyson spotted Anisha's movie collection and headed toward the entertainment center.

"Thirsty?" Anisha asked, her head stuck in the refrigerator.

"Yeah. Whatcha got?"

Anisha could feel him watching her. She turned around to see that he had abandoned his search of the movies and was leaning on the bar separating the small kitchen from the living room area. She pushed around several bottles, then rearranged two containers of leftovers while she built up the nerve to meet his glance. She briefly closed her eyes, hoping his appearance wasn't a figment of her imagination.

She glanced over her shoulder. Tyson was definitely still there. Every muscle of him. "Whatcha want?"

Tyson pointed to a pitcher on the top shelf. "What about the classic?"

"The classic it is." Anisha poured two tall glasses of Kool-Aid and handed them to Tyson. She grabbed a stack of napkins and two plates and joined him on the couch.

"Appreciate it," Tyson said. He opened the container to reveal three piles of mild, hot, and lemon pepper wings. He rubbed his open palms together in satisfaction. "Good food, good company, and a good movie. So what's showing at Anisha's Multiplex Theatre tonight?"

"I don't know. What are you in the mood for?" Anisha stood up and perused her movie collection for the second time that day, despite the fact that she could've rattled off her entire collection from memory.

"Looks like you've got everything over there." Tyson walked over and playfully bumped Anisha with his hip. "Mind if I make the choice?"

"Go ahead," Anisha agreed. She liked a man with initiative—a man not afraid to take control. She made herself a plate and waited for Tyson to make a decision. His choice would tell her something about him, she thought.

"Ready?" he asked over his shoulder.

"Let's roll." Anisha pulled the coffee table closer to the couch so their food would be within reach.

Within a few seconds, the opening credits flashed on the screen, and Anisha logged a mental note. *Adventurous with a good sense of humor.* She stole a glimpse of Tyson out of the corner of her eye and caught him doing the same, but they both acted like they didn't notice. Instead, they turned their attention to the television, balanced a plate of wings on their laps, and watched the drama of the two unlikely detective partners unfold.

With her eyes still glued on the television, Anisha reached for her glass and barely avoided tipping it over. The splashes lifted from her glass and landed on the leather cover of her Bible. She carefully wiped it off and shoved it into an end table drawer.

Tomorrow, Lord. I promise, she thought. *Me and You.*

$\mathcal{A}$ nisha rolled out of bed at almost eleven o'clock, and her body immediately yearned for a relaxing bath. She rarely slept past eight o'clock on Saturdays, but it had been two in the morning before Tyson left. She dragged herself into the bathroom and leaned over to the tub faucet, adjusting the water until she found the perfect temperature. Warm enough to make her ease in cautiously, but not so hot that the steam turned her bathroom into a sauna.

Anisha poured a capful of bubble bath into the tub and tuned her bathroom radio to her favorite jazz station. She stepped into the water and sank down until the bubbles covered her shoulders, then closed her eyes and slipped away to the night before.

After the movie ended, she and Tyson had sat on the couch in deep conversation. Anisha soaked up as much as she could about the man whom, until then, she'd only really known on the surface. She listened intently while Tyson shared his vision of starting a nonprofit organization to mentor young at-risk males in one of the rough southwest Atlanta neighborhoods. In the meantime, he worked as a computer tech consultant and volunteered as a counselor for the Boys to Men Youth Program housed in the building he eventually wanted to renovate for his own full-time program.

"And what about you?" Tyson turned the tables on her after he'd laid out his own dreams. "What's your passion?"

Anisha sat in deep contemplation, her gaze empty. "I can't really say I've found what drives me. You know, you have all these plans when you're a kid. The possibilities seem endless. But somewhere along the way in life, you lose the ability to dream. Or you dream but you're paralyzed by fear. Fear of failure, maybe even fear of success."

Anisha tossed her words around. Tyson's questions had challenged her, and she wasn't sure she could make sense of her own thoughts.

"I guess if I could choose one thing I wanted in my life right now, it would be to dream without limits again. As far as my passion or calling? Whatever you want to call it," she said, "I'm not sure I know."

Tyson dug deeper. "Did you ever dream about having a family?"

"Oh yeah. I had it all planned out." Anisha counted the steps on her fingers. "I was going to be married by at least twenty-five. Travel to a different country every summer with my husband. Have my own business so I could work from home. And have one—maybe two—kids by now. So according to *my* plan, I'm already three years behind schedule on the husband and rounding the corner to number four."

"I feel you," Tyson said. "I thought I was close to getting married at one point in my life."

"Really?" Anisha lifted her eyebrows.

"Yeah. To a girl I dated in college." Tyson searched her eyes and seemed to sense he could continue. "Sometimes you get comfortable in a situation even though you know it's not good for you. We were going in two opposite directions anyway, but that doesn't always ease the pain. Hurt is hurt." He paused for reflection. "I think I lost out on the whole college experience. I could've been doing other things, enjoying college, been with somebody else." He shrugged his shoulders. "But you can't go back and change things, only move forward.

Life is too short to settle. Besides, if God allows a person to leave your life, there must be a purpose."

Tyson left Anisha dangling from his last words. She wanted to pick up the conversation, but words evaded her, so she waited for him to break the silence.

He stared intently into her eyes, almost as if he was trying to search her soul. "So what about you? Any heartbreaks?"

Anisha picked at an imaginary piece of lint on her shirt sleeve. "More than I care to share," she replied.

"I can respect that. No pressure," Tyson said, glancing down at his watch. "Man. Can you believe it's almost two o'clock?" He stood up to pack up their leftovers on the coffee table. "I had no intention of being here this late."

Anisha looked down at her watch. Sure enough, two o'clock had arrived with no warning from yawning or drowsy eyelids. She wasn't the least bit tired, even though she'd been fighting sleep hours earlier when the sun had barely taken its slumber for the night.

"I guess time flies when you're in good company," Anisha said. "We'll have to do it again but get an earlier start and finish on things next time." *I did it again. Where is this boldness coming from today?*

"Definitely." Tyson let himself out and stopped on the front stoop. "I'll see you later," he said, backing down the sidewalk, his hands stuffed into his pockets like a sheepish schoolboy.

"Bye," Anisha whispered when Tyson had almost reached the end of her walkway. She backed into the house and slumped against the door. When she was sure he had pulled away, she peeked out of the blinds and followed his taillights until they disappeared.

The doorbell snatched Anisha from her daydream and dropped her back into reality. The shoulder-high foamy suds in her bubble bath had been replaced by a tub of cloudy water.

"That's gotta be Sherri," she said, then jumped out of the tub and grabbed a towel. Anisha flung it around her body, wet footprints following her down the hall and into the bedroom where she peeked through the blinds to catch a glimpse of her unexpected visitor. Just as she thought, Sherri was standing on the small porch, impatiently shifting her weight from one hip to the other while talking to the door.

"Hurry up and open this door, girl. I'm burning up out here," Sherri bellowed, the May sun beating down on her neck.

Even wearing heels, Sherri had to stand on her tiptoes in order to press her eyeball to the peephole. "Okay, Anisha. Act crazy if you want to, and you'll never get Tyson's message. I saw him at the gas station a minute ago, and for all you know he's on his way over right now."

For a brief moment Anisha watched Sherri saunter away from the front door. Sherri could very well be lying through her teeth, but she wasn't taking any chances.

Anisha made a mad dash through the living room and banged her little toe on the edge of the breakfast bar. She swallowed a four-letter word pushing to escape through her lips, grabbed her stubbed toe, and hopped the short distance to the door. She could only imagine how ridiculous she looked.

Anisha threw the door open and noticed Sherri quicken her pace. The tap of her heels on the concrete had escalated to a loud thud.

"Girl, don't play with me," Anisha threatened from the doorway. "You'd better bring your little self back in here and tell me what Tyson said."

Sherri stopped midstride, swung her body around, and caught sight of her friend peeping out the door wearing an oversized pink shower cap. The stern look on Sherri's face melted and amusement spread across it. She was the spitting image of a Cheshire cat. Evidently Anisha's one-handed struggle to hold a towel around her and use the other to point a demanding finger was enough to convince Sherri to come inside.

"Pitiful," Sherri said, shaking her head. She ran back up the sidewalk and dipped inside before Anisha could change her mind and make her meet the door face to face. Again. She plopped on the couch and picked up a *Black Enterprise* magazine.

"And?" Anisha propped her hands on her hips.

Sherri thumbed through the magazine's glossy pages. "And, what?"

"And what did Tyson say, that's what. What else would I be talking about?"

"I don't know. What *did* Tyson say? You were the one with him last night, not me. I would've known a lot sooner if you'd answered my calls. Caller ID messes a sister up every time."

"I should've known you were lying." Anisha dismissed Sherri with a flick of her hand. "It was no big deal. We just watched a couple of movies and talked," Anisha said, freeing her hair from the shower cap.

"Uh-huh. Whatever. Stop playing and give up the dirt." Sherri sat back against the couch and crossed her arms and legs. "You're dying to tell somebody, and it might as well be me." She looked intent on extracting information from Anisha even if she had to wait it out.

"First of all," Anisha stalled, "I know you didn't make a special trip over here this morning just to get all up in my business."

"Girl, please. I'm not that desperate. I'm headed out to the mall, and you're coming with me."

Anisha held her hands up in objection. "Not today. I've got too much to do."

"Like what? Sit around and hope Tyson calls again? You need to help me find some sandals to show off these cute little toes of mine." Sherri lifted her leg high enough for Anisha to get a good look at the hot pink polish from her latest pedicure. "But getting back to last night. Are you going to tell me about Mr. Randall's visit or what?"

"Scoot over, Ms. Nosy," Anisha said. She tightened the towel around her and perched on the edge of the couch while she recounted the story to Sherri, being careful not to leave out a single detail. For once Sherri didn't interrupt until Anisha was finished reliving the moments.

"Hold up." The words flew from Sherri's mouth as soon as Anisha's lips closed. "I know you didn't say he left at two this morning. He had no business over here that late."

"Oh, so you're my mama now?" Anisha asked, standing up and heading toward her bedroom.

"No, I'm not trying to be your mama; I'm telling you like a real friend. First it starts with staying late, then he starts spending the night on the couch, then it moves to spending the night and sleeping in the same bed, and then before you know it, bam! He's stolen the cookie from the cookie jar—"

"Sherri, puhhleeezzz. You don't even know Tyson like that."

"And you don't either, remember?"

Anisha ignored Sherri and jumped to defend herself. "One late night over and you've already put the man in my bed. We talked, just like I said. Talked and that was it. And if I recall correctly, less than twenty-four hours ago, *you* were the one who agreed with him coming over."

"Well, yeah, before I knew he would be over here until the crack of dawn. You set the standard for how you expect and deserve for him to treat you now, and you won't have to worry about him cutting a fool later. I don't mean to come off as trying to be your mama. I love you. We made a vow to hold each other accountable, and I'm helping you protect your heart. Besides, I'm sure Tyson looks nothing like Jesus."

Anisha eyed Sherri with a perplexed look. "What?"

Sherri threw her hands in the air in a dramatic fashion. "It's just me and Jesus tonight," Sherri mimicked. "Remember that?" She grabbed a pillow from the couch and swatted Anisha's rear end. "You stood Jesus up for Tyson."

She's right.

"No, I didn't." Anisha rolled her eyes and picked up her shower cap from the floor. *Was Sherri right? Stood up? I wouldn't exactly use those words.* "I'm going to get ready."

"See," Sherri yelled after her. "You only walk away when you know I'm right." She threw a pillow down the hall at Anisha. "And hurry up. We've got sales to find."

Anisha disappeared down the hall and into her bedroom and reappeared about twenty minutes later wearing a beige linen sundress with a belt tied loosely around her waist. She smoothed one side of her hair behind her ear, slung a purse across her shoulder, and set a pair of shades on the bridge of her nose. "Are you ready?" she asked, peering over the top of her shades.

"You were about to get left," Sherri fussed.

"Whatever." Anisha flung open the door and bounded down the steps toward Sherri's car. "Lock the door, please."

Sherri yanked the door—it had a tendency to swell in heat—closed, but not before hearing the phone ringing inside. Anisha fumbled for the keys in the bottom of her purse, but Sherri pushed her back down the steps.

"You go back inside and you *will* get left. He'll call back."

"It could be anybody," Anisha said.

"Yeah, it could be. And the only other anybody it could be is standing right here."

"I'm not even thinking about Tyson." Anisha pouted and reluctantly made her way to Sherri's car.

"Well, if you're not, then how did you know who I was talking about?" Sherri jumped into the car and left Anisha to sulk in the middle of the sidewalk. Sherri rolled down the passenger window and said, "It's too hot to be playing out here. Let's go."

Anisha surrendered. She opened the car door and slid into the passenger's seat. Her best friend knew her well. It had been a while since she'd shared a mutual interest with a man. She was hoping it was Tyson. She wanted to hear his voice.

If you would only long to hear My voice. But it's a still, small voice you can only hear if you draw closer to Me. I have so much to share, and if we would spend more time together, you'd learn more about both of us.

Sherri backed out of the parking space and began a slow crawl through the neighborhood. She twisted off the top of a soda bottle, making an awkward attempt to sip, steer, and shift gears.

"Why are there so many doggone speed bumps in this complex?" she asked between gulps, easing over another one of the raised slabs in the road. Less than fifty yards away, two boys racing on dirt bikes darted from behind a row of bushes, whipped across the street, and jumped a nearby curb.

"That's why," Anisha said. She pulled down the sun visor mirror, then dug around in her purse for a tube of lipstick, unaware Sherri was picking up speed as she crossed what used to be the last speed bump before the management added an extra one earlier during the week.

At the last minute, Anisha remembered the newly installed speed bump near the complex mailboxes. "Wait," she cautioned, but the warning came too late. The car jolted over the cement mass, sending Sherri's red soda splashing against the window, down the steering wheel, and into her lap.

Anisha scrambled for napkins in the glove compartment while Sherri steered the car against the curb.

"Oh no!" Sherri yelled, grabbing the napkins from Anisha. She wiped down the car's interior and attempted to soak the spreading red stain from her light yellow capris and matching tank top. "I need to go change. I'm a complete mess," she said, pulling the wet shirt away from her skin.

The usual twenty-minute ride to Sherri's was prolonged by an overturned tractor-trailer on the highway. It wasn't unusual for Atlanta, an ever-sprawling city where traffic was always unpredictable. Three of the four southbound lanes of I-285 were closed, bringing traffic to a complete halt at times. The afternoon sun had nearly lulled Anisha to sleep by the time they reached Sherri's apartment.

"You coming in?" Sherri asked.

"I'm tired," Anisha said. "I'll wait out here."

"That's what happens when you let men stay overnight at your house," Sherri said, grabbing her purse from the backseat. "You're tired the next day."

"Tyson did not stay the night."

Sherri rolled down the window and took the key out of the ignition. "He came over on Friday night and left on Saturday morning," Sherri teased. "To me, that's overnight."

Anisha unbuckled her seat belt and reclined the seat. "Am I going to hear about this all day?"

"Probably."

The clicking of Sherri's heels grew distant as she ran down the sidewalk and up a flight of stairs to her apartment. Anisha closed her eyes and tuned out the rush of the cars on the nearby highway. She dozed off, enjoying the warmth of the sun tickling her face. Minutes later when she felt its warmth subside, Anisha assumed the sun was playing hide-and-seek behind a cloud.

"Hey, Miss Sleeping Beauty. How 'bout a kiss?"

Anisha nearly jumped out of the car. She was met by a mouth full of gold teeth. Tarnished gold teeth at that. She hit the button to roll up the window, but realized the keys weren't in the ignition.

The intruder held up both his hands and backed away from the window. "Calm down, sweetheart. I ain't tryin' to hurt you." He stepped back, hoisted his baggy jeans higher on his waist and leaned against a car parked beside Sherri's. "So, how can I get to know you, Miss Sleeping Beauty?"

"I'm flattered, but I have a man." Anisha hated to lie, but she'd learned that sometimes it was the only way to avoid a foul-mouthed comeback and prevent being insulted with names men wouldn't dare call their own mamas.

She reached for her purse and opened the car door. Sherri had taken the keys with her, so the windows would have to stay down. *Too bad.* She got out of the car, hit the locks anyway, then noticed another guy leaning against the bumper who seemed uninterested in his friend's quest. Anisha looked back to the smirking face that belonged to the set of fake gold caps, his eyes now roaming over her body.

Anisha forced out a cordial acknowledgment. "Have a good day." She slammed the car door and made hurried strides toward Sherri's apartment. She fought to keep her legs from running.

"Can I call you if your man's not actin' right?"

"That won't happen," she answered without turning around. "I've got it under control."

"Mmmm. I like that," he hollered after her.

Anisha trotted up the flight of stairs and burst into Sherri's apartment without knocking. She headed straight into Sherri's room and yelled out her name when she didn't see her.

"I'm in here," a voice called from the closet. Sherri wriggled out of the overstuffed closet wearing wide-legged linen pants and an embroidered asymmetrical tunic.

"Cute," Anisha said.

"Consignment shop." Sherri twirled around, then held out each leg and modeled the shoes for Anisha. "Which one?"

Anisha pointed to the low-heeled slide on Sherri's left foot, and Sherri disappeared back into the closet to find its missing mate.

"What are you doing in here anyway?" Sherri asked.

"Let's just say I was awakened out of my dream into a nightmare." Anisha said, patting tiny beads of sweat from her brow. "Got any bottled water and napkins?" Anisha decided to wet the napkins to wipe up the probably now sticky pop in the car.

"Bottom shelf of the fridge, and the napkins are in the cabinet. Can you grab two bottles of water? I think I've had my share of soda today."

The doorbell rang as soon as Anisha walked into the kitchen.

"Can you get that?" Sherri hollered. "I'll be ready in a minute."

Anisha opened the front door and was met by her gold-toothed admirer again. She sucked her teeth and pulled the door close to her body so he couldn't see into the apartment.

"Well, ain't this a trip?" he said, hoisting his pants up from the crotch.

Irritation surfaced in her voice. "Look, if you followed me up here, please know I *will* call the police." She stepped back and tried to push the door closed, but he caught it with his hand and held it open.

"Feisty little thing, ain't ya?" he said, eyeing Anisha as he ran his tongue around his lips. "As much as I wish I was here to scoop you up, me and my boy are here for Tamara and Veronica."

"I'll tell them you're here."

Her quick movements caught him off guard, and she closed and locked the door before he had time to react. She grabbed the two bottled waters from the fridge and the napkins to clean the car and went back into Sherri's room with disgust plastered on her face.

"Your roommates have some thugs waiting outside for them."

Sherri pounded on her thin bedroom wall and yelled to her roommate. "Veronica, your company is here."

Veronica appeared from the back bedroom and sashayed down the hall in a pair of black stilettos, a mini jean skirt, and a halter top that looked to Anisha to be two sizes too small. Anisha had posted herself against Sherri's bedroom door frame and watched Veronica stomp back to Sherri's doorway when she saw her guests weren't waiting in the living room.

"Where?" Veronica barked.

"Outside," Sherri shot back.

Veronica spat out a string of curse words and stormed back through the living room to open the door.

Veronica said something about needing a few more minutes to finish getting ready. She walked by, performing her best strut down the carpeted runway, back into her bedroom. Anisha rolled her eyes before she could catch herself. She had no right to turn up her nose at anybody, but she still didn't see how Sherri tolerated Tamara and Veronica. She'd tried to make Sherri see her relationship with them wasn't getting her anywhere in life and needed to be cut. Snip. Seemed easy enough for her. She didn't care how long they had been friends; when the season was over, it was over.

Anisha knew Sherri had grown attached to her childhood buddies because the three had grown up together, and when they'd moved to Atlanta from Jacksonville, Florida, three years ago, Sherri was a natural choice to be their third roommate.

Anisha recalled how Sherri had reasoned that she needed relief from her financial strain and how having two roommates would help her make ends meet. She'd told Anisha she could be a good influence in their lives, but three years had passed, and Anisha still hadn't seen a change. But, Anisha decided, now was not the time to share her thoughts.

"Ready?" Sherri shoved closed one of her many dresser drawers that was bursting at the seams.

Anisha grabbed her purse and followed Sherri to the front door. She hated to come into any kind of contact with her admirer again, but unless she planned to jump out of the window, she had no choice. Men like him made Tyson even more appealing.

❧

The balls of Anisha's feet throbbed. She was close to limping when she finally arrived home that night. The sandals she'd endured all day were definitely for fashion, not comfort. She stripped them off and slipped into a pair of fluffy bedroom shoes as soon as she walked in the door. She shuffled through the apartment, scrolling through her caller ID.

Tyson had called twice while she was out but never left a message. She hoped he would call again and was granted her wish when he called later during the evening, right after she'd treated herself to an invigorating foot soak.

"Sherri musta dragged me to every outlet ever built within fifty miles of Atlanta," Anisha said, filling Tyson in on her exhausting day. "I guess it would be different if I had come back home with a couple of pair of shoes like she did, but I've got my purse strings pulled too tight right now."

"Why?"

"I'm saving for a down payment on a house," Anisha said.

"It's good to know you're a woman who knows what she wants. Most women are waiting on a man to take care of 'em," Tyson joked. "Like they're looking for a knight in shining armor."

"I'm not *most* women."

"Oh, I definitely know that."

"And besides, there's nothing wrong with a woman getting swept off her feet. In fact, every woman should. But who's to say a woman shouldn't bring some assets to the table instead of just liabilities?"

Anisha said. As much of a romantic as she was, she was just as committed to being practical.

Anisha and Tyson chatted for over an hour and picked up some of the conversation they'd shared the night before. Self-motivation had always been a part of Anisha's nature, but Tyson made her think out of the box.

Tyson suggested they catch a movie, but after such a long day with Sherri, Anisha couldn't imagine staying awake in a dark movie theatre, even if it was with Tyson. Besides, she'd promised her time tonight to God. She wasn't about to let Sherri hold that over her head again, so she opted for a rain check.

They bade their good-byes, and Anisha slowly placed the phone back on the receiver. She turned off the television and opened the end table drawer to find her Bible. It lay untouched in the same spot where she'd put it the night before.

Anisha stretched across the couch and flipped through the Bible's well-worn pages. Many of her favorite passages had been marked. Some places were wrinkled by tears of pain, others by tears of joy. Her fingers led her to Esther, one of her favorite books, and she balled herself up on the couch to unwind and enjoy God's presence through the Word.

She had read countless times about Esther's humble beginnings and of how, out of the hundreds of beautiful virgins sent before the king, Esther stood out above all the others. Esther had spent an entire year of her life preparing for the moment she would be presented to him.

Anisha's pampering had never extended beyond home treatments. She longed for the time when she could treat herself to regular massages and mud facials. She let herself daydream about what it would be like to be prepared for her mate. Anisha read the entire book of Esther before she turned in for the night. She changed into her pajamas and crawled into the bed, allowing the satin sheets to envelop her.

Although her physical body was fatigued and screamed for rest, Anisha couldn't seem to get settled. She tossed and turned for several minutes but found no comfort until she scooted down the length of the bed and knelt by the bedside to pray.

"God, I don't always do what's right, but my heart's desire is to get to know You better. You've always been there for me, and I want to be a person You can count on to lead others to Christ. I want more of You. I won't put anyone or anything in front of my relationship with You. I want Your voice to be so clear in my life that I won't be distracted and lose focus on Your will for my life. Cover my relationships. Cover my family. Stand strong in our lives so You'll get all of the glory, because all things work together for the good of them who love You. And I love You. And like Esther, if there's a king out there for me, prepare me to be a queen. Do what You need to do, and I promise to do my part. Amen."

That's exactly what I wanted to hear.

3

$\mathcal{M}$ost Saturday activities at the E.L. Clifton Recreation Center brought the entire southwest Atlanta neighborhood out of their houses and off the street corners. Renovation of the center used to be a major priority for the district's redevelopment plans, until the city's budget cuts put a halt to the project and the community's hopes. Now the only finished construction was a fenced-off playground area currently crawling with children of all ages—from scampering toddlers to middle-schoolers pretending to be too grown up to have childish fun. Across the way, parents kept a watchful eye on their kids while cheering for the teams from the set of rusty bleachers beside the basketball court.

After days of gentle persuasion, and then outright begging, Anisha had finally convinced Sherri to meet her at the center, where Tyson's Boys to Men Youth Program's basketball tournament was being held. Since rough games of trash-talking street ball were being played at both ends of the court, Anisha pulled her lawn chair onto a small patch of grass near half-court so she could watch the parking lot for Sherri's arrival and still see Tyson's game. She opened a large golf umbrella to shield herself from the sun's blazing rays, though it wasn't much help for the steam rising off the asphalt court.

The heat showed no mercy to the panting players, leaving their sleeveless T-shirts clinging to their sweat-drenched chests and backs. Anisha was impressed with Tyson's ability on the court. She didn't catch his eye until the end of the first game, and he motioned with a finger that he would be over to her momentarily. At the same time, she was relieved to see Sherri's car roll into the parking lot. She watched her friend traipse through the maze of parked cars. Even for a hot day out at the basketball court, Sherri was dressed to the nines and as usual caught the eyes of a few gawking male spectators as she made her way over.

"Scoot over and let me get a piece of this shade," Sherri said, opening her own lawn chair and inching it close to Anisha. She shielded her eyes and scouted the basketball court. "I don't see Tyson," she said, looking around.

"Well, hey to you too," Anisha said, adjusting the umbrella over them both. Anisha pointed to the far end of the court. "Over there."

Tyson's team was waiting for the next round to start, and he and two other counselors were roughhousing with a group of hyper boys, trying to steal their basketballs. Tyson held his ball at arm's length above his head, far beyond the youngsters' reach.

"He must really love working with these kids," Sherri said.

"These boys are practically his life." Anisha watched Tyson in admiration. "They're all he talks about."

During the week, Tyson and the other volunteer counselors focused on academics, but on Saturdays the boys could participate in special recreation and mentoring activities. Even the boys who didn't want to commit to the program during the week were welcomed with open arms on Saturdays. The counselors thought if they showed them unconditional love, the boys would eventually have a change of heart, and they usually did.

Anisha commended Tyson's commitment. "He spends most of his free time down here."

"Seems like over the last month you've become his extracurricular activity instead," Sherri said.

Anisha felt herself blush. Ever since their first movie night together they'd enjoyed each other's company at least two days during the week and more times than not on the weekend.

Tyson threw his ball into the air and let the rowdy boys scramble for it before jogging toward Sherri and Anisha. The women sat eyeing his every move.

"The muscles are in full effect today," Sherri said.

"Shut up, girl," Anisha whispered.

Tyson came to a stop in front of the girls and stooped under their man-made shade. "Hi, ladies," he said, blowing each of them a kiss. He wiped the sweat from his brow. "It's nice to see my fans here."

"Don't flatter yourself," Sherri said. She held out her hand and examined her cuticles.

Anisha rolled her eyes and elbowed Sherri in the side. "Please don't get her started."

"You know I only said it to get Ms. Feisty here stirred up." He pinched Sherri's cheek and belted out a laugh.

Sherri smacked her lips and playfully slapped his hand away.

"So what's up, ladies? Do you want to grab a bite to eat after me and my boys finish off these last couple of teams?"

"Sure." Anisha agreed without hesitation, but Sherri was quick to decline Tyson's offer.

"I've got food waiting for me at home. You guys are by yourselves today," Sherri answered.

"She's afraid she'll be a third wheel," Anisha blurted out. She felt Sherri's eyes boring into the side of her head but ignored her and sipped on her water bottle.

"If that's the only problem, we can always add another wheel." Tyson winked his eye and, before Sherri could object, stood up and spotted one of his teammates. "Hey X! Let me holla' at you for a second, man."

"No, you didn't," Sherri said. She shifted in her chair and cupped her forehead in her hands.

"Yes, he did," Anisha said, snickering between sips of water.

The tall, muscular man lay on the ground a short distance away with a basketball tucked under his neck as a pillow. He sat up and threw his ball onto the court before striding toward them, his body flexing like a lion on the prowl. He adjusted the string on his shorts before squatting down beside Tyson.

"Ladies, this is Xavier Collins," Tyson said.

Xavier extended his hand to Sherri first.

"This is the third wheel, Sherri," Tyson continued.

"Don't mind him," Sherri said, slipping her fingers into Xavier's waiting hand. "Nice to meet you."

"Likewise," he said.

Xavier kissed Sherri's hand and locked her eyes in a tantalizing gaze. Neither broke their stare until Tyson cleared his throat and waited for their attention so he could proceed with his introductions.

"And this is Anisha," Tyson continued.

Xavier shook Anisha's hand a little harder than necessary and left it dangling in midair. It was obvious his focus was still on Sherri.

Anisha looked over at Sherri and then Tyson with a raised brow.

Tyson slapped Xavier on the shoulder and shook him until he stole his attention. "We're going to grab some food after we finish here. You down?" Tyson asked.

"I'm down. I'm gonna need replenishing after we whip up on these boys." Xavier and Tyson slapped hands and stood up.

Tyson shrugged his shoulders at Anisha and Sherri. "What can I say? The two best players out here on the same team? Unstoppable, baby. Unstoppable." Tyson jogged off backward toward the court and pointed at Xavier. "I didn't know you had it in you."

Xavier acknowledged the ladies before leaving, and though he spoke to both of them, his eyes were locked on Sherri. "I'll see y'all after the game."

Anisha and Sherri watched their admirers until they were out of hearing range.

"You know I'm going to get your boy, right?" Sherri said. "I can't believe he pulled that on me." She pulled her shades out of her purse and offered Anisha a stick of gum.

"I would probably fall for your sorry attempt to act mad if Xavier wasn't such a fine specimen," Anisha said, popping the gum into her mouth. "But considering the athletic build, cocoa brown skin, cute little goatee, and the toothpaste-commercial smile, I'm sure you'll make it through the night just fine."

Sherri leaned back on the arm of her chair so she could get a good look at Anisha. "Well, would you listen to Ms. Saint? The missionary board wouldn't appreciate you sizing up men."

Anisha slid her own sunglasses from the top of her head and set them on her face. She looked in the direction where Tyson and Xavier were warming up for the next game. "I'm saved, not blind."

Tyson stuffed his sweaty clothes into his gym bag and slammed the rusty locker door. He sprayed cologne across his chest and on his neck before buttoning up his shirt, then finished his grooming routine and met Xavier in the hallway outside of the locker room.

"So what's up with Anisha?" Xavier asked Tyson, his voice echoing down the empty hallway. "You trying to make her your woman?"

"Why does it have to be all that?" Tyson adjusted his gym bag on his shoulder. He was hoping his remark would shut down Xavier's probing, but he was wrong.

"Since I've been here, I ain't never even so much as heard you mention a woman's name."

"And?"

"And I was starting to wonder . . ."

Tyson held up his hand. "You got the wrong one, bruh."

"All I know is out of the blue, you've got this fine woman—with her fine friend, I might add—sitting in the sun all day long, and you're trying to tell me there's not at least a little something going on?" Xavier stared at Tyson in disbelief.

Tyson kept his eyes on the double doors at the end of the dark hallway, avoiding Xavier's look of inspection. He'd never been one to let the other counselors know too much of his personal business, and he wasn't about to start now.

Xavier was more of an acquaintance than anything. Their similarities and interests didn't go far past their volunteer work at the Center, but Tyson had been trying to make an effort to be a light in Xavier's life. He could tell by Xavier's demeanor that an aggressive approach would send him running, so Tyson dropped in subtle messages when he could. He wanted to squash Xavier's perception of the stereotypical, superspiritual, hypocritical Christian.

"We've been out a few times over the last month," he said after some thought. "We're trying to see what the other is about."

Tyson showed no signs of sharing more than he already had, so Xavier dropped the subject. "Okay, I feel you. I'll let it rest for now."

They pushed the building's exit doors open and squinted at the sunlight that flooded their eyes and the dark hallway.

Anisha and Sherri were waiting in Anisha's car. After an afternoon of sitting in the unyielding heat, the girls had retreated to the air-conditioned vehicle while the victorious teammates went to shower and change. The ladies swung their car doors open as the men approached.

"It's amazing what a little soap and water can do," Anisha said, walking around and leaning against the hood of the car.

"Oh, you've got jokes now." Tyson pulled Anisha close to his chest and squeezed her tightly. She didn't resist.

"And does her accomplice have anything to add?" Xavier said, his voice floating above Sherri's head.

Sherri looked around, startled to see Xavier had approached her from behind. "Hey, I'm an innocent bystander."

Anisha and Tyson walked across the parking lot toward Tyson's SUV, tossing around restaurant options. Xavier and Sherri tagged behind them in awkward conversation at first.

"I say we go to Mick's downtown on Peachtree," Tyson suggested. "At least that way if the wait is too long, we can always find somewhere to eat down at the Underground or in Buckhead."

"Works for me," Anisha agreed.

She looked back at Xavier and Sherri and was glad to notice that their tension seemed to be easing. She couldn't hear what Xavier was saying but saw he'd captured Sherri's full attention. They were taking slow, deliberate steps and didn't seem to be in a rush. Xavier towered over Sherri. As he talked, he ran his fingers along the outline of his goatee.

Flirtations in effect, Anisha thought.

"I hope Mick's is okay," Tyson said when they reached his car.

Xavier and Sherri looked at each other and nodded in agreement.

"Good," Tyson said. "We'll chauffeur you ladies there and make sure to return you safely." Tyson opened the front passenger door for Anisha, and Xavier followed suit and helped Sherri into the backseat.

Tyson took the neighborhood route to the highway. He honked at the neighborhood kids still at play and sometimes slowed down to a crawl so he could chat through the window with the nosy parents and watchful grandmothers sitting on the porch. Once they got to the highway ramp, Tyson picked up speed, and they cruised down Interstate 85 toward downtown Atlanta. He slipped a CD in the player, and a melody of gospel jazz tunes filled the car, until they found a parking place close to the downtown restaurant.

The dinner crowds hadn't started to arrive, so their party of four was seated immediately. The hostess led them to a small nook near a back restaurant window, and a waitress served their appetizers and entrees within thirty minutes. They talked comfortably between the four of them, at times breaking off into personal conversations between the two couples. Their easygoing natures helped pass the time until their stomachs were full and their plates empty.

Tyson pushed his chair back and patted his full stomach. "That's what I call good eatin'," he said, reaching for his last gulp of sweet tea. His plate showed no trace of the meal he'd devoured. "All I need now is a pillow, and I'll be set for the night."

"Uh-oh. Looks like the syndrome is starting to set in," Xavier said. "Let's get this brother out of here before we have to carry him."

The girls laughed.

"Remember, you promised to get us back safely," Sherri reminded him. "You can't do that driving with one eye open."

The waitress approached with the check and placed it facedown in front of Tyson. He snatched it up and reached for the wallet in his back pocket. "It's on me," Tyson said, leaving enough money for the bill and a tip.

"Thanks," Sherri and Anisha chimed simultaneously.

"Yeah, thanks," Xavier said, stuffing his wallet back into his pocket.

Tyson pointed at Xavier. "Only because I owe you one anyway." They reached up and dapped each other across the table, then helped the ladies out of their seats.

Patrons began to pack the restaurant as the evening hours approached. Anisha and Sherri pushed through the crowd first with Xavier and Tyson following behind.

"Tyson?" A female's voice floated above the rumbling crowd.

Anisha instinctively glanced behind her and saw the voice's owner appear through the crowd, waving her hand in the air. A little girl with big round eyes, who looked to be about five or six years old, was clinging to the woman's leg. Her hair, the color of desert sand, was smoothed back into two tight ponytails that hung on either side of her head.

Tyson was visibly startled, but Anisha noticed his attempt to act indifferent. He stopped to greet them, but Anisha thought it best if she waited outside.

While she waited, Anisha resisted the urge to watch for Tyson through the glass door from where she was standing. She walked closer to Sherri and Xavier who were standing at the street corner. They stared at the star-sprinkled sky that shared its night canvas with the lights from the Atlanta skyline. Anisha tried to focus on the architecture of the surrounding office buildings so she could slow her racing imagination.

It's no big deal, probably an old friend. Like he didn't have friends before me. He's not my man like that anyway. Stop acting so insecure.

When Anisha could no longer resist, she walked closer to the door and casually glanced back into the restaurant.

Tyson had knelt down to talk to the little girl with the big eyes. The child was still hanging on to what Anisha assumed was her mother's leg, but she was giggling, revealing a snaggle-toothed smile.

Nothing. It's nothing. Anisha strolled back to the curb and was relieved when Tyson's face appeared a couple of minutes later.

"You guys ready?" Tyson asked.

He walked up behind Anisha, and she felt his hands on her shoulders. He gently steered her body down the sidewalk and, by the time they reached the car, had snuggled her into an embrace.

Anisha waited for him to identify the mystery woman, but he never did. She shrugged it off and decided instead to enjoy the moment.

Nevertheless, the ride back to the Clifton Center was noticeably different to Anisha. Although Sherri and Xavier whispered constantly in the backseat, she and Tyson shared little conversation. He focused on the road and drummed his fingers on the steering wheel to the rhythm of another CD he'd slid in the player. For some reason, Anisha didn't think Tyson was just enjoying the music. He seemed to be deep in thought.

When they pulled onto the property at the center, the parking lot was abandoned except for the girls' cars. Tyson pulled into the empty space between them.

"Delivered as promised," Tyson said, shifting his body to face Anisha.

"Looks like this is a ship we need to jump," Xavier said from the back.

Sherri stifled a yawn. "It's been real, guys," she said, hopping out and closing the back passenger door. She leaned on the edge of Anisha's open window. "I'll talk to you when you get home, which I assume will be *soon*."

"If I don't fall asleep here first," Anisha said, leaning back against the headrest. "Drive safely. I'll buzz you later."

"All right, girl." Sherri reached across Anisha and pounded fists with Tyson. "Thanks for dragging me along. I had a nice time."

"Good. I'm glad you came." Tyson lowered his voice to a whisper. "And I'm sure Xavier is, too."

"Now I'm really leaving." Sherri walked around to her car where Xavier was waiting. They bid their good-byes with a little small talk and a friendly hug before leaving.

Tyson and Anisha watched the taillights of their friends' cars disappear down the street.

"I've had you away from home all day, haven't I, Ms. Blake?" Tyson reached over and placed his hand on top of Anisha's.

She returned the gesture and rested her free hand on top of his. His hands were warm to the touch, and even though his grip was light, she felt his strength. His body language spoke volumes. She exhaled and opened her heart to let him in.

"It made no sense to let a beautiful day like this go to waste by sitting inside," Anisha said. "Thanks for inviting me."

"It was my pleasure. And my team thanks you."

"Your team? What do they have to do with anything?"

"I wouldn't have played as hard if I hadn't had to impress you. Not to mention, you kept the players on the other team distracted."

Anisha lowered her head and twirled a strand of hair around her finger. Tyson's compliments brought out her bashful side. "You're too much," she said, rubbing her hand along the texture of the dashboard. "I guess we need to get home and get ready for church in the morning."

Tyson closed his eyes and bobbed his head like he was nodding off. "If I'm as tired in the morning as I am right now, I'll be attending Bedside Baptist."

"Okay, Bedside Baptist! You make sure you get your butt up and make it to church!"

"Only because you said so," Tyson said. He lifted Anisha's hand to his lips and planted a soft kiss on her knuckles. "That's for the hand Xavier missed."

Anisha's hair flapped across her face as she sped down Interstate 20 toward her side of town. Tyson trailed not far behind, as he'd insisted on following her all the way home to make sure she arrived safely.

She still couldn't shake the look she'd seen on Tyson's face earlier, but she wasn't going to worry about another woman. If there was anything to it, she'd learn about it soon enough. She pushed the thoughts out of her mind.

Anisha held her hand out of the window and let the wind whip through her open fingers. She turned up the volume on the radio and crooned with Marvin Gaye and Tammi Terrell as their melody blared through the speakers from the oldies station.

*A*nisha had decided to attend the early morning Sunday worship service and arrived home before eleven o'clock to watch her favorite Lifetime's movie marathon. Her growling stomach grew more impatient as two o'clock approached. She was expecting Sherri for their weekly Sunday meal together—their traditional bonding time before another hectic week swept them into their busy schedules.

"Come in, girl. It's open," Anisha shouted at the sound of the doorbell.

When her friend didn't burst through the door like she usually did, Anisha yelled at the top of her lungs, figuring Sherri hadn't heard the first time. "I said it's unlocked."

The doorknob turned slowly, and Tyson peeked his head into the apartment. Anisha jumped up from the couch and smoothed back her rustled hair.

"Tyson?"

"You really shouldn't make a habit of leaving your door unlocked."

He lingered at the door, waiting for a welcoming invitation from Anisha.

"I thought you were Sherri." She motioned for him to come inside.

Tyson's voice was apologetic. "I should've called before stopping by. We just got out of church, and I was passing your subdivision. Do you mind?"

"Not at all." She shook a finger in jest. "Just don't make it a habit."

"I mean, I can leave if you want me to," Tyson stammered. "You know, if it's a bad time or something. I really didn't mean to intrude." He felt for his keys in his pocket.

Anisha softened her stern expression. "Don't mind me. I'm kidding. I'm actually waiting for Sherri to get here to eat, so you're more than welcome to join us."

Anisha moved a pile of magazines from the couch to the end table so Tyson could sit down. "So I see you didn't attend Bedside Baptist after all," she said.

"And have you beat me up for skipping church?"

Tyson finally left his post at the door and held his arms open, a sign he wanted her inside of them. She willingly fell into his embrace, but before she could lose herself in his world, her thoughts were interrupted by the sound of Sherri's voice from outside.

"Speaking of your trusty sidekick," Tyson said.

Anisha adjusted the blinds and watched Sherri trot up the sidewalk. Her five-foot four-inch frame was round and curvaceous compared to Anisha's lean figure.

Anisha greeted Sherri at the door and tried to drop an inconspicuous signal about their unexpected company. Sherri was so involved in her own private rendition of the latest Kirk Franklin hit that she didn't notice and rushed past Anisha into the apartment. She stopped in her tracks at the sight of Tyson.

"Hi, Tyson." She averted her gaze to Anisha while she spoke to him. "I didn't know you were joining us."

"I was in the neighborhood," Tyson said, as if he had to explain. He stood up and reached for the two grocery bags Sherri was carrying. "Can I get those for you?"

"Thanks, but I can manage. I'll set these down right here." She heaved the bags onto the counter and turned to Anisha. "I forgot a change of clothes. Can I borrow a T-shirt or something?"

"Yeah." Anisha turned to Tyson, who had quickly engaged himself in a magazine article to avoid any further disdainful looks from Sherri. "Can you give us a second? We'll be right back."

Sherri rode the back of Anisha's heels into her bedroom. Anisha eased the bedroom door closed and turned to Sherri, who had found a place on the edge of the bed and was loosening the sandal straps wrapped around her ankles. After taking a minute to dig around in her bottom dresser drawer, Anisha finally broke the silence.

"Go ahead and say it," she said, tossing a T-shirt and pair of footies to Sherri.

"There's nothing to say. This is your place, and you can have who you want over here whenever you want to," Sherri said, pulling the T-shirt over her head. "But I've never known you to be down with unexpected visitors. I hope you checked him on it."

"Oh, you know I did." Anisha exaggerated her reaction to Tyson's unannounced visit. "He offered to leave, but I invited him to stay. I'm flattered he stopped by. At least he was thinking about me."

"Or your food. You're only flattered because it's Tyson. What if Victor had pulled something like this? He wouldn't be sitting out on that couch right now."

Anisha didn't want to think about Victor, a pursuer from church that she'd had to dodge for a while. He'd been smitten by Anisha for two years and showed no signs of throwing in the towel. Rejection only made Victor try harder. Poor boy, he never had a chance.

"I'm not going to start in on Tyson," Sherri promised while she put on a pair of footies. "But the brother needs to know he doesn't have it like that yet. Or does he?"

Even though the door was closed, Anisha spoke barely above a whisper.

"We're still learning about each other, so don't even go there."

"And speaking of *going there,* don't set yourself up for Tyson to *go there,* if you know what I mean," Sherri said.

"Oh no, here we go again." Anisha heaved a loud sigh.

Sherri ignored her agitation. "You know what Pastor says. If you need a license to drive a car and you need a license to do hair, surely you need a license to go into the Promised Land."

Anisha walked to the bedroom door and paused before turning the knob. "I'm going to open this door, and you're going to go out there and be on your best behavior."

Sherri held up three fingers like she was pledging a Scout's honor. "Fine. But as long as he knows he needs a license." Sherri followed Anisha and raised her voice loud enough to draw Tyson's attention. "You need a license, boy."

"Huh?" Tyson glimpsed up from his magazine with a puzzled expression on his face.

"Nothing," Anisha said.

They piled their plates with smothered chicken breasts, French style green beans, creamed corn, and cornbread. Anisha pulled out three television trays, and the hungry diners found a spot in front of the television. Tyson said grace before the three tore into their Sunday meal.

During commercials, Sherri took advantage of the time to interrogate Tyson, all the while ignoring Anisha's looks of rebuke. By the time Tyson excused himself to the restroom, Anisha had reached the point of irritation.

"What do you think you're doing?"

"I'm merely gathering a little bit of information about him, so you'll know what you're working with. Collecting some data."

"If anybody needs to be collecting data, it's me. And rest assured, I'm getting the job done."

"Looks like somebody's getting upset." Sherri threw her hands in the air. "I'll back off, but only because you insist."

"Yes, I insist."

"But one more thing."

"What is it?"

"I still haven't found out how much he makes!"

"Girl, if you—"

"I'm kidding, I'm kidding." Sherri laughed to ease the tension.

Anisha heard the bathroom door click, and she put a finger to her lips. "Remember what I said. No more cross-examinations."

Tyson walked back into the living room and immediately picked up their empty plates. "You ladies have been so gracious today. Let me get the dishes for you."

"Thanks," they both chimed.

"No. Thank *you*." Tyson disappeared into the kitchen, and the girls grabbed a spot together on the couch. They listened to the sound of running water filling the sink and the clanging of dishes.

"Is he trying to work his way in there, or what?" Sherri asked.

Anisha pushed Sherri's shoulder hard enough to cause her to lose her balance and tip over. "Shhhhh. Let the man do his thing."

When Tyson finished cleaning the kitchen and came to rejoin them, Sherri stood up and looked around for her purse.

"Well, I guess it's time for us to be going," Sherri said.

Us? Anisha glanced at her watch and was surprised to see it was only five o'clock, much earlier than Sherri had ever left before. She always stayed until at least eight every Sunday.

"Yeah," Tyson said, catching the hint. "We wouldn't want to wear out our welcome."

"No, that would be for you," Sherri said, playfully poking her finger into his chest. "Mine is never worn." She swung her purse across her shoulder and winked an eye at Tyson.

Tyson laughed. "Now I know it's time for me to go. You've been riding my back all day."

"Please don't get her started," Anisha begged. "You've only experienced a taste of what she can unleash. But the bark is much worse than the bite."

"Let's go, Tyson." Sherri propped one hand on her hip and gestured the other toward the door.

"Guess that's my cue," he said to Anisha. "I'll see you later, baby." He kissed Anisha on the cheek, then turned and offered his arm to Sherri.

"May I have the honor of escorting you to your car, princess?"

"Yes, you may. But don't think you're getting any points for this," Sherri said. "Chivalry is a basic requirement." Sherri slipped her hand into the bend of his arm and let Tyson lead her to the car.

Tyson looked over his shoulder and winked at Anisha.

She shook her head and waved them away. "Bye. Be safe."

Anisha went back into the house to tidy up a bit and was interrupted by the doorbell a few minutes later. *No wonder Tyson had winked at me,* she thought, smoothing her appearance before opening the door. To her surprise, a smiling Sherri stood on her front stoop instead of Tyson.

"Waaaaassssuuup?! Surely you didn't think I was gone for the night." Sherri tossed her purse on the couch and went directly to the refrigerator. "That was to send Tyson on his way. You know our Sundays are a tradition."

"I should've known it was you," Anisha said.

"Could you do a better job of hiding the disappointment on your face, please? You wanted Tyson, but you got me," Sherri said, tilting her head to the side and filling her dimples with her index fingers. She pulled a stuffed grocery bag from the freezer and unpacked it.

"I didn't even see you put that bag in there," Anisha said. She picked up a jar of caramel sauce and twisted off the cap. "This stuff should be illegal," she said, inhaling the sweet scent wafting from the open jar.

They filled their bowls with French vanilla ice cream and doused it with an array of toppings until their desserts nearly dripped over the side.

"Girl, Pastor Armstrong got down today at the second service," Sherri said between greedy licks of her spoon. "You missed it." Sherri clapped in amusement before continuing with her story.

"He said that some of us singles should have a pair of golden arches outside of our doors because we let people do romantic drive-thrus on us without the commitment of marriage."

Anisha got so pumped when her pastor didn't hold his tongue. She loved watching the reaction of holier-than-thou religious folks who seemed to do no wrong. They always sat flabbergasted with their mouths open in disbelief at his boldness.

"You know I'm mad I missed it," Anisha said.

They both fell over, laughing at their pastor's boldness.

The Lifetime movies were no longer an interest to the two inseparable friends. They entertained each other with memories they'd shared together and reflected on how they'd watched each other mature over the years. Each had childhood friends, college buddies, and even family they'd known much longer, but none came close to the bond of their friendship. Neither claimed to be perfect. Their promise to God and each other was to try their best to walk upright and hold each other accountable.

Eventually, Sherri steered the conversation back to Anisha and Tyson. Sherri knew Anisha's habit of playing hard and tough, but she also knew her friend's knees would weaken if the right brother came along with the right words. Anisha could be gullible. And all it would take was a brother to come along with the right words, and he could steal her friend's heart. Sherri had comforted Anisha through her share of heartaches, and she planned on hawking Tyson to make sure he wasn't going to leave her friend wounded—her heart crushed by another.

"So what are you feeling about him?" Sherri searched Anisha's face for a true answer. "I mean, the man pops up over here without an invitation, and you didn't send him along his merry little way. It's evident he's got pull."

"The boy has got it going on—don't get me wrong. The fact that he loves God sends him to the top of the list. I've had a little crush on him for a while anyway," Anisha admitted. She buried her face between her hands.

Sherri wasn't surprised. "I knew it. I saw how you tried to play it off whenever he was around. I can't believe you didn't come out and tell me! You know your secrets are safe with me."

"Now who are *you* trying to fool? I know you wouldn't have told anybody, but you would've been trying to drop subtle little hints to Tyson. I didn't need your assistance with this one," Anisha said.

"Evidently not," Sherri said. "Tyson caught the vibes by himself."

"Vibes? What vibes? I wasn't throwing off any vibes to him."

"You were throwing off something, because old boy was like a deer stunned by headlights. He didn't even know what hit him."

"He was stunned by the light all right. The light of Jesus!"

"Keep the light shining, girlfriend." Sherri jumped up and paced in front of Anisha like a preacher delivering a soul-stirring sermon. "You know you can see right through some things if you hold them up to the light. You can tell what's counterfeit and what's real if you hold it up to the light. And the light will keep you out of dark situations." Sherri picked up a magazine to use as a makeshift Bible and dabbed her forehead with a napkin.

Anisha stood with one hand on her hip and the other raised in the air. "Hallelujah. Preach it, sista." She waved her hand frantically.

Sherri collapsed against the wall laughing, and Anisha flopped down on the couch.

"Let me get my stuff so I can get out of here. I'll bring your shirt back next week."

"And my footies," Anisha reminded her.

"And your stinkin' footies," Sherri said.

Anisha picked up the dish towel and poised herself to throw it.

Sherri screamed and slammed the door before Anisha could get to her.

Anisha ran to the door. "I'll get you. You've gotta come back."

"Yeah, but it won't be tonight," Sherri said, jumping into her car. "I'm gone this time for real. Adios, mi amiga!"

Anisha turned off the television and dimmed the lights. Conversations with Sherri always made her think. She liked Tyson more than she let on, and the feelings scared her. *Lord, help me to guard my heart.*

Anisha had experienced these feelings before. The secret crush. The butterflies in the stomach. The innocent friendship that somehow too quickly evolved in her mind into a romance.

Anisha climbed into bed with her thoughts. She turned on the bedside lamp and slipped under the sheets. She didn't care that it was barely past eight o'clock. She wanted to settle her mind. No television. No radio. No nothing.

The Bible on her nightstand almost seemed to glow. Anisha reached for it and opened the Book. It was as if God Himself had turned the pages to the fourth chapter of Proverbs. Her eyes fell on the twenty-third verse: *Keep your heart with all diligence for out of it spring the issues of life,* she read. "Are You trying to tell me something?" she asked, looking up.

Draw closer to Me, and you'll find out.

Anisha read through the entire fourth chapter and reviewed the Scriptures her pastor had referenced during his sermon. She read as much as her heavy eyelids would allow and whispered a prayer before sleep overwhelmed her.

*A*nisha pushed the sheets down and wiped the sleep from her eyes so she could see the clock across the room. Three minutes after six. She moaned and pulled the sheets back up to her neck. Nothing was worse than waking up minutes before your alarm clock was set to go off, especially on a Monday morning. She closed her eyes and tried to capture twelve more minutes of sleep.

When the alarm sounded, she stretched her limbs as wide as her body permitted, then threw her legs over the edge of the bed. Anisha stumbled to the bathroom and let her nightgown fall into a crumpled pile at her feet.

There's got to be something better than getting up this early to go and work for somebody else.

There sure is.

Anisha turned on the shower and stepped under the warm stream of water. She let the water cascade down her body and carry her grumbling down the drain with it.

In forty minutes, Anisha was nearly ready to head out and beat Atlanta's morning rush hour traffic. She slipped into a crisp suit fresh from the cleaners and scooted into the kitchen with a pair of pumps and her briefcase in tow. She popped two pieces of wheat bread into the toaster and was making a bowl of cereal when the phone rang.

She looked at the microwave clock. *Who could be calling me this early?* Calls this early were either bad news or the wrong number.

"Hello?" Apprehension hung on Anisha's voice.

"Good morning." Tyson's voice rolled from the other end.

"Well, good morning to you," Anisha cooed. "To what do I owe this pleasure?"

"No reason except that you're special," Tyson said. "I'm calling to wish you a good day today. Is that all right with you, Ms. Blake?"

"Perfectly fine with me, Mr. Randall." Anisha playfully twisted the phone cord around her fingers. She watched her bread pop out of the toaster, but the phone cord was too short for her to continue making her breakfast. She could deal with cold toast if she had to.

"I don't want to hold you. Get back to doing your thing, and maybe I'll catch up with you this evening."

"That would be nice."

"Talk to you later."

"Bye." Anisha lingered a minute before hanging up the phone. She shook her head and tried to wake herself out of a dream. "Definitely real," she said, smiling.

Anisha floated through the rest of her day. The coworkers who usually annoyed her didn't seem to matter at all. She was so busy handling her clients' requests and putting together reports that she didn't have time to call Sherri until lunch.

Anisha's position as a junior account executive for Dudley & Associates, a small advertising agency, involved her acting as a liaison with Dudley's clients. Her job was to communicate the clients' vision for their various products or services to her colleagues, who handled the creative direction for TV, radio, and print advertisements. She enjoyed turning on the television, flipping through a magazine, or driving past a billboard, and realizing that she had played a role in bringing that to fruition.

"It seems like we've got a little pursuit going on." Sherri laughed into the phone.

Anisha sat at her desk with her lunch container in front of her. She swirled around the remains of her leftovers with her spoon.

"You can't blame a man for seeing something he wants and going after it," Anisha said.

"And it seems he's not wasting a bit of time. I'm surprised he didn't happen to stop by for breakfast. We know his track record."

"Shheerrrriiiiii!"

"Okay, okay. I'm going to leave that man alone today." Sherri must've heard the muffled voice of one of Anisha's coworkers in the background. "Is that your cue?"

"I've got to go, girl. We're being called into a meeting."

"With all those meetings, you probably know enough to run the company and then some."

"You're telling me." Anisha stood up and stuffed her arms with a legal pad, her organizer, two file folders, and a bottle of water. "Let me get out of here, girl. I've got to stay on top of my game."

"Call me later. I'm sure you'll have another Tyson story to tell."

"Okay."

Anisha sat in the conference room and listened to the senior account executives toss around ideas about a strategic plan for marketing their newest client. *Is that the best they can do?*

The wheels in her head were spinning at lightning speed. She furiously jotted down notes on her legal pad, but her mind ran faster than her hand could write. The forty-five-minute presentation finally ended, and Curt, the senior account manager, opened the floor for suggestions from the junior account executives. Anisha was the first to stand. She straightened her suit jacket and with boldness she had never exhibited before at work walked to the front of the room. Her adrenaline was pumping so high that at first she didn't notice she'd left her notes. Unshaken, she confidently addressed her colleagues about how she thought the firm could best serve their client. It wasn't until she finished that she felt herself breathe again.

"Anyone else?" Curt went back to the podium and looked around at the faces seated around the large mahogany conference table. Her colleagues appeared stunned as they looked around at each other. Anisha supposed they were as surprised as she was at the assertiveness that had surfaced in her.

"If that's all, then it's a wrap for today," Curt said. "We'll pick up in the morning and make some final decisions. Thank you for your input, Anisha. Well done."

Anisha nodded her head in acknowledgment as everyone rushed to file out of the conference room. She took her time gathering her belongings until she was the only person remaining. "Thank You, Lord," she whispered. "You worked it like only You can." She turned off the lights and pulled the door closed behind her.

Sherri's right, Anisha reflected. *I could run this company.*

It's already in you. You're equipped, and as soon as you're really ready to do it, we've got some work to do.

*B*randy Sullivan pumped the foot lever of the salon chair and swiveled it around until Mrs. Jamison faced her. She slid the small-barreled iron out of the hot stove and carefully began curling the short coif. Brandy looked at the small clock at her station. It was almost two o'clock, and she still hadn't had time to stop for lunch. As soon as she finished with Mrs. Jamison, she'd have to slip out to grab a bite to eat and stop by the check cashing place. She needed to make a payment on her already past-due phone bill, or it would be disconnected by the day's end.

None of the words leaving Mrs. Jamison's mouth were making it to Brandy's ears. As usual, Mrs. Jamison was probably talking about her son. She was in the salon every other Tuesday like clockwork, always talking about how the Lord was going to save her wayward son, Kenny. How Kenny had promised he was really going to turn his life around this time. Kenny this. Kenny that.

Brandy raked through Mrs. Jamison's hair with a wide-toothed comb. As far as she was concerned, this woman had ridiculous faith.

Mrs. Jamison was convinced God could do anything. But Brandy wondered, when did faith cross over the line to foolishness?

Maybe if she had that kind of faith she could wish Tyson back into her life, Brandy thought. For four days, his face seized her thoughts every time she closed her eyes. Until the other night, she hadn't seen him since the week after she'd brought Ayana home from the hospital.

Brandy had thought her eyes had deceived her on Saturday night at the restaurant, but she didn't have time to second-guess herself. She'd pushed through the crowd to get closer to Tyson but missed grabbing his arm by inches. She'd called his name, fearing he might disappear for another six years. Her heart fluttered the instant their eyes met, and she still hadn't recovered from seeing him unexpectedly.

"Okay, Mrs. Jamison. You're all done." Brandy loosened the cape from around Mrs. Jamison and shook off the fine gray hairs she'd tapered from her neck.

"Thank you, baby." The tall, sophisticated woman bore a strong resemblance to the legendary jazz singer Nancy Wilson. She eyed her reflection from different angles and refreshed her lipstick. "You always keep me looking as sharp as these young girls. My husband better watch out."

Mrs. Jamison reached into her purse and pulled out a couple of crisp bills and a brochure. "Here's the information for the women's conference at my church I've been telling you about. You always find an excuse to say you can't come to church, but I think you'll enjoy this conference. They're having a special session for the single ladies."

Brandy opened the brochure and skimmed over the photographs and bios of the list of speakers. Getting all dressed up to sit in church all day wasn't her kind of thing. "Mrs. Jamison, I don't have anything to wear to something like this."

"This isn't a fashion show. Our church isn't like that. You come with what you have, and if anybody has a problem with it, tell them they can bless you with some new clothes."

Brandy refolded the glossy trifold and noticed the church's name printed boldly on the outside: Grace Worship Center. Didn't Tyson say he went there? She'd asked him if he was still doing the church thing and could almost swear he'd said he attended a church called Grace Worship. It had to be the same one.

Brandy's plan was clear. Tyson definitely wouldn't be at the women's conference, so there was no point in going. But if she visited during any of the other services, she was bound to run into him sooner or later. Hopefully sooner.

Brandy looked into Mrs. Jamison's hopeful face, and although she knew her motives were wrong, she finally said the words Mrs. Jamison had waited to hear for over a year.

"I can't make it to this women's conference, but I'll come with you this Sunday. I promise."

Mrs. Jamison beamed. She pulled Brandy into a motherly embrace, squeezing her until Brandy pulled away slightly. "And they have children's church for kids Ayana's age. I know she'll love it. Can I go in the back and tell my little lovebug?"

Brandy led Mrs. Jamison to the back of the salon to see her daughter. She and another stylist used one of the rooms as a play area for their children. Neither single mother made enough to afford decent day care, but both made too much money to qualify for government assistance.

As Brandy approached the door, she noticed the room was unusually quiet; there were no sounds of laughter or squeals of excitement. When Brandy entered the room, she saw her daughter slumped over a desk, her body shaking from the intensity of her sobs. She ran to Ayana and wiped her tear-streaked face with the back of her hand, then cuddled her to calm her shivering body.

"Tell Mommy what's wrong."

Ayana gulped for air, her bottom lip quivering. "Sidney . . ."

"Sidney, what?" Brandy rocked Ayana until her sobs began to wane.

"Sidney said I couldn't make a card for Father's Day because I didn't have a daddy. She said Uncle James didn't want a card from me because he's not my daddy."

Brandy glared at the accused culprit, who'd withdrawn to the corner in fear of getting scolded. If Brandy could have jacked her up by her neck, she would have, but she remained calm. She knew kids had a tendency to say things they didn't realize would be hurtful. Plus Mrs. Jamison was standing right behind her.

"That's not true. Uncle James would love for you to make him a card." Brandy dumped a box of crayons on the table and pulled out a piece of bright yellow construction paper. "Make your card, baby," she said, kissing her daughter's forehead.

Ayana's tears melted Brandy's heart. All the more reason she needed Tyson in her life. In their lives.

Anisha adjusted the pillow to cushion her back against the bed's headboard. She'd recently returned from a brief meeting with Tyson at the center and was sorting through some old sponsorship package examples she'd saved over the years.

Now it all made sense why she couldn't bring herself to trash the marketing materials that caught her eye. She'd kept a running file in case she ever needed to refer to them for a work project, but they were proving to be more beneficial for other purposes. She could very well find her own use for them once her own business was up and running, Anisha thought.

The volunteers at the center were in desperate need for someone to assist them with the proposal packages for the Rites of Passage Holiday Gala they were planning in December, so Anisha was offering her services and expertise. At no charge, of course. Her payment was the joy in seeing Tyson's vision revealed.

Anisha sifted through the entire folder and set aside materials that most closely matched the center's goals, sponsorship ranges, and sparse budget. With a little time, she could easily devise a tailor-made sponsorship package, complete with a matching program booklet for the night of the event.

As the night settled, Anisha wound up her activities and decided to call Sherri. She hadn't talked to her since the afternoon before, so she didn't have the chance to tell her friend how she'd shown her stuff at the meeting. She tried to verbalize to Sherri all that had transpired, but the words to describe her exhilaration evaded her.

"It was like I wasn't even moving my own lips," Anisha said.

"I know they were tripping. What did they say?" Sherri asked.

"My manager told me I did a nice job, but I think everybody else was too stunned."

"Except God. He knew it was already in you."

"I guess you're right, Sherri. And remember yesterday when you told me I knew enough to run the company? It's like my eyes opened to something new. When I was leaving the conference room, I saw myself standing at a podium conducting a meeting. And it wasn't at Dudley & Associates, either. I was running my own."

Anisha closed her eyes and tried to visualize the scene again.

"I'm going to start writing down everything that's been running through my mind for the past two days," she said. "It's like something has been stirred up."

"Well, I wish something would get stirred up in me," Sherri said. "I've been stagnant for years, and I feel like life is passing me by. I need a change in my life. This life I'm living is for the birds."

Anisha heard the frustration swell in Sherri's voice and stepped in to affirm her. "It can change today. God wants you to have an abundant life, and it's not beyond your reach. I know, if you pray about it, God will reveal the plan He has for your life. It's already been determined, but it's our job to go after it. The Word says He can do exceedingly above all we ask or think; I say ask big and think with no limits."

Anisha knew Sherri was covering the phone to muffle the sound of her crying. When Sherri finally responded, the pain was evident in her voice.

"It's easy for you to say right now. You're putting things in order to buy a house, a godly man is pursuing you—as he well should—and now you've got this renewed passion for life. But what's happening for me? You tell me, 'cause evidently I'm not seeing it."

"Maybe that's the problem. If *you* don't see a change happening in your life, it'll never happen. We've got to start expecting more than our current circumstances. God is moving in our lives. Yours and mine. My journey won't be your journey, and your journey won't be mine. Things happen at different times in people's lives."

Sherri laughed between sniffles. "Pastor Armstrong ought to let you preach this Sunday. I'm sorry, Anisha. I don't know where all that drama came from. It must be time for my cycle, 'cause I'm on an emotional roller coaster."

"Everybody has one of those days," Anisha said. "As long as you don't stay there. And as long as I'm around, you won't. And as long as you're around, I won't. We're in this together."

"That's right, girl. Together. Destiny awaits us," Sherri said.

"I know that's right. And she's been waiting a little too long."

"Love ya, girl."

"I love you, too," Anisha said. "And you better call me if you need me. I don't care what time it is."

Anisha hung up the phone and hauled a large plastic container out of her closet. She sat with it in the middle of the floor and scrounged through the office supplies she'd collected over the years. Anisha pulled out a yellow composition book and, using a black marker and her best penmanship, wrote on the cover in large bold letters, then held the book at arm's length to admire her work. VISION.

Anisha reached for her Bible and thumbed through the pages until she found the highlighted verses she was looking for. She flipped the notebook to the inside cover and copied the Scripture from Habakkuk 2:2–3. *Write the vision and make it plain on tablets, that he may run who reads it. For the vision is yet for an appointed time; but at the end it will speak, and it will not lie. Though it tarries, wait for it; because it will surely come, it will not tarry.*

Anisha gathered her belongings, went into the living room, and spread everything out on the floor. She scribbled incessantly until soreness crept through her wrist and fingers. She didn't worry about organizing her thoughts. To free them from her mind was enough for now.

Before an hour passed, Anisha had covered nearly ten pages. When she felt she'd finished for the night, she jotted down a prayer under the night's work.

Lord, I believe those things You've shown me. I know it's up to me to give life to the words You've spoken, so keep me focused on You. I pray Your will be done in my life.

If anyone or anything hinders or tries to abort the vision, remove them. I want to do and be all You have ordained. I trust Your plan and Your process for my life. Amen.

Remember your prayers if things get tight. You asked for My will, My way.

Sherri closed her bedroom door to drown out the sound of the music videos Veronica was watching in the living room. She was sick and tired of being sick and tired. From the outside looking in, she knew no one would suspect she was in inner turmoil. But wearing the facade was draining her. She was living two lives. The one she wanted others to see and then the *real* one.

She knew all Anisha said was true. There's a season to everything. But when would it be her time? She wanted to awaken to her destiny too, and she definitely wouldn't mind a man to share it with.

*A*nisha scanned the congregation for a sign of Tyson in the crowded pews. It was only a few minutes before the start of Bible study, and she was anxious to be seated before praise and worship began. Tyson was supposed to save her a seat since she'd had to stay at work late for a meeting. The couple was beginning to attend worship services more frequently together, and it was evident to the both of them that their friendship had moved to another level.

Anisha's life had been a whirlwind for the past two and a half months. Ever since she'd impressed the senior account managers at the strategic planning meeting, her workload and confidence had grown. She felt promotion was certain on her horizon, and she gave her job 100 percent of her effort. Most weekends she brought work home so she could stay a step ahead of the game. With the extra time she was spending on work and the nights helping Tyson, not only with the gala, but now with his business plan to expand the mentor program into a full-time program, there was barely time for anything else besides church.

Some people stood with their hands raised in submission, already engulfed in their own personal worship though service hadn't begun. Others knelt at the altar in prayer or brought their gifts of tithes and offerings to the front. Being in the midst of them rejuvenated Anisha's tired body and spirit. No, she thought. She couldn't forsake her fellowship with other believers even though her mind had told her to go home earlier.

But what about your fellowship with Me?

Anisha spotted the back of Tyson's head about ten pews from the front. As usual before service, he was buried in his Bible. As she floated down the purple-carpeted aisle she saw Sherri and her other former pew partners—Monica, Kendall, Felicie, and Angie—sitting a few rows behind him.

"Sherri," she whispered and waved excitedly at her friend.

Anisha noticed how Sherri's face lit up but faded when she realized she was passing her pew. Anisha knew she owed Sherri some quality time. She'd practically pushed her out the door two Sundays ago right after they'd eaten lunch. But she'd had to. Tyson was waiting outside for her.

I'll make sure we hook up on Saturday, Anisha thought as she slid onto the pew beside Tyson.

The dynamic praise and worship set the atmosphere for the congregation to receive the Word from their shepherd. Pastor Armstrong approached the pulpit with humility. The flock God had chosen for him to lead sincerely respected his integrity. He opened his sermon with a prayer, then immediately delved into the night's message.

Pastor Armstrong's sermon was a continuation of a series he'd been teaching about God's process of molding His children to be vessels fit to be used by Him. Her pastor's words resonated in Anisha's mind.

"No one is exempt from pain," he explained. "Even the righteous experience tribulation, and it's meant to make you stronger. It may seem like the situation is tearing you down, but like the old saying goes, 'No pain, no gain.'

"Don't get me wrong," he continued. "There will be times of peace and rest too, but then God will cause you to experience a period of adversity and discomfort. It's a cycle for God to mature you and to take you to the next level in Him."

Anisha jotted down key notes and Scriptures during Pastor Armstrong's message so she could review them when she had time.

I should come before your other pursuits. Where's your heart if spending time with Me isn't a priority?

Anisha always had good intentions to go back to her notes and study, but lately the pages of her Bible rarely saw the light of day except on Sundays and Wednesdays. Anisha listened to Pastor Armstrong's message and felt in her heart that God wanted more of her love. He needed more of her time and more of her attention. He wanted more of her. She felt the tug of her soul longing after God's presence.

Pastor Armstrong's fervor and passion escalated as he ministered the Word.

"God may take us on a journey through pain and tribulation, but in the end, if you don't know anything else, you'll know the peace that surpasses all understanding. Not only will you know *about* God, but you'll also come to know God for yourself. Your perspective will change, and you'll see things through God's eyes and want His will for your life more than your own desires. You'll grow to a point where you view things differently."

Pastor Armstrong walked to the edge of the pulpit and jumped down onto the main floor. He paced down the aisles and stopped at the end of the pew where Tyson and Anisha were sitting.

"Watch this," he said, his gaze stopping on Anisha's. "You'll mature to the point that even though someone is mistreating you, you'll pray for him or her and go the extra mile to love rather than walk away."

❦

After the benediction, some members of the congregation filed out into the vestibule, while others walked around and quietly fellowshiped in the sanctuary.

Anisha waved at a dignified couple who stood holding hands at the doors leading out to the vestibule. The two smiled in admiration as Tyson and Anisha approached them. Deacon Russell Davenport was a dark-skinned man of average height. His fairly thin build was slightly interrupted by a growing midsection. His wife, Carolyn, was at least two inches taller than he—nearly four inches when she wore heels— but what Deacon Davenport lacked in height he made up for in character. The constant gleam in Sister Davenport's small, almond-shaped eyes reflected the immensity of honor she held for her husband.

The Davenports were in their early forties, and their maturity equaled that of a couple more advanced in years. They had become an instrumental influence in Tyson's life since he'd started taking the financial stewardship class taught at the church by the deacon.

Sister Davenport extended her arms to Anisha and pulled her into a tight embrace, bringing Anisha an unexplainable comfort. She felt their souls connect.

Sister Davenport stepped back and looked at Anisha. "Your face sure is glowing tonight," she said.

"Oh, stop it." Anisha blushed and covered her face with her Bible.

"It wouldn't have anything to do with the man over there talking to my husband, would it?"

Anisha followed Sister Davenport's gaze over to the two men who had moved a few feet away and were engaged in animated conversation. From the corner of her eye, she could see Sister Davenport watching her. Anisha tried not to reveal any emotion, but the warm flush she felt rise in her face again told the story anyway.

"Russell and I were talking the other week after you two left the house," Sister Davenport said, lowering her voice. "He said Tyson has been acting like a different man over the last three months. But I have a secret to confess. When you and Tyson came to the house to pick up his materials for class, he really just wanted us to meet you. He'd already called ahead of time and told Russell he wanted us to meet his special lady friend."

Anisha remembered their visit to the Davenports' house one Saturday almost two weeks ago. They'd had plans for the night, but Tyson was persistent about stopping to pick up a study guide for class. At the time, Anisha couldn't understand why Tyson couldn't get it the next morning at church, but Sister Davenport had spilled the secret.

Sister Davenport continued, "After being on a consecration for a year, I'm sure the Lord gave him plenty of direction. He knows what he wants."

A year's consecration? Anisha smiled and nodded at Sister Davenport, never giving her a hint she was telling her things she had no idea about. *Must be the reason it took him so long to approach me.*

"Anisha?"

She turned around to the voice of Deacon Davenport.

"How are you, doll?" They exchanged friendly hugs, then the deacon grabbed his wife's hand. "We've got to get out of here, baby," he urged. "If we leave now, I can still catch the end of the game." He pulled Sister Davenport toward the vestibule doors.

"I'll talk to you all later," Sister Davenport said to Tyson and Anisha. "We've been meaning to invite you guys over for dinner, so let's plan on Sunday."

"That would be nice," Anisha said, shooing Sister Davenport along. "You better hurry."

Sister Davenport smiled and rolled her eyes. She hooked an arm around her husband's waist and followed his hasty stride out of the church.

Tyson and Anisha wove through the chatty crowd in the vestibule. Anisha lagged behind, looking for Sherri. She wished it were Sherri she'd seen instead of who she saw walking in her direction.

Anisha immediately recognized the face from Mick's restaurant—the same one who had stopped Tyson. She didn't even know the girl, but the sight of her dropped a funny feeling in her stomach. Again. She had a glowing bronze complexion and hair that looked like it belonged on the head of a model in a shampoo commercial. As before, the little girl with the round eyes was attached to her like a permanent fixture on her leg.

Anisha looked up at Tyson and saw his face held just as much surprise.

"Hi. How are you?" Tyson asked, stopping briefly as their paths met.

"Fine, thanks," she answered, without so much as a glance at Anisha to acknowledge her presence. Her eyes were fixed on Tyson.

"Hey, cutie," Tyson gently pinched the small child's cheek.

Anisha anticipated an introduction, but Tyson started toward the exit again as quickly as he'd stopped. She tried to steer Tyson into an explanation as they walked through the parking lot toward her car.

"She looked familiar."

"Huh?" Tyson took Anisha's hand and led her through a maze of parked cars.

"I said she—"

"Hey, y'all."

Sherri's voice broke Anisha's probing. Seeing her friend's head poking outside her car window brought a smile to Anisha's face, and she temporarily forgot about her concern.

"What's up, girl?"

"I'm surprised you recognize a sister," Sherri joked. She pecked Anisha on the cheek, then acknowledged Tyson with a handshake and a witty remark. "You're the reason Anisha has cut our Sunday brunches for the past two weeks," she said to him. "I'm starting not to like you."

"You know you love me," Tyson grabbed her finger and pretended to bite it.

Sherri snatched her finger out of his grasp. "Whatever," she said teasingly. "Call me," she told Anisha. Sherri started up her car and navigated through the parking lot toward the main road.

"Do you think Sherri really has a problem with me?" Tyson asked. He opened Anisha's car door and helped her get in. He leaned on the open door frame and stared down at her.

"You know how Sherri is," Anisha reassured him. "She was only playing."

"She may try to act like it, but I don't think she's always kidding."

"I think I know her a little better than you, but if it'll make you feel better, I'll ask her about it."

"No need. I just wanted to know what you thought."

"Okay," Anisha said, shrugging her shoulders. "I'll talk to you tomorrow."

"Actually, I was planning on giving you a buzz tonight. We need to talk."

Anisha hated those words. *We need to talk.* She'd never known it to be followed by pleasant conversation.

"What's wrong? You wanna talk now?"

Tyson loosened Anisha's grip on the steering wheel and kissed her fingertips. "Call ya when I get home."

"Fine," Anisha uttered in frustration. People initiating a conversation before they were ready to address it really irritated her more than that 'we need to talk' phrase. What difference would waiting until later make?

Tyson must have sensed the annoyance in Anisha's voice. He lifted her fingertips to his lips again, then lightly tapped the hood of her car before walking away.

Anisha forced a weak smile and pulled off. Though slightly perturbed, she tried to focus her thoughts on the sermon but couldn't. She found the short drive home a welcome convenience.

Anisha hung out her clothes for work and readied herself for bed while she awaited Tyson's phone call. She stepped into the shower and heard the phone ring over the running water. She was in no rush to answer it. She knew it was Tyson, but she didn't know if she wanted to hear what he had to say.

"We need to talk," she said aloud, scrubbing the soapy washcloth on her shoulders. Saying the words again only made her cringe.

Anisha's thoughts traveled back to her conversation with Sister

Davenport, the brief confrontation with Tyson's mystery friend, and then to Sherri.

Will Tyson tell me about his consecration period? What made him do it anyway? How could that girl have the audacity to ignore me? She acted like I wasn't even there. Was I wrong for not stepping up and saying something first? Would that have been being the bigger woman, or would I have been trying to make a point? I need to talk to my girl. She denied it, but there's a possibility Tyson is right. Sherri could be trying to hide her true feelings behind the guise of a joke.

Anisha only let her worrying invade her thoughts for a moment. She was physically and mentally exhausted by the time she finally climbed into bed. She buried her head under a pillow and, despite her former anxiousness, now hoped Tyson would postpone his call until the next day. The ringing phone quickly banished the possibility.

"Hello," she answered, her voice already covered with sleep.

"You asleep already?"

"Not yet."

"I'm sorry. If you're too tired we can talk later, but if you can hold out a little longer, I'd really like to talk to you now."

"Of course I can stay up for you," Anisha said, sitting up and adjusting two pillows behind her back. She kicked the covers to the bottom of the bed and stretched out her legs.

"Do you remember that time we went out to eat with Sherri and Xavier a few months ago?"

"Yeah."

"Well, when we were leaving the restaurant, I ran into my exgirlfriend Brandy and her daughter, Ayana. I haven't seen her in about five or six years, so needless to say I was pretty shocked." Tyson paused for a moment as if waiting for Anisha's response, but when he didn't get one, he picked up his story. "When we were leaving Bible study tonight, I saw her again. Shock number two."

Anisha waited patiently while Tyson seemed to gather his thoughts.

"There's something about our relationship I haven't shared with many people," he said. "It's not like I was trying to hide anything, but since it was in my past I didn't see a reason to bring it up until I was sure our relationship was growing."

Anisha held her breath. *If this man tells me Ayana is his daughter, I don't know what I'm gonna do. Oh God, please don't let him tell me that. I can't deal with any baby's mama drama.*

"Are you there?" Tyson asked.

"I'm here," she managed to say.

"Brandy is the girl I dated in college that I told you about. To make a long story short, we didn't go our separate ways just because we were growing apart. We reached a point where we'd break up every other month. Until Brandy told me she was pregnant. We decided we were going to stop acting immature and make a commitment to raise our child and be a family."

Pregnant? Our child? Family? Anisha's stomach knotted.

"You okay?" Tyson asked.

"Uh-huh. Go ahead."

"At the time there was nothing I didn't try to provide for her. I bought whatever she needed for the baby and anything I thought she wanted. I was a senior in my last semester trying to work a part-time job and finish school."

Tyson got sidetracked and rambled on about everything he'd bought for the child. Anisha wanted to edge him on to the point but let him carry on until he was ready to discuss the real issue.

Tyson breathed a heavy sigh into the phone. "I was at work when Brandy went into labor, so her mom took her to the hospital," he recalled. "It was at the end of the day, and traffic was already backed up on I-85, so by the time I got there she was already in delivery and too many people were in the room. I ended up staying in the waiting room for over an hour with another guy. I think his name was Chad or Chris. Something like that."

Anisha slid beneath the coolness of her covers. She inhaled and exhaled slowly, trying to slow her palpitating heart back to its normal pace. It didn't work.

"Turns out the same guy I was waiting with was there for Brandy, too. Ayana was his daughter, not mine, and Brandy waited until that day to tell me," Tyson said. "She claimed she had wanted to tell me before, but she was scared. So I was there with the rest of the family looking like an idiot, to say the least. In my mind I was thinking we could work it out anyway, and I'd raise the baby as my own. She didn't give me a chance. Said she felt like the baby's real father was more established and could give her more. So she went for the man with the wallet instead of the man with the heart."

Anisha could hear the lingering pain in Tyson's voice. She knew her thoughts were selfish, but she was relieved the ordeal had turned out the way it did. She cast out her thoughts and focused on being the shoulder Tyson needed to lean on. She struggled to find the right words to say.

"It's her loss," Anisha consoled him. "God sees things we can't, and He knows what's best."

"Maybe seeing her tonight started to open up an old wound," Tyson said. "Me and God had a talk on the way home, and I've got a peace about it. I mean, I'm not trippin' over her or anything. Like I said before, it sorta threw me off seeing her again tonight."

"So do you think she just happened to show up at the church? Or maybe she goes to the church. With so many people and two services, it's possible you never ran into her before."

Anisha knew what she thought. The night at the restaurant was a coincidence. Tonight was planned, whether Tyson could see it or not. True, it had been a while since they ran into her the first night, but every snake could lie in wait until it was time to strike.

"I guess," Tyson said. "But now that I think about it, when I saw her at the restaurant she asked if I was still going to church, and I probably told her where."

Bingo.

"I don't know. I don't remember what I said."

Tyson's voice sounded agitated, so Anisha didn't push further.

"Regardless, at least she's somewhere where the true gospel is being taught," Anisha said. She felt it was the right thing to say, even though she didn't really mean it. As far as she was concerned, Brandy needed to go somewhere else. Anywhere else. She didn't want the drama.

"Enough about that," Tyson said, dropping the subject. "I had to get all of it off my chest. I'm tired, and I know you're tired. I'll call you tomorrow if I get a chance. I've got to go down to the center to take care of some business as soon as I get off work."

"Okay. And thanks for sharing. You didn't have to do that."

"Yes, I did," Tyson assured her. "I wanted to."

"I'll talk to you tomorrow," Anisha said.

"All right, love. Sleep tight," he whispered.

Anisha reached over to her nightstand and hung up the phone. She pulled her knees to her chest and closed her eyes. *He called me love.*

Brandy stroked the top of her daughter's head as they lay in the full-sized bed together. She remembered a time when she had to line pillows behind Ayana's back or had to push the bed against the wall for fear her small body would roll off the bed during the night. Soon there would barely be room for the both of them.

Brandy leaned over and kissed the closed eyelids of her sleeping child. The light brush of Ayana's breath warmed her cheek. Her daughter was the reason she lived, and Brandy was determined to make a better life for the two of them.

"Mommy is going to do her best for you, baby," Brandy whispered.

It had taken nearly two months of visiting the church off and on, but it had finally happened. She'd finally run into Tyson. Tonight she'd noticed the strong maturing of his face. His jaw line was stronger and his eyes more intense than the face she remembered.

Brandy stretched her arms above her head and contracted all of her muscles as tightly as she could before letting her body go limp again. She wished those same eyes were staring at her right now the way they used to, reassuring her that he would always take care of everything she needed. She remembered the dreams they'd shared to be a family. They were going to be young parents, but Tyson had promised to give their child the best life he could.

There wasn't a day from the moment Tyson had found out she

was pregnant that he didn't rub her stomach and talk to the growing child he'd thought was his own. She hadn't meant to slip up with Chris. He'd crept in when she was vulnerable and she and Tyson were going through one of their reoccurring breakup stages.

She hadn't known how to tell Tyson the truth. He didn't make things easy by coming over with a gift every day. She'd been confused. And her life hadn't changed much since then.

Brandy felt the bed shift slightly under Ayana's weight. Ayana stretched and kicked until she freed herself from the bedsheets that swaddled the length of her body. Brandy pulled the covers off of both of them and pushed them to the end of the bed. Even in the dark, Brandy knew her daughter's thumb had made its way into her mouth. She could hear the faint suckling as Ayana lulled herself back to sleep.

Ayana deserves her own room with a daybed and a matching dresser, Brandy thought. She wished Ayana could experience the simple things in life that children enjoyed. She wanted her to have a desk where she could sit and create colorful works of art, then plaster them like wallpaper on the refrigerator. She deserved to be in an after-school program with other children instead of having to play in the little room in the back of the salon.

And more than anything else, Ayana needed what every little girl her age should have—a loving father. Someone who could carry her piggyback through the park. Someone whose arms she could jump into when he came home from work. Someone who could rule with a stern hand when she was out of line, but who Ayana could wrap around her little finger. Someone to read her bedtime stories before tucking her in for the night.

Brandy wiped away the tears sliding down her cheeks. She had mistakenly believed she could secure Ayana's future by staying with Chris. Even though Tyson was more emotionally stable at the time, Chris was more financially secure. He'd inherited a large sum of money when his grandfather died, and he was making plans to invest a little and use the rest to start his own business. But the dream never became a reality, and Brandy ended up living a nightmare instead. Chris had a hidden drug addiction that drained his bank accounts and then sucked Brandy's small savings dry.

She'd depended on Chris for everything, and after she became a mother and a makeshift wife, she never bothered to finish the last semester she needed to graduate with her accounting degree. Funny how someone who was supposed to be able to manage money had done such a bad job at it. Her dreams, her money, and her self-esteem all walked out the door with Chris when he left. Ayana was only two at the time. The day was forever etched in Brandy's mind.

Brandy kissed Ayana's forehead again. The pastor at Grace Worship had been talking about how God answers prayers. She needed to convince God that Tyson was supposed to be her man in the first place, and it was only right that he be hers again. His current—soon to be ex—girlfriend would have to understand.

*T*hursday rolled on like any other day for Tyson. His en-
gineer-wired mind ticked like clockwork from the time
he arrived at his office at seven-thirty that morning until he finally
wrapped up the day at six. The demanding schedule and projects didn't
leave much room for his mind to wander to anything else. Until now.

Tyson drummed his pencil on the desk. He hadn't accomplished
much since arriving at the center more than two hours ago. He sat at
the computer screen, wearing the same blank look on his face he'd worn
for the last ten minutes.

Why Brandy? Why now? He had a feeling in his chest he couldn't describe. A sort of anxiety had crept in last night and refused to leave.
And then there was Anisha. He was learning more about the woman
he'd watched for over a year. She hadn't tripped when he'd talked to her
last night. He knew she was probably a little unnerved by it, but she
was willing to let the past stay in the past.

Tap. Tap. Tyson looked up at the sound of the light rap on the door.
Xavier stood in the doorway carrying a stack of manila file folders.

"What's up, man?" Xavier walked inside the office and dropped the folders on Tyson's desk. "I've walked past your office twice in the last ten minutes, and you've been staring at the computer screen like it's on," he said, rapping the monitor with his fist.

Tyson swiveled his chair around and pushed the power switch on the CPU behind him. "Thinking, man."

"Well, I hope you've been thinking about some more companies who can sponsor this gala for the boys. Six months really wasn't a lot of time to pull this thing together in the first place."

"I know," Tyson said. "Anisha helped the committee put together a sponsorship package, and I'm going to mail ten of those in the morning. Hopefully by Saturday I'll have some more strong prospects and be able to send out ten more next week." Tyson clicked through the icons on his desktop until the database of his prospective sponsors opened across his monitor screen. "I'll make some follow-up calls over the next couple of weeks, and we'll see what we've got from there."

"Sounds like a plan to me." Xavier picked up his folders and tucked them securely under his arm. "Do your job," Xavier said, backing up, and on the way out picked up a crumpled piece of paper from the floor and tossed it at Tyson.

A sudden agitation surfaced in Tyson's voice. "Have you ever known a time when I haven't? You make sure you do *your* job."

"Man, you've got to give me something to work with," Xavier retaliated. "You trippin'." He walked away and left Tyson to simmer.

Tyson propped his elbows on the desk and buried his face in his palms. He hadn't meant to lash out at Xavier, but his mounting frustrations were overtaking his usual easygoing manner. He'd probably set the trust in their relationship back another six months. He hoped he hadn't bought into being the hypocritical Christian he'd fought so hard to defend himself against.

Tyson reached for the phone and methodically dialed Deacon Davenport's number. He was relieved to hear the patriarchal voice answer after only two rings.

"Hello?"

"Hey, Deac."

"Tyson, how's it going, man?"

"To tell the truth, Deac, not too good. Got a minute?"

"As many as you need."

Tyson closed his office door to fend off any unnecessary interruptions.

"Yesterday," he started, "things couldn't have been better. But now I've got so much invading my mind,. I can't stay focused on anything."

Tyson recounted the events that had brought him up to his current dilemma. He told the deacon about his relationship with Brandy and the act of betrayal that finally ended their relationship. He openly shared how the emotional breakdown had brought him to a true relationship with God.

"It took a lot out of me, but it made me a better man," Tyson said. He leaned back on the headrest of his high-backed leather chair. He squeezed his eyes together until he saw white lights dancing around the darkness of his closed lids. He wasn't prepared for the sting of tears threatening to slide through the cracks of his eyelids. He squeezed his eyes even tighter and swallowed the rising lump in his throat. He didn't want the evidence of his true pain to surface in his voice.

The two men sat in silence. Tyson was relieved to finally unload the burden that had weighed him down all day. He relaxed his shoulders and exhaled slowly.

"Let's pray first," Deacon Davenport suggested. "Do you mind?"

"Of course not," Tyson said.

Deacon Davenport cleared his throat, and Tyson pictured what his mentor must have been doing. Was he on his knees or stretched out in his recliner? As silly as Tyson knew he would look if somebody walked in his office, he decided to crawl under his desk and position himself for prayer. He didn't have time to worry about people's opinions.

Tyson always appreciated Deacon Davenport's prayers, whether they were praying together or in class. It was like Deacon's voice transformed. It sounded like the Holy Spirit sat on his vocal cords and God used his mouth.

"Lord, I pray for a release for Tyson from his past," Deacon Davenport said, "Let it not be a hindrance to him but an experience to push him into his future. Father, we've all made a mess of some things in our lives, but You can turn our mess into our message. Nothing catches You by surprise, not even our mistakes.

"Clear up any confusion in his life, and keep his mind steadfast on You. Make him a better man. Make *us* better men. *We* need Your wisdom in all things. All things, Father. God, crush the seeds of bitterness and rejection that may have been planted in his old relationships, so it won't spring up in his new relationship and strangle the life out of it. In Your Son's matchless name we pray. Amen."

"Amen," Tyson added.

Bitterness? Rejection? The words collided in Tyson's mind. Deacon had him wrong, but he decided not to address it with him. He needed to refocus so he could get back to business. Tyson massaged his temples to ease the pressure of a threatening headache. He was probably thinking too hard.

"Thanks, Deacon." Tyson sighed. "You know how to call down the fire when a brother needs it. I feel better knowing someone with a clear mind is getting a prayer through."

"Your prayers are getting through. You gotta be patient and quiet enough to hear your answer." Deacon Davenport lowered his voice. "I've got a pair of ears walking into the room."

Tyson heard Sister Davenport's voice in the background. "Baby, who's that?"

"See, what did I tell ya?" Deacon Davenport chuckled. "If you need me, I'm here. I'll still be praying for you, and I'm not just saying that."

"Later, Deac," Tyson said.

He crawled from under the desk and hung up the phone. He thought about calling Anisha but decided against it. He'd wait and call tomorrow.

Tyson turned around to his computer and lost himself in his work. As the time crept to midnight, he customized, packaged, and addressed all ten of the sponsorship packages and had them ready for the morning mail. When he finally opened his office door, he found all of the offices empty. The rest of the volunteers had retired for the night, and the building was void of all signs of life. The silence was broken only by the sound of the humming refrigerator in the snack room.

Tyson double-checked all of the doors to make sure they were locked, then walked to his car that sat under the single streetlight in the abandoned parking lot. He slid into the driver's seat and looked out into the darkness.

"God, what's this about?" he asked aloud.

Tyson was growing to care for Anisha more each day, so he wondered why seeing Brandy brought conflicting thoughts in his mind. Brandy made her choice years ago when she felt he didn't meet her standards. He may not have had all she wanted then, but he was more of a man now. The man who had lost Brandy's heart but was trying to gain Anisha's. Of that, he was sure.

The more he thought about it, maybe Deacon Davenport was right. There was a level of rejection there, but the past was the past. What could be done about it now?

*A*nisha and Sherri strolled through the quaint Atlanta sub-urban community of downtown Decatur amidst the rows of independent novelty and clothing shops. After Sherri's remark at Bible study on Wednesday, Anisha had made a point to schedule a girl's Saturday out with her. She didn't want her best friend to feel she'd been deserted.

Even at ten o'clock in the morning, the community was bustling with movement. A group of men in coordinating blue shirts and tan shorts scurried around pulling extension cords and speakers across the plush lawn in front of the Decatur courtyard. A white banner with bold blue letters foretold the night's activities: Funk Jazz On The Lawn.

Sherri sucked the last of her frappuccino, then pulled out the long green straw to lick off the whipped cream. "So old girl *happened* to show up at church? I don't buy it. You know she tracked your boy down."

Anisha took a sip of her fruit smoothie before answering. "My thoughts exactly. I know that and you know that, but you know men. Tyson acted like he didn't see the connection."

"I don't see why," Sherri said, stopping in front of a novelty shop on East Ponce to admire the items in the display window. "He's the one who told her what church he went to."

Anisha finished off the last of her smoothie and tossed the empty cup into a nearby trash can. "Right now I don't have time to worry about it. That was about three months ago when we saw her at Mick's downtown. The girl is free to go to any church she wants to. She may really need a relationship with God," Anisha said, trying to convince herself as much as she was trying to convince Sherri.

"And I know something else she may need if she starts acting up," Sherri said. "A good butt whippin'."

"I should have known better than to get you started."

"Exactly. Don't start none, won't be none. Show me who she is, and I'll make it plain to her." Sherri balled up her fists and jabbed her best boxing punches.

"You're a mess," Anisha said, pushing past Sherri and walking into the store. "First of all, do not embarrass me here. Secondly, it's not even that deep. Tyson told me about it, so evidently there's nothing to hide." *God, I hope not.*

The girls were welcomed with a cheerful greeting from a short, middle-aged woman. Her round face was topped with pink, spiked hair and framed with a pair of horn-rimmed glasses, and her vintage clothes looked deliberately mismatched.

Sherri picked up a set of Chinese stress balls from a table and made an unsuccessful attempt to roll them through her fingers. "Number one, I'm much too cute to embarrass you or me." She held up two fingers in front of her face. "And secondly, I'm only telling you so you can let me know if we need to call in the troops."

Anisha rested her hand on her friend's shoulder and held the other over her brow in a military salute. "You will be the first to know, Ms. President."

Anisha squeezed down the narrow aisles of the small shop. She picked up several different hand painted frames and thumbed through a collection of handmade cards. "Some of this stuff is so creative," she said, rubbing her hand across an embossed picture album with raised lettering.

Sherri walked toward her with a small wire object. She set the twisted contraption resembling the shape of a body in front of Anisha. "That's not the word I would have used," she whispered. She twisted the small white tag so she could read the price. "Twenty-three dollars?" she exclaimed, her voice raising slightly above a whisper.

"This is someone's passion," Anisha said, picking it up. "And as crazy as it looks to somebody else, the artist took a chance on it. How much you wanna bet somebody will buy it?"

"It sure won't be me," Sherri said.

Anisha walked toward a basket of fabric-covered journals. She stooped down to the basket and sorted through the journals until she discovered one to her liking. "This looks like it was made for me," she said, standing and showing the book to Sherri. It was covered in a deep purple material with a gold cross appliqué stitched on the front cover.

"Oh, that's beautiful. Almost too pretty to write in," Sherri said. "But it does make you want to hide all of your deepest secrets and dreams on the pages."

Anisha's face bubbled with excitement. "Why can't we?" Anisha bent over the basket again and resurfaced with a journal for Sherri, similar in style, but in bronze and blue. "These are our prayer journals," she explained. "Whatever you want to tell God. Whatever you want to ask Him about. Any intimate conversations. Any prayer."

"That's a good idea." Sherri pulled the journal to her chest. "You know writing is cathartic. It has a way of cleansing your soul."

Anisha and Sherri took their treasures up front to the lady tending the cash register. As they reached the counter, the woman hollered out a welcome to two women trying to maneuver their supersized baby strollers through the door. She wrapped Anisha and Sherri's journals in pink tissue paper and carefully slid them into gift bags.

"Thanks," they both said, then headed toward the door, content with their purchases.

"This is so cute. I've got to have it," someone in the store said.

Anisha's eyes searched for the reason for the voice's delight. One of the ladies who'd entered the store was holding the wire-shaped figurine up for her friend to admire. Anisha nodded her head toward the couple as she pushed on the door heading out to the street. "See? What did I tell you?" she said to Sherri.

"It proves to me anything is possible," Sherri said.

"You're right about that, girl. Do your thing."

"As soon as I know what it is, I will. But you, on the other hand, know at least one thing God has called you to do. So how's your business plan coming along?"

"It's coming," Anisha stammered. It had been nearly two months since she'd thought extensively about it or written anything in her vision notebook. She'd been too busy making sure Tyson had everything together for the gala and his mentoring program. It was taking quite a bit of time to pull together his business plan, marketing program, and now the program curriculum.

Anisha could tell by the look on Sherri's face that she was tempted to climb onto her proverbial soapbox. Her look was caught somewhere between disgust and disappointment.

"God didn't stir up the gift so you could sit on it," Sherri said.

"You're right," Anisha said. There was no room for discussion. Besides, she wasn't up for it. Today was supposed to be for some girlfriend bonding. "I'm gonna get on it," she promised Sherri and herself.

Anisha and Sherri stopped at the corner of East Ponce and Church Streets. The heat triggered sweat beads to form across their noses, and they looked for another shop to duck into for shelter.

Sherri shielded her eyes from the sun and tried to stir an imaginary breeze by briskly fanning herself. "I love Georgia, but if I could trade in this heat for a few months of mild temperatures, I'd do it in a second," Sherri complained. "Either we need to go into another one of these little shops or find our way to somewhere with some AC."

"You're so pitiful," Anisha said. "You should live in Colorado or somewhere. This *is* Hotlanta, you know."

"If I lived in Colorado, you wouldn't have the privilege of knowing me."

Anisha wrapped her arm around Sherri's shoulders. "You're right." Anisha gasped sarcastically. "What in the world was I thinking?" She looked up and down the streets that were busy with the hustle of people running Saturday midmorning errands and others escaping the bustling big city life. Foot traffic on the sidewalks was beginning to pick up pace, too, with families dragging along their pets and children.

"What's the menu for tomorrow's dinner?" Sherri asked. "I'm going to the store later on this afternoon."

Anisha hated to break the news now after such a bonding moment. Better now than later, she thought.

"Actually, the Davenports invited me and Tyson over for dinner after church," Anisha explained hesitantly.

"I see. That's why you were so anxious for us to get together this morning," Sherri said. "You knew you would be ditching me for the third time in a row tomorrow." She lifted Anisha's arm from around her shoulder and turned to look her friend in the eyes. She smiled to show there weren't any hard feelings.

"Go with your man, girl. I know I would. We had our time today."

"Let's go to the little place up the street a ways where you can make your own pottery," Anisha suggested after some thought. "We've been saying we were going to for a while."

"No time like the present," Sherri agreed. "Can we walk in without a reservation?"

"I'm not sure, but it's worth a try."

The aura inside the pottery shop was soothing. The calming scent of lavender swirled around the room, and the handcrafted clay vases scattered around the room were full of fresh flowers.

After a few minutes of explanation from the instructor, Anisha and Sherri were posted on stools in front of lifeless lumps of gray clay.

"Remember," the instructor reiterated, "the clay is totally in your hands. It has no choice but to conform to however you shape it. Gentle molding works, but sometimes you have to apply a little pressure to get the shape you want."

The instructor placed a bowl of water on the small table between them. "If the clay gets too dry, it will become resistant to molding, so you have to add a little water to it." The instructor stood before them, her hands clasped in front of her chest like a pleased schoolteacher. "After you've finished, we'll coat it with a glaze that acts like a seal to give the pottery its texture and brilliance. Lastly," she said clapping her hands together, "we'll put your pieces in the fire."

"Won't the fire melt the pottery?" Anisha asked.

"No, because the glaze is for protection too. It gives the pottery both shine and resistance."

Anisha and Sherri worked in silence as they attempted their first hand at pottery making. They worked slowly and deliberately to fashion the pieces to the image they envisioned.

"Every piece is an original," the instructor said. "Even if someone tries to duplicate your work, there will never be another one exactly like it." She walked behind Anisha and Sherri, observing their work. "Very nice," she said. "Would you girls like a little music while you work?"

"Have any jazz?" Sherri asked, her eyes never leaving the clay lump transforming before her.

"Of course. It's the best music to work to." The instructor disappeared behind a doorway covered with a string of beads, and soon the music spilled into the store.

"We can take our creations to the little store up the street and make a killing." Sherri giggled. "You can make enough money for the down payment on your house, and I'll take a couple of months off from work to figure out what I want to do with my life—or should I say what *God* wants me to do with my life."

"Sure," Anisha mumbled. She was lost in thought. She dipped her hand in the basin of water and carefully smoothed a bubble forming in her clay.

Your life is like clay in My hands. I take special care in molding you into the woman I created you to be.

Anisha turned to Sherri. "I was reflecting about how God molds our lives," she said. "He's the potter, and we're the clay. He's fashioned each of us into an original design, and He knows exactly what it takes to get us into shape. He uses pressure when He needs to, but He also adds a little water—His Word—so we'll conform to His image easier."

"But don't forget the most important part of the process," Sherri added. She dropped her fingers into the bowl by her stool and flicked water on her creation.

"What?" Anisha asked.

"Into the fire."

*T*yson and Anisha turned into the subdivision entrance of the extravagant neighborhood of Cascade Heights. Each of the custom-built houses sat on an expansive lawn with meticulous landscaping, a far cry from the concrete that took up the majority of the landscaping in their neighborhood.

The Davenports' house was nestled in a cul-de-sac on one of the streets farthest from the main road. Tyson pulled into the driveway and parked his car beside Sister Davenport's pearl-white Mercedes Benz.

Anisha opened the car door and was ready to get out until Tyson reached over her and pulled the door shut.

"Where are you going?" he asked, jumping out of the car and running around the rear bumper. He opened the passenger door and bowed down. "Now you may exit, my lady," he said in his best English accent and offered a hand to Anisha.

"How cordial of you, sir." Anisha attempted to imitate the foreign dialect as she accepted Tyson's waiting hand and stepped from the car.

Evidently Sister Davenport had spotted the arrival of her visitors. She was waiting on the porch as Tyson and Anisha walked hand in hand toward her. The aroma of the Sunday dinner floated from the house and mingled with the fragrance of the rose bushes lining the walkway.

"Make yourself comfortable in the family room," Sister Davenport said. "I'm heating up the food now. Russell went upstairs to get out of his suit. He'll be back down in a second."

Tyson led Anisha to one of the least formal rooms in the house. A wide-screen television and entertainment center was built into one of the walls, and the soft pastel colors that accented the décor gave the den a cozy feeling. Tyson found his place on one of the sofas, and Anisha ventured over to inspect a collection of photographs on the fireplace mantle. She picked up a picture of two girls with identical smiles sitting on a porch swing. It was one of many photos spread along the mantle that seemed to chronicle the girls' lives from infancy to adulthood.

"These must be their daughters," Anisha said to Tyson.

"Yep. Those are my babies," Sister Davenport said, walking into the room. "They're sophomores in college right now. Yolanda is up at the University of Maryland, and Raquel is studying at the University of Miami. Those girls are so busy being grown they rarely come home anymore unless it's a major holiday. I tell you, they're two peas in a pod." Sister Davenport picked up a photo of the girls in their cap-and-gown regalia, taken at their high school graduation. She ran her finger along the silver frame. "I can't believe they went to school so far away from each other."

"It's usually hard to separate twins," Anisha said.

"They're not twins," Sister Davenport said, putting the photo back on the mantle.

"Oh," Anisha said flatly. *Maybe one of the girls was held back a grade,* Anisha thought. *How else would they have graduated from high school at the same time?*

They heard Deacon Davenport thump down the stairs and moments later appear in the family room. He'd replaced his black pin-striped suit with a white polo shirt and a starched pair of khakis. "How long before we can grub?" Deacon Davenport asked, rubbing the chubby pouch extending over his belt.

Sister Davenport walked over and stood behind her husband. "Patience, patience," she said, massaging his shoulders.

"Uh-oh, little lady. Don't get nothing started." Deacon Davenport circled his shoulders, obviously enjoying the pressure of his wife's touch. "We might have to leave our company alone for a while."

"Russell! I can't believe you said that in front of these kids." Sister Davenport caught him off guard with a light push on his back. He tipped over slightly but regained his balance. "They're not kids; they're grown adults. They know how they got into this world."

"I know they do, but please spare them any unnecessary details and save me from any more embarrassment."

Embarrassment was still on Sister Davenport's face as she walked over to Anisha and took her hand. "Did you hear the oven timer buzzing? I think we better go check on the food."

As Sister Davenport passed her husband, Anisha saw her pinch his rear with her free hand. Deacon Davenport yelped and whirled around with a look of astonishment, but his wife's countenance showed no sign of guilt.

Sister Davenport looked at Anisha and shrugged her shoulders, unaware that Anisha had seen her in the act. "You'll never figure men out, honey."

Sister Davenport led Anisha into the kitchen and grabbed the ringing phone from the counter. She engaged in lively chatter with the caller, all the while directing Anisha with exaggerated hand motions and whispered instructions. By the time Sister Davenport hung up the phone, Anisha had found the set of dinnerware and was setting the table.

"That was my girlfriend, Vivian," Sister Davenport said, pulling four sets of cutlery from the drawer. "Did I introduce you to her at church before?"

"Not that I can recall."

"She's excited about our big Labor Day cookout we have every year. She's bringing a young lady she calls her adopted daughter, so you two will have to meet. I think Vivian said you all were probably around the same age. "

Anisha folded a cloth napkin and set it out beside one of the place settings. "Okay," she said. "I can't wait to meet her."

❦

Deacon Davenport scooped a generous second helping of mashed potatoes onto his plate before passing the bowl to Tyson. "Are you going to help me finish these off?" he asked Tyson, reaching for the dish of steamed squash and zucchini.

Tyson held up his hand to decline. "That's it for me, Deac. I need to save a little room for a helping of peach cobbler."

"I didn't tell you we had peach cobbler," Sister Davenport said, standing up to gather the empty dinner plates.

"No, but somebody else did, and *he* shall remain nameless."

"Wasn't me. Musta been Jesus." Deacon Davenport leaned over to Tyson. "Don't get me in trouble, man. I've got to live with this woman."

When Sister Davenport and Anisha disappeared into the kitchen, Deacon Davenport lowered his voice out of range from any wandering ears from the other room.

"So have you gotten your head straight since we talked the other night? The whole Brandy thing?"

"Yeah," Tyson said. "Like I said before, running into her at church threw me off for a minute. I was more concerned about making Anisha comfortable. I don't want to risk her pulling away from me." Tyson didn't want to get into a deep discussion. There wasn't a need to address any old issues with Brandy. She was the past, and he was trying to stay concerned with the future.

Sister Davenport and Anisha returned with plates of warm peach cobbler and French vanilla ice cream and set them down before the men.

"Round two," Deacon Davenport said, rubbing his stomach.

❦

Deacon Davenport swirled the crust on the end of his fork through the remaining peach syrup on his plate. He chucked it into his mouth and chased it down with a cold glass of water. "How are your boys doing down at the center?" he asked Tyson.

"They're fine. If I've learned anything from working there for the last two years, it's that kids hold you to your word. Me and Xavier have been doing everything in our power to make sure the gala in December is a success. If I show the neighborhood and corporate community that the program is effecting positive change in the youth, then I don't think it'll be a problem getting funding to make it a full-time, year-round program. Seeing the boys for a couple of hours a day during the school year and two Saturdays out of the month ain't enough. We've got to destroy some of the mind-sets they've grown up with."

Tyson continued sharing his vision of the program with the Davenports. It was a dream he'd shared plenty of times with Anisha, but she bubbled with pride whenever he talked about it, as if it were her first time hearing it. She didn't know who was more excited. They had been working overtime to finish his business plan for distribution to the sponsors who were attending the gala. Tyson was determined to put one in the hand of every potential investor.

"I wouldn't have gotten this far with the proposal if it hadn't been for Ms. Executive here." Tyson reached across the table and took Anisha's hand. "I told her what I wanted to do, and she's been able to pull the pieces together and run with it."

Anisha shook her head in modesty. "It's no big deal, really. Tyson is exaggerating."

"Maybe not to you because it's your natural gift," Sister Davenport said. "But don't take it for granted. People are always looking for strong writers and visionaries with creative minds. If nothing else, you can bring in some extra income on the side."

Anisha marveled at God's tactics of using other people to speak His desires to her. *Okay, God. I think You've made Your point clear. I promise I'll work on it this week.*

"Actually, I am interested in starting my own business," Anisha shared for the first time to someone other than her immediate family, Tyson, and Sherri. Maybe if she told more people about her vision, she'd be driven to stick to the task. "I don't know when I'll be ready to launch it, but I know it's what I'm supposed to do. I'm still working on getting the details together."

"If God told you to do it, baby, you make sure you do it," Sister Davenport said. "He'll move anything and anyone out of the way who's blocking your focus or hindering you from His assignment for you. Don't let anyone drown out the voice of God."

Anisha left the last corner of her peach cobbler on her plate. It didn't taste as sweet. Evidently her mind was playing tricks on her. The Enemy was trying to play games and confuse her. Why was she thinking about Tyson? He was anything but a hindrance. He believed in her dreams, prayed over her vision, and was a good man. He was God sent, wasn't he?

Sherri fumbled to open the door. She didn't know which was worse—her headache from being so tired or the hunger pains shooting through her stomach. After Anisha announced yesterday that she was missing yet another Sunday brunch, Sherri had come home Saturday night and prepared her own feast.

She threw her pocketbook on the couch and went directly to the refrigerator so she could start warming her food. Before long, the pot roast with red potatoes and baby carrots simmered in the oven, and a pot of lima beans sat warming on the stove. Sherri changed out of her dress as quickly as she could. The aroma made her taste buds dance so hard she forgot about sleep.

Sherri stacked her plate, poured a tall glass of iced tea, and decided to eat at the dining table instead of with her usual tray in front of the television. She heard the click of one of her roommates' bedroom door and watched Veronica drag into the kitchen.

"Morning," Sherri said between bites of pot roast.

"Hey." Veronica groaned and pulled two glasses from the cupboard. She filled them with orange juice and, slurping from one of the glasses, eyed Sherri at the dining table. "I take it your little friend Anisha has a man now."

Sherri laid her fork down and stopped eating. "What makes you say that?"

"You've been at home after church for the past few weeks, and I know y'all always eat together. What other reason would she have for kicking your butt to the curb?"

Sherri picked up her fork and stabbed a potato a little harder than she intended, sending it bouncing off the plate and rolling onto the place mat. She ignored it and sawed at a piece of pot roast, hoping Veronica would disappear back down the hall. Realizing Veronica had no intentions of budging until she was addressed, Sherri offered an explanation. A very brief one.

"She's been busy."

Veronica huffed and shook her head in disbelief. "Yeah, she's been busy all right. Busy with her man." She sipped from one of the glasses and looked at Sherri with a smug look that Sherri wished she could've slapped off her face. Veronica strutted down the hallway and disappeared into her room.

Sherri rolled her eyes and pushed her food around on her plate. She refused to let Veronica spoil her meal. Before she could try to regain her composure, she heard one of the back bedroom doors click open again. Sherri was relieved when Tamara walked into view.

"Morning," Sherri said in her second attempt to hold a decent conversation with a member of her household.

Tamara pulled out a chair and sat across from Sherri. "Good morning." Her microbraids were pulled into a high ponytail, and with her usual layers of makeup scrubbed from her face, she looked younger than her age of thirty years. She pulled the oversized sleep shirt that hid the true contour of her body down over her knees. "How was church today?"

"Awesome as usual. Pastor Armstrong ministered on how the words you speak can make or break your life."

"I could use some preachin' like that," Tamara said, covering her mouth and stifling a yawn.

"You ought to come with me one Sunday," Sherri said. She walked to the cupboard and pulled out another plate. She loaded it with generous portions of the Sunday meal.

"I need to get myself together before I can go to anybody's church," Tamara said after some thought.

"Girl, if I'd waited to get myself together, I still wouldn't be in church to this day," Sherri said. She set the plate in front of Tamara.

"Mmmm, thanks." Tamara heaped a spoonful of lima beans into her mouth. "All I can promise is I'll think about it."

"Good enough for me."

Tamara and Sherri tossed around polite conversation, indulging in their Sunday meal until their conversation was disrupted. The voice of an unidentified man chuckled with Veronica from the end of the hallway. Sherri looked at Tamara, who had sunk down into the kitchen chair and was fiddling with a place mat. She darted her eyes around the room, looking at everything but Sherri's face.

Sherri didn't have to wait long for the answer to the question bouncing around in her mind. A tall, light-skinned brother with a bald head and deep-set eyes trailed Veronica through the living room and to the front door. The stale smell of liquor and cigarettes lingered behind him.

"Be back in a minute," Veronica said, opening the door for the visitor. He slunk out of the door, obviously unaware he'd have a gawking audience at his departure.

"And that would be who?"

"I think his name is Marcus," Tamara said.

"Think? The real question is, does Veronica even know?" Sherri didn't give Tamara time to muster up an excuse for her roommate's shameless act. "She can't bring random men in here to spend the night. There are two other people in this house, and that's not safe," Sherri yelled, slamming the dishes in the sink.

A glass shattered from the impact of one of the dishes. Sherri was caught between frustration and fury. Despite the circumstances, she had to get her emotions in check. She knew Tamara was watching her every move and formulating her own opinion about "church folk." She couldn't preach one thing and show another. Hypocrisy could kill her testimony.

Tamara helped Sherri pack the leftovers and arrange them in the refrigerator. She wanted to say something. Anything. But she knew from years of experience that a silent Sherri was better left alone.

Her two friends were so different from each other now. Sherri had changed, but she didn't think it was for the worst like Veronica always complained about. Sherri seemed happier about life. Tamara saw a look in her eyes that she wanted for herself. A sparkle of joy, even though at the present time it was cloaked by anger.

Tamara finished washing and drying the dishes, then wiped her damp hands on her T-shirt. She ran a damp cloth across the kitchen table and pushed in the chairs. She glanced over at Sherri, who had retired to the couch and was reading her Bible.

"You never did tell me what time church starts," Tamara said.

"There's a service at eight and another at eleven," Sherri said.

"Oh, okay." Tamara pulled the ponytail holder from her hair and let the burgundy braids fall to her shoulders. "Thanks for the food," she said, twisting a single braid around her finger. "That's the best I've eaten in a long time."

"Thanks for your company. I needed it as much as you needed a good meal," Sherri said.

She marked the page she was reading with her Bible's ribbon and walked over to hug Tamara.

Tamara didn't resist.

*A*nisha opened the drawer to her nightstand and took out the yellow notebook. The word VISION stared back at her. She thumbed through the pages until she found her last dated entry. July 22. It had been over a month since she'd last written, much less even read through her notes. She uncapped the ballpoint pen clipped to the front of the notebook cover and carefully printed the date on the page. *August 26.*

"God, I really want to do this," she said aloud. "My job is great and I'm thankful for it, but I can't spend the rest of my life working for somebody else. That isn't for me. God, how do You want me to move forward?"

Have you prayed for direction? Are you willing to be a yielded vessel so I can use you?

Anisha stared at the blank page for a few moments before closing her eyes and uttering a prayer.

"Lord, I'm sorry for not staying on task. I'm sure You're tired of hearing the same thing and the same excuses," she said.

Anisha continued with a prayer asking for God's direction, grace, and mercy. When she opened her eyes, the wheels in her mind immediately began to turn. Anisha grabbed her organizer from her attaché, then retreated outside to the patio without her cordless phone. Any calls, including Tyson's, would have to wait. She flipped to the notes section and mapped out her objectives. She furiously scribbled down an action plan and to-do list to complete for the next three months. *Draft business plan outline. Business license info from Chamber of Commerce. Research company names. Update resume and portfolio. Set up separate savings account.* The list continued for two pages. Before dusk fell, Anisha had completed her list and assigned a deadline to each task.

She sat back and reviewed the pages she'd written. She realized how prayer had taken the stress and uncertainty out of her work. Instead of struggling to figure things out, her prayers had opened up her spirit to receive the dictation from God's voice. It was His plan anyway.

Anisha closed the book and stared out into the twilight. There was nothing like the feeling of accomplishment. Though her work may have been a small step on a long journey, she was a step closer to her destiny than she'd been earlier that day.

She gathered her belongings and had gone back into the house when she remembered that she hadn't invited Sherri to the Davenports' cookout yet. She meant to do it after leaving the Davenports' the evening before, but she and Tyson had stayed over the rest of the afternoon and then went with them to a movie. She was so exhausted by the time she made it home that she fell asleep on the couch, clothes and all.

She'd intended to call Sherri from work, but personal phone calls right now were out of the question. With the closed-door meetings she'd been noticing around the office, Anisha had made it a point to stay on top of her game. Curt and the rest of the management had noticed. She was often called upon to take up some of the slack and overload from the other junior account executives. It was an honor, but sometimes a burdensome one that she hoped would soon reap some benefits. She expected the trade-off to be a promotion lined with deeper pockets.

"Hello?" Sherri's voice sounded mellow.

"What's up? You already in bed?"

"Not yet. I'm writing in my prayer journal. I can't wait for the day when I can look back and all these prayers have been answered."

"You and me both," Anisha said. "Look, I'm not going to keep you. I'm calling to invite you to the Davenports' Labor Day cookout next Monday."

"I don't even know them."

"It doesn't matter. They told me to bring somebody with me."

"Who's going to be there?"

"I don't know. Probably some people from the church."

"They're not going to sit around and sing hymns, are they?" Sherri asked.

"Girl, please. Don't let the Davenports fool you. They've got more spunk than the both of us put together. Now, are you coming or what?"

"I don't know. I'll have to think about it."

"What's there to think about? Are you gonna sit around the house all Labor Day?"

"Who said I'll be sitting around the house?"

"Okay then, Miss Social Bee. Where are you going?"

There was silence on Sherri's end.

"That's what I thought," Anisha said. "And Tyson is bringing Xavier," she slipped in.

"Then I'm definitely not coming."

"Don't start this again. Why not? He's just coming along for the ride."

"We exchanged numbers the night we met, and he never called me," Sherri complained.

"Did you call him?"

"No." Sherri huffed. "Do I need to call your attention back to our dating commandment number four? 'Thou shalt not pursue a man.'"

Since Anisha and Sherri had experienced their share of relationship problems during the years of their friendship, they had devised their own list of relationship dos and don'ts. Rules and boundaries for dating they'd adopted but only seemed to remember when it was convenient to prove a point.

"I make a motion to add an amendment to that," Anisha said. "Calling him doesn't necessarily mean you're chasing him. Now, if you've called him repeatedly and he's not calling you back, then that would be considered chasing."

"Correction," Sherri said. "That would be considered stalking."

"Come on, Sherri. Don't make me resort to begging."

"Fine. I'll go. But don't try to make this into a matchmaking session."

"Please. I'm giving you someone to harmonize with when we sing the hymn selections."

"Great," Sherri muttered. "I can't wait."

"Good-bye, Miss Drama," Anisha said.

Anisha opened the drawer to her nightstand and pulled out her prayer journal. Sherri's mention of it had jogged her memory. Its pages were as empty as her vision notebook had been. The reality of it all almost brought tears to her eyes. Every time she made a promise to God, she never kept it. She'd taken all those notes last week at Bible study and hadn't looked at them since. She flipped to the third page of her journal. Her time with God had lost priority in her life. She couldn't remember the last time she'd risen early in the morning for her own private devotions. She and the Father.

Anisha prayed and penned some thoughts into her journal. The time alone was refreshing. Times like these were infrequent, and now, lying in her bed with nothing but her thoughts, she realized again how much she missed it and needed it.

❦

*A*tlanta's broiling weather had taken a pleasant turn over the weekend and welcomed the Labor Day holiday with temperatures in the midseventies and the occasional tickle of a light breeze.

Tyson and Xavier arrived at Anisha's apartment promptly at four fifteen, and in twenty minutes they were winding through Sherri's complex to her building. Anisha pushed speed dial on her cell phone and called Sherri.

Sherri answered after one ring, bade Anisha to "come up," and hung up before Anisha had a chance to respond.

Anisha conversed with the silent phone. "Hey, are you ready?" She paused for a little added effect. "Okay, I'm coming." Anisha jumped out of the rear passenger door. "Be right back," she said to Tyson and Xavier.

Xavier elbowed Tyson in his side and looked back at Anisha. "How long is this gonna take?"

"As long as necessary. Do a little male bonding or something." Anisha bumped the car door closed with a swing of her hips. She scurried to the second floor apartment and found Sherri waiting with the door open.

"Aren't you cute?" Anisha said, admiring Sherri's red wrap-style sundress. "Tell me why I had to come all the way up here?"

"I didn't want to walk down by myself. I felt like everybody would be staring at me."

"Everybody meaning Xavier? You're going to have his eyes popping out of his head for sure," she said, slapping a high five with Sherri.

"How does he look?" Sherri asked.

"What do you think? The brother is looking good—like that's a surprise."

Sherri smoothed the sides of her dress down along her thighs and adjusted the knot tied on her left hip. "Are you sure I look all right?"

"Better than all right. You look mahvelous, dahlin', so calm down and let's go. And don't worry, you're sitting in the backseat with me, so you don't have to worry about any awkward conversations."

"You know you're my girl."

"I knew how you'd want it. Let's go."

Sherri's rambunctious roommates could be heard coming through the breezeway as Sherri went back inside to grab her purse. Veronica appeared at the top of the stairwell, and Tamara shadowed a few steps behind her boisterous companion.

"Can you say fine with a capital F?" Veronica asked. She slipped her newly infused weave over her shoulder. "I wonder who those two cuties are coming for?"

Anisha turned around with a smug look on her face. "That would be us," she said.

You're representing Me.

Anisha knew better than to act so uppity, especially since they hadn't intentionally provoked a venomous response. She changed her tone of voice and tried to make up for her rudeness. "Hi, ladies. How are you?"

Veronica rolled her eyes and threw up her hand in disgust as she brushed past Anisha without uttering a word. Tamara, at least, made an effort to be courteous.

"Hi, Anisha. Good seeing you. It's been a while," she said, giving her an awkward but warmhearted hug. "Y'all have a good time," she said as Sherri reappeared with her purse slung over her shoulder.

"Thanks."

Anisha and Sherri walked downstairs to the parking lot.

"Tamara seems friendlier than usual," Anisha noticed.

"I think she's finally getting a little tired of fooling with Veronica," Sherri said. "She asked me about church a couple of weeks ago. I think she may actually come soon."

"Maybe there's a reason why you had to live with them after all. Somebody had to show them an example."

"Now, isn't that what I've been saying all along?"

Anisha squinted from the brightness of the sun and pointed in the direction of the car.

"We're over there."

Tyson and Xavier had both of the doors waiting open as the ladies approached.

"Your chariot awaits, ladies," Tyson said.

Anisha and Sherri slid into the backseat, grinned at each other, and buckled themselves in.

Xavier leaned on the armrest between the two front seats and directed his attention to Sherri. "I shouldn't be surprised at how stunning you look today."

"Thanks." Sherri smiled. *And the same to you.*

"Okay, okay." Tyson turned the ignition and tossed a leather CD case into Xavier's lap. "Turn off the mack game and find us something to listen to."

Endless rows of cars lined the Davenports' street and the cul-de-sac in front of their home. The smell of barbecue wrapped itself around their nostrils as soon as the couples opened their doors. They followed a low bass thump into the expansive backyard. From the looks of the people congregated there, it was evident the Davenports had a diverse group of friends. People of all ages and races milled around. In the far corner of the backyard, a group of old schoolers were making their best attempt at the electric slide, adding a dose of their own improvisation wherever and whenever they found it necessary. Another section of the yard had been set up for board games and dominoes with two tables for cards. Couples of awaiting spades teams stood behind the seated players and taunted them, pushing for the next round of losers to be eliminated.

"Now this is a barbecue," Tyson said, taking in the sights. "Do you see Deac or Sister Davenport?" he asked Anisha, checking the faces of each chattering group for his father figure. "Oh, there he is," Tyson said, pointing to one of the card tables.

The deacon was waiting for the next team of spades players to be unseated. Although Deacon Davenport's back was turned, he was easily recognizable by his wide-legged stance and the tendency he had to stand with his hands clasped behind his back like he did when waiting for the offering basket to wind through the pews.

Tyson walked up to Deacon Davenport from the back and landed a slap on his shoulder. "Deac! What's up, man?"

Deacon Davenport's enthusiasm was apparent at the sight of Tyson and his friends. "What's going on? Y'all just now getting here?"

"Yeah. And we probably should've gotten here earlier. This is some barbecue." Tyson marveled again at all the activities and people.

"My wife loves this kind of stuff," the deacon said. "We throw the Labor Day cookout for the whole neighborhood every year."

"Looks more like the whole city," Anisha said, stepping up and hugging Deacon Davenport. She turned around to Sherri and pulled her closer so she could be introduced. "This is my best friend, Sherri. She goes to Grace Worship too."

"I knew your face looked familiar," Deacon Davenport said. "Nice to meet you."

"You too," Sherri said pleasantly. "Your home is beautiful."

"Thank you so much," Deacon Davenport said. "God has truly

blessed us, and we like to have our family and friends over whenever we can. That's what makes it a home."

Tyson introduced Xavier, and the men gabbed about the progress of the spades tournament.

Deacon Davenport pointed to two men sitting across from each other at one of the spades tables. "I'm hanging around waiting for somebody to beat these two amateurs."

"Amateurs!" one of the men hollered, his buggy eyes never leaving the cards being thrown on the table. He slapped an ace of spades on the table, scooped up the other cards into a stack, and added them to a growing row in front of him. "I'll show you an amateur."

"Me and Parham will show you skill," Deacon said about his partner, who was standing behind the seated boaster.

Wendell Parham was a rugged-looking man with a thick Southern drawl. He reached across the table over the heads of the seated players and slapped hands with Deacon Davenport. "Sho' you right," Parham agreed. "We'll let our game speak for itself."

"Hey X," Tyson said. "You wanna get in on the rotation at this table?"

Xavier rubbed his hands together and stepped closer to stand on the other side of Deacon Davenport. "I'm in."

"What do you know about busting spades?" Deacon Davenport teased in good nature to Xavier. "You're a young chap. You've still got milk behind your ears." He reached up, flipped Xavier's earlobe, and sniffed his fingertips, then turned and did the same to Tyson. "Similac." He chuckled at his own humor, then turned his attention to Sherri and Anisha. "Carolyn should be somewhere inside if you want to look for her. Make yourself comfortable. There's food everywhere."

Anisha and Sherri wandered around to look for Sister Davenport. They found her in the kitchen dipping relish out of a jar and into a large bowl of potato salad.

"Can we give you a hand?" Anisha asked, washing her hands.

Sister Davenport looked up from the growing mass of potatoes and wiped the wooden spoon on the side of the bowl. "Hey, precious. No, I'm fine. This is usually Vivian's job, but she's running late because she had to pick up some people."

Sister Davenport wiped her hands on the end of her apron, then wrapped an arm around each girl's waist, pulling them into her side. "And you must be Sherri. I'm so glad you came. It's nice to finally meet you."

"You too. Thanks for inviting me."

"Are you sure you don't need help? We don't mind," Anisha offered again.

"I'm all right. It'll only take me a second. You girls go ahead and fix yourselves something to eat."

Anisha and Sherri went outside to indulge in the generous spread of meats, pasta salads, desserts, and the usual barbecue foods. They made themselves a plate and found an empty bench at one of the picnic tables.

Anisha spooned potato salad into her mouth and chewed slowly, savoring its taste before saying, "See, what did I tell you? The Davenports know how to have a good time."

Sherri pulled a piece of barbecued chicken from the bone and watched the rest of the tender meat fall off. She nodded toward the spades table and said, "Look at your boys over there. They're acting like they've known those men forever. Does Tyson know them?"

"I have no idea. But you know men are like that. Women are the ones who have to size each other up before we even speak."

Anisha and Sherri enjoyed chatting with the new and familiar faces rotating through and sharing their picnic table. They were still amazed at the immensity of it all. The earlier group of dancers in the corner of the yard had surrendered their space to a new group who were attempting the backbreaking feats of limbo.

Sherri gathered their empty plates and crumpled napkins to dump in the trash can. "What's the plan for your birthday on Saturday? I know Tyson's got you for at least one day over the weekend, but can I get a time slot in your appointment book, please?"

"I think I can pencil you in for Saturday night. Or should we take our Sunday brunch out on the road?"

"What's Tyson got planned?" Sherri asked.

"Your guess is as good as mine. We're going out on Friday night, but he's not giving up any information. He only told me what to wear, and that was it."

"A man who can build a little suspense. I have to give it to him—he's working hard."

"The suspense is about to drive me crazy. I have no idea what to wear, and I've only got four more days to find something."

Sherri swatted at an annoying gnat flying around her head. "I thought you said he told you what to wear."

"He said, 'More than what you'd wear to church, but not too formal.' What's that supposed to mean? I need specifics."

"Girlfriend, you're going to have to work with whatcha got. Enjoy the mystery of it all." Sherri swung at the gnat again. It was evident it had found joy in being a nuisance to her. "Okay, I've had enough of the great outdoors for a while."

"Let's go inside to check on Sister Davenport one more time to make sure she's okay; then we can mingle a little bit," Anisha suggested.

They entered the house through the sliding patio doors and were met by a totally different crowd of faces than they'd seen an hour before. They watched excitement escalate when familiar faces recognized each other and pleasantries exchanged during new introductions. Anisha and Sherri maneuvered through the crowd, talking to each other, but still catching pieces of other people's conversations.

"Congratulations. When are you due?"

"When did she get married?"

"Honey, my job is working my last nerve . . ."

"I wish my husband *would* do something crazy like . . ."

Anisha heard her name float over the conversations and looked around to see Sister Davenport's head bobbing over the crowd and her hand motioning them to come to her. Anisha grabbed Sherri's hand and maneuvered through the crowd until they stood in front of Sister Davenport.

"I wanted you all to meet Vivian and the young lady she brought with her," she said, her voice full of excitement. "Vivian?" Sister Davenport called out to the foyer.

"Let me drop these purses in here," the woman said from behind the open closet door.

The door closed, and Vivian Jamison stood smiling, anxious to introduce her guest. Anisha heard Sister Davenport introduce Mrs. Jamison, but her eyes were locked on the familiar face beside her. Anisha quickly wiped the look of astonishment off her face. She could tell by the girl's expression that she was equally surprised. Little did anyone know, introducing them to each other wasn't really necessary. They had never been formally introduced, but they both knew exactly who the other was.

Vivian Jamison rambled on. "She's my stylist at the Cutz Hair Salon in Stone Mountain."

"I might have to give you a call," Sherri said. "I'm looking for a new beautician."

I don't think so, Anisha thought. *Not going to happen.*

The ladies walked back down the foyer to join the festivities in the rest of the house, and Anisha tapped Sherri's side when they were out of the silence of the hallway.

"That's her," Anisha mouthed as she brushed past Sherri and followed behind Sister Davenport.

Sherri looked confused. "Her who?" she whispered.

Anisha's words were brief. "Brandy," she mumbled. "Tyson's ex."

Anisha calculated her moves like an expert chess player. She knew they couldn't break for an immediate exit, but a private conference with her friend was in order. She waited until Mrs. Jamison and Sister Davenport were distracted with other introductions and made eye contact with Sherri. Anisha slipped into the bathroom down the hall, knowing Sherri would soon follow.

Anisha sat on the closed toilet seat cover and rested her elbows on her knees. She buried her face in the palms of her hands and shook her head. "After six years of being out of the picture, why is old girl suddenly making a grand reappearance now?"

She looked up and searched Sherri's face for consolation and an answer. Sherri rubbed her hand along the nape of her neck. She looked to be in deep thought. Anisha knew Sherri was staying calm for her sake—for once not contributing to the drama.

"Don't start tripping," Sherri said. "If their relationship was supposed to work out, it would've happened six years ago. Tyson has moved on with his life, and the only woman he's concerned about right now is you."

Anisha got up and stood behind Sherri in the bathroom mirror. "You sound confident enough for the both of us."

"There's nothing like a secure woman, so go out there and be Anisha. If Tyson is crazy enough to act a fool, then it's his loss."

Anisha rifled through her purse for a comb and a tube of lipstick. She freshened up and calmed herself down before deciding to go back out. "Okay, I'm going out now, but don't come out with me yet. Wait a minute."

"I know the routine."

Sherri opened the door and pushed Anisha out into the hallway. She waited until the click of Anisha's heels across the hardwood floors faded and she was sure she had made it into the plush carpeted area of the living room before walking out.

Sherri walked out onto the raised deck and filled a cup with fresh-squeezed lemonade to quench her thirst. She leaned over the wooden rail and saw Tyson, Xavier, Deacon Davenport, and Mr. Parham finally matched head to head at the spades table. The dance floor in the corner of the yard had been transformed once again and had a Soul Train line in the making. Sherri giggled at a Gerald Levert wannabe performing his best choreographed moves and then went back to her surveillance.

She slid her shades from her head and rested them comfortably on her nose so she could scan the area below to see if Brandy was trying to prey on Tyson. She'd told Anisha it was nothing to worry about, and she believed that was true. Still, doing a little investigation of her own wouldn't hurt.

She didn't spot Brandy but did notice her little girl holding the hand of Mrs. Jamison and cautiously approaching a small group of children who were involved in a dizzying game of ring-around-the-rosy. Sherri's search for a hovering mother was interrupted as she sensed the approach of a visitor into her solitary spot on the deck.

"Would you mind a little company?" A hand with short, stubby fingers extended toward Sherri. "Calvin Wright." He introduced himself and cupped one of Sherri's hands between his.

"Sherri Dawson." Her eyes unconsciously wandered from his round, childlike face to his equally round belly, and she prayed he hadn't noticed her roaming eyes through the dark shades. She shifted her eyes back to his face and offered a polite smile before easily sliding her hand out of his grasp.

Sherri tried keeping one eye on Calvin and the other out for Brandy without seeming rude but realized she couldn't do both. She temporarily suspended her lookout search and opted to be entertained by her admirer. She snapped back into the tail end of his sentence.

". . . a nice chance to get away from the campus and dining hall food."

"I'm sorry. Where did you say you were in school?"

"I'm in seminary. I'll be graduating in the summer and going back home to Mississippi to copastor with my father at our family's church."

Calvin could carry on a conversation without anyone else's input. Sherri could tell he was doing his best to impress her, and he soon caught the hint that she was entertaining him only to be friendly.

"How long are you going to stand here and humor me?" Calvin asked.

"What do you mean?"

"I mean I know I'm not your so-called type, so you're not taking me seriously."

"Not true," Sherri lied.

"Very true. I can tell you're the kind of lady who's attracted to men who look like they walked off a professional football field. You're probably used to someone towering over you and looking down into your eyes. Roughnecks probably."

"But—" Sherri began.

"Shhh." Calvin held his finger to his lips and shook his head. "I'm not judging you for your preference, but at least tell me if I'm on the right track. Did I hit the nail on the head? Be honest."

"Maybe."

"That's what I thought," he said, leaning on the edge of the railing. "Well, Ms. Dawson, I might not have all the physical attributes you want, but there's one indisputable thing I do have. Confidence." He ran his hand down the front of his chest and tugged the bottom of his shirt down over his stomach.

Sherri's eyes darted around the backyard before lifting her shades to let her eyes meet Calvin's. She prodded him. "And how much confidence do you have?"

"Enough to know I've sparked your curiosity about me, and you want to know more."

"Is that so?"

"I'm confident it is."

Sherri hadn't noticed that they had company on the patio until Anisha cleared her throat and caught their attention. Sherri introduced Calvin and Anisha, then picked up her cup of lemonade from the banister, ready to follow Anisha back into the house. "Nice meeting you," she said, offering her free hand to Calvin.

"I'm sure we'll speak again before the night is over."

"You think so?"

"Oh, I'm confident about it, sweetheart. *Very* confident."

Anisha raised an eyebrow at Sherri before turning and leading the way back into the house. Once they were safely out of hearing range, she said, "I couldn't tell if you needed rescuing or not. But now I think ol' boy had it under control."

"A little attention is better than nothing, ain't it?"

Finally. Brandy knew that Sherri girl was staking her out for her friend. She was relieved when someone came along to divert her attention so she could focus on finding Tyson without her every move being followed.

Tyson was engulfed in a card game, so she wouldn't try to get to him now. She found a strategic spot at a table across from him, knowing if he happened to look up, he couldn't help but see her.

⁂

Tyson slapped a high spade on the table, securing the last book he and Xavier needed to at least meet their bid and win the game. "X-man," he said, "how 'bout we grab a bite to eat and get back to this later?"

"I feel you," Xavier said.

Tyson and Xavier conceded their winning seats to the next waiting partners so they could tackle the food table housed under one of the canopies. Tyson turned to swing his leg over the picnic bench and caught a glimpse of Brandy. With his leg still suspended in mid-air, he lost his balance and caught himself on the edge of the wooden table. "Ouch," he winced, pricking a splinter from his forefinger.

"What's up with you, man?" Xavier asked. "You look like you saw a ghost."

"Close to it." Tyson wanted to pretend he hadn't seen her, but their eyes had already connected.

14

*A*nisha pulled the facade down tighter over her face and
pretended all was well. She pasted on a plastic smile and
mingled around the room. The crowd at the Davenports had dwindled
to about fifty stragglers over the last two hours, making it easier for
her to watch Brandy's roaming. Looking at Brandy made her think
about the Scripture describing Satan . . . *your adversary the devil, as a
roaring lion, walketh about, seeking whom he may devour.*

Anisha knew they were harsh words, calling Brandy the devil and
all when she didn't even know her. But she didn't have to know her to
sense her intentions were sinister. Anisha's instinct was pretty keen.

When Tyson had finally come inside to eat earlier, he'd found his
way to Anisha. Though he hadn't mentioned the situation, Anisha
had been with him long enough to read his mood and expressions.
She knew they'd talk when the time was appropriate. But until then,
Anisha hoped her true feelings wouldn't soak through this facade. It
was getting harder to simulate the I'm-so-secure-your-ex-girlfriend-
here-doesn't-bother-me role.

Lord, Anisha prayed silently, *this relationship has been drama free.*

Please keep it that way. For some reason, Anisha felt her prayer had detoured and made a U-turn on its way to heaven. There was that intuition again. She hoped it was a lie this time. There was always a first time for everything.

❈

This God thing really does work, Brandy thought. He'd answered her prayer and was bringing Tyson back around to her life, slowly but surely. She would have to calculate her moves carefully. Tyson had to be lured away and caught at the right time. Maybe she'd pray to God that he and his girlfriend would have a fight, and he'd go out for a ride and somehow run into her. Yeah, that's what she'd pray.

Brandy knew she didn't need much time with him. Just long enough to plant a seed in his mind about how good their times together used to be and the things they'd shared together. The seed would take root on its own, and all she'd have to do was water it.

Drip. *"Tyson, remember when . . . Drop . . . Tyson, remember how . . . I'll never forget the time we . . ."*

Brandy bounced Ayana on her lap and plaited an unraveled ponytail. From her seat in the living room, she could see into the kitchen where Anisha and Tyson were sitting at the table. Anisha had pulled her chair close to Tyson's and was rubbing his back. Brandy snickered to herself. *Let up a little, sweetheart. I know you're trying to stake your claim because I'm here.*

She watched Mrs. Jamison float around like the social butterfly she was. She loved that woman like a mother, but goodness, she wished Mrs. Jamison would stop trying to push her to bond with Anisha. How many times did she have to remind her that they were the same age and Anisha was a young woman who had a relationship with the Lord? If Mrs. Jamison thought she could jumpstart a sisterhood like the one she shared with Sister Davenport, she was sadly mistaken. It wasn't an option. Not when she was after Anisha's man.

❈

Sherri wondered which one of her players would move his pawn first. There was one empty seat left at the kitchen table, waiting for the one who dared to approach her.

Xavier's approach, she knew, would be smooth and calculated. He played his game from afar, making his most critical moves with his eyes. During the cookout, Anisha had filled her in on the scoop about Xavier. According to Tyson, he was a decent guy but probably had a ways to measure up to Sherri's standards.

But Mr. Confidence, on the other hand, didn't live up to his name when he was in head-to-head competition.

Sherri examined both of their demeanors. Xavier was easy on the eyes, but Calvin stimulated her mind. He had already cornered her several times during the course of the evening. What could it hurt? Anisha had convinced her to break out of her comfort zone and give the brotha a chance. At a most convenient time, she'd pulled out dating commandment number thirty-two. "Don't reject a man based on his looks alone."

Either way, it was better than her usual date with the couch on Friday nights. Was it wrong for a sister to want a free meal?

This was something that should happen to a player, Tyson thought. *Man plays women for most of his life. Man finally finds woman he loves and wants to commit to. One of man's ex-girlfriends shows up to try and shake up his plan.*

Tyson knew Anisha was a mature woman. She was probably disturbed by the whole situation, but she'd hold her peace until they'd had a chance to talk. She wasn't one to make a scene. But there was no sense in that anyway. It wasn't like any of this was his doing.

In a few minutes, Tyson would suggest they make their exit. Even Deacon Davenport wasn't going to believe this one.

*A*nisha leaned over from the edge of the bed and wrapped the shoe's leather strap up her calf. She walked over to the full-length mirror so she could admire the dress she'd spent every lunch hour during the week searching for. She'd almost thought her favorite department stores and boutiques had forsaken her until she saw it. There, hanging between some slightly tattered and picked-over clearance items, the bronze cocktail dress with spaghetti straps screamed her name. Somehow, the perfect dress had found its home within the fashion rejects. It begged her to rescue it from its doom of being packed in a dingy cardboard box and shipped back to the warehouse to make room for the upcoming winter selections. There—on the hanger and in the store's dressing room—it was perfect.

Now, staring at herself in the mirror, Anisha wasn't so sure. She fingered the beads sewn across the bodice. Was it too formal for tonight's occasion? Anisha pushed the unnecessary worry to the back of her mind. She was too excited about the mystery of the night to be worried over clothes. Tonight was especially planned for her, and she was going to enjoy every second of it.

Anisha went into the bathroom and gently untied the silk scarf that held her pinned-up coif. A few soft ringlets cascaded down to frame her face, and one fell at the nape of her neck. The dress could capture its own audience. There was no need to overdo the accessories. She clasped a dainty necklace around her neck and put in the matching set of earrings.

The doorbell rang as Anisha was putting the finishing touches on her makeup. She fanned a hand in front of her eye to dry the freshly applied mascara and squeezed a dime-sized drop of body shimmer lotion into her palms. She smoothed the creme across her shoulders and down her arms as she ran to the door.

Tyson gasped when Anisha opened the door. "Are you okay?" He grabbed her forearm and whirled her around 180 degrees, then back toward him.

All hint of excitement faded from Anisha's eyes like the abating glimmer of a shooting star.

"Oh, baby, it must have hurt"—Tyson pulled Anisha into his broad chest—"falling from heaven." He squeezed her tightly. "You look like an angel."

"Thank you." Anisha beamed, and her eyes soaked up the gleam they'd lost seconds before. "You don't look too bad yourself," she said, picking up a small beaded clutch and sheer chiffon wrap from the back of the love seat. She accepted Tyson's waiting arm and glided outside.

"Where are we going tonight?" Anisha asked, sliding into the passenger's seat. She knew it was a useless question. She'd been asking Tyson all week and could never get him to break. Tyson waited for her to adjust her dress and buckle her seat belt.

"How many times have I told you not to ask me that question again?" Tyson squeezed her knee and shut the door.

She loved the faint trail of cologne he always left in the car. He walked around to the front of the car and opened the door, as his scent wrapped around her again.

"Ride baby," Tyson said and tuned the radio to his favorite jazz station. The sounds of the clarinet caressed and whined with the saxophone. As they drove down the highway, Tyson drummed his fingers on the steering wheel and every so often blew an imaginary trumpet or tickled the keys on an invisible piano.

When they exited at Peachtree Street in downtown Atlanta, Anisha was certain Tyson was taking her to eat at the Sun Dial Restaurant. The view from the revolving restaurant atop the Westin Peachtree Plaza was a picturesque scene of Atlanta's skyline. During at least an hour of dining, one could see Centennial Olympic Park, Georgia Tech University, Turner Stadium, and the lights of some of Atlanta's outlying neighborhoods. Anisha had always enjoyed the two-minute ride to the top in the glass elevators the most. She'd raved about it so many times before that evidently Tyson had finally gotten the hint.

Tyson cruised down the two hundred block of Peachtree Street three times. Anisha squirmed back and forth between looking out the window and looking at Tyson. She pressed her lips together, determined not to let a whimper squeeze through them. When her patience had reached its limit, Tyson finally abandoned his games and drove down Peachtree Street until he came to a stop in front of the Fox Theatre.

"We have to get to our seats before the lights go down. There's no late seating, and we'll be stuck outside until intermission."

Anisha glanced up at the lighted marquis. *PRESENTING THE ALVIN AILEY DANCERS.* She'd read the review article in the *Atlanta Journal-Constitution* to him weeks before, but at the time he'd acted more interested in watching the football game.

Anisha leaned over and kissed Tyson softly on both cheeks. "I thought you didn't like dance and theater or anything like that," she said between smooches.

Tyson shrugged his shoulders. "It's your day. Whatever makes you happy," he said. He planted a kiss on her forehead and buried his face in the bend of her neck before kissing her again on the cheek. "You can wait here while I go park." Tyson walked around to the passenger's side and opened the door.

"You're starting to spoil a girl." Anisha stepped out and let Tyson escort her to the veranda. "I could get used to this royal treatment."

"Why shouldn't you?"

❈

Anisha was captivated by the entire repertoire of the acclaimed dance theater company. From *Serving Nia, Revelations, Night Creature, Dance at the Gym,* and every performance in between, the dancers transformed themselves into living, breathing manifestations of the music. Anisha rarely spoke until the final curtain call.

"The view from the first row in the balcony was perfect." Anisha held onto Tyson's arm as they trekked back to the parking garage. "That was one of the most phenomenal performances I've ever seen," she said, sliding into the passenger's seat. The rhythm beating in her soul kept her reliving the magic and wishing her own body could express itself in such a way as the dancers.

Tyson's face was clad with satisfaction. "I thought we'd finish the night with an intimate dinner at one of my favorite places." He opened the glove compartment to fish around for his cell phone. "Our reservations are for ten," he said, eyeing the dashboard clock. "We may be a few minutes late. I'd better call so we don't lose them."

Tyson pushed the number three for the auto-dial programmed into his cell and must have noticed the puzzled look on Anisha's face. "Oh, I programmed the number in the phone before I left tonight in case I needed it." He drove the SUV down the three parking garage levels and waited for the bustling crowd to cross the street.

"Yes, I'm calling to confirm reservations for two under Randall," Tyson said. "Correct. Ten o'clock. We're running a little late, so it'll be closer to ten-fifteen."

Anisha attempted the off-limits question once more, knowing she'd only get the usual lighthearted scolding. "Where are we going?"

"Did you forget tonight's rule that quick?" He reached over and squeezed her lower thigh. "No questions, ride baby. You know you're in good hands with me."

Tyson sped down the highway and, to Anisha's surprise, got off the interstate at the exit leading to his place. His apartment complex was immediately on the right corner, and he whipped into the entrance before Anisha had a chance to object. "I need to stop by home for a quick second," Tyson explained.

Anisha looked at the dashboard clock and then at Tyson.

"We've got time," Tyson said. "It'll only take a minute." Tyson pushed the gate opener over his visor and slowed until the iron gate swung open wide enough for him to zip through.

"Hey," Anisha said, trying to see past Tyson to a car crossing a speed bump at the visitor's exit gate. "Is that Xavier?"

"I doubt it," Tyson said. He sped through the partially open gate, barely taking notice of the other car. "He doesn't even live on this side of town." Tyson parked the car in his allocated space and sprinted into his first-floor apartment.

Anisha watched Tyson's shadow and followed each lighted room as he entered it and watched the same shadow disappear as he left each room. It was ten fifteen, and unless Tyson hurried, they'd lose their reservation. When another five minutes passed, Anisha noticed only the living room appeared to have a faint glimmer of light.

What in the world is taking so long? Anisha grabbed her purse and dashed to the door. She knocked twice, opened the door, and froze in her tracks.

An array of white candles lined every surface in the spacious living room and kitchen area. Tea lights, votives, floating candles, pillars, scented candles, candlesticks, and tapers. Every shape and every size. The flames cast dancing shadows along the walls. A small table for two was adorned with a deep purple tablecloth and a crystal vase with a single white rose. The prepared meal was already served on dinner plates, complete with a bottle of sparkling white grape juice on ice.

Tyson peeled Anisha's grip from her purse. He slid the wrap from her shoulders and set her belongings on the coffee table.

Anisha's voice was barely audible behind her covered mouth. "Oh, baby!" Anisha gushed as Tyson ushered her to the table. "How did you pull all of this off?" she asked. "That *was* Xavier, wasn't it?"

Tyson placed his hand on Anisha's elbow and led her to the table. It wasn't until she sat down that she noticed the place cards with their names penned in calligraphy. Tyson sat across from Anisha and reached around the crystal vase to take her hand. His gentle squeeze relayed a message to Anisha that he need not verbalize. Following Tyson's lead, she bowed her head in prayer.

"No man has ever cooked for me before," Anisha said, cutting into the salmon filet.

"I wish I could take all the credit, but I had a little help." Tyson tasted the steamed vegetable medley and nodded in satisfaction.

"The fact you pulled it all together is enough for me."

"You know, Anisha, I wasn't quite sure when to share this with you, but . . .

Oh boy, what is he about to say? Anisha wondered.

"I really want God's will for my life, and I don't want that to be just some cliché that I say. Because of that, I just finished a yearlong consecration, so that I could really focus and hear from Him."

"Tyson, I feel really blessed that I'm a part of your life, and my desire is to be in His will as well. I thank God that you thought enough of me to share that part of your walk with me. Thank you for everything," Anisha whispered. "The night was special to me, and you're special to me."

"Nothing is too much for the woman I love," he said, winking at her.

The woman he loves, Anisha thought. *I am the woman Tyson Randall loves.*

Tyson made it a point to make his affection clear to her the night after the Davenports' cookout and the whole fiasco with Brandy. Yes, that night he'd told Anisha that he cared for her, and her only. But tonight, he'd professed his love.

Anisha awoke with a start. She sat up and instinctively reached down for her comforter. It took her a couple of seconds to catch her bearings and realize she was still at Tyson's apartment. She squinted at her wristwatch. Two thirteen?

Anisha swung her feet to the floor and wiped the blur from her eyes. She fastened a bobby pin dangling from a curl and saw Tyson in the kitchen blowing out the candles that hadn't already extinguished themselves.

"Hey, sleepyhead," he said, snuffing out the last taper candle.

"Hi." Anisha stood up and stretched. "I'm sorry I dozed off. You must have fed me too much."

Tyson cleared the table while Anisha sat on the arm of the couch. "It's already late. You might as well go back to sleep. I'll take you back home first thing in the morning."

I know it's late but it doesn't look right.

"But Tyson, I don't think—"

"It's okay. I'll give you something to sleep in, and you can stay out here or go to my room. Wherever you're most comfortable. I'll sleep where you don't."

Anisha.

"It *is* late," Anisha reasoned. *It's not like we're going to do anything.* "First thing?"

"First thing."

Anisha washed her faced and slipped into one of Tyson's oversized tees. She opened the bathroom door and peeked down the hall. She saw a faint light escaping under the crack of Tyson's bedroom door. Anisha tiptoed down the hall, using the streetlight shining through the blinds of the sliding door to find her way back to the living room. She'd opted to sleep on the couch. Sleeping in Tyson's bed, even if he wasn't in there, seemed wrong.

Anisha adjusted the extra pillow and wrapped herself inside the covers Tyson left on the couch for her. She pulled the linty blanket up to her chin and stared into the darkness. She could have sworn she heard Sherri's voice.

"First it starts with staying late; then he starts spending the night on the couch . . . " Anisha tried to shake the voice from her head, then pulled the comforter over her to try and drown it out. Funny how Sherri's voice suddenly sounded like God's.

*A*fter the special evening with Tyson, Anisha couldn't imagine that anything more exciting could happen for her birthday. The night was perfect. Well, almost. Her stay at Tyson's was innocent, but she still didn't like the feeling it left her with. She was disappointed in herself, but more than anything, she felt she'd disappointed God. She didn't want to compromise her standards and end up in a predicament she'd regret.

Anisha fluffed one of the throw pillows and tossed it back to the end of the couch. She peeked out of the living room blinds for a sign of Sherri. She could practically see the heat bouncing off the asphalt in the parking lot and could tell by the grungy look of the kids who were taking full advantage of their Saturday freedom that it was a scorcher outside.

She and Sherri were supposed to catch lunch and then a matinee. With no sight of her, Anisha plopped on the couch and opened her Bible to review the text from the past Wednesday's Bible study.

"Chapter fifty-five, verse eleven," Anisha recalled, thumbing through the pages of the book of Isaiah. She read the Scripture aloud.

So shall My word be that goes forth from My mouth; it shall not return to Me void, but it shall accomplish what I please, and it shall prosper in the thing for which I sent it.

Anisha leaned back and closed her eyes in meditation. She repeated the Scripture over and over in her mind and relaxed in the peace and serenity that had overtaken the room. At that precise moment, she felt God's manifested presence closer than she had in months.

You are the Word I sent forth. You should be My walking Word so people whom you come in contact with will experience Me.

Hearing the words in her spirit sent warmth through her body. *Sent forth to do what?* Her business was only a small piece of the puzzle, Anisha sensed, and she needed another piece. She dozed off with the thought still on her mind and was awakened by the doorbell.

"About time," Anisha said and swung the door open.

"Stop jiving around, soul sista, and let us in your crib." Sherri swaggered into the apartment, an Afro wig swaying with each step.

Their other friends from church sashayed in behind her wearing identical Afro wigs and large silver hoop earrings almost half the size of their heads. Kendall, Monica, and Angie were decked out in bell-bottom jeans and go-go boots, while Sherri and Felicia modeled dark denim skirts with frayed hems.

The look was fitting to Anisha's taste in music and her occasional fashion trends. The girls always teased Anisha that she should've been an adult during the seventies—during the times when Hank Aaron hit his historic home run and Muhammad Ali knocked out George Foreman to regain his heavyweight title. She knew the words to every Marvin Gaye and Tammi Terrell song and dared any passenger in her car to switch her preset radio stations from anything other than the R&B oldie tunes of the local classic soul radio station.

"Where in the world did you find these African dashikis?" Anisha tugged on the sleeve of Kendall's multicolored tunic.

"I made them," Sherri said, reaching into her shoulder bag and pulling out a matching tunic and a long wrap skirt. "And here's one for the birthday girl." She dug through the bag again and drew out another Afro wig and pair of hoop earrings.

"What a minute," Anisha said, holding up her dashiki with the Nefertiti silhouette stitched across the front. "You made this? I didn't even know you could sew. I knew you were a fashion diva, but I never knew you were a designer too."

"Please, Anisha. I threw them together. It didn't take much talent."

Monica swung the end of the silver links belted around her waist. "Ummm. Excuse me but can we talk about this later?" She lightly shoved Anisha toward her bedroom. "Go get diva-fied."

Anisha skipped to her bedroom to convert her outfit into the seventies and returned looking like she'd walked off the set of *Shaft*. The girls had set up lava lamps and rolled out shag rugs, and in a matter of minutes, her apartment had been transformed.

"Pardon me, ladies, but can I get some tunes to groove to? It's time to get down." Anisha broke out into her best dance renditions of the Monkey and the Four Corners, the only two dances her mother still hung onto and proudly displayed whenever one of "her songs" came on.

Felicia turned around from where she was fiddling with the television and joined Anisha in a hip-bumping dance. "Diva-licious!" she screamed.

Sherri dropped the string of beads she was draping over the window. "Hand me the camera, Monica. This is a Kodak moment."

Anisha struck the signature *Dance Fever* pose and squealed in delight. "I'm loving this."

Monica tossed Sherri the camera, then started a chant of "Go 'Nisha. It's your birthday. Go 'Nisha. It's your birthday."

The chorus of their voices shook their eardrums while they danced. Finally they got back to the decorating business at hand. Sherri and Kendall pushed the coffee table back against the wall to make room for an orange shag rug, the last of their retro accessories. Felicia went back to the television and shoved a tape into the VCR. The familiar sitcom tune of *Good Times* spilled from the television.

"How about we spend a little time with J.J. and Thelma?" Felicia asked.

Anisha picked up the tapes and sat in front of the TV. "Where in the world did you find these?"

"Girl, it's amazing what you find watching television late at night," Felicia said.

"Excuse me, Miss Diva," Monica said, tapping Anisha's shoulder. "I think you've forgotten you're wearing a rather large obstruction on top of your head."

"My bad," Anisha said, reclining across the shag rug.

The girls chose their favorite episodes about the family in the Chicago projects who could never manage to dig themselves out of their financial pit but always found the good times with each other. They watched three episodes before taking a break and beginning Anisha's interrogation about her night with Tyson.

"So fill us in."

"Was it more of a romantic night or an adventurous night?"

"Where did he take you?"

"Did y'all behave yourselves?"

Anisha mused while they threw a flurry of questions around quicker than she could answer them. "Are you finished?" She sat up, crossed her legs Indian style, and patted her round Afro. A grin spread across her face as she eyed her captive audience. "Now that I have your undivided attention, I can proceed."

Anisha recounted her night with Tyson. She painted a picture with words that thrust the girls on the stage at the Fox Theatre and seated them at the table with Tyson for dinner.

"And then to top it all off," she finished, "last night he told me he loved me."

"He what?"

"More or less. He didn't flat-out say the words 'I love you,' but he did say, and I quote, 'Nothing is too much for the woman I love.'"

"Oh, that's it." Felicia threw her hands in the air. "You've got the boy's nose wide open. He's hooked like a wide-mouthed bass on a fishing pole."

"Sounds like this is starting to get serious," Angie said.

"*Starting* to get serious?" Kendall added. "When's the last time you saw this woman at Singles Ministry?"

Anisha's mouth dropped open. "What's Singles Ministry got to do with anything?"

Kendall looked around the circle in hopes somebody else would step up to the plate. When they didn't, she did it herself. "People can always tell when the regulars get a man. They disappear off the scene like they're married instead of dating. Girl, you still need the teaching to make sure you're keeping your relationship in God's order. You don't want to end up laying up at the boy's house or something."

Anisha's heart jumped. *Okay, God. I hear You.*

"Uh-hum. True." Angie chimed in in agreement with Kendall. "But I can't say I blame you, Anisha. Enjoy the relationship. A man like Tyson is a blessing. Bump the single life. You're trying to get down that aisle, girl!"

Anisha was glad someone had come to her defense. She looked at Sherri, who appeared disinterested in the conversation. She hadn't joined in the girls' harmless teasing, but Anisha already knew Sherri's stand. She'd never argued Tyson wasn't a good man; she just thought Anisha needed to balance her life. Tyson's end of her scale was carrying too much weight.

"How long have y'all been seeing each other?"

"Five months," Anisha answered.

"And he's using the L word already?"

"He only said what I've been thinking," Anisha admitted. "I love him, too." Anisha picked up the remote. "Anyway, girls, we got a few more episodes of *Good Times* to watch, and y'all are interrupting my flow. This is supposed to be time with my girls. Enough about Tyson for now."

Monica cupped her hand to her ear. "Y'all hear something?"

The girls fell silent and strained their ears.

"What is it?" Anisha asked.

"I think I hear wedding bells," Monica teased.

*S*herri watched the curriculum from the Atlanta Art and Fashion Institute Web site spit out of the printer. She added the pages to the growing stack of papers on the desk. The winter session at the Institute would be starting next month, and she was prepared to do whatever it took to earn her associate degree in fashion design.

She hole punched the stack of papers and clipped them inside a three-ring notebook. The clash of the metal rings meeting together reminded her of a judge's gavel. The verdict was in, and her mind was made up. It was now or never. If it meant taking part-time classes at night, she'd do it. If it meant weekend classes, she'd make the sacrifice.

Sherri couldn't believe her passion had been in front of her face for all these years. She'd never considered her natural eye for fashion as the key to taking her to the next level. Just as she'd spoken a word and opened Anisha's eyes to a world of possibilities, Anisha had done the same for her. Her gift had been lying dormant, waiting to be realized and awakened.

Ever since Sherri made the girls' dashikis for Anisha's seventies birthday bash last month, she'd wanted to learn more. Her innate talent coupled with the skills she'd learned in her high school home economics class were enough to throw together the simple tunic pattern but not enough to design the clothing line she was envisioning, especially tailored for curvy, petite women like herself.

Sherri had deliberately altered her lifestyle over the last month so she could hone her skills before starting classes at the Institute. She'd given up her routine nights of sitting in front of the tube and convinced her aunt Jean to let her come over and use her sewing machine to practice. She had added quite a few simple pieces to her personal wardrobe.

Sherri was disturbed by the phone ringing. It was unusual for her to get a call so early on Saturday morning unless it was Anisha calling from the center. Sherri knew they usually had those volunteer meetings for the gala early in the mornings, and Anisha was always there. Every weekend like clockwork.

Sherri couldn't seem to convince Anisha that she didn't fault her for helping Tyson with things down at the center. She just wanted Anisha to see that she had a vision of her own that she was neglecting. Again. Even the girls had said they noticed Anisha had lost her own life to live inside Tyson's world. But how many times did she have to talk to her friend before her eyes were opened? She was done with it. At least until next week.

Sherri dove across the bed and decided to catch the phone before it could ring for a fourth time. If it were a monotone voice reading a script to sell vinyl siding, she'd put the poor man out of his misery and hang up the phone before he got too deep into his spiel.

"Hello?"

"Good morning. Is Sherri there?"

"Speaking." It didn't sound like a telemarketer. The voice was familiar, but Sherri couldn't match it with a face.

"What's up? This is Xavier. Sorry to call you so early, but I wanted to catch you before I left for the center."

He paused briefly as if waiting for a response. He continued when he didn't get one. After all, he'd asked her out a few weeks ago and ended up standing her up. He'd waited until the next day to call her back with some lame excuse.

"I was thinking we could grab a bite to eat later on tonight if you're not busy. Give us a chance to get to know each other a little more without an audience."

"I'm not sure what my evening is looking like right now," Sherri said. "I've got some things I need to take care of today." *Dating commandment number seven: Thou shalt never seem desperate.* "Maybe if you call me when you're leaving, I can meet you somewhere if I'm already out."

She gave Xavier her cell phone number, and he promised to call her around eight.

"Ain't that a blip," Sherri said, hanging up the phone. Her infatuation with Xavier was fading. After a few brief phone conversations with him, she realized his character was nowhere near as captivating as his looks. Nevertheless, it was nice to hear a man's voice, even if it was a sporadic occurrence.

Sherri flipped over on her stomach and closed her eyes.

"God, thank You for answering my prayers and revealing to me what was already inside of me," she prayed. "Direct my steps, because You know what's best. You can see from the beginning to the end of what You have for my life. But God, I really want to enroll in this fashion design program, so if it's Your plan too, I don't mind. Amen."

Sherri jumped up and headed to the kitchen for a light breakfast. Tamara was sitting on the couch in the living room with the lights and the television off. The early morning sun seeped through the closed blinds, offering enough light for Sherri to see Tamara's tear-streaked face.

"Morning, Tam." Sherri grabbed a banana from the fruit bowl on the kitchen table and poured herself and Tamara a glass of orange juice. "You okay?"

Sherri handed her roommate the glass and sat down beside her. Tamara took a small sip, then put the glass on the plant stand beside her.

"Yeah. I couldn't sleep last night, so I came in here early this morning." Tamara pulled her knees to her chest and rested her chin on top of them. "I don't know. I can't put my finger on what's wrong. I've been restless all week."

A single tear crept from Tamara's eye and rolled down her cheek. She brushed it away with her pinky finger, but not before it was followed by a stream of tears that rushed out like water through a broken dam.

"Do you want to talk about it?" Sherri asked, rubbing her roommate's back.

Tamara shook her head and buried her face in her hands.

Sherri went to the bathroom and came back with a handful of tissue.

"Why don't you put on some clothes and come out with me this morning?" Sherri suggested. "You probably need to get out of the house for a while."

"I think I will." Tamara patted the side of her face with the soggy tissue. "Are you sure it's okay?"

"I insist. When's the last time we hung out? It's long overdue."

Tamara reached for her glass and downed the rest of the juice. "Thank you, Sherri. I mean that."

"Are you sure you don't want to talk?"

"No, really. I'm okay."

Sherri put an arm around Tamara's shoulders and rested her head on her shoulder. "I'm always here for you. Don't forget it."

"I won't."

"And I haven't forgotten you said you'd come to church with me," Sherri said. "You promised."

"No, I promised I'd *think* about it, but I haven't counted it out," Tamara said, getting up and grabbing an apple from the fruit bowl. "I'll be ready in thirty minutes."

Sherri kicked the door open with her foot and backed into the apartment carrying the heavy Singer sewing machine box with Tamara's help.

"Okay. Put it down here. We can push it the rest of the way." She looked down at the machine and shook her head. "I can't believe

Auntie Jean. When she told me she had something for me to pick up, I never imagined it would be my own sewing machine."

Tamara tossed her purse on the couch and flopped down beside it. "She really believes in you."

"Either that or she's tired of me coming to her house every day," Sherri said, dropping down on the couch beside Tamara.

"Whatever the reason, I can't wait to show off my outfit." Tamara pulled out the pattern she'd chosen during their trip to the fabric store.

"Don't be so anxious to parade around," Sherri said. "This is the first time I'm making anything like that for somebody other than myself."

"I'm confident in you. Why don't you show a little confidence in yourself? Besides, I'm your free walking advertisement, so you would want to hook it up."

"Free?" Sherri said. "Who said anything about free?"

"After all those times I slapped a perm in all that long hair before you jumped on the Halle Berry bandwagon and cut it off? Girl, please. It's the least you can do."

The muffled sound of Sherri's cell phone rang from the bottom of her purse. "Okay, okay. But only because it's you," she said, dumping the contents out of her purse so she could quiet the ring. *If it were Xavier, at least he'd call this time if he had to cancel,* she thought. Sherri finally found the cell, and she dipped into her room to take the call in private.

"Hello?"

"Is this Sherri?"

"Yes, it is." *Definitely not Xavier's voice.* "May I ask who's speaking?"

"This is Calvin Wright. But better known to you as Mr. Confidence."

Dang. She'd forgotten she'd given him her cell phone number. "Well, Mr. Confidence, you've been more like Mr. Absent. For a man who acted so persistent, you sure took your time calling. How long has it been? Over a month now?"

"I'm not going to offer you any excuses, only an apology."

Calvin and Sherri chatted until their conversation was interrupted by Xavier's call. She dumped the call with Calvin. She'd deal with

Mr. Confidence later. She made plans to meet Xavier an hour later at the Cajun Bayou for a taste of Louisiana cuisine.

Sherri went into the living room to push the sewing machine the rest of the way into her room. "Girl, I ain't trying to kick you to the curb, but I've got a dinner date," she told Tamara.

"I ain't mad at ya. Do your thang, girl. Just don't pull a Veronica on us."

"Real funny," Sherri said, dipping into her room. "Don't worry about that."

Sherri showered, slipped into a cute, funky dress she'd found on sale, and was out the door in record time. It was good to get out of the house for something besides a rendezvous with the girls. Finally a little action in her life.

Sherri pulled into the restaurant parking lot and saw Xavier's midnight blue Mustang already parked near the entrance. She pulled through the valet parking line and jumped out of the car. The waiting valet accepted her keys, and Sherri stuffed the claim ticket in her purse as she entered the restaurant.

In the dimness of the restaurant, Sherri could see the servers and hostesses scurrying around dressed in all black. She'd never patronized the restaurant at night, but she loved the lunch menu and thought the live jazz music she'd heard they had on Saturday nights would be a nice touch.

The hostess led her to a small booth in the back. Xavier stood when he noticed Sherri approaching the table. He flashed his signature smile at her and helped her remove her jacket. He looked even better than she remembered.

"How are you?" he asked.

"Good."

Xavier waited until she was seated before sliding into the booth. At least he had some gentlemanly attributes, Sherri decided. Her impression of him that she'd gathered from their phone conversations wasn't what she'd expected, so she figured she'd give him a chance to redeem himself.

The waitress came almost immediately. She was a short, thin girl with a figure that looked a tad bit disproportionate to Sherri. *Probably because her bustline screamed plastic surgery,* Sherri thought. She left them with two menus and returned shortly with their drink orders.

"So, tell me about yourself, Sherri Dawson."

"What do you want to know?" she asked, tasting her sweet tea. She added a lemon and an extra packet of sugar. She tasted it again and, finding it to her liking, took a long sip.

Xavier settled down lower into his seat and crossed his arms across his broad chest.

"Well?" Sherri asked again.

As was his habit, Xavier traced the outline of his mustache and goatee. "Whatever you want to tell me."

"Since that's the case, I plead the fifth. Your turn."

"That ain't fair."

"When has life ever been fair? Your turn."

"Fine. I'm not scared to answer questions."

The waitress appeared out of thin air again to take their orders. Her overexaggerated attempt at customer service was working on Sherri's nerves. She could have sworn the waitress had undone another button on her already low-cut blouse. *Her breasts must be new,* Sherri thought.

Since neither of them was extremely hungry, Xavier and Sherri each ordered a house salad and decided to share a seafood platter. Xavier placed the order and, when the waitress left, leaned forward with his elbows on the table. He fixed his eyes on Sherri. They were seductive, almost hypnotizing.

A girl could get into trouble looking into those eyes, Sherri thought.

"Go ahead, prosecutor," Xavier prompted. "I'm waiting."

Sherri drummed her fingers on the table in contemplation. "Are you sure you're ready for my examination? I can be pretty tough on a brother."

Xavier held a steady hand out across the table. "Do I look like I'm shaking?" he asked and took a long guzzle of his light beer.

Sherri watched the beer bottle leave his lips and clank on the table in front of her. She wasn't too enthused about him drinking, but she doubted their acquaintanceship would ever turn into anything serious. She was there to get out of the house and have a good time. No strings attached.

Sherri zeroed in on her target. "So what do you do besides volunteer at the center?"

"I'm in training at the fire academy for the city of Atlanta."

"So you'll be one of our fearless public servicemen in uniform?"

"Something like that. Next question."

"How old are you?"

"Thirty-one."

"Where are you from?"

"Georgia native. Born and bred."

Sherri pried further. "What church do you attend?"

"Depends."

"On what?" She couldn't wait to hear this answer.

"On who's on TV when I wake up."

Strike one, she thought.

"What's that look for?" Xavier asked, taking another swig of his beer.

"What look?"

"The look like I'm a straight-up heathen. Do I have to be a church boy to be about something?"

"I never said that."

"You didn't have to. Your face told on you."

"Why are you worried about what I think? I thought you weren't scared."

"I'm not. Go ahead."

"What's your vision?"

"Twenty-twenty."

"Uh-hum." *Strike two.* Her singles minister always cautioned the ladies to ask the brothers about their vision. If he talked about his sight instead of his ambition in life, the woman was in for some serious work. Or serious trouble.

"What's my sight got to do with anything?"

"Nothing," Sherri said, waving her comment off. "Crazy personal fetish." If he didn't understand, she wasn't going to waste her energy explaining.

"Hold up a minute. You mean you get to sit and drill me, and I can't ask one single question?"

"Fine," Sherri conceded. "One question."

"If that's all I get, I'd better save it until I know I've got a good one."

A middle-aged woman wearing a bright blue, knee-length beaded dress sauntered onto the small stage area to join the band. It was obvious by her hairdo and outfit that she was stuck in a time warp, most likely from her younger days. Regardless, the crooner played her voice like a well-tuned instrument. By the end of the second song, the waitress was bringing out an array of shrimp, crawfish, deviled crabs, and blackened catfish. She set down two plates and refilled Sherri's iced tea.

"Can I get you anything else?" she asked Xavier, her eyes roaming over his biceps.

"I think we're okay. You need anything else, Sherri?"

"No, I'm fine. We shouldn't need anything else for a while," she hinted.

Xavier tore into the crab legs. Sherri noticed he didn't offer for them to say grace together and hadn't even prayed a blessing over his own food. She bowed her head anyway, and when she looked up after her grace, he was still stuffing his face.

Xavier wiped the cocktail sauce from the corner of his mouth. "Your girl is a permanent fixture down at the center. She was still there when I left this evening. I think she's more crunk about this whole gala and mentoring program thing than Tyson."

"Tell me about it." Sherri rolled her eyes before she could catch herself. Fortunately, Xavier was too busy cracking a crab leg and hadn't noticed. See? Proof again that everybody else noticed, but Anisha was too blinded by love.

Xavier dipped the crabmeat in melted butter and inhaled it. "I've never known Tyson to even talk about meeting a woman's peeps, much less go out of town to meet 'em."

Sherri concentrated on not letting her expression show her thoughts. She stuffed her mouth with a piece of shrimp so she wouldn't have to respond. *How could Anisha neglect to share something like that with her and subject her to hearing about it from this outsider?*

Maybe she'd forgotten to mention it. They hadn't really talked much since Anisha's birthday. Like Xavier had said, Anisha practically lived at the center, and she was tied up with preparing for her classes at the Atlanta Art and Fashion Institute. But that kind of information shouldn't be withheld from a best friend. As far as Sherri was concerned, she should've been the first to know. She guessed she shouldn't be surprised. Her friendship with Anisha was slipping between her fingers, and she couldn't seem to get a firm grasp on it. Tyson had a solid pull, and it didn't look like he'd be letting go anytime soon.

Xavier droned on, and Sherri grew more disappointed as she continued to notice the lack of depth to his conversation. He was eye-candy good for entertainment purposes, but that was about it. She was relieved when the waitress returned with the check and gave it to Xavier. She could almost swear that she saw a telephone number on the other side of the receipt, but she could have been wrong. It *was* dim in the restaurant, and she was looking *through* the thin receipt. Her assumption may have been a little over the top, but considering the actions of the waitress that night, Sherri wouldn't put it past her.

"You all take it easy," the waitress said, turning around and practically knocking her hips out of joint with an overexaggerated, supposedly sexy gait.

Xavier left enough money on the table for the bill and tip and escorted Sherri to the valet waiting area.

Sherri noticed that he didn't seem to be pulling out his keys or doing anything that signaled he was leaving. "Isn't that your car parked out front?" she asked, slipping a dollar bill into the valet's hand.

"Yeah, but I need to run back in to the restroom." Xavier kissed her on the cheek and closed her door. He waited until she pulled off, and from the rearview mirror Sherri saw him dip back into the restaurant. *Yep,* her instinct confirmed, *that was definitely a phone number.*

For that lack of intellectual stimulation, she could have stayed at home with a pizza and the instruction manual to her new sewing machine. She pulled out of the parking lot and headed for the highway. She still had time to go home and start cutting out Tamara's dress pattern.

*T*he sound of a horn blared through Anisha's closed car windows. She'd planned on taking care of some Christmas shopping during the post–Thanksgiving Day sales, but the impatient commuters and Friday's exhaustion from working overtime all week zapped what little energy she had left.

"There's definitely got to be something more than this," Anisha complained. She slammed her fist on the steering wheel in frustration. She was stuck in bumper-to-bumper rush-hour traffic. And as usual for a Friday evening, I-285 looked more like a parking lot than a freeway.

Cars crept along at a snail's pace. She'd already been in traffic for thirty-five minutes and was still less than halfway home. She slipped Sunday's sermon CD into the player again. She didn't care that she'd heard it four times that week already. Her spirit needed it. The sound of Pastor Armstrong's strong voice drowned out the horn-blaring of the irritated drivers around her.

Anisha had been meditating on the words of her pastor's sermon all week. The words reverberated like an echo through her mind, even when she wasn't playing the tape.

"Life is more about God than you," Pastor Armstrong said. "Every challenge you face is even preordained. God knows everything, and He doesn't throw out things randomly. We should be trying to fit into God's plan, not have Him fit into ours."

It was as if God Himself was speaking to Anisha, and she knew He was through the voice of her pastor. She didn't try to hold back the tears swelling in her eyes. She didn't know why she was crying, and as the tears rolled down her cheeks she didn't bother stopping them from salting her lips.

She refocused herself on Pastor Armstrong's voice.

"Don't let your emotions distract you and cause you to lose sight of God's plan for your life," he said.

Anisha found an old fast-food napkin in her glove compartment and wiped her face.

"Lord, why do I keep coming back to this same point inside when everything on the outside seems to be together?"

You need to know My plan for your life. No one else can complete you.

Thoughts of Tyson raided her mind, but they didn't make sense. They weren't bad thoughts, per se, but they left her in a state of confusion. Tyson was all she had ever prayed for. He was a good man for her, and the past six months had been more exciting than she'd ever imagined a relationship could be.

How many times would she make a promise to God and then break it? She was tired of having good intentions but circling around to the same place. She always claimed that she'd be obedient to God. It was an easy vow to make when her thoughts lined up with what she felt He wanted her to do. But she was in a battle between two wills—her will and God's will. And it wasn't even to say that Tyson wasn't the one, but whether it was the season for them to be together. The way she saw it, God's timing was just as important as His directions.

Sherri figured she'd probably be at home alone again tonight. She was hoping to hear from Xavier, but he hadn't called her all week. When she tried to call him, his cell phone always transferred straight to his voice mail. She wished she had his home number, but he didn't have one. He said it was much more economical for him to only carry a cell phone, since he was at the fire station most of the time anyway.

As usual, Sherri's roommates were heading out to the club. She wasn't in the sewing mood and would do almost anything to get out of her apartment's four walls.

Maybe she'd surprise her roommates and venture out with them. Veronica, especially, since she always griped she was out of touch. She said Sherri thought herself better than others since she "got into church," as she'd put it.

"You act like you ain't never stepped foot in the club before," Veronica had said before. "We remember your B.C. days—you know, before you got saved."

But to keep peace in the house, Sherri always refrained from making malicious remarks.

Sherri went to her room, squeezed into her closet, and came out with a black knit skirt, body shirt, and brick red leather jacket. She heard cabinet doors opening and glasses clinking as she headed toward the kitchen.

Veronica poured two glasses of whatever was still wrapped in a brown paper bag. "It's supposed to be slammin' tonight," Veronica crooned. "And it'll be even better once I get my buzz on."

Sherri's stomach turned, and her chest tightened. The knot in her chest wouldn't loosen even when she tried taking deep breaths. The Holy Spirit inside of her was grieved, and she knew it. What was her real purpose for going? Did she really want to show them an example of Christ and how she could relate to their struggles, or was she looking for a way to escape her own misery?

Sherri slipped back into her room and hung her clothes back in the closet. She dug her coziest pair of cotton pajamas from the bottom drawer of her armoire, grabbed the fluffiest pillow from her bed, and headed for the living room sofa.

"Have a little Communion?" Veronica asked when she turned and saw Sherri plop down on the sofa. She lifted her glass in the air. "We can even make it official with some crackers." Veronica rolled over in laughter, but Tamara winced.

"You have your way to have fun, and I have mine," Sherri said, picking up the remote and surfing through the television channels.

"If you call fun being cooped up in this house every weekend laying on a lumpy sofa instead of in the arms of a strong man, then I feel sorry for ya," Veronica said.

"At least I'm on the same sofa every week," Sherri shot back. "And don't make me get into that tonight." She didn't mean to let her thoughts push their way from her brain to her lips, but for once she was glad she did. She'd had enough of Veronica's smart-aleck remarks. And to think she was about to take a step backward just to prove something to them. It wasn't worth it.

Veronica stood with her mouth open and hands propped on her hips, obviously taken aback at Sherri's words. Too astonished to respond, she picked up her glass and headed back to her room. "Whatever," she mumbled. "Come on, Tam."

Tamara had been leaning against the kitchen counter, silently watching the rift. She set her glass down on the counter and followed Veronica. Tamara hung her head and examined the imaginary scuff marks on her shoes, careful not to make eye contact with Sherri as she passed.

The forty-five minutes before her roommates left seemed like hours to Sherri. Before, she'd complained about being alone, but now she couldn't wait for them to leave. And when they finally did, they did so without saying so much as a word. Veronica slammed noisily through the living room on her way out the door, and Tamara tiptoed behind her. Tamara turned around to shut the door, and for a brief second, her eyes met Sherri's disappointed gaze.

As soon as the door closed, Sherri picked up the phone to call Anisha. She hung up when she heard Anisha's voice on the answering machine. *Probably with Tyson,* she thought. Sherri dragged her all-too-worn covers and pillow down the hall toward her room.

"It figures," she said, sulking.

Her reflection in the hallway mirror caught her attention. She stopped and stared at the sullen face looking back at her. "Look at you," she said to the face. "Is this what I'm giving Tamara and Veronica to look at?" She smoothed her hair and ran her fingers down the side of her face. "Is this the example I'm setting? If I thought living for the Lord meant living like this, I'd run the other way, too." The face in the mirror smiled and laughed back at her. "Forget this mess. I'm going out! Where? Who cares? I'll know when we get there."

Sherri headed to her closet and pulled out the outfit she'd started to wear to the club. "Saved for a much better occasion," she concluded.

She enjoyed a relaxing soak in a tub full of bubbles laced with skin-smoothing chamomile and sweet olive oil. She stepped out of tub renewed in spirit and feeling and looking like a new woman. She rubbed lotion across her body, pausing only to examine the flawless hot pink polish on her toes. She threw a few curls in her short crop and added a little makeup to her face for a natural look. Her new face was much more alert and inviting than the reflection she had spoken to earlier.

"Now don't you look better?"

She beamed in the mirror, then went to her closet and pulled out two more prized possessions. At the end of last winter, she'd found the perfect purse and boots to match her brick-red leather jacket. She'd waited nearly a year to break out the set.

"I am looking much too cute for the club tonight anyway," Sherri decided. She threw her purse over her shoulder and sashayed toward the door. She kept prancing down the stairwell even when she heard the phone ringing. She thought about stopping in case it was Xavier but decided against it. Bump him right now too. Even though the last few times she'd talked to him he didn't seem so bad. He had a lot of growing to do when it came to his spiritual life, but she couldn't necessarily fault him. Everybody needed someone to help guide them from darkness into the light, didn't they? She'd try to reach him on his cell later.

Anisha wondered where Sherri could have gone. She hung up the phone when it was apparent Sherri wasn't answering. It wasn't like her to be out on a Friday night unless she was braving the holiday shopping crowds instead of running for cover as she'd chosen to do. Anisha tossed the cordless on her bed. She wouldn't be surprised if Sherri had gone to bed early or turned the ringer off so she could focus on sewing some new pattern.

Anisha had jotted down a shopping list during her long commute and stopped at the grocery store before going home. She peeled out of her work clothes before unpacking the groceries and filling her empty pantry shelves. She'd become a stranger to her own house.

Tonight Tyson was home getting well-deserved rest. He'd put in long hours on his regular job all week and was still trying to tie up loose ends for what they'd finally decided to call the "Rites of Passage Holiday Gala." Both left him physically and mentally exhausted, and with only two weeks left before the big event, he needed as much rest as he could get.

When Anisha stopped by his apartment on the way home earlier that evening, she convinced him he needed a break.

"Use this weekend to get yourself back together," she'd told him. "I want to make sure you stay around as long as possible," she said, latching her arms around his neck.

Tyson wrapped his arms around Anisha's waist and pulled her close enough for the tips of their noses to touch. "I'll rest much better if you're here," he said. His lips tickled hers like the light dusting of a dove's feathers.

Anisha felt a tingle rise from her toes, and she playfully squirmed out of his clutch. "No, you won't get any rest if I'm here," she'd said, poking her index finger into his chest. "I don't want to hear from you this weekend," she said. She pecked him on the cheek and scooted for the door. She ran outside and didn't turn around until she was safe in the car. "Rest," she'd yelled and sped off to the grocery store.

Anisha lined the boxes of cereal, instant oatmeal, and other snacks on the bottom pantry shelf. She'd thought about Sherri when she'd bought a bag of sour cream and cheddar potato chips. Give Sherri a bag of those chips and a soda on a lazy afternoon, and she would settle in on the couch for a movie—content for the remainder of the day.

It had been a while since Anisha had had a heart-to-heart with her best friend. They promised they would never let a man come between their relationship, and she was guilty of committing the ultimate friendship crime and breaking a dating commandment. But people's lives changed, and the dynamics of a friendship don't necessarily stay the same forever. It was part of life. Dating Commandment number twenty-eight would have to be amended.

Anisha had never had a man who wanted to spend as much time with her as she did with him. Tyson was that man. He was full of adventure and always had a surprise up his sleeve. Even now her birthday evening brought a smile to her face. It was a night she'd never forget—the night when he'd first expressed his love for her.

Anisha stuffed the last pack of meat into the refrigerator and then went into the laundry room. She separated a few piles of clothes, dumped in a load of whites, and collapsed across the bed. She tried calling Sherri one more time but didn't get an answer.

"Hey, Sherri. I was just thinking about you," Anisha said on the answering machine. Give me a call when you get a chance. Talk to you later. Love ya." Anisha hung up and tried Sherri's cell phone. "No Tyson or Sherri tonight."

But I'm here. Let's share some time together.

They weren't supposed to be there with her tonight, Anisha decided. And she wasn't alone; God was already there.

Anisha pressed the power button on her stereo remote and set the CD player to random selection. The discs rotated and blared the beats of one of her favorite Fred Hammond CDs. She was sure the music was disturbing her neighbors, but at the moment she didn't care. She sang as loud as her vocal cords would allow.

Anisha crooned and danced in a way she hadn't done in ages, unconcerned about who may have heard or been watching through the open blinds. The disc changer rotated again, stopping on a ballad by Yolanda Adams.

Anisha felt warmth move through her body. She lost herself in praise and wouldn't stop, even when her muscles reminded her that she hadn't worked her body in a while. She couldn't stop. She leaped and swayed until her legs could no longer carry her weight.

Look at My baby girl, praising Me. Now if I could get some worship.

Finally Anisha collapsed in exhaustion and lay prostrate on her bedroom floor. The presence of the Lord in the room wrapped itself around her like a warm towel on an aching body.

"God, You've stayed so faithful to me." Anisha cried so hard that her eyes began to swell. "You've been so patient. How can You love me like You do? Nothing should be more important than our relationship. Help me, Lord. Help me to hear and obey Your voice even when it hurts."

Anisha was disappointed in herself, but she knew God didn't condemn her. In His loving way, He showed her the areas of her life that needed work. She worked on building other areas in her life—her career, her relationships—but she neglected her spiritual needs. She needed to spend more time with God, and she knew it. He'd become an afterthought when He should've been the first thought. From this point forward, she would put Him first.

"Lord, hold me to my promise," she cried.

*A*fter months of planning, the Rites of Passage Holiday Gala was proving to be an astounding success. Every sponsorship table had been purchased, and those who couldn't afford to purchase a table contributed money at other sponsorship levels. The black-tie event at the ritzy hotel was a first-time experience for some of the boys and their families. They were thankful to Tyson and the rest of the program counselors for giving them the opportunity to step outside of their worlds.

The banquet hall chandelier hung in the middle of the ballroom, casting the illusion of a fiery sun suspended in midair. The tables, decorated in white linen with matching seat covers, were arranged in a semicircle around a hardwood dance floor area. Esteemed guests and leaders in the community were seated on a raised platform on either side of the podium.

Anisha sat at the sponsorship table that Deacon Davenport and his partner at their engineering firm had purchased. She couldn't contain her excitement when Tyson approached the podium to read the charge issued to the young mentees. During the presentation, each mentee was presented a certificate for his commitment to the program. The counselors charged their mentees to incorporate all they had learned, and would continue to learn, into their daily lives. They commissioned them to teach their peers by example.

Anisha could sense that all eyes at her table landed on her at some time during Tyson's presentation. Deacon and Sister Davenport, Sherri, and even Monica, Kendall, Angie, and Felicia had come to support him.

Proud mothers cried as they watched the initiation ceremony of their once-disrespectful boys groomed into well-mannered gentlemen. All night the boys exhibited the highest respect and chivalry to the guests and to one another. And thanks to the patronage of a local formal wear chain, each of them was outfitted in a black tuxedo. Their physical appearances and attitudes had been transformed for the night, and Tyson was prayerful that their attitudes would remain transformed long after the tuxedos were returned.

Anisha's girlfriends crowded around her after the gala ended.

"I have to give it to you, Anisha," Sherri said. "Now I can tell why you were so engulfed in this whole thing. That ceremony was touching. And the little boys looked soooooo cute! Makes me wish I had a son."

"I'm not gonna go that far." Monica laughed. "But I was extremely impressed."

"I'll tell Tyson you said so," Anisha said.

"Tyson?" Felicia waved the program booklet in the air. "Girl, they should've dedicated a full page in this book to you."

"Felicia, if you're riding with me, you better come on," Sherri said. Sherri hugged Anisha and promised to call her later. "Give Tyson my love. I've got to get out of here and finish my homework. If I don't stay ahead over the weekend, I'll get behind."

"I'm so proud of you, Sherri." Anisha pulled her into an embrace. "I know we haven't talked much lately, but I'm always thinking about you," she said low enough for only Sherri to hear. "I'm gonna be bragging about how I knew you before your fashions made it to the New York runway." She gave Sherri a slight nudge toward the door. "Go ahead and go home. I don't want to keep you from doing your thing."

Anisha bade the rest of the girls and the Davenports good-bye and promised to keep them updated on anything that might happen after they'd left.

As the night drew to a close, Tyson and the boys posed for pictures for a photographer from one of the city's local newspapers. Afterward, Tyson hobnobbed with representatives from the companies and foundations who had helped to sponsor the gala.

Anisha waited at one of the back tables in the hotel banquet room. Even from where she was sitting, she could tell Tyson had captured the company representatives with his natural charisma. He moved among them effortlessly, shaking hands and working the floor with confidence. Anisha had the inside scoop and could tell he was spending extra time with those he'd pinpointed as strong prospects to fund the program.

At ten o'clock, Tyson escorted the last guest out and came back inside with a beaming smile. Anisha stood to greet him.

"Looks good, baby," he said, wrapping his arms around her and lifting her off the floor. He set her down and led her to the middle of the empty dance floor that hours earlier had been bustling with young men leading their mothers, aunts, or grandmothers in ballroom dances.

"That proposal is what did it. They said there wasn't a single question they had that wasn't covered in it." Tyson kissed Anisha tenderly on the lips. "Thank you." He turned around to the deejay, who was starting to disconnect his equipment. "Could you play one more before you pack up?"

"Gotcha, man." The deejay reached into a milk crate, twirled a vinyl record between his fingertips, then put it on the turntable. He carefully dropped the needle on the rotating disc, and the sound of the Luther Vandross classic "Here and Now" filled the room.

Tyson rested his cheek on the side of Anisha's temple as they slow-danced and dragged into their own world. He whispered in her ear, "Everything is falling into place, baby. I've got two definite investors for the full-time program, and their contributions alone will carry us through the first year. Anything else confirmed from this point on can go into reserves."

Anisha laid her head on his chest and closed her eyes. She'd prayed for a man who loved the Lord. A businessman with drive, and a man whom she could share dreams with. Here he was. Her answered prayer.

Tyson hugged her closer. "This is no longer a dream; it's a reality," he said. "At the beginning of the year I'll be out of the corporate rat race. The next time I pull long hours it'll be to build my vision. God's vision."

Anisha squeezed her arms around Tyson's waist. "You deserve it, sweetheart. This is a new chapter in your life. I'm excited for you."

"I've got another chapter I'm looking forward to starting, too."

"Oh really?" Anisha lifted her head and looked into Tyson's eyes.

"Really."

"And what's this chapter about?"

"A certain lady in my life."

Anisha laid her head back on his chest. "Mmmmm. Sounds interesting."

Anisha wondered if Tyson was hinting at marriage and, if so, when he was thinking this new chapter would begin. After repeated instances of heartache, it looked as if her prayers for a knight in shining armor were being answered.

*A*yana's questions about having a father were becoming a daily weight on Brandy's mind. Now her daughter was fantasizing about the stacks of Christmas presents she'd have to open if only she had a daddy. Saturday morning television programs, inundated with all the toy commercials between the cartoons, shifted Ayana into full gear.

"If I had a daddy, I bet he'd get me that," she'd yell and clap. "Mommy, do daddies buy those?" she'd ask, jumping in front of the television and pointing to the latest life-size baby doll on roller skates.

Brandy's response was always the same. "Mommy can buy it for you."

Brandy hadn't run into Tyson since seeing him at the Davenports' cookout in September. For three months she'd been lingering around the vestibule after church and hadn't caught so much as a glimpse. She'd alternated between the early morning service and the afternoon service, and still nothing.

Brandy weighed her options. She'd already tried the obvious route, but Tyson's number was unlisted. She didn't know where he worked now, and asking Mrs. Jamison to ask her friends the Davenports was out of the question.

The only remaining logical option was to call Tyson's mother. His mother had gotten remarried during his college sophomore year to her high school sweetheart, Steve Brooks. To Tyson's dismay, his stepfather moved his mother to Tallahassee, Florida, where he owned an auto sales business. Steve had a house custom built and said he always planned to stay there until he died or got moved to an old folks home, whichever came first. Brandy figured there was very little chance they'd moved or changed their phone number. Even after all these years, the number was still engraved in her memory.

If she called his mother now, nothing would seem suspicious. It was Christmas Eve, and people always caught up with old family and friends around the holidays. Yet Brandy was hesitant about calling his mom, because she wasn't sure how she would react. After the drama at the hospital, his mother had still been reserved the first few times Brandy had spoken to her. Not only was Tyson expecting a daughter, but she'd been expecting her first grandchild. Tyson wasn't the only person Brandy had hurt and deceived.

Despite her reservations, Brandy convinced herself that destiny had allowed her and Tyson's paths to cross again. If he happened to be home during the holidays, that would make things all the better.

What have I got to lose?

Brandy walked into the living room to check on Ayana, catching her in a picture-perfect moment. She was standing on her tiptoes in red fleece pajamas trying to pull her favorite Rudolph ornament off the Christmas tree. Brandy crept up behind her and scooped her up in her arms before Ayana could snag the reindeer made from clothespins.

"Mommmmyyyy," Ayana screamed, kicking her feet in delight. She wrapped her arms around her mother's neck until her feet were safe on the sofa. "How many more days?" she asked, jumping up and down on the sagging cushions.

"One more day."

Ayana jumped up and down again, shifting the cushions on the sofa. "Can I call Grandma?" she said, her eyes twinkling like the lights on the Christmas tree.

"As soon as you get out of the bathtub."

Brandy carried Ayana into the bathroom and set her on the toilet seat. She pushed back the clear vinyl shower curtain with bright images of tropical fish and seahorses and turned on the water. She held her hand under the spigot, testing the water for the right temperature. Ayana loved playing in the bathtub. It was her favorite room since she'd picked the décor herself. She'd chosen everything from the bright yellow toilet seat cover and bath mats to the tropical shower curtain and colorful fish-shaped appliqués pasted on the walls.

Brandy helped Ayana undress and left her in the tub with some toys to keep her occupied. She pulled the bathroom door closed, leaving a small crack so she could still hear Ayana from the bedroom.

She picked up the phone and immediately dialed the number before her nerves could get the best of her. The phone rang five times, and not even an answering machine picked up. As she was about to hang up, a groggy voice answered.

"I'm sorry for waking you up, sir," Brandy said. She didn't want to identify herself. "Is Mrs. Brooks available?"

"Naw. Not right now, but she'll be back in about an hour. Do you want to hang up and call back to leave a message on the voice mail?"

"Uh, no. Actually, this is one of Tyson's old friends from college, and I was trying to get in touch with him."

Brandy took advantage of the sleepy man's incoherence and asked him for Tyson's number. He rattled it off; then Brandy thanked him and quickly hung up the phone. She knew he'd forget the call before his head hit the pillow.

Brandy picked up the phone again and listened to the drone of the dial, urging her to make a decision. She punched the keypad and pressed the phone to her ear. *I'm calling your daddy, Ayana,* she wanted to say.

*A*nisha drove her mother's car to the airport to pick up Tyson on Christmas Eve morning. At the last minute, she'd decided to take a few extra vacation days and escape to the simplicity of her hometown in High Point, North Carolina. She'd needed to escape the office.

It seemed the workload of all the junior account executives, except hers, had changed. There were days she'd stay until nearly eight o'clock at night and still feel she hadn't put a dent in the assignments dumped in her in-box. Sometimes Anisha wondered if showing them her abilities had worked against her. She was expected to do twice the amount of work and draft reports in half the time. Not only that, but she'd noticed the frequency of closed-door meetings for the past month. It was all suspicious to her, but none of the other junior execs seemed to recognize it.

But her schedule was in her own hands this week. She would rather stay up all night with her brother and sister watching movies at her mom's house and fall asleep on the couch. She was happy going to her grandmother's for breakfast and making a piece of cheese toast in the oven while Grans sipped on a cup of coffee and ate a bacon and egg sandwich on white bread. It was heaven.

Anisha merged over into the fast lane on Interstate 40. Although it was the eve of a holiday, the heaviest traffic in the city was no comparison to Atlanta's lightest traffic days. Anisha arrived at the airport in twenty-five minutes, wheeled into an empty parking space, stuck a quarter in the meter, and ran inside.

She'd told Tyson to meet her at the baggage claim. The entire Triad International Airport could probably fit inside one of the terminals in Atlanta's airport with room to spare. She knew Tyson wouldn't have any trouble finding his way around, seeing as there was only one row of terminals leading straight to baggage claim.

The electronic board showed Flight 8357 arriving from Atlanta was on time for its 10:37 a.m. arrival. Anisha sat down in a chair across from the baggage conveyer belt that would be carrying Tyson's suitcase. She passed time by watching a red garment bag circling the conveyer belt. By the time the bag completed its fourth rotation, she looked up to see Tyson riding down the escalator.

It was all Anisha could do to prevent herself from breaking into a sprint. She tried to walk calmly, but her legs pushed her to move faster. She stopped and let Tyson finish the short walk alone.

"Hey, baby." He held her as if she'd disappear if he let go.

Anisha held on to him until she realized the onlookers were probably perturbed by their lengthy public display of affection.

"So, this is the big Triad?" Tyson asked.

"A far cry from the ATL, isn't it?"

"From what I saw out of the plane window and from the looks of this miniature airport, I would say so."

"Let's grab your bag and get on the road. I want to run by the mall before we go home."

"This is the only one I have," he said, lifting up the roller bag he was pulling behind him. "We're only here for four days. Shoot, I could've fit a week's worth of clothes in here if I'd had to."

"Of course—you're a man. What was I thinking?" Anisha asked, clutching his hand and leading him toward the parking lot.

"So where's your family?'

"Everybody's at home. I didn't want them to bum rush you as soon as you got off the plane, so I convinced them to stay at home. I have some last-minute shopping to do. Don't worry. You'll meet them soon enough."

Anisha pulled in close to the porch and shifted the gear into park. She grinned at the sight of her sister standing in the doorway.

"Looks like you have an official greeting committee," she said, opening the car door. "Don't let my family wear you out. They can be a little worrisome at times. I've already warned them, but I can't promise they'll behave."

Tyson opened his door and walked around to the trunk. "Babe, it's all right. I should be the one stressed out, not you."

"Are you?"

"Am I what? Stressed?" Tyson hoisted his luggage from the trunk. "Not at all."

They headed for the doorway where Anisha's mother had joined her sister.

"Well, hello, Tyson," Margaret Blake said, holding the door wide enough for him to roll in his luggage and for Anisha to squeeze through with her shopping bags. "I'm glad to see your flight made it in safely."

Tyson slid into the welcoming arms of Ms. Blake for a motherly hug. "Thank you, ma'am. It's nice of you to have me."

The younger spitting image of Anisha stepped up and extended a hand. "And I'm Dominique, but you can call me Nikki."

"I've heard a lot about you," Tyson said.

"Don't believe anything but the good stuff," Nikki said.

"Tyson, you can put your things in the family room downstairs," Mrs. Blake said. "There's a sleeper sofa down there, and I left some fresh linen and towels for you."

"Thank you," Tyson said.

Anisha intertwined her fingers between Tyson's and laid her head on his shoulder. "Is lunch ready?" she asked.

"Yes, but we're waiting for Travis and Grans to get here."

"Where are they?"

"I don't know where your grandma is right now, but she said she'd be here around lunchtime. Ever since she got that new car, we can't keep her out of the streets. And you ought to know your brother is out somewhere with Jesse and Anthony. They picked him up right after you left this morning."

Anisha led Tyson down the hallway and opened the door to the stairs that led to the basement. It had been remodeled into a family room with a sitting area, a small kitchen table, and its own half bath.

Tyson leaned his suitcase against the wall and pulled off his coat. "This is like a private apartment down here. It's even got a separate entrance?" he asked, noticing the large bolted door.

"Pretty much." Anisha motioned to all the furniture and extra amenities. "My dad hung out with us a lot down here. After he died, when I was eight, it became an empty, large room with gray cement floors."

"Do you remember much about him?" Tyson asked.

"Yeah, I think back sometimes about playing board games with him, going out for ice cream—you know, simple stuff."

"Sometimes it's the little things that stick with us the most," Tyson said comfortingly.

"Yeah, you're right," Anisha said, smiling.

"Anyway, Nikki, Travis, and I decided to turn this space into the neighborhood roller rink. Travis and Nikki used to invite all their friends over on the weekends, and I'd charge them fifty cents to get in. We made skate tapes by dubbing songs off the radio, and when it got hot down here, we'd pull out a cooler of orange and grape sodas. Charged 'em twenty-five cents a pop. Chips too. Ma remodeled after I went to college."

"I can't believe you were hustling the neighborhood kids for their money."

"That wasn't a hustle. We were operating a business. Entrepreneurship has always been in my blood."

"Call it what you want," Tyson said. "You were a hustler." He kissed the top of her head. "It's cool to be here, getting to know your family. Going to see my stepdad's parents in Connecticut was not what I wanted to do this Christmas. Plus with the kind of weather they have there I didn't want to chance getting stranded."

"You don't have a relationship with his family?" Anisha asked.

"Not like that. Remember, I was in college when they got married, so it's not like I was always around him."

"Oh. When do they fly out?"

"Tomorrow morning."

Anisha held up her hand to quiet Tyson and strained to identify the new voice belonging to the extra pair of feet entering upstairs. "That's Grans. I'm going up."

"I'll be up in a minute. I'm getting hot in this turtleneck."

"Okay." Anisha bounded up the stairs and closed the door behind her. "Hey, Grans."

Anisha walked up behind her grandmother and play swatted her on the behind.

Joyce Edgars—lovingly known as Grans to young and old alike—had her salt-and-pepper hair pulled back into her signature chignon. The well-used apron was pulled tightly around her round middle section, and even though she was only wearing a T-shirt and some slacks, she still was adorned with her favorite pearl necklace.

Grans turned around and landed a slight hit on Anisha's behind before she could dodge out of her grandmother's reach. "You're not too old for me to turn you over my knee." Not being one to beat around the bush, Grans asked, "Where's your friend?"

"Getting settled downstairs. He'll be up in a minute." Anisha lifted the lids of two pots on the stove. "I'm hungry, Ma. Travis isn't back yet?"

"Give him a few more minutes, and then if he's not here we'll go ahead and eat."

"What are we having?" Anisha stirred the beans in the pots with a spoon. "These don't look ready."

"They're not. That's for later. Nikki fixed a light lunch since we're having such a big dinner."

"Since you're so concerned about it," Nikki said to Anisha, "you can help me get everything out of the fridge."

Anisha opened the fridge and pulled out a covered tray. "And what do we have here?" She put the tray on the island in the middle of the kitchen and folded back the plastic wrap to reveal an assorted arrangement of meat wraps and vegetable pitas.

Grans walked over and peeked around Anisha. "Looks healthy."

The creak of the door in the hallway announced Tyson's arrival. He walked into the kitchen wearing a fresh change of clothes. Anisha re-covered the pita tray and walked over to Tyson, steering him toward her grandmother with a nudge to his back.

"Tyson, this is my grandmother."

"Nice to meet you, ma'am."

Grans offered Tyson a hug full of motherly love. "I'm glad you came. Nobody should have to spend the holidays by themselves. 'Nisha tells me your people are going to Connecticut."

"Yes, ma'am."

"I don't blame you for not going. You could get up there and get stuck for weeks if it snows."

"My reasoning exactly," Tyson said, looking around the kitchen. He slapped his hands and rubbed them together. "Put me to work. What do you need help with?"

Anisha was going to suggest that Tyson help her, but Grans interjected. Her grandmother held onto her beliefs that women should take care of domestic issues in the kitchen and men were to handle the hard manual labor.

"You're a new guest, so you can relax for now," Grans said. "You can help Travis take care of some things later."

Tyson winked at Anisha and complied by pulling out a chair from the kitchen table. Anisha rolled her eyes and stuck out her tongue just as the front door opened and a herd of feet trampled into the foyer.

Travis filed in with his road buddies, Jesse and Anthony, behind him.

"Where's the food?"

"Let's eat."

"Wait a minute." Mrs. Blake put one hand up in the air to stop their stampede. She pointed a scolding finger at Jesse and Anthony. "I see y'all once in a blue moon when Travis comes home from school, and the first thing you do when you walk in my house is ask about food?"

"Naw, Mama. You know we love you," Jesse said, grabbing her from the side. Anthony clutched her from the other side, and they squeezed her into a human sandwich until she pleaded for mercy.

"One for you too, Grans," they said, doing the same to her.

"And we can't forget about baby sis," Anthony said.

Nikki wielded a knife she was using to cut the sandwiches. "Now you're going too far."

They backed away with their hands in the air. Jesse leaned against the counter, and a huge grin spread across his face when he noticed Anisha. "The love of my life. When are we getting married?"

"Next year," Anisha chimed with everybody else in the kitchen. It was the same answer she'd been giving him for the past fifteen years since his elementary school crush on his best friend's older sister first started.

Travis picked up a turkey wrap off the tray and stuffed it in his mouth.

"Wash your hands," Grans fussed.

"Sorry." He turned around and for the first time noticed Tyson sitting in the corner. "What's up, man?" he said, walking over and locking hands with him. "You must be Tyson."

Travis pointed to his friends. "That's Anthony, and this is Jesse, your competition."

Tyson pounded fists with both the boys. "You may have the home-court advantage, but this game is far from over," he said to Jesse.

"Oooohhhhh," Travis said, slapping hands with Tyson. "I like you already, man."

The house was full of lively chatter and activity. After lunch, the guys retreated downstairs, and the women finished cleaning the kitchen. Anisha had already anticipated her grandmother's conversation about Tyson, and it came as soon as he was clearly out of sight and hearing range.

Grans kept her voice low but loud enough to be heard over the clinking of the dishes in the sink. "Tyson seems to be a fine young man," she said, passing a plate to Anisha.

"He is, Grans." Anisha ran a dish towel over the dripping plate.

"What are his intentions for coming home with you?"

"Intentions?" Anisha looked over at her sister and mother who were pretending not to be listening to the conversation. Nikki kept wiping the same section of the kitchen counter, and her mother had found interest in a yellowing article clipped to the refrigerator.

"I've got seventy-two years notched on my belt, 'Nisha. You don't spend Christmas with just anybody, even if your family is out of town."

"I know he loves me. He not only says it; he shows it. And I love him too."

"Love is a strong word," Grans said. "It can be the most wonderful or the most painful experience in life. Sometimes both at the same time, especially if you love someone enough to let them go. But if it's God's will, they'll always come back."

"Yes, ma'am." Anisha pulled out the broom and dustpan and began working her way around the kitchen. If she could only sweep away her confusing feelings as easily. For a while she'd been thinking about her time with Tyson compared to what she spent in intimate time with God. If God seemed distant, she knew He wasn't the one who had moved.

Anisha thought she'd been released from any additional lecturing, but Grans continued.

"And sometimes it's all about timing," she said. "I'm not just talking about Tyson when I say this, but people can come with a whole lot of baggage they haven't unpacked yet, and you don't know about it until you've already given them the keys to move into your heart."

Oh, God, help me trust You. Anisha hoped that wasn't some kind of prophetic utterance from Grans. She had a way of dropping one of those from time to time.

⚜

Nighttime was settling in and so was the Blake household. Grans left to go home so she could finish making her mouth-watering sweet potato pies. Mrs. Blake and Nikki were in the living room doing last-minute gift wrapping, and Anisha and Tyson had escaped downstairs to enjoy some personal quality time.

Anisha sat on the outdated tweed sleeper sofa surfing through the cable movie channels while Tyson rummaged through the neatly folded clothes in his luggage.

"Come sit with me, baby," Anisha said, patting the empty space beside her on the couch.

Tyson zipped his suitcase and cuddled up beside Anisha. He ran his hand down the length of her hair. "I'm happy to be here with you."

"Not as happy as I am." She kissed the end of her finger and touched it to the tip of his nose.

"If I were at home right now, my mom would be passing out gifts."

"On Christmas Eve?" Anisha turned to face him.

"One gift per person. We've done it since I was little. I've always opened one gift on Christmas Eve night." He pulled his hand from around his back and held out a small, round box covered in purple satin.

Anisha pointed at herself, and Tyson nodded his head to her unspoken question.

She took the box from Tyson and cupped it in her hands. She ran her thumbs across the texture of the fabric, then shook her head and held the box back out to Tyson. "I'd rather wait until the morning."

Tyson pushed her hand away. "You'll still have a gift to open in the morning."

She smiled sheepishly at Tyson and lifted the top off the box without further hesitation. She gasped at the glittering pair of diamond studs sitting atop a bed of black velvet.

"Baby." It was the only word Anisha could muster up. She leaned over and kissed Tyson on both cheeks, the tip of his nose, and finally a slow kiss on his waiting lips.

"I guess I don't need these anymore," she said, handing Tyson the diamond studs so she could remove the small cubic zirconium earrings she was accustomed to wearing. She was suddenly embarrassed about the obviously fake impersonations and hurried to take them out of her ears as quickly as possible.

Anisha bounced to the bathroom mirror, and Tyson followed her. He handed her the box, and she took great care in placing the diamond studs in her ears.

"My ears even look different," she said, pulling her hair back from around her face.

"I'm glad you like them."

"Like them? I love them. And I love you too." Anisha turned around and wrapped her arms around Tyson's waist.

"I love you more," he whispered.

Anisha kept Tyson company until ten o'clock. She knew she was still expected to respect her mother's house, so after making sure he was comfortable, she went upstairs to join her mother and sister.

"Hey, get out!" Nikki yelled when Anisha walked into the living room. Nikki threw her body across a small stack of unwrapped gifts.

"Sorry!" Anisha yelled. She covered her eyes and backed up toward the hallway. "Where's Ma?"

"In her room. Bye."

"I'm going, I'm going." Anisha went down the photo-lined hallway and tapped lightly on her mom's open door.

Mrs. Blake was reclined across the bed with her attention divided between the newspaper and the television.

"Hey, 'Nish."

"See anything different about me?" Anisha tucked her hair behind her ears as a subtle hint.

Mrs. Blake shook her head after staring at her daughter for a moment. "Nope. Are you wearing a new shirt or something?"

Anisha went closer to her mother and tilted her head to show her pre-Christmas gifts. "From Tyson. Aren't they beautiful?"

"Ooh, nice," Mrs. Blake said, running her finger around the diamond stud. "He just gave these to you?"

"Yep. His family always opens one gift on Christmas Eve." Anisha lay across the bed, then curled up beside her mother. "He told me I had something else to open in the morning, and I can hardly wait." Anisha frowned. "But I couldn't afford anything like these earrings for him."

"Did you buy something from the heart?"

"I got him an engraved desk set for his office and some personalized stationery."

"I'm sure he'll appreciate it. The thought is worth more than any amount of money you can spend."

"You're right."

Mrs. Blake slid her feet under the covers. She smoothed the crown of Anisha's hair, then lifted Anisha's chin until their eyes met.

Anisha knew that look. It was the guise of a concerned mother who was about to impart a word of wisdom. She'd seen it many times before, and when she didn't heed the words that followed, she always regretted it. It took her nearly twenty-five years to realize that mothers were almost always right.

"I want you to think about what your grandmother said. You know she doesn't say things like that just to be talking."

"Yes, ma'am," Anisha said.

"Sometimes the line can get blurred between God's will and your own choice. And that's not only in relationships; that's in life, period. I've always taught you what the Word says, Anisha, and you're old enough to seek God for yourself." Mrs. Blake patted Anisha's back and clicked off the television. "Pray that God shows you things He wants you to do."

Anisha knew He already had. She felt like she was supposed to work on giving herself completely to God, cultivating a heart of devotion for

Him. But leaving Tyson now didn't make sense—not right now when everything was so perfect. She'd tossed the thought around in her head for weeks.

"Okay, Ma. I'm going to bed."

Anisha went into her old bedroom that had since been converted into a guest room. She closed the door behind her and crawled between the sheets with her clothes still on. Tears trailed down her face and wet the pillow. *Why now, God? Why now?*

What's more important to you? My will or yours?

Anisha awakened to the smell of country ham and butter biscuits. She pulled off the clothes she'd never changed out of and slipped on a robe and bedroom slippers. She padded down the hallway to the kitchen and found her grandmother bent over looking into the oven.

"Morning, Grans. What are you doing here so early?"

"Ain't no use in sleepin' the day away." She slipped on an oven mitt and slid a pan of biscuits from the oven.

It was only eight o'clock, but Anisha knew her grandmother had been awake for at least two hours. She'd always risen before the sun and probably always would. She said she liked to meet the Lord early in the morning. To her, it seemed like the rest of the world was still asleep, and she could have private time with her Maker.

"Your mama went to put some clothes on, and I think Tyson is up too. At least I heard water running downstairs."

"I guess I better go get dressed," Anisha said, popping a strip of bacon into her mouth. "Mmmmm." She smacked her lips. "That's good."

"Go on before I spank your behind."

"Ho, ho, ho!" Anisha held her stomach and reared back in a jolly laugh.

"Merry Christmas," Grans finished off.

Tyson couldn't remember Steve's parents' number, but if he knew his mom, she'd call and leave it on his voice mail. Their flight had left at six in the morning, so they would be arriving in Connecticut from Florida at about eight thirty.

Tyson unzipped his travel kit and dropped his razor in the black leather case. He patted a warm washcloth over his freshly shaven face. The scent of breakfast wafted downstairs and teased his appetite. He decided to wait for Anisha to come for him instead of venturing upstairs alone.

He turned on his cell and called to check his voice mail at home. The electronic woman's voice alerted him to two messages. As he'd thought, his mother called to leave Steve's parents' number and their flight information. Tyson had almost concluded the second message was a wrong number, because the caller seemed hesitant to speak.

"Ummm. Tyson. Tyson, this is Brandy. I got your number from your stepdad. Hope you don't mind. Ummm. I was calling to wish you a Merry Christmas. It's been nice running into you a couple of times. You were on my mind, so I thought I'd call and say hey. Anyway, you don't have to return my call, but you can if you'd like," she said, and left the number.

The electronic woman's voice spoke again. *To save this message, press two. To erase it, press three. To start over at the first message, press one.*

Tyson pressed two and hung up. He didn't have time to process his thoughts before there was a light tap on the door.

"Tyson?" Anisha called down to him. "Are you dressed?"

"I'm on my way up, babe." He tossed his cell phone into his suitcase and went upstairs to celebrate the holidays with Anisha's family.

*A*nisha ran the feather duster across the entertainment center. For some reason, cleaning up had a way of clearing her mind of distraction and setting her thoughts in order. She'd spent every waking moment since she came home after Christmas in prayer. She talked to God in the shower, while she was cleaning up, when she got into the car, and every time in between. Whenever her eyes were open, she was praying, and when they were closed, she was still doing the same.

God had definitely gotten Anisha's attention. Maybe it had taken the pearls of wisdom from the two women she adored the most to open her ears to God's voice. Her spirit was beginning to yearn more intensely for a deeper relationship with God.

Anisha picked up the glazed clay vase from the fireplace mantle and dusted it lightly. As she carefully set the piece down, she recalled the feeling she'd had when she made it. The forming and molding had taken some time, but the result was a beautiful sight to behold. Even now she couldn't believe the vase was the work of her own hands, fashioned specifically to her liking. Anisha knew it was how God felt about her, only He wasn't surprised at the end result.

Anisha pulled the vacuum from the closet and ran it through the carpeted rooms. Her grandmother was right. Love could feel exhilarating and painful all at the same time. But she loved Tyson enough, and God even more, to begin making God a priority in her life again. This time she meant it.

Anisha ran a sink full of water for her breakfast dishes. By the time she finished vacuuming and washing a few loads of clothes, it would be time to meet Sherri for dinner. Before, Anisha had been the one who was hard to catch, but with Sherri taking classes in the evenings, Anisha was the one who had to be penciled in on her best friend's schedule. After spending some quality time with Sherri, she planned on going to visit Tyson. Tonight she would talk to him. She knew he would understand how she was feeling. This wasn't an end to their relationship. They just needed to balance the time they spent together. *Isn't it healthy for couples to spend time apart sometimes? Wasn't it good to maintain a sense of individuality and have some personal space once in a while?*

Anisha sat at the stoplight and admired the tennis bracelet Tyson had given her to match the earrings. It looked especially elegant with her French manicured nails. By the things he'd said after the gala, she had thought the tennis bracelet was going to be an engagement ring. Fortunately or unfortunately, it wasn't. It may have swayed her decision and caused her to follow her own desires instead of the way God was leading her. Timing is what her grandmother had said. When and if Tyson ever proposed, it would be in God's timing.

Anisha pulled up to the valet parking at Paschal's Restaurant. She was elated to be meeting Sherri for dinner. Anisha saw Sherri through the front glass window, sitting on a bench against the wall. Sherri stood up and swung open the glass doors when she saw her friend approaching.

"Girl, I haven't seen you in forever," she said, hugging Anisha.

"I've only been gone six days," Anisha said.

"Yeah, but I hardly saw you at all before the gala, and then you left right after that. We've got a lot of catching up to do. Especially the details of your family's take on Tyson. Where is he, anyway?"

"Do you even have to ask? At the center, of course, where else? He's getting his office together." Anisha motioned to the young lady standing behind the front podium. "Two, please."

"Everything happened so fast for him," Sherri said.

The hostess led them to a booth and handed them each a menu.

Anisha slid into the plush leather seat. "That's what it looks like from the outside, but I know how hard he worked to make it happen. He lives and breathes that program."

"And now he's getting paid for his passion. Must be nice."

"You're telling me," Anisha said. "But shoot, girl. You're on your way to the same thing. How's class?"

"If I do another zig-zag or basting stitch, I swear I'm throwing my sewing machine out of the window."

"It can't be that bad."

"No, it's really not. Our instructors are stressing the fundamentals right now, but I'm ready to start designing the line for Short Ragz."

"Well, excuse me," Anisha said, snapping her fingers around in the air. "It's only been three weeks, and my girl has already got her clothing line in mind. Give them some time to teach those other folks what they're doing."

They continued looking over the menu and engaging in small talk until the waiter came to take their orders. Anisha hadn't mentioned Tyson's gifts to her, hoping Sherri would notice the bracelet dangling on her wrist, but they'd been in the restaurant for at least ten minutes and Sherri still hadn't said a word. Anisha thought she'd help her out and pretended to need a napkin from across the table. With exaggerated arm movements, Anisha rotated her wrist so the bracelet clanked against the side of Sherri's glass.

Sherri reached her hand out to steady her glass. "Dang, girl. You 'bout to knock my water over. What do you need from over here?"

Anisha shamelessly held her wrist out so Sherri could catch the glimmer of the brilliant diamonds. "Bam!"

Sherri pulled Anisha's arm closer to her face, nearly lifting Anisha's rear from the booth seat. "No, he didn't," Sherri exclaimed.

"Yes, he did. And these too." Anisha pushed her hair back from her ears so Sherri could see the diamond studs.

"No, he didn't." Sherri leaned in closer to examine the teardrop-shaped studs.

"Yes, he did." Anisha said, with a grin wide enough to cover her entire face. But when she thought about the conversation that was to ensue later on in the evening with Tyson, her smile faded. She bit her lips and closed her eyes to hold back the tears. "But I may give them back."

"Give 'em back?" Sherri looked shocked by her friend's sudden turn of emotions. "Is it Tyson? What did he do?"

"Nothing. Tyson didn't do anything. I'm the confused one. All week I've convinced myself this is a good thing. Don't get me wrong; I still think it is."

"Think what's a good thing? You've lost me, Anisha."

"Stepping back and giving each other some space," Anisha explained. "And don't tell me you told me so."

Duh, Sherri thought. "Come on, Anisha, I'm not going to say that. I may think it, but I'm not going to say it," Sherri joked to lighten the mood. "But seriously, you and Tyson are two grown adults who can handle the changes that come with relationships. People grow and sometimes need a little growing room. The game's not over; you're taking a time-out."

"Cute analogy, Sherri. Is that what I'm supposed to tell Tyson? Give him some kind of male symbolism to relate to?"

"Hey, whatever works. Need I jog your memory to our dating commandment number eight? 'Thou shall give each other breathing room.'"

"I know, but Tyson is everything I could've asked for," Anisha said, squeezing a lemon into her ice water. "Eight months ago he said he wanted to get the program up and running full-time by the beginning of the year, and he did it. On the other hand, I'm no further along with my business plan than I was six months ago, but it's not Tyson's fault. I haven't been staying focused like I should have."

"Don't tell me; tell him," Sherri said. "Pray before you talk to him so he won't take it the wrong way."

"Girl, I've been praying so much lately that God probably gave me extra credit."

The waiter came to the table with their meals and two extra plates. It was their habit to order completely different meals and ask for extra plates so they could taste test each other's food. He set a steaming plate of gumbo, green beans, and macaroni and cheese in front of Anisha and a plate of roasted chicken, turnip greens, and sweet potatoes before Sherri.

"Let's talk about something else," Anisha said after they prayed over the food. She spooned up some gumbo and blew on it until the steam tapered off. "Like you. You and Xavier still hanging?"

Sherri shrugged her shoulders. "Whenever he has time, basically. His commitment to the fire academy is probably as demanding as Tyson's time at the center. But drop Xavier for a minute, and let me tell you about my visit from Calvin first."

Anisha's eyes nearly bugged out of her head. "You mean Mr. Confidence came over?"

"Yes."

"Were your roommates there?"

"No. Thank God, they were still out of town."

Anisha fanned her hand to egg on Sherri's story. "So what happened?"

"You're not gonna believe it," Sherri said. She put her fork down and crossed her arms on the table. "First of all, from the moment he walked in the door, he kept hinting around about how hungry he was and how the dining hall food was nothing like home cooking."

"So did you offer him anything?"

"What do you think? I didn't want him to think I was going to be his drive-through restaurant."

"You can't make a conclusion about the man because he was hungry."

"Let me finish," Sherri said before taking a sip of water. "I was willing to overlook his rash attempt to get a free meal and give him another chance, until he dove on my floor like a wet seal out of water."

Anisha covered her mouth with her napkin to keep from spewing tea across the table. She choked down the gulp, and Sherri waited for her to recover from her coughing episode. Anisha looked around the restaurant to see if anyone was watching after her near choking incidence.

"He did what?" Anisha whispered. "Please tell me you're lying."

"I wish I could. We were watching an episode of some old sitcom that he apparently found extremely hilarious. Before I knew it, he had rolled from my couch, onto the floor, and was kicking his feet and barking like a seal. I lie to you not."

"I can't even imagine. That's one I would have to see for myself."

"Trust me. You don't want to. And if you do, it won't be at my house. Needless to say, it was his first and his last visit. Mr. Wright was all wrong."

Anisha let out a soft chuckle and then a sigh. Her mouth smiled, but the distance in her eyes showed her thoughts were afar off. She picked over her food, taking small bites of the macaroni and cheese she would have normally devoured by now.

Sherri signaled for the waiter and asked for two to-go containers. "You need to go see Tyson," she told Anisha. "Tyson loves you, and everything will be okay."

Anisha lowered her head to shield her face from any onlookers in the restaurant. She pressed her napkin against her closed eyes and waited for the swelling tears to subside. "I know." She sniffed. "I know." *God, please let him understand.*

Tyson swung around in his high-backed leather chair and looked around at his office. *Power of Man,* one of his favorite prints by Kevin A. Williams, hung on the freshly painted walls. It was a Christmas gift from his mom and Steve, along with the two bronze lion bookends.

Next week, January 6, would begin his first official day as the new director of the Boys to Men Youth Program. He closed his eyes and leaned back against the headrest. He'd finished his work for the night and was only there to wait for Anisha to stop by. She'd sounded fine when they'd talked earlier this morning, but a few minutes ago, she sounded concerned, almost sad. *Women and their emotions,* he thought when he hung up the phone. *No telling what it is.*

Tyson sorted through his drawers and worked on cleaning out his file until he saw the glare of headlights stream through his office blinds. He walked down the dimly lit hall to unlock the front door for Anisha.

"Hi," Anisha said.

Tyson noticed how she avoided eye contact with him when she came inside. She handed him a Styrofoam container.

"Leftovers," she said.

"Thanks, babe." He kissed her lightly on the forehead and then locked the door behind him. He lifted the container lid to see what looked like an entire meal to him. "Did you even eat anything?" he asked.

"I wasn't very hungry."

"Feeling okay?" He lifted her chin and tried to look into her eyes.

"Kinda," she said, turning her head aside.

Anisha followed Tyson down the hall to his office and sat in one of the chairs near the door. Tyson leaned against the edge of the desk to face her and under the office light first noticed her swollen eyes. He jumped up and ran over to Anisha, cradling her face between his hands. He brushed away her tears that were beginning to fall.

"There's no easy way to say this. I can't verbalize or attempt to describe what I'm feeling." Anisha stopped to catch her breath. Tyson didn't speak, only stared at her with hopes her eyes would tell the story she couldn't.

"I just need some space." She wiped her nose with a piece of tissue that was balled up in her coat pocket. "I need some time to figure out what's going on in my life. What's not going on that should be. I know it must feel good for you to have accomplished a dream, and I want the same feeling. I haven't stayed focused long enough to make any progress with my business or anything else. I wasn't praying or spending time with God like I should have."

Tyson stepped back and looked at Anisha with astonishment etched across his face. "Are you trying to say I've been a distraction? I thought you wanted to help me with my business. Now all of a sudden I'm keeping you from attaining your dreams?"

"I never said that. I'm only trying to—"

"Trying to what? I thought you were happy for me, Anisha. You've watched this vision come alive with me, and now you want to walk away?"

"You never let me finish," Anisha pleaded. "I was only going to say we needed to balance the time we spend together. Neither one of us needs to put the other before God." Anisha got up and walked around Tyson's desk to sit in his chair. "We need space from each other. I need space until I can sort out my feelings and spend the time with God that He wants from me right now."

Tyson went over to stand behind her. He leaned over the back of the chair and massaged Anisha's shoulders. "You're right, and I'm sorry. What's a little time for the person I want to spend forever with?" He pulled another fresh Kleenex from the box and handed it to Anisha. He swirled the chair around until she faced him. "I love you, and I'm sorry. I was only thinking about myself. That was selfish."

Anisha breathed a sigh of relief. "Thank you, baby. I knew I could count on you to understand," she said, standing up to hug him. "I'm exhausted, and I just wanna go home and chill out." She reached for his hand and held onto his assuring grip as they walked to the front of the building.

Tyson walked Anisha to her car and made sure she was off safely. He needed to shut down his computer and grab his briefcase before leaving. He went back into the office to gather his belongings. He punched in the combination to the safe under his desk and pulled out a purple velvet bag. He reached inside the bag for the small black box it was protecting. The box held the third piece to the set he'd already given Anisha for Christmas. He looked at the diamond ring he was saving for his planned proposal at the stroke of midnight on New Year's.

"I guess now's not the time," he said, closing the safe door.

*A*nisha hung her full-length wool coat on the hanger in her cubicle. She tossed the matching fleece gloves and hat set on an empty chair and turned on her computer. She dug around in her purse for a compact to examine her face. It had been a rough night. Her conversation with Tyson replayed in her mind from the time she went to sleep until the time she woke up that morning.

She'd applied more makeup than usual this morning to mask the puffy under-eye circles. If anybody asked, she'd tell them she had allergies. *No, that won't work. People don't have allergies in December.*

The voices coming down the hall startled Anisha. She thought she was the only person in the office. She ducked down in her cubicle until she could identify who it was. Probably the janitors.

"Unfortunately change is inevitable."

It's Curt. Anisha was careful not to shift one muscle, seeing that a squeaking chair in the dead, silent office would give her away. Being in the office early wasn't a problem, but how would she explain her hiding? It looked too suspicious.

"I don't want to let them go either," Curt said. "They're young, creative, and promising. But financially, the company can't take them into the next year."

"But the new fiscal year doesn't begin until next September. Can't we wait to see if we can recover?"

Who was that? It sounded like Richard from human resources.

"Look, Richard. The decision has already been made not to carry them into the next calendar year. Go ahead and get their separation notices ready for today so we can get this over with."

Anisha crouched lower until the footsteps padded in their separate directions and she heard the click of both office doors closing. She rose slowly, unaware until then that she'd even been holding her breath. Who was "them"? Young and creative. He had to be talking about the junior account executives. There were seven of them in the office, and the conversation could have easily been about anybody.

Oh, God. So this was the reason for all of those closed-door meetings. How can they let people go days before the new year? What about the courtesy of at least two weeks' notice?

Anisha grabbed her purse and prepared to make a quiet escape to the ladies' room. She could stay there for about fifteen minutes until someone else came into the office or until she could make an unsuspicious return. She pulled her coat off the hanger and slipped down the hall and into the bathroom, easing the door closed behind her. She sat on one of the benches in the ladies' lounge and called Sherri from her cell.

"Hello?"

"Sherri!"

"Anisha? Why are you whispering? Where are you?"

"I'm in the bathroom at work. I think I heard a conversation about something I wasn't supposed to know—at least not until later."

"Like what?" Sherri asked.

"They're letting some of the junior account executives go. I didn't hear who, but they're doing it today."

"Today? That's ugly. You don't know who's getting laid off, so there's no reason to start freaking out. Prepare yourself to handle the situation, whatever the outcome," Sherri consoled.

"You're right, Sherri. I'm not going to worry about it. I know more about these clients than some of the account managers do. All of the overtime and extra reports had to account for something. Evidently they were trying to see who had the skills to handle extra assignments. I've been pulling my weight and then some on the team."

"So you're okay?"

"About as well as can be expected."

"Call me later, and keep me posted on what's going on."

"You know I will."

Anisha glanced at her watch. In another ten minutes, her colleague Katherine would probably be in the office. She arrived like clockwork, always carrying a steaming cup of latte from the café downstairs. She and Anisha were always the first to arrive. Anisha battled with whether she should talk to Katherine or wait for an announcement.

Anisha walked back to her cubicle and purposefully made a little extra noise to announce her arrival. She pulled out the paperwork for Bradworth Inc. Her report was due by the end of the day, and she was determined to stay focused despite the uncertainties. She buried her head in the folder, reviewing the numbers and making edits.

"Morning, Anisha." Anisha looked up minutes later when Katherine came in. She was her usual cheerful self.

"How are you?"

"Cold, but good." She held the cup under her red, cold-bitten nose to warm her face and walked over to peer over Anisha's shoulder.

"Is that the report for Bradworth? You've been working on it forever."

"Forever is right. It's due today."

"Well, I'll leave you alone and let you get to work."

They peered over the cubicle wall when they heard an office door open down the hall. Curt stepped around the corner and into their view.

"Good morning, ladies."

"Good morning," they said.

"Katherine, could I see you in my office, please?"

"Sure. Give me a second." She pulled off her coat and threw it on her desk. "I wonder what this is all about," she whispered to Anisha as she walked down the hall.

Anisha shrugged her shoulders. "And the drama begins," she said to herself, watching Katherine float down the hall unaware of what awaited her.

Ten minutes later a sullen Katherine appeared. Her eyes were glazed over, and her pale face had splotches of pink flushing across her cheeks. She looked almost hypnotized, moving to her desk with robotic movements.

"Katherine?" Anisha jumped up and went into Katherine's cubicle.

"They let me go. As of this moment, I am no longer employed by Dudley & Associates." The coffee on her desk had lost its steam and aroma.

Anisha rubbed her colleague's back, and for the first time since she'd heard the news, Katherine let her tears of disappointment fall.

"This was the best job I've had since college. I saw myself progressing here. I worked my butt off for these people, and this is the gratitude they show me? Laying me off without a notice?" Her face looked distressed. "I don't have a savings or anything. I'm barely making ends meet as it is."

Anisha was at a loss for words. In silence, she helped Katherine clean her desktop, purge her personal files from her computer, and pack her belongings.

"You've got my home number and e-mail, so use it," Anisha said as she walked Katherine to the parking lot. "With your talent, you'll find another job in no time."

"Can I list you as one of my references?" Katherine forced a laugh and dumped her box on the front seat.

"I'll do better than that. When I get my business up and running, you can work for me."

"I'll take your word on that. Bye, Anisha. Keep Curt in his place."

Anisha went through the emotional drain of watching two other assistants get handed their walking papers by lunchtime. The tension in the office wasn't encouraging a productive work environment, so Anisha was relieved at the opportunity to steal away from the office during lunchtime. She dialed Sherri's work number as soon as she got into her car.

"What did they say?" Sherri asked after Anisha filled her in about what went down all morning.

"Nothing yet. I guess they'll wait until the end of the day to call the last men standing into a meeting and let us know what's going on."

"That's dirty."

"Unfortunately, that's the breaks when you work for somebody else."

"Enough about those crazy people at Dudley & Associates. How are you doing after the talk with Tyson last night?"

"I'm making it. I was up most of the night wrestling with sleep and my decision. That's how I ended up coming into the office earlier than usual and being alerted to all the drama going on today. I've been so distracted with things at work that I haven't had the opportunity to think about it much."

"Sorry to bring it up."

"Don't worry about it. I know you're just checking up on me."

"Day by day. It's all you can do. Take it day by day. Where's that Scripture? Somewhere in Matthew where it says, 'Don't worry about tomorrow, because tomorrow will take care of itself.'"

"Mmmmm," Anisha agreed. "Now that's a word to live by."

She paused to consider the power of the Scripture. God Himself knew His people could get bogged down in worry and said it was a waste of time. Worrying about things that hadn't even happened wouldn't change the situation anyway.

Anisha blared her horn at a careless driver who swept into her lane without signaling. "I'm out of the office for lunch. Hopefully, we're through with the drama for the day."

"Okay, call me later," Sherri said. "I'll be at home finishing a dress I promised Tamara months ago before Christmas. She said whenever I finished it, she'd come to church with me."

"The best church you've shown her is the time you've spent with her and the love you're showing her. The building is only a formality, but you've been showing her God's love working through you. She may be determining her acceptance of God based on what she sees in you."

"Remember that when you get back to the office."

"Tell me about it," Anisha said, pulling into the parking lot of one of her favorite eateries. "I'll talk to you later."

Anisha wrapped a scarf around her neck and pressed through the chill to get inside the restaurant. Only the thought of eating one of their famous orders of chili in the sourdough bread bowl could've convinced her to battle the blistering winds outside, and every employee in downtown must have felt the same way. Anisha pushed through the crowd to the back of the line for the long—but well worth it—wait for the chili bowl.

Anisha surveyed the patrons in the restaurant. She could clue in on a person, watch their mannerisms, and construct her own story with her imagination. She'd think about things like why the girl over in the back made exaggerated movements that made her oversized breasts bounce around on her small body. *They must be new.* She noticed that the guy whom the girl was pawing looked a lot like Xavier—Xavier? There was no mistake about it. That *was* him. Anisha dipped behind the broad shoulders of the man standing in line in front of her. She'd seen all she needed to see.

Arriving back at the office, Anisha immediately printed out two copies of her report. She placed one in a presentation folder for Curt and slid the other into one of her own files. Curt's office door was closed, so she left his report in the bin hanging on the wall outside of his door. She went back to her desk, typed out a quick e-mail to let him know the report was ready, and slumped down into her office chair to enjoy her lunch and the latest copy of *Newsweek*.

By the end of the day, Anisha's desk was more organized and in better working order than it had been for the last month. No one had come to dump loads of work in her in-box. Everything was filed in its proper place, all e-mails had been answered, and she'd completed her to-do list for the next day. Things seemed to be slowing down since it was the day before the New Year's holiday, and work probably wouldn't pick up pace again until the beginning of the year. The calm was a welcome luxury. The only thing that bothered her was the fact that they still hadn't called in the remaining junior account executives to debrief them on the day's happenings and what was to be expected with their extra workloads.

By five thirty, Anisha had decided her uncertainties were being pushed into the next day and Curt was avoiding a meeting until he could concoct a convincing speech of reconciliation. She shut down her computer and wrapped herself up to face the cold.

The alerting tone of her intercom system buzzed through the phone.

"Anisha?"

"Yes, Curt?"

"Can I see you in my office before you leave today?"

I've been sitting here all day, and you want to call me as soon as I get ready to leave? "Sure. I'll come right now."

"Thanks."

Anisha pulled off her coat, hat, and gloves and tossed them on her desk. If there were any changes Curt wanted made to her report, she would be in the office at least another hour. So much for an easy day.

Anisha walked into Curt's office, and he motioned for her to close the door. She sat on the edge of the chair across from him, crossed her legs, and rested her hands on one knee—her signature pose that she meant serious business.

"Since I've been at Dudley & Associates, I've never seen or worked with a junior account executive more driven than you. You take the initiative to do whatever's necessary to learn more about the business and the industry."

Anisha nodded her head in agreement. She could attest to her hard work and planned on riding her drive straight to a promotion as an account executive.

"In these changing times we can't always see the shifts that will call for changes in personnel."

Anisha kept eye contact with Curt so he could see she understood. It probably wasn't easy for him to explain he would have to dump an extra load of work on her. If they agreed to at least give her a raise compatible with the work, she would be satisfied for the time being.

"Unfortunately . . ."

No, God. Please. No. Anisha watched his crooked bottom lip moving in slow motion but could only hear her own voice echoing between her ears. She clenched her jaws tight and slid her back into the curve of the chair.

"*Blah . . . blah . . . blah . . .* and I've written a strong recommendation for you." Curt slid the letter on Dudley & Associates letterhead across his mahogany desk.

Anisha wanted to hurl it back at him and tell him what he could do with it. She might have done it if she knew it wouldn't drift lazily through the air instead of smacking him in the forehead like she wished. She picked up the letter and quickly skimmed the blur of words across the page.

Be an example.

"I appreciate your kind words, Curt, and even this letter of recommendation," she said, taking the manila folder he was giving her. "But what I'm trying to understand is why you kept me here until the end of the day when everyone else was notified this morning. Could it be because you wanted to make sure the project was finished before you fired me?" The rhetorical question rolled off her tongue like venom.

Be an example.

"I've given 100 percent to this job and nothing less. I've taken projects usually assigned to your best account executives and done a comparable, if not better, job than they. You could've at least had the decency to let me and everyone else know ahead of time."

You're representing Me.

188

Anisha stood up and straightened her skirt. She'd better stop while she was ahead. Before her mouth wrote a check her butt couldn't cash. "Things should've been handled differently."

She extended her hand to Curt and walked out after a strong, affirmative handshake. She didn't need to be told to go to human resources for her release interview and separation papers. She had watched others go through the process all day.

Within a few minutes, Anisha was walking out of the glass double doors of the fifteen-story office tower. She dropped a small cardboard box of her personal belongings into her trunk, then sat in the car waiting for it to warm up. When she pulled off the property, she finally let the first tear escape.

Anisha fell across the bed and dangled her feet over the edge. She kicked her pumps off and crossed her hands under her head. She'd tried calling everyone on her way home. Her mother. Grans. Sherri. Even Tyson. Why wasn't anyone around when she needed them?

I am.

Anisha felt tense. She wasn't sure which emotion would push itself to the surface first. Anger. Pity. Sadness. Panic.

"This is the last thing I expected to be dealing with today, God. Wasn't Tyson enough? Do You have to take away everything important to me?"

Anisha closed her eyes and replayed the day's events and what she would have said to Curt if she could do it over again. The phone interrupted her thoughts, and she was happy to hear the comforting voice of her mother.

"'Nisha?"

"Hey. Ma."

"Hey. What's going on? You didn't sound too good on your message."

Anisha couldn't answer. She began sobbing hysterically and could barely catch her breath to speak.

"Anisha, get hold of yourself and calm down," her mother coaxed. She waited for Anisha's wailing to subside. "Now, what in the world is it?"

"I got laid off, Ma. After I had been at work all day, Curt had the nerve to call me into his office and give me some sorry lecture about how they had to make changes."

"I'm sorry, baby." Her mother's words expressed the empathy she knew her mother really felt. "Were you the only one?"

"No. But they let the other junior execs go earlier this morning. That's what makes me so mad. They used me to make sure I finished a report I was working on. That was wrong."

"Yes, they were. But we can't control other people's actions; we can only control how we respond to them."

Anisha digested her mother's words and thought about how she had acted. She should have left them with a better impression. She went into the bathroom and rolled a wad of tissue around her hand. She stood in front of the mirror and patted the remnants of her breakdown from her face.

"How does your money look?" her mother asked.

"I've got some money in my savings account, but it was supposed to be for the down payment on a house."

"Count it a blessing, Anisha. You could have nothing. Some people get laid off and don't have anything to fall back on. They may have children and spouses to take care of, too. Be thankful and know God's going to take care of you. He has all this time."

Anisha was ashamed she hadn't recognized the blessing even in the midst of her trial. She thought about Katherine and how she'd cried because she didn't have anything saved. Anisha was overwhelmingly grateful. She was glad her mother could see the best of what seemed to be the worst situation and offer a new perspective on things.

Grans called her right after she hung up the phone with her mother. Even she led Anisha to peace in the midst of a storm.

"Before you go to bed, find you a good Scripture like Matthew 6:26. Your spirit will have something to meditate on while you sleep."

"Yes, ma'am."

"This might have caught you by surprise, but it didn't catch God by surprise."

"Yes, ma'am," Anisha said.

She changed clothes and forced herself to make something for dinner. She picked over a taco salad while she mulled over updating an old copy of her resume. When the page was covered with rephrased bullet points, Anisha abandoned the paper on the kitchen table, dumped the rest of her uneaten salad in the trash, and crawled into bed. Even though it was the night for some of her favorite television shows, her thoughts were far from escaping into the unbelievable lives of sitcom characters. She had her own drama—her real-world situations to handle.

She reached for her Bible in her nightstand and looked for the Scripture her grandmother had given her to read. She memorized verses easier when she read them aloud. *"Look at the birds of the air, for they neither sow nor reap nor gather into barns; yet your heavenly Father feeds them. Are you not of more value than they?"*

Anisha closed her Bible and hit the power button on her television remote. "I would hope so," she said, closing her eyes.

The faint chirping of a bird outside her window opened up Anisha's eyes to tears of joy. God cared so much He'd sent a special messenger.

Sherri pulled the tattered ironing board from the hall closet and into her room. She picked up the pieces of fabric lying on the floor that had been carefully pinned onto a pattern and threw them in the trunk beside her sewing table. Scrap pieces of fabric and thread spools were strewn around the room. She kicked some, stepped over others, and made a mental note to put cleaning up her room at the top of her priority list.

The ironing board legs screamed as she released the latch and stretched it out for its duty. Sherri plugged in the iron and called Anisha while she waited for it to heat up.

"Hey, girl. I'm calling to check on you," Sherri said when Anisha finally answered the phone. "Whatcha up to?"

"Nothing but looking through this useless pile of classifieds," Anisha said, obviously bored with what had become a meaningless and fruitless task.

"You haven't found *anything* you're interested in?"

"Two months, one week, and four days of looking in this stupid paper, and I have yet to find one lead to follow. I'm about to resort to one of these 'EARN MONEY SITTING AT HOME' ads. That's one skill I've perfected by now." Anisha yawned and smacked her lips. "What are you doing? You sound like you're outta breath."

"I am. I'm supposed to be meeting Xavier at that new sports bar down on Memorial Drive, and I lost track of time. We're going to catch one of the basketball games. It's sad—I don't even know who's playing."

Sherri held up her jeans for inspection and turned up the knob on the iron to increase the temperature. She'd need the maximum heat to steam the wrinkles out of the scrunched fabric.

"Xavier? I thought you were through with him after I told you about seeing him with some girl that day downtown."

Sherri stretched one of the jean legs across the ironing board. "We settled all that. She was his cousin, Renee."

"And you believe him?"

"Not initially. But he had her call me, so it's all good."

"Uh-huh. Whatever," Anisha mumbled.

Sherri ignored Anisha's doubtful and sarcastic tone and focused on ironing out the stubborn wrinkles. "So have you tried surfing the Internet?" Sherri asked, changing the subject.

"Yep. I posted my resume on some of the job Web sites. I guess I'll have to wait and see what happens."

"Wait? Why? Can't you market yourself to some of these companies as a freelancer or a consultant?"

"That's a good idea and all, but right now I need some steady income."

"Who said it wouldn't be steady? You're speaking negative things before you even get started. As much as you complained about work having control over your life, you should be the first person to step out and start something for yourself."

"Yeah, but it's a lot easier said than done. I'm the one watching my savings account dwindle away."

Sherri slipped into her crisply ironed jeans, fingered combed her short tresses, and freshened up her makeup while Anisha droned on about what *wasn't* happening in her life. Besides the fact Sherri was running late, she didn't want to join in Anisha's pity party. She hadn't heard from Xavier in two weeks and was anxious to be able to finally spend some time with him again.

Sherri waited until she could squeeze in a word and disrupt Anisha's "woe is me" dialogue. "Okay 'Nisha. I don't want to cut you off but I've really got to get out of here."

"All right."

Sherri sensed Anisha's irritation and tried to sweeten her abrupt end to their conversation. "You and Tyson going out tonight?"

"He's got a couple of his boys from the center spending the night with him this weekend, so he had to get some work done before they come tomorrow."

"Oh," Sherri said.

Sherri noticed how Tyson had started giving Anisha some lame excuse when it came to them spending quality time together lately. Regardless of her previous admiration of Tyson, Sherri decided this whole situation of Anisha needing time to focus on her own life had exposed his selfishness. He was growing distant, and Sherri wondered if Anisha realized it, too. Based on his track record with her birthday and Christmas, Sherri was sure he'd take it over the top for Valentine's Day, but his effort was minimal, to say the least.

Sherri felt she'd fulfilled her listening friend quota and could wean herself from the conversation. "I'll give you a call tomorrow. Are you stopping by before you leave to go out of town on Sunday?"

"I promised, didn't I?"

"Good," Sherri said, pulling on her black peacoat. "Remember what I said about this whole job thing, though. There might be a reason why you can't find another job. Maybe being laid off was to push you out of your comfort zone."

"Maybe," Anisha considered. "Guess I won't know until I step out of the boat and try to walk on the water." Anisha sighed, and Sherri knew her friend was hesitantly ending the conversation. "Bye. Talk to you later."

Sherri grabbed her purse and bolted to the door before deciding to go back and check on Tamara. She tapped on her closed bedroom door and waited for Tamara's permission to enter.

"Hey," Sherri said, peeking inside.

Tamara was sitting in the middle of the bed with a book opened across her lap. A collection of library books and a stack of brochures were scattered along her side and at her feet. She folded the corner of the page she was reading and closed the book. Tamara scrunched down into her pillows and stretched her arms above her head.

Sherri walked in and sat on the edge of Tamara's bed. "You going out tonight?"

"No. Not tonight." Tamara pushed up the sleeves of her sweatshirt and took off her glasses. She rubbed her eyes until she could focus on Sherri.

"I'm looking over this information about massage therapy school. I think I can swing the evening classes after work like you do."

Sherri picked up one of the many brochures on the bed and skimmed it. She turned around to Tamara and gave her a high five. "You can do it, girl," she said, adding an extra dose of encouragement to Tamara's recipe for her new life.

Sherri was impressed with Tamara's newfound drive. Her whole attitude about life had changed in the past month. When Sherri had finally finished the suit she'd promised Tamara, Tamara surprised her and decided to wear it to New Year's watch night service at Grace Worship. It was the first time Tamara had stepped into a church in five years. Over the years she'd even skipped the guilt-driven Easter, Mother's Day, and Christmas services.

It was like Tamara had changed overnight. She was coming to church with Sherri more frequently, even to Bible study once. But Sherri wasn't worried about Tamara's having perfect attendance at church. She was more concerned that she had a heart open to receive God's unconditional love.

Sherri got up and walked to the door. "Where's Veronica?"

"I don't know," Tamara said, shaking her head with a look of annoyance. "She's got an attitude with me right now, so I'm leaving her alone for a couple of days. You know how she is. She'll get over it."

"I won't even ask," Sherri said, rolling her eyes. "I'm out. See you later."

"Be good," Tamara yelled after her.

"Of course."

Sherri eased the bedroom door shut and left Tamara to the task of mapping out her dream.

When Sherri finally arrived at the Time Out Bar and Grill, she circled the small parking lot three times before spotting a recently vacated space. She squeezed into the tight space and opened the driver's door slowly to prevent the March wind from whipping it against the sleek silver Jaguar parked beside her.

Sherri pulled the collar of her jacket tight around her neck and ran inside the lively sports bar. There seemed to be as many televisions inside as there were people. Most of the people in the bar were sporting the paraphernalia or at least the colors of their favorite team. A table of die-hard New York Knicks fans, causing a friendly ruckus in the middle of the bar with another table of Los Angeles Lakers fans, tossed around a life-sized blow-up doll suited in a basketball jersey and shorts. Sherri was glad her light pink shirt was hidden for the meantime and covered the fact she was a rookie spectator.

Sherri couldn't spot Xavier from where she was standing, and she was hesitant to walk through the jumbled maze of bar tables and stools to try to find him.

"OOOOOOOOHHHH." The wail rolled over the crowd. Sherri turned around to see the instant replay of a three-hundred-sixty-degree slam dunk by one of the players. The men practically flounced on top of each other every time the replay flashed on the screen. Even the women were going wild. Sherri watched the television closest to her and pretended to be absorbed in the game. It was a sad thing she didn't even recognize the player who had performed the gravity-defying feat. She wasn't even interested that much in basketball. She'd only come because Xavier had suggested it, and she had to get her time in whenever she could.

Sherri jumped when she felt a sudden poke in her side. She swung around, prepared to lay a smack across the face of a frisky old man if necessary.

Xavier jumped back. "Whoa there, little mama. Calm yourself down."

"Never do that to a woman standing alone in the middle of a bar," Sherri scolded him playfully.

Xavier bent over and stuck out his cheek for Sherri to kiss.

"Where are you sitting?" she asked. "This place is packed."

"I know. I can't find any empty seats. I already checked way in the back, and there's nothing there."

Sherri scoped the area again and didn't see anything either. Those committed bar patrons who didn't have seats were content to stand at occupied tables or linger near the bar so they could be in the middle of the action.

Sherri hooked her hand through Xavier's arm. "What do you want to do?" she asked him. "Can we go to your place?"

"You live closer; why can't we go to yours?"

"We could, but the television in my room isn't really big. The one in the living room went on the blink a couple of weeks ago."

"Look, I don't care about all that. I'm just trying to see the game. If you don't want to go to your house, then I'll stay here. I can grab a beer and stand up over there near the bar somewhere. I'm just trying to make sure *you're* comfortable."

Sherri heard the frustration rise in his voice. She didn't want to risk making him mad and cause him to shut down. "Okay, fine," Sherri agreed hesitantly, as she remembered the untidiness of her room. "Let's at least get something to eat."

Xavier followed Sherri to the take-out counter at the front of the bar. With the bar being overcrowded and short staffed, it was some time before their order was brought out. As the half-time commentary began, a different server than the one who had originally taken their order appeared and slammed a white plastic bag on the counter. She jerked Xavier's money out of his hand, shot her eyes at Sherri, then back at Xavier.

Sherri searched Xavier's countenance for an explanation, but his expression never changed.

The woman pounded the keys on the cash register and fumbled to count out the correct change. "See you found another trick, Xavier."

Trick? Sherri's mouth fell open. *I know she didn't say trick.* Sherri looked behind her to see if the woman could've been referring to someone who might have walked up behind them. The next couple in line tried to pretend they were engrossed in each other, but Sherri knew they were only trying to save her from any additional embarrassment. They were standing so close that it was almost impossible for them not to have caught an earful.

Sherri latched on to Xavier's waist in a purposeful attempt to infuriate the woman even more. She steadied herself and bit down on her lip. She had too much class to stoop to that level and make a scene in the packed restaurant.

Xavier snatched his change and stuffed it in his pocket. "You're the only trick I know." He smirked. He pulled Sherri toward the door and left with the woman's eyes burning through the back of his neck.

"Old flame. She's never been able to let go," Xavier muttered to Sherri when they were outside. "Don't worry about her." He leaned down and kissed Sherri on the cheek. "Come on, we can make it before third quarter is over."

Sherri had gathered the remains of her latest sewing assignment and piled them on her chair and around her working station. Xavier had kicked off his shoes and was stretched out on the bed. He'd complained of the stuffiness in the room earlier and had long since peeled off his bulky sweatshirt. His white undershirt clung to his chiseled biceps. She ran her hand over his arm to see if it felt as solid as it looked.

"Maybe we can catch a movie tomorrow," Sherri suggested.

"Tomorrow's not a good day. I got some stuff to handle with the fellas."

"All day? What about tomorrow night?"

"Look, I ain't making no promises I can't keep, and then you'll be all bent out of shape." Xavier maneuvered his hand underneath the edge of Sherri's shirt to the small of her back. "Why can't you lay back and enjoy the moment? You want time together, and you're getting it now."

"I don't understand why—"

Xavier's eyes were melting her defense.

"Baby girl, tonight we're together—that's all that matters." He gently pulled her down beside him. It felt as if their bodies were being drawn together by a magnetic force she couldn't control. That she didn't want to control.

God, please. I know it's wrong. But to be able to feel the touch of a man. I promise I won't go all the way.

Sherri's eyes darted around the dark room. She made out the shape of her sewing machine table and moved to the next object that caught her eye. A large black figure hovered in the air. Her breathing quickened, then stabilized when she realized it was only the silhouette of a suit she'd hung above the closet door.

Her eyes adjusted to the darkness, and Sherri made out Xavier's face. Lying there with content smeared across his face, the sound of his low snore irritated her. She shook his shoulder. When he didn't move, she shoved him harder.

What have I done? Oh, God. I'm sorry.

"You've got to go," Sherri whispered frantically to Xavier.

What if Tamara and Veronica knew? She was sure they'd heard Xavier come in. Tamara at least. *She probably knows someone is in here with me. Oh, God, I'm sorry.*

Xavier rolled over and thrashed his arm about, looking for Sherri's body. She shoved him off. "No. You've got to go." Sherri rolled off the bed and groped around for Xavier's clothes in the dark. She found his pants and threw them on top of his head. She elevated her voice to a notch above a whisper. "Now."

"What's your problem?" Xavier grunted. "Come lay down." He tossed his clothes back on the floor and tried to pull the sheet over his head, but Sherri snatched it from his grip. She thought fast and smart, pulling from her Rolodex of experiences that men hate drama and unnecessary emotion. She knew Xavier couldn't see her face in the dark, so she wasn't worried about conjuring up any fake tears.

"I don't know why I'm feeling this way," Sherri said, making her voice quiver.

"Dang. What now?" Xavier threw himself to the edge of the bed and pulled his legs into his jeans. "I'm leaving. Are you happy now?" He muttered some things under his breath Sherri couldn't make out and didn't care to know. She was just glad he was leaving.

Sherri stood under the shower in the dark and ran the soapy washcloth down her arm. She held her head back and let the water pound against her face. The darkness felt safe. Turning on the light meant she would have to look at herself and face the reality of what had happened. She'd wait until the morning broke.

There was no distinction between the water from the showerhead and the soaking from her own tears. She grabbed the metal rack on the inside of the shower as her body shook, heavy with regret. It was no use. Only God could wash it away.

"Mommy, let's call Grandma. Pleaassseee. I wanna call Grandma."

Ayana jumped up and down on the bed, rocking Brandy's body like a ship tossing on waves. She plopped down on her knees, missing Brandy's head by inches.

"Ayana, please stop," Brandy yelled. "Mommy's trying to get a little rest before we have to go to the shop." Brandy searched her thoughts for something to keep Ayana occupied. "Can you put some books in your bag for me?" Brandy said in a more coaxing tone.

"I don't wanna. I wanna call Grandma, Mommy," Ayana whined.

"If we call her, then will you get your books so Mommy can get some rest?"

"Yes." Ayana nodded her head and folded her arms across her chest, happy that her repeated begging had finally produced the result she wanted.

Brandy picked up the phone from the nightstand and started to dial her mother's number. Although it wasn't even eight in the morning, Brandy was sure her mother was already piddling around the house, finding some menial tasks to keep her hands busy.

"No, Mommy! Let me do it," Ayana said, bouncing across the bed again.

Brandy handed her the phone and waited while Ayana found each number Brandy recited.

"Hey, Grandma," Ayana squealed. She pressed her ear to the phone as if the act would lay her cheek against her grandmother's face. Ayana's mouth flew a mile per minute whenever she was afforded the chance to talk to her grandmother. Since Ayana was growing older, Brandy had learned to keep one ear on her conversations, because she was quick to share information Brandy would rather she keep quiet about. Like the time when Brandy couldn't pay the electricity bill before the service was disconnected. The next week Ayana had proudly announced to her grandmother, "Me and Mommy played camping, and Mommy used the candles so we could see at night." In her childhood innocence, Ayana had no idea she had unleashed a reign of lashings Brandy dealt with for over a week.

Brandy sat up on the bed and leaned closer to the receiver snuggled against Ayana's face, but she couldn't make out her mother's babbling on the other end. Ayana's own chattering had ceased for a moment, and she was now answering a string of yes-and-no questions. What they were, Brandy could only imagine. But her thoughts hadn't wandered too far away when a question escaped from Ayana's mouth that nearly knocked Brandy off the bed.

"Grandma, why doesn't my mommy have a daddy either? Like me. Can you get a daddy for mommy *and* a daddy for me?"

Brandy fell back on the bed and immediately massaged her temples. She might as well start early to stave off the migraine that was sure to arise. Whatever her mother was saying, she was bringing a smile to Ayana's face.

"Tell Grandma you have to go now," Brandy whispered to her daughter. But it was too late.

"Okay, Grandma," Ayana said. She handed Brandy the phone and bounded down the hall to the living room.

Brandy took a deep breath and slowly exhaled before putting the phone to her ear. "Hello, Mother," Brandy said, bracing herself for the imminent lashing.

"Didn't you say you ran into Tyson some months ago? Why didn't you talk to him? You should have been trying to see if he was married or something. At least you'd know if you had a chance. Ayana is starting to need some fatherly love or something."

Brandy closed her eyes and imagined her mother was the nurturing type. "Yes, Mother, I'm doing fine," Brandy said, answering the question she wanted to hear instead of responding to the harangue spitting from her mother's lips.

"If you'd stayed with him in the first place, you wouldn't be in the situation you're in now. I don't like my granddaughter having to go and sit at the salon all day. Especially on a Saturday when she should be romping around with other children. Seems like those chemicals from the perms or something could be doing something to her brain."

"Ma, Ayana's brain is fine."

"You never know. They always coming out with something new. First it was asbestos; then it was lead paint. You never know what's happening to your body from all this stuff they got around now."

Brandy thought it was best to keep silent so she wouldn't disrespect her mother. If it wasn't for Ayana, she wasn't so sure their strained mother-daughter ties wouldn't be severed by now.

She knew her mother was bitter about life, but instead of digging out the weeds of the betrayal she'd experienced, her mother had allowed them to take root, wrap themselves around her emotions, and choke the very life out of her being. And all because Brandy's father had walked out.

Brandy could feel the pain. She had gone and was still going through the same issues herself because of Chris and her father. Brandy never figured out why it had taken her dad eight years to figure out that he wasn't equipped to be a father and a husband. Like the Hollywood script of the original "made for television" movies, he left one morning for work, crept home at least once during the day to pack some of his personal belongings, and never came back. End of story, beginning of pain.

Her mother had never trusted another man and had instilled the same fear of abandonment into Brandy—until she'd met Tyson. Tyson had vowed to stick by her even when she'd messed up. It was her own fault she'd lost him. And for years her mother always made a point to remind her.

"You never explained to her why one day she had a father and the next day she woke up and he wasn't there," her mother said. "I was truthful with you. At least I was straight about your good-for-nothin' daddy," she spat.

Here we go again, Brandy thought. As much as she hated to admit it, her mother had a point. She didn't know how to talk to Ayana about her father's disappearing act. Her main focus now was to purge all memories Ayana had about Chris and replace them with new ones. It's not like she wasn't trying to give her daughter a family life.

Tyson bruised her ego when he never returned her call from the message she'd left at Christmas. She guessed the old girl really had him wrapped around her finger.

Brandy concluded her approach needed to be more aggressive, and she only had one more chance to quiet her own conscience and her mother's constant nagging. Desperate times called for desperate measures. She'd saved a clipping from a small neighborhood newspaper Mrs. Jamison had brought into the salon. Buried on the bottom right corner of page seven, Mrs. Jamison had spotted an article about the revitalization of a boys' mentoring program. She was impressed with the photograph of the young men dressed in tuxedos and had shown it to Brandy. When she'd noticed Tyson standing among the boys, Brandy had feigned interest in a story on the adjoining page and asked Mrs. Jamison for the paper.

"Don't you want what's best for Ayana?" her mother asked, barging her way back into Brandy's thoughts.

No. I want her to live a sour life like you. "Yes, Mother. I'm doing the best I can. It's hard being a single parent."

"You act like you're telling me something I don't know. I went through months of not knowing how I was going to pay . . ."

Why did I have to say that? Brandy thought. *Part two of today's tirade.*

Her mother ran out of breath and insults. She became so frustrated with Brandy's unresponsiveness she ended the conversation on her own. Brandy hung up the phone and tossed out the idea of getting any sleep. She tip-toed into the living room and found Ayana entertaining herself with two black Barbie dolls in swimsuits and an empty shoe box as a makeshift swimming pool.

Brandy went into the bathroom to run a warm bath for Ayana. Her mother had added a pinch of salt to an already open wound. Getting Tyson back was no longer just an issue for Ayana, but Brandy would prove to her mother that she wouldn't be destined for a life of loneliness.

Brandy walked back into the cramped bedroom, pulled out her nightstand drawer, and found the clipping from the *Community Outlook* newspaper. The caption under the photo was impressive: *The vision of volunteer Tyson Randall is helping to restore hope and dreams with the full-time Boys to Men Youth Mentoring Program.*

The article listed all the information she needed to make another attempt to contact Tyson. If she could catch him by surprise, he couldn't avoid as like he'd done at the Davenports' cookout. There was no way around it. The shop would be closed on Monday, and she'd have plenty of time to make an unexpected visit to the E.L. Clifton Recreation Center—with Ayana in tow.

Tyson had hoped another Saturday morning wouldn't find him at the Center yet again. He'd dreamed of getting to this point one day, but he wasn't sure if he'd taken a realistic look at the cost that he'd have to pay to walk in the shoes as director and owner. The weight he was carrying wouldn't seem as heavy if Anisha was around to encourage and push him like she'd always done. He missed her presence around the office, her motivation, and her input. But she'd asked for some space to get focused, and he didn't want to be a distraction.

Two hours passed before he finally picked up the phone and dialed in the password to check the Center's general voice mail. He found a legal pad and pen in his desk drawer and prepared to deal with the business and personal issues he knew had been left on the voice mail since Friday afternoon.

He'd only given his home and pager numbers to a select few of the volunteer parents. It was hard, but he tried to separate his work life from his personal life. Since he'd walked into the program full-time, he'd become like a surrogate father to the majority of the boys in the program. Already, he'd sat in on a parent-teacher conference at the near-by middle school when a single, working mom couldn't make it. He'd even had to act as a character witness for Jerome, a fifteen-year-old who'd been taken to the juvenile detention center for repeated fighting in school. Jerome acted up for attention, and Tyson couldn't bear to throw up his hands and walk away when Jerome needed him most. Jerome's mother was known for the revolving door of men she'd keep company with for a while and try to force to develop a relationship with her son.

Tyson's bond with his father had always been tight until he died of a massive heart attack when Tyson was fourteen. Tyson was grateful for the morals his father had instilled in him. It had taken some time to see Steve replace his father in his mother's life. Since Tyson had been in college when his mother remarried, Steve had turned out to be more of a friend than a patriarch. When Tyson had needed fatherly direction, God had been faithful in placing strong men in his life like one of his college English professors and now Deacon Davenport.

Tyson heard Jerome's mother's familiar crackly voice. Not again. He had his own issues to deal with.

Like Anisha.

It was a scenario his emotions had experienced before. He'd given Anisha his all, like he'd given Brandy, but she'd chosen to walk away at a critical time in his life. A woman he thought he'd spend the rest of his life with deserted him. Again.

No matter Anisha said she needed some time. That was probably to soften the blow. But space is what she wanted, and space is what she'd get.

Tyson rushed through his breakfast of a banana, protein bar, and pint of orange juice that was stuffed in his gym bag. By the time he listened to the twelfth and final message, his mental capacity was only cognizant enough to pack up and meet Deacon Davenport for their one-thirty tee time at the golf club.

⚜

The chill hand of winter had robbed the golf course of its usual spring and summer lushness, but the grounds were still manicured and well kept in anticipation of the arrival of spring three weeks around the corner. The giant oaks surrounding the property towered over everything in the revitalized community. It was no question the lush Bermuda fairways and Crenshaw Bentgrass greens would reappear once Mother Nature's clock summoned their arrival.

Tyson tucked his white collared shirt into his navy blue slacks and pulled the fitted Titlist cap down low on his brow. He swung his golf bag over his shoulder and stuffed his white leather playing gloves into his back pocket.

Deacon Davenport was an avid golfer, hitting the greens for a round of golf at least twice a week. Tyson usually only managed to get to the course about once a week, but he had taken up playing with the deacon more frequently so he could escape duties at the Center. It helped him relieve stress, and studying Deacon Davenport's technique had challenged Tyson to step up his own game.

Tyson went into the clubhouse locker room and slipped on his softspike golf shoes. He threw his tennis shoes into Deacon Davenport's locker and slammed it closed. Deacon Davenport walked in as Tyson was reapplying the lock.

"I saw you coming into the clubhouse when I was pulling into the parking lot," Deacon Davenport said, walking in and wiggling the rest of his upper body into a windbreaker. "I figured you were coming in here to get ready for today's whippin'."

Tyson flexed his knuckles and stuck a hand into his playing glove. "Maybe for now, Deac, but my game's coming up."

Tyson and Deacon Davenport walked out onto the greens and met their assigned caddy. He was a stocky adolescent who appeared to be around fifteen or sixteen, though his muscular stature could have played double for a pro football player. He easily hoisted their golf bags into the cart and pulled onto the cart path.

Deacon Davenport looked at Tyson with a raised brow as he pulled on his playing gloves. "Why haven't I been seeing you at church lately? Have you been going to the early service or something?"

"Actually, Deac, I haven't been to church in almost a month."

"Tyson, now you—"

"Hold up, Deac—let me explain. Every day there's a challenge at the Center, and Sunday is the only day I have to recuperate and get myself prepared for the week. I need to be able to make wise decisions during the week, and I can't do that worn-out like I've been."

"Exactly why you need to be at church sometimes. I'm not saying you're not entitled to miss a Sunday every now and then, but the Enemy can use your tiredness to attack when your defenses are down. I'm surprised Anisha didn't stay on your case about skipping out. She's a wise young woman if I've ever seen one."

"I can't argue about that, Deac, but Anisha's not around right now."

Deacon Davenport adjusted the brim of his cap. "What do you mean she's not around? What happened between you two?"

"Nothing happened," Tyson said. "Maybe I shouldn't have put it like that."

The caddy cut a sharp corner, and Tyson gripped the side of the cart.

"When we got back from Christmas with her family, she came to me and said she needed some space to stay focused on some things and hear from God," Tyson said. "She said she'd been neglecting some things she was supposed to be taking care of. More or less I was a distraction in her life. She didn't say it that way, but she might as well have."

"So you took her words and twisted them to what you wanted to hear?"

"Point blank, Deac. She needs some space, so I'm only giving it to her."

When the caddy pulled the golf cart to a stop, Tyson jumped out onto the greens and strode toward the first hole. "I don't have time to deal with that, Deac. I've got a business to handle now."

Deacon Davenport shook his head and grabbed a driving iron from his bag. "You're going to risk losing a good thing because a woman wants to spend time with God and get direction for her life? I think the real issue is she hurt your ego."

Tyson set his ball on the tee. He concentrated on his stance, planting his feet shoulder-width apart. He squared his shoulders and followed through with a powerful swing, sending the ball whizzing through the air.

"Good shot," Deacon Davenport said. He turned toward the young caddy and asked him, "Do you have a girlfriend, young man?"

The boy looked surprised that someone was addressing him about something other than a driving iron or putter. He straightened his back as if he'd been called to attention by a drill sergeant.

"Yes, sir."

"Of everything your girlfriend may want from you, what do you think she wants the most?"

"My support and affection, sir."

Deacon Davenport eyed Tyson, who was leaning his body weight against his club, waiting for Deacon Davenport to take his shot. "Out of the mouths of babes," Deacon Davenport said, setting his ball on the tee. "Why don't you call Anisha tonight and take her out to dinner at the Waterside Restaurant up at Stone Mountain or something nice? I think she'd enjoy that. You probably haven't been acting the best lately."

"Can't happen tonight, Deac. I've got two brothers from the Center coming to my house tonight cause their mom has to work third shift."

"Maybe you can take her out for lunch after church tomorrow."

"I don't think I'm going to feel like dragging those boys to church. They're not patient enough to sit through an entire service. Plus, Anisha's leaving early in the morning to go home for a few weeks."

Deacon Davenport propped his club on his shoulder. "Man, I thought you loved her. And you're letting her leave without making sure she knows she has your support, even if your ego is bruised?"

"I do love her, Deac."

"Let me tell you something about love. Love means putting your selfish feelings aside and making sacrifices if you think it will make the other person happy. That's love. Love doesn't pout."

Tyson wasn't up for the in-your-face confrontation the deacon seemed bent on dishing out today. He was here to clear his mind, not participate in a counseling session.

*S*herri wasn't in the mood to deal with anyone, but she'd made Anisha promise to stop by before she left for North Carolina. She was afraid Anisha would sense what had taken place the night before.

Sherri flung her curtains open to let in the March sun. She'd awakened with an urgency to clean up and rearrange her bedroom furniture. It was the first time in days she'd been able to walk around in her room without stepping over stuff, and the new look was refreshing.

Sherri positioned her full-length mirror on an empty wall space beside her dresser. She looked at the bags that had taken residence under her usually bright eyes. All this external cleaning and rearranging still hadn't changed what had happened. No amount of dusting and scrubbing could wash it away. She needed to pray. She surrendered to the inner voice and crawled onto her bed, meditating on the Lord.

Sherri cried out to the Lord and shoved her face into her pillow. She balled her body up into a fetal position. It was how she felt. Helpless as a baby, crying out for the touch of her father.

"Lord, if I could take it back, I would. I'm ashamed of how I dishonored my body. Your body. This body I had sanctified and consecrated for You. Lord, I repent for falling out of Your will, and I ask for Your forgiveness. Heal my mind. Renew my passion for You so I won't sin against You again."

Sherri wished she could rewind time and go back to the sports bar. She would've left Xavier there and not given in to his attitude. Or even if she did and they ended up at her house, she would've stopped him the minute he touched her in a suggestive manner. She wouldn't have let his lips or his hands roam over her body. But it was done now. And even though she'd prayed, she found herself waging a mental battle to forgive herself.

⁂

"Well, what do you want, Anisha? Didn't you tell Tyson you needed time for you?" Sherri was sitting with her legs folded, looking at her friend stretched across the floor.

Anisha covered her face with the corner of the comforter so her voice was barely audible. She spoke more to herself than to Sherri. "I've got all these feelings jumbled up on the inside right now, and nothing makes sense. I'm confused about everything."

"Taking some time away right now is the best decision you can make. The world is not going to stop turning if you leave Atlanta for a few weeks. Enjoy the opportunity you have to spend some time with your family. Once your business is up and running, you might be too busy, and you'll wish you would have taken advantage of your free time."

"What if people don't think I have enough experience? All I know is something needs to turn over, because the funds are getting low."

"Oh ye of little faith," Sherri said, shaking her head. She threw her hands in the air. "Fine. If you don't want to believe in yourself, go ahead and throw your business plan out of the window. Go back and find another job that's going to pay you what *they* think you're worth. Then you can work your butt off for them for years, and then they can let you go at their own whim. Go ahead, Anisha. Go back to putting your destiny in somebody else's hands."

Anisha ran her fingers through her hair, then pushed it behind her ears. "I wish I could find myself without worrying about whether I'll lose Tyson in the process. He's become so distant lately. He doesn't make time for me like he used to. He's not even making an effort to see me before I leave to go home."

"If it's truly meant for y'all to be together, he'll still be there in the end. If you're really serious about this time alone, don't worry about what's going on with Tyson. Let God handle that. He knows what's best for you anyway, so believe that He's made the right decision for you."

"You're right. Sometimes I need someone to remind me I'm doing the right thing even when it starts getting tight."

"I've yet to see the time when following God's voice was wrong. The process may hurt, but in the end you'll see the purpose for it was all worth it." *If only I'd followed His voice last night.*

Anisha got up and sat on the bed beside Sherri. She pulled her legs to her chest and rested her chin on her knees. "I hope Tyson sees."

"Even if he doesn't, you make sure you do. You're focusing on Anisha right now, remember?"

"I know, Sherri, but please, can I keep it real for a minute?"

"Like anything I can say is going to stop you," Sherri joked.

"I never really realized how I'd lost myself in Tyson's world until I took a step back and was suddenly by myself again. I mean, my heart practically jumps out of my chest whenever the phone rings because I'm hoping it will be him. We spend a little time together, but it's still not as much as I expected. I only wanted a little space, not a chasm."

Anisha kept ranting when Sherri didn't respond.

"It's like he went on about his business, and he's not even affected by it. And here I am going through all these changes."

"Face it, Anisha. Men don't act the same way we do about things. It's not to say he's not thinking about you or he doesn't care. He's thrown all his emotions into focusing on his business."

Anisha huffed. "How can two human beings be made so completely different? Men should think like women. It would make the world a much better place."

"No. It would make the world an emotional mess," Sherri said.

"Look, Anisha. God wants what's best for you. And right now what's best for you is quality time with Him."

"I don't even know how to spend time with God anymore. I know you can always read and pray, but there's got to be more. I think I've been lacking true intimacy that comes with a committed relationship."

Committed relationship. Sherri didn't remember the last time she'd been in one of those. Not like Xavier, the relationship man of convenience.

"Think of God as your lover," Sherri said. "When you knew you were spending time with Tyson, what did you do? You probably made sure you bathed in some scented oil or put on your favorite body lotions so you'd smell like heaven." Sherri ran her nose down Anisha's forearm and said, "Sort of like I smell now."

Anisha laughed. "Girl, you're a mess. Now go ahead and set up the atmosphere."

Sherri walked over to her stereo and turned on the CD player. "When you're spending time with your special someone, you set up a candlelight dinner, put on a little jazz, whatever." She pushed the play button, and the CD started on cue.

"Oh, here you go," Anisha said, shaking her head at her friend's antics.

"Why can't you do that for God?" she asked, twirling around the room. "You can't tell me every time you and Tyson were together you had to go out and do something. Most of the time you were happy just to be with him, letting him hold you. Talking wasn't even necessary. Bask in God's presence, girl. I guarantee you Tyson could never match it."

"Is that what you do?"

"Not like I should. I'm preaching to myself too." *If only you knew how I needed Him to hold me now.*

She was too ashamed to share her wrongdoing, even with her best friend. She knew the Bible said to confess your faults to one another so you could be healed, but knowing it and having the guts to do it were two different things. She'd broken their number one ultimate dating commandment. "Never ever let the man in the Promised Land."

Me and God will handle this between the two of us, Sherri thought.

Sherri sighed. "I've got to admit. I was a little jealous over you and Tyson. I mean, old boy swooped in out of the blue and took my place like that," she said, snapping her fingers.

"Tyson, take your place? Please, you're my girl for life."

"Could've fooled me. But we're not going to go there."

"Please don't. I'm trying to leave Atlanta on a good note."

Sherri belted out a high-pitched squawk.

Anisha pushed herself off the floor. "That's definitely not the note I meant," she said, covering her ears. "Let me get out of here, chica. I'm trying to pull out by at least five in the morning."

"Why can't you leave like regular people at around eight or nine?"

"Because if I leave at five, I'll get home when it's still breakfast time, and Grans will have something waiting for me before she leaves for church."

"To be so small, you're always thinking about food."

"You know it."

Anisha pulled her purse on her shoulder. "I love you, girl. Sisters for life," she said, holding out her pinkie finger.

Sherri hooked her pinkie onto Anisha's. "Sisters for life."

After Sherri watched Anisha make it safely to her car, she came back inside the apartment and called Xavier's cell phone. As usual, she was met with his voice mail message. It was the fourth time she had called that day, and he hadn't bothered to return the first three messages.

Sherri threw the phone on the floor. If she ever needed God before, she needed Him now. *Right now at this very moment, God.*

Sherri knew God had forgiven her. She just couldn't forgive herself. And she couldn't let it go until Xavier knew how she felt.

Anisha woke before the sun and stuffed at least three weeks' worth of clothes into a suitcase. She hadn't even left her apartment, and she already felt a sense of rejuvenation. She jumped into the shower, then threw on her favorite pair of sweats. She wanted to be comfortable for the five-hour ride to North Carolina. She threw a handful of CDs and a couple of Pastor Armstrong's sermon tapes into her duffel bag, then lugged all her belongings out to the front stoop.

"Good-bye, old life," she said, standing in the doorway. "When I get back, I'll be a changed woman."

Anisha dumped her suitcase in the trunk and threw the duffel bag on the front seat. Being laid off wasn't always a bad thing. The lack of extra finances was definitely an inconvenience, but she could live comfortably off of her savings for at least another month, maybe two. She thought about what Sherri had said and had come to appreciate the freedom. If she was working, it was doubtful she'd be making this trip unless it was a major holiday.

Sometimes adversities are blessings in disguise, Anisha thought, patting her foot on the gas to rev the engine. She decided to call Tyson. When they'd talked late last night, he'd made her promise to call when she was about to get on the road.

"Good morning," Anisha whispered when Tyson answered his phone. "I wouldn't have called you this early if you hadn't told me to."

"That's okay. Where are you?"

Anisha switched the rear button to high. "I'm still at home. I'm about to leave right now." *Ask me to stop by.*

"Okay, well, be safe. Call me when you get there or if you get sleepy on the way."

"I will," she said, hoping Tyson would hear the disappointment in her voice. He didn't.

"Are you going to church today?"

"No. The boys were up past midnight. I'm going to let them sleep in."

"I guess I better go ahead and get on the road."

"All right then. Tell everybody I said hello."

"Bye." Anisha threw her car into gear and started to speed through the complex. *Calm yourself down, girl. It's not that serious.* She turned on the radio and tuned to the twenty-four-hour gospel station. Singing God's promises always helped to calm her down. The sky was prepared to drop its dark blanket in preparation for the sunrise of a new day. Anisha hit the highway and prepared for the lone ride down Interstate 85. The new beginning of the day reminded her that nighttime didn't last forever. Things would get better.

Today's the day, Brandy thought. She looped a pink ribbon around each of Ayana's spiral-curled ponytails. She'd let Ayana choose her own outfit for their "special day," as Brandy described it. It was no surprise she'd pulled out her favorite bright yellow shirt with the smiling pink flower on the front, paired, of course, with the jeans that had the same smiling flower embroidered down the right leg.

"Now," Brandy said, turning Ayana around so she could admire the picture-perfect image she'd sought to convey. It was worth keeping Ayana out of school for today. How far could a first grader get behind in one day?

"You look so pretty, baby." Brandy kissed Ayana on her Vaseline-shined cheek, then handed her a pair of white tennis shoes. "Can you put these on while Mommy changes clothes and gets ready?"

"Yes, Mommy," Ayana said, taking one of the shoes and sitting on the floor.

Brandy dropped the other shoe at her daughter's side. "And then what are you going to do?"

"Sit still like a big girl and not get dirty," Ayana said, repeating the instructions that had been drilled into her head during her press and curl.

"Good," Brandy said, disappearing into the bedroom.

She analyzed the two outfits spread across the bed. If Tyson's taste hadn't changed, he'd appreciate the way the flare-leg jeans hugged her without cutting off the circulation to the rest of her legs. She held up a light blue fitted sweater that she usually paired with one of her favorite brown miniskirts and knee-high leather boots. Of course, he'd always commented on how shades of brown played against her bronzed skin.

After careful consideration of how Tyson would react to her—even if only in his mind—Brandy decided on the jeans and a red V-neck shirt. The leather skirt was probably overdoing it, since this was supposed to look like a spontaneous visit instead of a premeditated plan.

If she timed her visit right, she would arrive late enough for Tyson to be thinking about lunch and early enough that the boys would be coming to the Center for the after-school program. An eleven o'clock appearance would give her enough time to stir up the good memories and then casually suggest they grab a bite to eat. Two friends for old time's sake.

Brandy pulled out the rollers she'd slept in all night and ran a wide-toothed comb through her honey-blonde streaked locks. The large rollers had given her hair an incredible amount of body, and she was glad she'd grown her hair out over the last two years. Being a beautician wasn't what she wanted to do for the rest of her life, but it definitely had its benefits.

Brandy dabbed the pad from her compact across her face and lined her eyes with smoky gray eyeliner. It added a more alluring touch to her almond-shaped eyes.

"What do you have to lose?" Brandy asked her reflection. If Tyson blew her off and kept their encounter as casual as possible, she'd throw out the white flag and concede the victory to Anisha. But if she could at least get him to take up lunch with her, she'd know she had a hook in the water.

Brandy grabbed Ayana's bag and stuffed it with a few books, a coloring book, and a box of crayons. She walked into the living room to find Ayana fighting sleep, her head bobbing as she tried to keep one eye half-open on *Sesame Street*.

Brandy sat down on the couch beside her and slipped Ayana's arm into her jacket.

"Am I going to school now, Mommy?" she asked, noticing her Minnie Mouse book bag on her mother's lap.

"No, baby. I'm bringing some books with us for you to look at."

"Can I take my flash cards too?"

"Yes, baby." Brandy retrieved Ayana's flash cards from the kitchen table and zipped them in the book bag's side pocket. She steered Ayana's limp body into the breezeway and locked the door behind them.

Brandy pulled her late model Toyota Camry into the parking lot of the E.L. Clifton Recreation Center and parked beside an older model Buick LeSabre. Of the other three cars in the parking lot, she figured the SUV was Tyson's.

The receptionist she had talked to earlier had given her precise directions, and she'd followed them straight there without any trouble. That was rare, considering her less-than-accurate sense of direction. This day was meant to be.

Brandy checked her makeup in the rearview mirror and stole a glance at Ayana in the backseat. For the entire thirty-minute ride, she'd been adding and subtracting the ladybugs, bumblebees, and other insects lined across her math flash cards.

"What have you got to lose?" Brandy asked herself aloud again.

"What, Mommy?" Ayana asked, unbuckling her seat belt.

"Nothing, baby. Let's get out." Brandy opened the door and lifted the seat lever so Ayana could crawl out from the backseat. She slid her book bag on her back and grabbed her mother's waiting hand.

Brandy gripped Ayana's small hand as if she were trying to extract an ounce of strength from her. She was doing this for herself, yes, but Ayana needed Tyson more than she did. *Right?*

She walked into the building and knew the voice she had talked to that morning belonged to the older lady at the receptionist desk. Her long drawl was consistent with her unhurried movements. It was as if she considered each turn of her body before making it.

"How can I help you?"

"I'm here to see Tyson Randall."

The woman stood up and peered over the counter at Ayana. "Are you aware this program is for young boys only?" she asked Brandy.

"Yes, ma'am, but I'm not here about the program. I'm an old friend."

"Oh, okay. Is he expecting you?"

Enough with the questions already. Does every visitor get this kind of interrogation? "No, ma'am, he's not. I'm stopping through."

"Let me see if Tyson is available. You and this precious little girl can sit right over there until I get back," she said, pointing to a pair of chairs.

Brandy looked around the lobby. Although the outside of the building still left much to be desired, she could tell a lot of work had recently gone into renovating the inside of the building. The walls hadn't suffered any smudges yet from grimy hands fresh off the playground. Inspirational quotes and photos of historical figures decorated a single wall with the words HOPE—DREAM—ACHIEVE painted across the top.

It wasn't long before Brandy heard the old lady's voice coming back down the hallway. "If you get those files to me before lunch, I can have the report finished by the end of the day."

Brandy heard Tyson.

"I don't know what I'd do without you, Ms. Francine," he said. "I need to take you to my house to get some stuff in order."

Brandy sat up straight in her chair, then decided to stand for her unexpected visit. The anticipation of his presence gripped her before he came around the corner. Her legs froze, and she suddenly became bashful when her desire stood in front of her with no obstacles but her own sudden nervousness.

Tyson's jaw dropped, and he looked back and forth between her and Ms. Francine.

Brandy eyed Ms. Francine, who seemed to be trying to assess if it was a reunion she should've helped facilitate or if she should've dug around for more information first.

"Hi." Brandy finally managed to squeak out a greeting that didn't seem sufficient for the occasion. She wished she'd thought of something more engaging.

"This is definitely unexpected," Tyson said, walking over and giving her a polite hug. "How are you?"

"I'm good," Brandy said, more relaxed.

He bent down and tugged lightly on one of Ayana's ponytails. "Hey, cutie."

Brandy pulled Ayana's thumb out of her mouth. "Say hello to Mr. Tyson."

Ayana whispered, "Hello, Mr. Tyson," then stuck her thumb back in her mouth.

"Why don't you come on back?" Tyson offered.

Brandy readily agreed, happy to be leaving the watchful eye of Ms. Francine. She picked up Ayana's book bag and followed Tyson down the hall. The hallway was lined with bulletin boards boasting of the boys' personal achievements and displaying their artwork and projects from classes at the center.

"Was there a teacher workday in your district?"

"Oh, no. We had a rough weekend, and she was really tired this morning, so I kept her out," Brandy lied. "This is a nice office," she said, sitting down across from Tyson's desk and helping Ayana hoist herself up into the chair beside her.

Tyson slid into his office chair and saved the document he'd been working on. "Thanks," he said, swirling back around to Brandy. "You must have a flexible job."

"Actually, I work at a salon, and we're closed on Mondays."

"Oh, okay."

"I know what you're thinking," she said, answering the curious look on his face. "Why do I work at a salon?"

"The thought crossed my mind."

"I never finished my last semester to get my degree," Brandy said.

She'd never felt embarrassed about it before, but suddenly it brought her shame.

"Oh yeah. I almost forgot you had your cosmetology license before you started at CAU."

"Yeah. When I was still in that phase trying to find myself. It kept plenty of money in my pocket, hooking up the girls in my dorm, though."

Tyson cut to the chase. "What brings you here?"

"Actually, I've been thinking about swinging by for a while. I saw an article in the paper a few months ago and promised myself I was going to check out your program the next time I had some free time. Then after you didn't call me back at Christmas—"

"Yeah, about that. It wasn't a good time, you know. I was so busy getting things up and running with the Center. I guess it eventually slipped my mind." He picked up a squishy stress ball and rolled it between his palms.

"I understand," Brandy said. "Plus, it's not like I don't know you have someone in your life."

Tyson tossed the ball into the air and watched it miss his hands and bounce into a corner. "Besides, I didn't think it would be proper to call you back and have your friend answer the phone. What was his name? Umm—Charles? How's he?"

"Chris. And I wouldn't know how he is. Haven't known for four years. He pulled one of my dad's moves."

Tyson's face was more sympathetic. "Sorry to hear it."

"Don't be," Brandy said. "I guess it would be right for me to ask about Alicia. How is she?" She could play the old forget-the-name game, too.

"Anisha. And she's fine. Taking care of business."

Perfect. Preoccupied, Brandy thought. "You don't think she'll swing by for lunch or anything, do you? I'd hate to start any unnecessary drama."

"Oh, it's straight. She's out of town for a few weeks."

Could the cards be stacked any better in my favor? Brandy pulled her chair closer to the edge of Tyson's desk. She folded her arms across his desk and leaned in as close as her balance would allow.

"I ran into the both of you quite a few times, you know," she said. "Have you ever thought about that?"

"About what? Us running into each other?"

"Yeah."

"Coincidence, I guess."

"Do you really believe in coincidences?"

"Depends," Tyson said, getting up to rescue his stress ball from the corner.

Brandy sensed his uneasiness and decided not to take the aggressive route. She'd stick to her original plan. Slow and steady.

Over the next hour, Brandy and Tyson caught each other up on six years of their lives and had taken several walks down memory lane.

"We had the best time that night," Brandy said, remembering a moonlit Luther Vandross concert they'd attended at the Chastain Park Amphitheater. The fishing line had been cast.

It neared the hour of school dismissal, and Brandy tried to think of a tactful way to invite Tyson to join them for lunch.

As if reading her mother's mind, Ayana stood up and dropped her cards on the floor. She jumped into Brandy's lap and hooked her arms around her neck.

"I'm hungry, Mommy. Can we go eat now?"

Brandy rubbed Ayana's stomach and shook her head. "Little tummies can't wait for food," she said to Tyson. "I guess we better get going. Maybe we'll chat later." She paused briefly, then said, "Unless you'd like to join us?"

Tyson looked down at his watch. "I guess it won't hurt to get out of the office before the boys get here." He swiveled his chair around to the file cabinet behind him. "Let me get these files together for Ms. Francine, and I'll be ready."

"Great," Brandy said, picking up the scattered flash cards on the floor. There was the hook. The only thing left to do was reel him in.

As Tyson grabbed his keys from his top desk drawer, the phone rang. "Let me catch this," he said to Brandy. Tyson was quick with the caller. "Hey, how's everything? Yeah, I'm on my way out, and by the time I get back the boys will be coming in. Can I call you later tonight? Okay. You too."

Brandy took Ayana's hand and walked back down the hall of achievements with Tyson behind her. Her picture should be up there. She'd accomplished what she'd come to do. It had been easier than she'd thought it would be.

You too? Anisha wasn't thrilled with the way Tyson had rushed her off the phone earlier during the week. It had gnawed at her nerves since he'd said it. Whenever she said, "I love you," he always said, "I love you more." No matter when. No matter where. It was the same with her. It's what they always said.

She didn't like the person he'd become over the past month and a half. He was pulling away from her. He wasn't being the kind, caring man she knew. Or maybe this test of their relationship had revealed his true character. Inside, she refused to believe Tyson wasn't a good man. But she wanted the man back she'd grown to love. Maybe work had stressed him out.

Anisha hadn't realized how much she missed her family and the tranquility of not being in a bustling city. When she arrived Sunday morning, Grans had breakfast waiting at her house as Anisha had figured. She had chowed down a hefty breakfast, while Grans slurped her typical Sunday morning cup of black coffee before whisking away to church service. Later that day, her mother and sister had joined them at dinner, feasting on good times, pleasant memories, and soul food.

Since then, Anisha had spent the rest of the week resting at her mother's house.

Now, after a routine week of Nikki being in class and her mother at work, the house was too quiet. She surfed through the channels and realized what a waste of money cable was during the daytime. After two hours, she'd had her fill of repetitive court television shows and the warmed-over topics on talk shows.

You too? Anisha wondered what or who had kept Tyson from saying their habitual phrase. A business partner, maybe, but their presence had never stopped him before. Anisha reprimanded her thoughts and decided to review the first completed draft of her business plan. She only needed to make a few small edits, and then she'd let her brain rest for a couple of days. By next Monday, she'd be prepared to start marketing herself as a consultant. The market was ripe with employers who could benefit from the work of a contracted instead of full-time employee. Many organizations, especially nonprofits, needed seasonal workers for temporary projects.

Anisha booted up her laptop and stretched across the couch in the den. She reread the first page of her executive summary and realized the words weren't going to change until her thoughts gave her fingers some work to do on the keys. But her thoughts were too wrapped around Tyson, and the quietness of the house gave her mind too much playing ground.

Anisha closed her laptop and packed an overnight bag to take to Grans' house. Maybe she'd find her creative juices with a change of scenery. She scribbled a note to her mother and left it on the kitchen counter.

Grans' driveway was one of two on a small country road that hadn't been paved. Anisha pulled into the driveway, and she knew the crackling of the gravel beneath her tires had announced her arrival. When she was younger, everything about the house seemed so massive, but driving up to it now, it reminded her of something in a child's picture book. The only thing that had grown with her was the umbrella tree towering in the yard near the back porch. She remembered many a trip out to the tree when it was small enough for her to break off the thin twigs to be used as one of her own switches. She'd always tried to choose the flimsy twig that looked like it would inflict the least amount of pain, but no matter how small, the swat of the limb across her legs always left her with a powerful sting and a lesson learned.

Anisha pulled her car under the shade of the umbrella tree. She looked at Grans' silhouette standing in the glass storm door. The sun cast a reflection onto the door, giving her the appearance of a glowing angel.

Grans opened the door for Anisha to squeeze past with her laptop case and duffel bag.

"It's too late for breakfast and too early for lunch, so what brings you here?"

Anisha kissed Grans on the cheek as she scooted past her. "Grans, I can't believe you said that." Anisha dropped her belongings at the end of the chaise lounge and plopped down beside them.

"I don't see why not. You like to eat as much as I like to cook."

"Good. Then you'll have your chance tonight and in the morning, because I'm spending the night."

"That should be easy enough. Tonight you can eat leftovers from yesterday, and in the morning you're going to have to fend for yourself. I've got a doctor's appointment."

"Poor little me," Anisha said, hanging over the edge of the chaise. "I'll wither away into nothingness until you come revive me with a pan of fried okra."

"Child, you could be making this family a load of money with the acting job you're pulling off."

"Acting is not my thing, Grans, but I'll make my millions another way." Anisha hoisted her laptop bag onto her shoulder and went into the kitchen. She pushed aside a place mat and flower arrangement on the table so she'd have sufficient working space.

Grans followed her into the kitchen and busied herself with wiping off the kitchen counters. "What's all that stuff for?"

"I'm working on a business plan. I figure I might as well be my own boss so I won't have to worry about getting the boot again."

"All things work together for the good of them who love the Lord,"

Grans said, stopping her cleanup work and leaning against the counter. "You do love the Lord, don't you?"

"Yes, ma'am."

"Well, all right then. Maybe it was God's plan for you to get let go from your job. Otherwise you might not be working as hard to get this thing together for yourself."

"Same thing Sherri said."

Grans pulled out the chair beside Anisha and eased down into the seat. "Seems like my knee starts acting up when I stand up for a long time." She leaned over so she could see Anisha's laptop. "A computer you can carry around like a pocketbook. I'll do fine with a pencil and piece of paper."

Grans pulled a wilted petal off of one of the flowers on her table arrangement. "Who's at your mama's house?"

"Nobody," Anisha said, pushing the power button on her laptop. "I had to come up here so I could concentrate."

"What's on your mind so heavy?"

Anisha was hesitant about sharing her relationship problems with her grandmother. She wasn't sure she could relate. After her husband's death, Grans was never interested in being in another relationship. At least that's what she'd always said. She was more concerned with raising her children and helping folks in the community.

Grans read Anisha's mind. "Is it Tyson?"

"Yes, Grans. But I don't want to—"

"You think your grandfather wasn't a man? Whether it's 1949, 1999, or 2009, some things don't change. A man is a man is a man."

Grans' advice would probably be as good as anybody else's, if not better, Anisha thought. But on the other hand, she was too drained to endure another emotional hangover. She'd had enough private sessions that week already.

"He's been acting really standoffish," Anisha explained. "Especially this week. I feel we're growing apart. I didn't think this would happen because I needed time with God. Tyson is the first person I'd expected to understand."

Grans tapped her finger on the table. "I can't tell you exactly what he's thinking, 'cause God made men with a mind I've yet to figure out." Grans chuckled at her own admission before she continued. "The Bible says to seek the kingdom of God first and all His righteousness, then things would be added unto you. That includes your business, prosperity, Tyson." She reached over and patted Anisha's hand. "Your peace."

Grans' reassurances were refreshing, and Anisha worked tirelessly into the evening until her business plan was as close to perfection as she could get it. She'd also cut and pasted parts of the plan into another document and pieced together a business proposal. If a position caught her eye, she'd send the proposal of her services with her resume. It was worth a shot.

Anisha hung up the phone, frustrated after another empty conversation with Tyson. There was a time when they were comfortable in silence, but now any lull in conversation was awkward. They struggled to keep a conversation flowing.

Her first instinct was to call Sherri and search for some kind of justification for Tyson's actions. She resisted the urge, one reason being that Sherri was currently at work, the other that she didn't want to bother Sherri with her "Tyson" problems. Sherri was carrying more than enough burdens with work and school and didn't need an extra weight helping Anisha with her disarrayed love life.

Anisha reached into her pocket and pulled out the Scripture from Jeremiah she'd written on an index card. *For I know the thoughts that I think toward you, says the Lord, thoughts of peace and not of evil, to give you a future and a hope.*

"Anisha," Nikki called out and knocked on the closed guest room door. "Are you coming with me and Ma to the movies?"

"I don't feel like it," Anisha yelled, not bothering to invite Nikki inside. Nevertheless, her sister took it upon herself to barge in and make herself welcome on the end of the bed.

"Look, ever since you've been here, Ma has been into this whole mother-daughter bonding thing," Nikki said. "So you might as well suck it up and make the best of it. You know how she gets when she's all love-dovey and sentimental."

Anisha sucked her teeth. "Okay, fine." She looked at Nikki's jeans and smiled. She knew her sister hated when they dressed even remotely similar. "I have a pair of jeans just like those," Anisha said, sorting through the clothes she'd hung in the closet. "I think I'll wear them."

"Great." Nikki's voice was riddled with sarcasm. "Do you always have to make us look like the Bobbsey Twins?"

"We're bonding, remember?"

"Whatever," Nikki said, grabbing a stick of gum off the dresser. "We're leaving in ten minutes."

Anisha slipped into her pair of jeans and pulled on a trendy top she found at one of the teen stores in the mall. She pulled her hair back into a barrette and put on a pair of silver hoop earrings. Not only did she change her clothes, but Anisha also promised to change her attitude for the night. Her trip home was supposed to be refreshing. She was supposed to be enjoying time with her family, getting things in order for her business, and spending intimate time with God. Those were the goals before her when she left Atlanta, and she was going to accomplish them by disciplining her mind. It might take time, but she was determined to stay on the potter's wheel.

"Regardless of the pressure, Lord," Anisha prayed aloud, "I'm staying on this wheel until I'm the woman You've created me to be." It was going to be a painful process if God had to strip Tyson from her life, but if she wanted God's will for her life in every area—and she did—what other choice did she have?

Anisha walked into the living room where her mother and sister were engulfed in a conversation about where Nikki should apply for an internship.

"Okay, people, let's get a move on it. We don't want to be late," she said, beckoning them with her hand and sauntering down the foyer.

"I see the hermit has resurfaced," Nikki said to her mother.

"About time." Mrs. Blake burst into a performance of the chorus of "Ladies' Night" by Kool and the Gang.

"Save it for our property only, Mother. Pleeezzzz don't embarrass me in public," Nikki said, running down the front steps to the car. "What's up with this habit you and your daughter have of bursting out with these old school songs? Don't you know any songs from church?"

Anisha laughed at her sister. She did have a point, but she joined in the chorus with her mother anyway. When Mrs. Blake broke into her signature dance, Anisha joined her, despite her sister's attempt to press them to the car. She felt better already.

*T*yson knew it was time that he call Anisha. He was treating her in a way she didn't deserve, and he could tell by their last conversation that she was searching to see where his head was. Even he didn't know. That was the problem. He loved Anisha and didn't want to hurt her, but what if it was his destiny to be back with Brandy? Maybe Anisha going to North Carolina and Brandy finding him was God's will. What if? Maybe God had stopped his proposal before he got caught up in a marriage God didn't intend to happen. It wasn't a question of whether Anisha was a good woman; it was whether she was *his* good woman.

He wheeled slowly through the lot looking for the Cutz Hair Salon along the strip of sandwich, nail, and beauty supply stores. Brandy was supposed to be finishing her last client at around eight, and he was picking up her and Ayana to grab a bite to eat. What was the harm in two old friends getting together?

Brandy was being supportive while he dealt with his uncertainties concerning Anisha. She'd helped him to see that Anisha's need for space wasn't necessarily a bad thing. They could both use the time to re-evaluate what they wanted in their lives. If Anisha needed the space to get close to God, perhaps there were some personal issues she needed to deal with that he didn't know anything about. Brandy thought it was God's way of protecting his heart.

Tyson parallel parked in an illegal curb space in front of a fire hydrant. He called the salon number scribbled on the paper with his directions and asked the gum-popping receptionist if he could speak to Brandy.

"Hi. I'm outside. Are you ready?" he asked when she came to the phone.

"Give me a minute to clean around my station. Can you come inside and get Ayana?"

"I'm illegally parked, so I better not. Send her out, and I'll go ahead and get her buckled in."

Tyson leaned against the car and waited for Ayana. He saw her run to the glass door and use all her weight to push the heavy salon door open. The brown wooden beads on the ends of her cornrows bounced against her back as she skipped out the door. She bounded toward Tyson and jumped into his arms, wrapping her knobby legs around his waist.

"Mr. Tyson," she screamed. "Can we go see the dancing bears at Pizza Den?"

"What did your mom say?" Tyson asked, opening the car door and setting her in the backseat.

"She said I have to ask you." Ayana examined the bead on the end of her braided style. "Pleeeezzz," she begged, sticking the tip of her braid into Tyson's ear while he tried to buckle her seat belt.

Tyson pretended to ignore her and kept readjusting the seat belt until her small body was secure and comfortable.

"Pleezzzz," Ayana poked the small bead around the top of his head, circling his eyes, nose, and mouth.

Tyson pretended to walk away, then dove back into the rear seat, tickling Ayana until she could barely catch her breath.

"Are you going to be good?" he asked, ceasing his tickle attack long enough for her to squeak out, "No!"

Tyson ran his fingers across Ayana's stomach and under her armpits. She wriggled around, kicking and screaming in delight, but couldn't dodge his reach because of the seat belt.

"Are you going to be good?" Tyson asked again, his fingers suspended in the air, ready to descend upon her guarded tummy.

"Mommmyyyy!" Ayana screamed at the sight of her mother's face peeking over Tyson's shoulder.

"What are you guys doing?" Brandy asked.

"Mr. Tyson is tickkkuulllinnn me," Ayana said, still laughing uncontrollably.

"Who, me?" Tyson backed away from the car with his hands up. "I wasn't doing anything."

"Uh, huh. Yes you did, Mr. Tyson. Yes you did."

"I'll get Mr. Tyson later," Brandy said, nudging Tyson in the side. She flipped her shampooed locks over her shoulder. "Ayana wants to go to the Pizza Den."

"I heard," Tyson said, opening the door for Brandy and helping her into his vehicle. "That'll work for me."

On the way, Ayana entertained Brandy and Tyson with her class's new sing-along songs about lemon drops and raindrops. She'd found great joy in teaching them the words and accompanying clapping rhythms. By the time they pulled up to the restaurant with the herds of parents trying to keep the reins on the enthusiastic kids running outside, Ayana had conducted a successful rehearsal.

"This place is packed," Tyson said. He backed into a space at the far end of the parking lot and pulled a brush out of the glove compartment. He ran the bristles across his hair, then pulled a piece of gum out of his pocket.

"Do you plan on hookin' up with someone inside?" Brandy joked, accepting a piece of gum from his packet. She popped it into her mouth and searched her pocketbook for a comb to start her own beauty regimen.

Tyson leaned back against his door and watched her paint her lips with a fresh coat of lipstick. She pumped scented lotion from a small bottle and rubbed it through her fingers and down her neck. She smelled like a sweet honeydew melon. Light and fresh like the body cream Anisha wore, Tyson thought.

"Look who's talking." Tyson reached over and smoothed a stray hair near her temple. "Your hair looks nice."

"Thanks," Brandy said, swinging her locks over her shoulder. "You ready?" She looked back at Ayana, who was singing with her eyes closed. "If I hear another line about a lemon drop I might get a cavity."

"You and me both," Tyson said, getting out of the car to help Brandy, then Ayana.

The Pizza Den was designed to look like a large cave built into the side of a mountain. Wooden signs along the cobblestone walkway leading to the entrance warned campers "Please Don't Feed The Bears" and to "Watch For Falling Rocks." Ayana ran ahead as far as the hands holding her on either side would allow until they finally reached the wooden door. "Beware of Fun Inside," the sign across the archway read.

Tyson swung open the door and followed Brandy into what looked like a miniature amusement park stuffed inside of a building. In one section, video games, interactive games, cages filled with plastic balls, inflatable jumpers, and a climbing wall that looked like the side of a mountain were situated around fake trees built from the floor up to the roof. Children ran around the area, largely unsupervised by their parents who Tyson assumed had abandoned them for a few minutes of adult interaction. But even the eating area reminded them they were still in a restaurant geared toward a child's imagination. Singing mechanical bears in overalls and plaid shirts plucked banjos, strummed fiddles, and blew harmonicas. Their mouths opened periodically in sync with the chorus blasting over the loud speakers.

Brandy yelled above the screaming kids. "You're probably not used to this sort of thing," she said to Tyson. "Sorry. Maybe we should've gone somewhere quieter."

"And have Ayana stuffed into a booth where she couldn't talk without impatient adults staring at our table the whole night?" He swooped Ayana up and put her onto his shoulders. "Don't worry about it."

"Thanks," Brandy said.

They followed a perky teenage hostess with two pigtails to an empty table. Ayana was too excited to sit down and begged Brandy to go to the inflatable jumper.

"Stay where I can see you," Brandy said, pulling off Ayana's jacket.

Ayana's face lit up. "Okay." She stripped off her tennis shoes and threw them under the table. "Pepperoni pizza, Mommy," she yelled as she skipped away.

"Looks like the decision is already made," Tyson said, picking up the menu. "Peg the Porcupine's Pepperoni Pizza?"

"I've seen you down many a suspicious dish," Brandy said, pointing a finger at Tyson. "Remember the time you ate that unidentifiable meat at that Chinese restaurant and ended up getting food poisoning? You were so pitiful."

Tyson shook his head at the memory. "I had a rough night, but you hung in there and let me act—"

"Like a baby," Brandy said.

"Actually, I was going to say like a wounded soldier, but a baby may be a pretty accurate description."

"Oh, it's extremely accurate."

"Okay," Tyson said, rubbing his chin with a look of playful revenge spread across his face. "Since you want to put my stuff on the table, let's talk about the girl who would rather eat dirt than apologize."

"Hey, I apologized whenever I was wrong."

"Yeah, but it was like pulling teeth. You know how you hated to be wrong."

"I was wrong plenty of times," Brandy said. She looked down at the table and ran a napkin across a brown stain on the table. "I was wrong for lying to you about Ayana being your daughter."

"That was years ago, Brandy. You don't have to go there right now."

"Yes, I do. I never apologized, and I've had to live with that. I promised myself if I ever had the chance, I would ask for your forgiveness. Can you accept me as a friend who made an immature decision?"

Tyson took Brandy's hands between his. Her eyes pleaded for him to heal the past wounds they had inflicted on each other. Brandy didn't appear to be the same woman who'd crushed the dreams he'd built around her. People changed. Even things that were important to him years ago didn't hold the same value as they did today.

"Only if you'll share a Peg the Porcupine's Pepperoni Pizza with me," Tyson said.

❦

Tyson threw his briefcase on top of the pile of clothes that had been waiting for a trip to the cleaners for over two weeks. His only clean suit hung on the back of his office door in case of an unexpected meeting. He unbuttoned his shirt and tossed it with the others. He changed into a pair of shorts and sat on the end of the workout bench in his room. Thoughts about Brandy and Anisha clashed in his head.

He pumped the barbell, watching his biceps bulge with each repetition of arm curls. Maybe Anisha had been placed in his life for a season, and they'd taken it beyond what God had intended. She was strong and goal oriented. They'd probably be too busy with their own personal ambitions to spend any time together, and the marriage would eventually fall apart. She seemed to be more of a career woman than she was a family woman.

Tyson leaned back and scooted under the bench press bar. If he truly thought about it, he couldn't blame Brandy for choosing Chris. He was Ayana's father and was more financially stable. There was no way she could've known his promises would turn out empty and he'd abandon her.

I can prove to be the man Brandy needed before, Tyson thought. *She knows me like no one else. And Ayana has taken to me easily.*

Tyson turned over on his stomach and hooked his legs under the leg lift and curled the bar until his thighs shook and weakened with exhaustion. Calling Anisha would be more grueling than any workout. He knew how she cried from the depths of her soul when she was hurt, and how he always wanted to hold her until she felt better. Being in two different states was best for both of them right now. The distance between them would help the intense emotions that usually followed a breakup.

Nine thirty wasn't too late to call her mother's house. He prayed Anisha would answer the phone so he wouldn't have to endure clawing his way through all the pleasantries, knowing the news he was about to deliver.

"Hello?"

Nikki or Anisha? Their voices were hard to distinguish over the phone. "Anisha?"

"No, Nikki. Who is this? Tyson?"

Exactly what he didn't want to happen. "What's up, Nik? Is your sister there?"

"Yeah. We just got back from the movies that we had to practically drag her out of the house to go see. She's been slipping back and forth out of a funk all week, so please whip your charm on her and do us all a favor."

Tyson forced out a chuckle. This wasn't going to be good.

"Hold on. I'll get her for you."

He heard Nikki belt out Anisha's name. "Your man's on the phone," she announced to the entire East Coast.

When Anisha answered the phone she sounded out of breath. "Hello?"

"Hey, 'Nish. What's going on?"

"Whew. I need to work out. I was downstairs and tried to skip the steps two at a time." She sighed and her voice softened. "It's good to hear your voice."

"Yours too." Tyson wished she wouldn't say things like that. *Not now.*

"Tyson, I've gotten so much accomplished this week. I finally finished my business plan and sent out a resume and proposal package to two companies."

Tyson took hold of the piece of rope she'd given him and tried to stretch it out into an excuse. "Getting away from Atlanta and from me has done you a lot of good, hasn't it?"

"Don't say that," Anisha said. "I miss you."

Her words weren't helping his mission. "Look, 'Nish. Can we talk?"

"Sure. What's on your mind?"

He could hear concern, almost apprehension, rising in her voice.

"I don't think we should be together right now. I know you said you needed some space, but maybe a relationship between us was never meant to be. I don't want to try and predict the future right now. We both need to reassess where our lives are taking us and see if we're going in the same direction. I mean, look how much you've accomplished without me distracting you."

Her voice fluttered, and he could tell she was trying to stave off a rain of tears.

"How could you call me on the phone and tell me something like this? I knew you were acting distant toward me, but you couldn't deal with it like a man, could you? You had to wait until you wouldn't have to look me in the face. You're a coward, Tyson."

He deserved her lashing, every name she spat out, and the outpouring of tears in between.

He hoped he was making the right decision.

30

Voice mail again. Sherri stuffed her cell phone back into her coat pocket and eased the classroom door open. She slipped into her seat in the back row and tried to will herself to pay attention and focus on the lesson about making pleats.

It had been nine days since she'd given her body to Xavier, and he hadn't had the decency to call on his own will or return any of her messages. *Focus, Sherri. Focus.* Fire academy or not, no one was that busy.

She pulled the Scripture she'd been meditating on to the forefront of her mind. *Whatever things are true, whatever things are noble, whatever things are just, whatever things are pure, whatever things are lovely, whatever things are of good report, if there is any virtue and if there is anything praiseworthy—meditate on these things.*

How could she meditate on those things when thoughts of Xavier kept invading her mind? That was the last call, she decided. *Enough is enough,* she thought, scolding herself. *You deserve better. It's done and you can't change it. Move on.*

If only she felt the freedom to call Anisha, she'd pour out her heart and let her friend help rebuild her womanhood. Her chastity.

"Ummm . . . excuse me." Sherri's classmate tapped Sherri on her shoulder and pointed to the other students who were getting out of their seats. "We're supposed to be breaking up into our groups."

"Oh yeah," Sherri mumbled. "Sorry." She looked around the room at the rest of her eclectic classmates who had moved to the various sewing stations assigned to their teams. She wondered if anyone else was dealing with an emotional turbulence.

She joined her team at their station and pulled one of the wooden stools closer to the machine so she could watch her group members practice before it was her turn. The methodical hum of the sewing machine soon lulled her attention away from class again. By the time it was her turn, everything about the class—her instructor staring over her shoulder, the excited chatter of the students—had irritated her already frayed nerves.

She pulled on a hanging string and the entire stitch unraveled. *Just like my emotions right now. One wrong choice and I'm unraveling.* Sherri repositioned the fabric and aligned it under the sewing machine needle.

One of her flamboyant male classmates patted her back. "It's okay, sweetheart. These things take practice."

"Thanks." Sherri knew she could sew circles around him on any given day. She took a deep breath and pressed her foot slowly on the sewing pedal. The first tear plopped and darkened a small round space on the brown fabric. "I'm sorry," she said to her classmates. "I don't feel well. I need to go."

She ran to the back of the room, grabbed her bag, and flew down the hallway to her car as fast as her legs would carry her. Before she realized it, she was flying down the highway. She pushed the auto dial on her cell phone and called Xavier again. *You have reached the voice mail box of . . .*

She disconnected the line and pushed the button to call again, only to hear the voice of the one who'd jilted her. She hung up and called again. And again. And again. And again. And again until she whipped into her parking space at home.

For seven years she'd held her celibacy. Now she knew why the bonds of fornication weren't worth it. She was tied to this man deeper than she could break out of on her own. If she had to stay up praying all night, this stronghold was going to be broken. Sex was supposed to be symbolic of an everlasting covenant between a married man and a woman, not an act of entertainment for two people who couldn't control their lusts.

Sherri was thankful when she opened the apartment door to only the lights seeping from under her roommates' closed bedroom doors.

"God, send Your Holy Spirit to comfort me. You said in my weakness, You would be made strong. I'm weak, Lord, and only Your strength can carry me through. I know You've forgiven me, but help me to forgive myself. Help me to press forward and learn from this mistake. I knew Xavier wasn't the man for me, but I allowed my loneliness to overrule Your will. Forgive me for trying to take my life into my own hands when You know and see all."

Sherri's ringing cell phone disrupted her prayer. Xavier's name flashed on the display, and she answered it with fury.

"Hello?"

"Yeah, what's up?"

"What do you mean what's up? It's nice to see your fingers are working again."

"I'm returning your calls. What's up with blowing up my phone? If I didn't call you back the first time, you should've known I was busy."

"So we have sex and now you pretend like you hardly know me?"

"If I recall correctly, you're the one who woke me up and was trying to sneak me out the door."

"You don't understand. I feel bad about what happened. I had made a commitment to God not to have sex again until I was married."

"And you actually thought you could do it? Come on, Sherri. I know you want to be a good Christian and all, but men and women have their needs. Sex is for men and women to enjoy themselves. You trying to tell me God don't want you to feel good? In fact, I know you were feeling good."

She cringed with regret. "I know God designed sex, Xavier, but it was meant for the confines of marriage."

"Look, it's over and done with. Pray to God, or whatever you need to do, if you're that upset about it."

"I don't even know why I expected you to understand." Sherri tried her best to be tough, but her tears spilled over before she could stop them.

"Look, I didn't call here for all this emotional drama. I wanted you and you wanted me. Ain't nothing wrong with that."

Words were useless. She knew she couldn't make him experience the same kind of conviction she was feeling. *Christ* lived in her. It was evident she hadn't considered who or what lived inside of Xavier.

The strength Sherri longed for finally stood up inside of her. "You know, Xavier," Sherri said, "we could go back and forth all day, and you'd still never get it. I made a mistake that has opened my eyes to a lot of things. I settled for a lot when dealing with you because I wanted somebody to give me some attention. But I'm worth more than that. I'm a diamond, and it's evident you can't afford to pay the price. So good-bye, and good riddance!"

Sherri furiously threw down her cell phone. As far as she was concerned, Xavier was dead.

The phone rang again instantly. He was calling to get in his last words, but she wasn't going out like that.

"What?" Sherri yelled.

The sobs Sherri heard from the other end caught her off guard. "Hello? Who is this?" She tried to talk over the escalating wails. "Anisha?"

"Sherri, Tyson dumped me. Over the phone like I was some kind of long distance company he was rejecting. I knew he was acting funny. If I'd never asked for space, he wouldn't be walking away now. He wouldn't be doing this to me."

Sherri searched for words sufficient enough to ease the pain her friend was feeling, but in the light of her own drama it was proving useless.

"I'm sorry, Anisha. I'm sorry you have to go through this right now, but God even orchestrated it so you could be at home right now around your family. There's nothing like a mother's comfort."

As the Lord led Sherri to minister to Anisha, she found the weight of her own problems became less cumbersome. That was what friends were for. To bear one another's burdens.

"There's a mountain at the end of this valley, Anisha. I have to keep reminding myself, too. Trials produce patience, and patience builds character."

"I've been so wrapped up in my own problems that I didn't ask about what's happening with you."

"Things could be better, but I'm trying to stay focused on school," Sherri said. "I finally cut Xavier."

"Thank God," Anisha said. "That alone has brightened my day already."

Not if you knew the whole story, Sherri thought.

"I'm sorry I even tried to play Miss Matchmaker. I wanted you to be with somebody because Tyson and I were together. Now look at both of us, back at square one again."

"That's not true. We've got some wisdom under our belt," Sherri said.

"And a little more gray hair to go with it," Anisha joked.

"You know I can always call Calvin."

"Unless you plan on being a seal trainer, I'd leave that one alone." Anisha laughed behind her sniffles.

"Tell me about it," Sherri said. "If we hang in there, every day will get easier. Who says it's over for you and Tyson anyway? Maybe it's not time. You have to be whole in yourself before God can put the two of you back together."

"Let's pray," Anisha said. "Do you want to have the honors?"

"Sure," Sherri said, kneeling with the phone at the end of her bed. She'd pick up where she'd left off before Xavier's phone call.

"Lord, be a fence around us," Sherri prayed. "Guide us and protect our hearts as we travel along this path You've chosen. We know all things work together for the good of those who love You. And we love You. You also said the prayers of the righteous man availeth much, and we present ourselves to You as righteous. You've forgiven our sins and made us brand-new. We can't thank You enough for Your loving kindness. We're nothing without You."

Sherri wanted to bear her soul to Anisha, but she knew her friend would partly blame herself for what had occurred. Besides, even though she knew Anisha would take her secret to the grave if Sherri asked her to, this might be one thing that only God would know.

*S*herri had become best friends with the toilet since about five o'clock that morning. Her throat burned from the acidic taste of the food that was no longer there. She watched every course of her dinner swirling down into the unknown. Spicy foods late at night weren't for her, she decided. This stomach virus had been getting the best of her for over a week. She winced again at the familiar churning in her stomach.

It took all the strength she could muster to pull on her clothes and make it to the car. On the way out the door, she grabbed a plastic grocery bag in case her stomach couldn't wait. Her boss wasn't going to allow another sick day unless she turned in a doctor's excuse, so she woke up early with the intention of being the first patient at the doctor's office.

Fortunately, the DeKalb Urgent Care Clinic was only one mile away, and the parking lot was practically empty when Sherri arrived. The two cars in the lot probably belonged to the front desk staff, Sherri thought. Minutes later she watched someone who she thought looked like a doctor wheel into the parking lot in a silver Mercedes

Benz. The woman who got out wobbled toward the clinic door wearing a maternity top and a pair of loose linen pants pulled above her very pregnant stomach.

When Sherri's dashboard clock hit eight o'clock, she dragged herself inside the clinic. The lady at the check-in desk was too chipper for Sherri's early morning taste, but Sherri appreciated her effort. She managed a weak smile and took the clipboard to complete the thesis-sized stack of forms on her life's medical history.

Sherri couldn't figure out for the life of her why it was taking so long for the doctor to see her. She'd been the first patient to arrive and had already had her temperature and blood pressure taken by the nurse, who left her in the cold exam room. Finally the doctor's stomach, followed by the rest of her body, came through the door.

The doctor looked down at the chart on her clipboard and then up at Sherri.

"Good morning. I'm Dr. McIntire." She reached a pale, freckled hand out to Sherri, then sat on the stool in front of the examination table. "Can you tell me about your symptoms?"

"Probably a stomach virus," Sherri explained. "I've been throwing up all week, and it's zapping my energy and giving me headaches."

Dr. McIntire nodded her head. "Any diarrhea or fever?"

Sherri furrowed her brow then shook her head. "No."

"Abdominal pain?"

Sherri pressed her lower abdomen. "Some slight cramping down here."

The doctor raised an eyebrow and flipped a page on Sherri's chart. "When was your last period?"

Sherri counted back in her head, growing more panicked with each week counted. "It should be starting any day now, so it must have been on the twenty-third."

"Are you usually regular?"

"Yes. But I've been under a lot of stress lately. Can't that throw off your cycle?"

"Sometimes. Any chance you're pregnant?"

"No." Sherri defended herself without thinking, but her conscience reminded her of the Xavier incident. *Please God.* "Maybe a small chance, but I doubt it."

"Well, which is it? Yes or no?"

Look woman, don't get smart. "I haven't been sexually active in seven years, but there was an incident about four weeks ago."

"All it takes is one time."

You don't think I know that. I don't need your high school sex education class speech right now.

Dr. McIntire closed Sherri's chart and sat down on the swivel stool beside the exam table. "Why don't I have a nurse get a urine sample first and when you get back I'll go ahead and examine you?"

"Why do you need a urine sample?" Sherri asked, though she was already fully aware of the obvious answer.

"With the symptoms you've mentioned, you might be pregnant. It's a good idea to check," she said, getting up and opening the exam room door.

She led Sherri down the hall to the nurses' station and whispered instructions to the woman sitting behind the desk.

Sherri took the small plastic cup from the nurse and went into the bathroom. When she finished, she put the cup inside the cubbyhole in the wall and went back to the examination room.

Dr. McIntire followed directly behind her. Sherri sat on the examination table, and the doctor placed the cold tip of the stethoscope on her back to listen to her lungs.

"Take a deep breath in and let it out," Dr. McIntire said, sliding the stethoscope across Sherri's back.

Sherri tried to calm herself when the doctor placed the instrument on her chest. She knew her heart was pounding.

Dr. McIntire noticed, too. "It's okay," she said, offering what was supposed to be a comforting smile.

No, it's not okay.

"Lie back on the exam table for me, please." Dr. McIntire lifted the bottom of Sherri's shirt and pressed her fingers around on Sherri's stomach. "Let me know if it hurts anywhere."

Dr. McIntire finished the exam and helped Sherri sit up on the table. "Everything feels normal," she said. "Let me go check on your results."

Sherri wished Dr. McIntire hadn't left her alone with her thoughts. *They should play jazz or classical music in the doctor's office,* she thought. Anything was better than the cold silence.

Dr. McIntire returned, looking down at her clipboard.

What's so important on that clipboard? Sherri thought. *It can't tell you anything I can't.*

"Your pregnancy test is positive," Dr. McIntire said, pausing as if she was giving time for the news to soak in. "Have you given any thought about what you want to do?"

Any thought? "No, no . . . no thought," Sherri stammered. "This was the last thing I expected." Her voice was barely audible, even in the silence of the exam room.

Sherri stared at Dr. McIntire's stomach. She could have sworn she saw her shirt suddenly jut out from the force of a small foot or elbow. Dr. McIntire grabbed the side of her stomach. Sherri was right.

"You're early, so you have some time to talk to your partner or a support system about what's best for you."

Dr. McIntire's suggestion hit Sherri in the throat. *Xavier? He bears no resemblance to being my partner, let alone a support system.*

Dr. McIntire reached into her lab coat pocket and gave Sherri a handful of brochures. "Here are some materials to help you think about your choices," she said.

Sherri thumbed through the stack. SINGLE PARENTHOOD. WHAT YOU SHOULD KNOW ABOUT ABORTION. I DIDN'T EXPECT THIS: HOW TO DEAL WITH UNPLANNED PREGNANCY. YOUR BABY AND YOU.

Dr. McIntire pulled a small blue box out of her other coat pocket. Sherri hated those pockets.

"These are prenatal vitamins I want you to take until you make your decision. It's very important that you have folic acid in your system during the first weeks of the baby's formation."

The baby. The words knocked the wind out of her.

Sherri stuffed the brochures and the box of prenatal vitamins down into the bottom of her purse and methodically walked out of the exam room. She didn't remember leaving the clinic or driving home.

Crackers were the only food Sherri's stomach could manage. Days of nausea had weakened her body and her reasoning. She didn't know if it was the morning sickness or nerves that were wreaking havoc on her body. She bent over the toilet for the third time in fifteen minutes. *I might as well get a pillow and stay in here all day.* She was glad it was Saturday, and she didn't have to worry about making it in to work. Sherri balled up on the bathroom floor. How was she going to handle another eight months of this? *Would* she handle another eight months of this?

Sherri had avoided calling Xavier, although she knew she needed to. He needed to know. Maybe if she could unload some of this burden, they'd figure out something together. By now, he would have recovered from the lashing she'd given him the last time they talked. He was responsible for the situation as much as she was.

She went down the hall and peeked into Tamara's room.

"Good morning, Tam."

"What's up, girl?" She looked at the hollowness of Sherri's eyes. "You okay?"

"Yeah. Can I borrow your cell phone for a minute?"

Tamara furrowed her brow. "Sure. It's over there on the dresser."

"Thanks. I'll bring it right back."

Sherri didn't bother to change clothes. She trekked outside to her car wearing her pajama bottoms, an oversized T-shirt, and flip-flops. If Xavier saw Sherri's cell or home phone number, it was highly probable that he'd ignore her altogether. She hesitantly dialed his number. She wasn't sure if she wanted him to answer.

"This is X," he answered.

His voice sent her emotions in overdrive. "This is Sherri—please don't hang up," she implored. She heard him huff into the phone. "We need to talk."

"About what?"

"I'm pregnant." There, she spit it out. No beating around the bush. It was what it was. Sherri was confused by the silence on the other end. She'd been sure he'd at least fly off into a fit of rage. Or denial.

"Did you hear me? I said I'm pregnant."

"Why you calling me?"

"Why do you think? 'Cause it has to be yours. You're the only person I've been with in seven years."

"Maybe it was Immaculate Conception, Ms. Holier Than Thou." *No he didn't.* "What am I supposed to do?"

"Do whatever you want, but I'm not taking care of any more kids."

"Any *more* kids?"

"I got three of my own and a brother can't get ahead dishing out child support to two women and playing house to keep another one out of my pockets."

This was talk-show material. Today's topic: Good girls who get jilted by bad boys. Sherri couldn't believe he had the audacity to mentor young men. *Tyson should enact a new policy of moral background checks,* she thought.

"That's not fair, Xavier. I can't believe you're saying this. How can you call yourself a mentor for young boys and you can't even stand up to your responsibility?" She remembered the scorned woman at the Time Out Bar and Grill. Evidently she had a reason to be. "It's not fair," Sherri said again.

"It takes two people to make a baby, so don't try to throw your responsibility sermon on me. And don't go into what you think is fair. I recall a certain someone telling me life wasn't fair. That wouldn't have been you, would it?"

The phone went silent. The call hadn't dropped. She knew he'd hung up. She redialed his cell phone, and it went straight into his voice mail.

Sherri crumpled over the steering wheel. She'd finally found her passion and was working hard at the fashion institute. She didn't see how having this baby was going to fit into her plan. What would her parents say? How would Veronica and Tamara look at her? She was supposed to be setting an example. She thought about her family's reaction. She couldn't perpetuate the tradition and join her other cousins in the plight of single motherhood. They expected more than that from her.

One night, God. Couldn't You have shown me a little grace and mercy on this? Regret consumed her. She'd chosen the sin but couldn't choose the consequence.

She had reread the brochures Dr. McIntire had given her enough times to know the pamphlet WHAT YOU SHOULD KNOW ABOUT ABORTION had a list of clinics on the back. One of them was bound to be open on Saturdays, so she'd call to make an appointment for Monday morning. Just in case.

"A re you going to revival service tomorrow?" Grans asked Anisha.

Anisha hated when Grans cornered her. She had a way of guilt tripping her into being at church from sunup to sundown. What ever happened to resting on the Sabbath day? God rested on the seventh. Couldn't these traditionalists get the hint?

"I don't know, Grans," Anisha said, stirring a pot of collard greens on the stove. "I'll think about it."

Grans opened the oven and checked the chicken. She pulled it out and peeled off the aluminum foil. "Hand me the mushroom soup, 'Nish," she said, poking a fork in the chicken. "Now you've got at least seven new recipes to practice when you get home. I don't see how you survive on hamburgers and deli sandwiches. You need to keep some vegetables in your system."

"Me and Sherri used to cook dinner every Sunday."

"Y'all need to do it more often. You keep on and you're going to be nothing but skin and bones after you get back home."

"Yes, Grans."

Grans recovered the dish and set the oven timer. "You can take full credit for this dinner tomorrow. As far as I'm concerned, I wasn't even here."

"So you're going to help me lie to them, Grans? I can't believe you."

"We're not lying to them. We're trickin' 'em."

"Since you put it like that, then I guess I'll have to go with your plan."

"Have I ever steered you wrong?"

"Nope, Grans. Never. Every word you say is like God Himself is speaking." Anisha held up a finger. "Except, of course, for the lies."

Grans snapped the dish towel at Anisha's behind. "Get out of here before I make you go get a switch off the tree."

"I'm going out to a tree, but it won't be for a switch," Anisha said, going to find an afghan in the linen closet.

Anisha retreated outside to relax under one of the apple trees in the backyard. Taking this time away from the bustle of the city was definitely one of the best decisions she could've made. It'd been a long time since she'd spent this kind of time with her family. God knew what she'd needed, and no paycheck could compensate for what she'd shared with them for the last two weeks. If her brother had been home from college, then all would be perfect. She was having a wonderful time with the women in her family. Still, a little testosterone added to the mix wouldn't have hurt.

Her work for today was done. Her devotions with God in the mornings made all the difference. Her mind was clear in the decisions she'd made. She even felt she knew which jobs to send her proposals to and which ones weren't worth it.

Anisha turned onto her back and watched the clouds float across the sky and transfigure themselves into different shapes. The wind, still slightly brisk, rustled the tree leaves and played nature's music. If this world were without crime and creepy things that crawled and slithered, Anisha thought, she'd spend the night under a blanket of stars.

Her Bible study that morning had been in the third chapter of Ecclesiastes. She opened her Bible to read the Scripture again. *To everything there is a season, a time for every purpose under heaven: A time to be born, and a time to die; a time to plant, and a time to pluck what is planted; a time to kill, and a time to heal; a time to break down, and a time to build up; a time to weep, and a time to laugh; a time to mourn, and a time to dance; a time to cast away stones, and a time to gather stones; a time to embrace, and a time to refrain from embracing; a time to gain, and a time to losev time to keep, and a time to throw away; a time to tear, and a time to sew; a time to keep silence, and a time to speak; a time to love, and a time to hate; a time of war, and a time peace.*

"God, help me to endure the winter season in my life until You send the spring," Anisha prayed.

⁂

Anisha was purposefully late coming back from visiting her cousin, Karen, so she could dodge Grans and her futile attempt to drag her to the Sunday evening revival service. It was ten o'clock, and Grans would be arriving back home soon. Even though Grans hated the bugs that congregated around the outside porch light, Anisha turned it on so Grans wouldn't have to find the steps in the pitch black darkness.

Anisha nodded on and off during the ten o'clock news. The news was less eventful than the daily murders, traffic accidents, and scandals of Atlanta's newscasts. She dozed off to sleep and was awakened by the doorbell at the front door. That was odd. It couldn't be Grans. She never used the front door.

Anisha looked out the peephole and saw Deacon Norman standing on the porch.

"I was hoping somebody would be here," he said, looking past Anisha and into the house. "Are you here by yourself?"

If someone else had asked her that, Anisha would have been suspicious, but Deacon Norman was a longtime family friend, and she could tell he meant no harm. His face actually looked concerned.

"Yes. I'm waiting for Grans to get home from revival." Anisha looked at his suit and the deacon's badge he was still wearing. "Are you coming from church?"

Deacon Norman put his hand on Anisha's arm. "Get your things and come with me. Your grandmother's been in an accident. They're taking her to the hospital."

"My mama." Anisha scrambled around for her purse, then picked up the kitchen phone. "I've got to call my mama."

Deacon Norman took the phone from Anisha's trembling hand and put it back on the receiver. "We'll call her in the car, and she can meet us there. We've got to go now." His voice was calm but urgent.

"What happened? Tell me what happened."

"Looks like a drunk driver was involved," Deacon Norman said.

He turned out all the lights in the house except in the kitchen, locked the door behind them, and escorted Anisha to his car. The quickest route to the hospital took them past the scene of the accident. A police car was still parked on the shoulder of the curvy country road, his lights on full bright to light the road for the man hooking Grans' car to the tow truck. A mass of twisted metal was being pulled out of the ravine off the shoulder of the road.

The police officer slowly directed Deacon Norman around the wreckage. Anisha pulled off her seat belt and tried to open the locked car door.

Deacon Norman reached over and patted Anisha's knee. "It's all right, baby. It's all right."

Anisha slumped down into the seat. She dialed her mother's number with a shaking hand, then handed the phone to Deacon Norman. She didn't trust her vocal cords to function. She rode dazed until they arrived at the hospital, and the nurse escorted them down the white, sterile corridors to room 248.

The high-pitched beep of the monitor was the only sound in the room. IV tubes ran from a pole and into Grans' arm. A tube ran into her nose from another machine. It didn't make sense for Anisha to see an artificial machine pumping life into a woman who had always been her lifeline. Grans had to feel her strength, so she wiped away the tears before cautiously approaching the hospital bed and picking up Grans' hand.

"Grans. It's 'Nish. I'm here with you. Mama is on the way."

Grans tried to open her eyes but couldn't. Anisha saw a slight gleam from her irises before they closed again. The areas around her eyes were bruised, and a large bandage hung from where they'd tried to cover a gash across her forehead.

A nurse walked over and changed the IV bag. "She's really weak from the accident, anesthesia, and the pain medicine. "

"Can she hear me?" Anisha asked.

"Most likely, but she can't respond."

"Everything's okay, Grans. You'll be fine."

Anisha didn't want to let go of Grans' hand because she needed to feel the warmth of her grandmother's body. It let her know Grans' motionless body still had life.

Mrs. Blake walked into the room with Nikki on her heels. Anisha could tell they'd both been crying on the ride over but had mustered the strength to contain themselves for the entrance into the room. Anisha walked into her mother's embrace and pulled Nikki in with them.

Her mother kept whispering into their ears that it would be okay, and Anisha used every ounce of faith she had to believe it.

"Did you call Travis?" Anisha asked, reaching into her pocket and pulling out a crumpled piece of tissue.

"Yes. But I talked to his roommate and had him drive Travis down. One accident is enough."

They walked to Grans' bedside together. The generations she'd birthed stood on each side and at the foot of her bed to pray. Mrs. Blake rubbed the back of her hand along her mother's face. She closed her eyes and uttered a prayer Anisha couldn't decipher. Anisha covered Grans' hands with one of her own while her mother was praying. She thought she felt a slight squeeze from Grans, but her eyes still didn't open.

A doctor walked into the room and asked to see Mrs. Blake. Anisha started to follow them, but her mother held her hand up and shook her head. Anisha and Nikki stayed by the bedside until their mother peeked inside the hospital room and motioned them into the hallway. Her eyes were swollen again.

"She has a lot of internal injuries, and she's losing a lot of blood. Because of all the damage, they can't perform surgery."

"What does that mean?" Anisha raised her voice and caught the attention of a passing attendant.

"They can't stop her internal bleeding."

"So she's lying in there bleeding to death, and you're telling me there's nothing they can do about it. They're not even going to try?"

Anisha saw her mother's body shiver. "They already did. They rushed her into surgery as soon as she got here, but there's too much bleeding."

Anisha collapsed against the wall and slid down to the floor. She buried her head between her knees. "So what are we supposed to do?"

"Pray."

Anisha wasn't satisfied with that answer, even though she knew it was the best one. If she was going to walk by faith, her prayers couldn't be based on what she saw. The tubes, the oxygen, the heart monitor. She couldn't go back into the room. Not right now.

Anisha grabbed her purse, then followed the maze of corridors back to the emergency room entrance. She went outside, sat on the curb, and tried to steady her fingers long enough to avoid misdialing on her cell phone.

It was nearly midnight, and Sherri's phone was busy. Anisha hoped she hadn't fallen back into dealing with Xavier. She hung up and called again, in case she'd dialed the wrong number. When she got the same response, she tried Sherri's cell, but it went straight into the voice mail. Strange, Anisha thought. Sherri's cell phone was always on.

Anisha's heart ached to call Tyson, but she wouldn't do it. She couldn't. It would only add another layer of pain. Losing him was a different kind of grief, but it was grief just the same.

Anisha saw Pastor Jennings and her great aunt Alice walking up the sidewalk to the emergency room entrance. She turned her head in hopes that they wouldn't notice her, and to her relief they didn't. She didn't feel like being bothered.

By two in the morning, the nurse and doctor had run all but Grans' immediate family out of the room. Anisha's legs were sore from curling her body up into the metal chair in the corner of the room. Anisha sat up and stretched her legs. She looked around the room, lit only by a miniature lamp hanging over the oxygen machine. Travis and Nikki were huddled against the wall in another corner of the room. Nikki was resting her head on Travis's shoulder. The incident had brought out another level of intimacy within their family in the past three hours. Her mother was stretched out in the antiquated pink recliner beside Grans' hospital bed. She had one of the thin bedsheets the nurse had given them balled up under her head.

Anisha stood up to stretch her legs and noticed Grans' eyes open. She wanted to shout and arouse the entire hospital, but Grans shook her head before she could awaken the others.

Anisha leaned over and kissed her gently on the cheek. "How do you feel?" she whispered.

"Not the best."

Anisha shivered at the sound of her grandmother's voice. It was weak, as if the life was dripping out of her.

"When you get out of here, I'm going to cook you a welcome home dinner of all the dishes you've taught me over the past few weeks," Anisha said.

"Lord willing."

Anisha bent over to her grandmother's ear. "Don't talk like that, Grans. God can heal you."

"I know He can. But my life is His to do as He pleases."

"I don't think God will take you away from us, Grans. What would we do without you?"

"Same thing you'd do with me. I've lived a good life."

"Grans, stop it."

"This ol' body ain't nothing but a shell. I'll have eternal life."

"You're saying that 'cause you feel bad. You'll feel better tomorrow."

Grans' voice grew faint. "Stand on faith, baby."

Anisha placed her hand on the top of Grans' head, being careful not to touch the areas that were covered by bandages.

"What's wrong, Grans? Do I need to call the nurse?"

"Just tired. Let me rest my eyes."

E ven though it's not the best thing for me right now in my eyes, I'm having this baby.

Sherri had cancelled her appointment at the abortion clinic. When she was finally stable enough to put a rein on her emotions, she'd decided against it. Whether she would keep the baby or give it up for adoption was the question now. She was sure there were plenty of eager couples who were looking to adopt a newborn.

Sherri pulled in front of the expansive light-brick building. They specialized in comprehensive women's health issues, the brochure said.

Sherri had reasoned with herself all night. She'd turned off the ringer and closed herself up in her room. How could she be responsible for the life of another human being? She barely kept up with her own. She knew the routine from watching her cousins' lives. Some of them had planned to go back to school, but weeks would turn into months, months into years, and years into never.

She'd gotten herself into this, and she was going to have to face it. God put the passion of design inside of her. It had taken this long to uncover it, but this was another obstacle that she would have to overcome. The more she thought about it, maybe it wasn't an obstacle but a blessing. Even if it was a blessing in disguise.

Sherri looked over her shoulder as she got out of the car. She wasn't sure why. Two squirrels darted into her path as she made her way to the front door. The world in its splendor was full of life. She was full of life—literally.

The atmosphere and aura inside even exceeded the frontage of the building. The lobby was alive with fresh greenery, and Impressionistic art hung on the walls.

Sherri thumbed through another clipboard full of medical forms. She checked and signed the numerous medical release and consent forms without bothering to read the small print.

She returned the clipboard to the front desk and found a chair in the corner away from any roaming eyes. She read through old copies of women's magazines until a lady opened the door leading to the back.

"Miss Dawson?" The woman looked over her red-rimmed glasses to see if she detected any movement.

Sherri threw the magazine she'd been looking at back on a table and darted toward the lady, who seemed anxious to make another loud announcement. *Why did she have to call her name so loud in the first place?*

The woman introduced herself as the counselor, and Sherri followed the pear-shaped woman back into a quaint corner office away from the examination rooms.

"Good morning, Ms. Dawson." She extended a wrinkled hand to Sherri. "I'm Marva, and I'll be helping you through your decision to adopt or keep your baby."

Sherri nodded her head. For a person who always had something to say, it seemed she was at a loss for words during her recent visits to the health care clinics.

"I see by your forms you have quite a collection of friends and family that will be able to help you as well."

"Yes," Sherri answered, her voice trembling. She felt faint all of a sudden. Little did the counselor know, Sherri's group of family and friends still weren't privy to the secret she held. Not even her mother.

The counselor paused and looked at Sherri. "Are you okay, Ms. Dawson?"

"Yes. Please go ahead."

"I know this can be an emotional time. If you'd like we can reschedule for another time and you—"

"No," Sherri insisted, sitting forward in the chair and crossing her hands on her lap.

"Is there someone here with you that you'd like to sit in on this part of the session?"

"No. I'll be fine. Please, go ahead."

Marva studied her face a moment before continuing. "Unless or until you find another doctor's office, we'll provide as much support as we can for you, but make sure to keep your support circle involved in this process."

There that word was again. *Support.* The one who was just as responsible as she was was missing in action. He should have been there to be her rock, but Xavier was about as stable as quicksand, and she'd fallen into his miry trap.

"We'll make sure you get the proper vitamins and nutrition during your pregnancy," Marva said. "I hope knowing that we're here to help you with everything will help you relax."

Looking down at Sherri's forms, Marva said, "I see you've indicated that you're interested in adoption. We have a list of African-American couples that are very interested in adopting." She handed Sherri a manila folder stuffed with papers. "Here's a list of things you need to read and complete in order to get started with the adoption process. Would you like to start right away?"

"Yes, please."

Sherri couldn't believe how easily the words flew from her mouth. She still wasn't sure what she wanted to do. She wasn't educated about the legal procedures, but she assumed she was safe as long as she didn't sign anything.

"Being that you're in about your fourth week makes it a good time to get all of the paperwork out of the way so that you can concentrate on staying healthy," Marva said, handing Sherri a video about the adoption process for her to take home. "Let's go ahead and get you set up in the exam room."

Sherri followed Marva down another side hallway and into an exam room. It was completely opposite from the room at the urgent care clinic she'd first visited. The artwork of islands on the wall and the elevator music floating softly throughout the clinic promoted a sense of calm.

Marva left Sherri in the room to change. Sherri slipped into a thin cotton gown and waited what seemed like hours for the routine tap on the door.

"Come in."

Marva peeked around the door, then walked in, followed by a medium-complexion woman with jet black hair. The woman looked to Sherri to be Greek or Italian because of her distinct features.

"This is Dr. Romano," Marva said.

"Hello, Ms. Dawson." The doctor's words rolled off her tongue with a heavy Italian accent. "How are you feeling today?"

"Fine," Sherri said, gripping her gown together at the back.

Dr. Romano proceeded to explain the comprehensive services the clinic would provide to Sherri while Marva listened in. Much of it was repetitive from Marva's session, and hearing it again made the situation even more real.

Sherri reclined on the exam room table and positioned her feet in the stirrups. Her body responded to the doctor's instructions, and she scooted down until the small of her back nearly hung over the edge of the table. With each step, the doctor's reassuring voice commented on how well Sherri was doing.

I really don't want you talking to me right now, Sherri thought.

Sherri tuned out the doctor's voice and tried to focus on the rhythms of the classical music she could faintly hear. Anything as long as it wasn't the doctor's voice or the other voices in her head.

"You're very healthy, and the baby seems to be doing fine in this stage of development," Dr. Romano assured Sherri. "I'm going to schedule you for an ultrasound in the next few weeks so we can keep a watch on the baby's development."

The words left Sherri's mouth before she realized it, pushing through her lips before she had the time to change her mind. Again.

"I'm keeping the baby."

⁂

Sherri walked straight out the clinic door, purposefully ignoring eye contact with anyone in the cozy waiting room. She wondered who else who had come considering adoption would decide to keep the baby as she had. Maybe it was the teenager sitting in the corner with her mother. Or the career woman who seemed irritated because she'd left her in-box full only to encounter another massive heap of paperwork.

Her car must have been on autopilot. It was the only explanation she had as to why she'd made it home safely. She'd been lost in the thoughts of single parenthood. It would be hard, but God would strengthen her.

Sherri buried herself in the bed for a nap. Tomorrow she'd proceed with her life as usual—if usual was possible. Work and class were waiting for her return. Pregnancy was not the end of her life, she thought; it was just the beginning of a new chapter in her life. The circumstances weren't ideal, but her child was still a blessing. God's gift.

Tamara knocked on Sherri's closed door; but didn't wait for an answer. "Is your ringer off or something?" Tamara asked, laying the phone on top of the covers pulled up to Sherri's neck.

"I forgot to turn it back on." Sherri groaned.

"It's Anisha, and she doesn't sound good."

*S*herri rode in the family limousine to the church. She'd heard Grans preach before of the longevity of the Blake family church. St. Paul's had stood on the same property for four generations.

Today Joyce Edgars was being returned to the same grounds she'd tread on as an energetic youth during summer vacation Bible school. Her empty body lay at rest at the same altar where she'd given her spiritual life to the Lord and her physical life to Moses Edgars, III.

Sherri swung open the door to the white stretch limousine and helped the waiting usher assist the family members out of the car and into the church. The family was outfitted mostly in whites, pastels, and bright spring colors. Anisha had insisted on it. The traditional black dress was too morbid. The funeral was supposed to be a celebration of Grans' life on earth and its continuation in heaven.

Sherri and a host of other family and close friends filed in behind the immediate family. The air conditioner pumped laboriously to cool the small church that was packed to capacity with mourners.

The choir began a thunderous praise song as the family neared the open casket. Sherri marveled at the strength Anisha portrayed. Since

Sherri had arrived, she'd watched Anisha become the cornerstone of the family. It was as if Grans had angel-delivered her strength to Anisha from heaven.

Sherri's knees weakened as she approached Grans' coffin. An usher must have noticed her falter, because she felt an arm catch her around the waist and steady her. The shrill of a baby's cry rose above the harmonic singing of the choir and the "amens" and "hallelujahs" from the congregation. Sherri's tears fell for the loss of Grans' life.

Sherri hugged Mrs. Blake and offered her condolences to the family on the front pew. Anisha stood up and grabbed Sherri in a strong embrace. Sherri felt compelled to confess her wrongdoing. How could I have thought Anisha would be judgmental? They lingered together until an usher pulled them apart and led Sherri to the fifth pew. She slid into the pew and tucked her chin to her chest. The usher laid a funeral home fan on her lap, and Sherri used it to cover her face.

Sherri put her hand on her stomach as nausea began to swirl around in her body. Her baby was one less thing Anisha needed to know about right now, but once Sherri saw her best friend, she wasn't sure how long she'd be able to contain herself.

She wiped a tissue down her face as her mouth grew pasty. She'd dropped a small pack of saltines into her purse in case there was a bout of morning sickness. She quietly ripped the package open and slipped one behind the fan and into her mouth.

Sherri kept her head lowered until Pastor Jennings ended his powerful eulogy.

"'For I am already being poured out as a drink offering, and the time of my departure is at hand,'" Pastor Jennings quoted from 2 Timothy. "'I have fought the good fight, I have finished the race, I have kept the faith.' Let all God's people say amen."

❖

The brief interment was held under the funeral home tent out back in the church cemetery. The white casket trimmed in gold was lowered into the ground beside the grave of the late Moses Edgars III.

A line of limousines and cars followed the funeral escort back to Grans' house for the repast. St. Paul's missionary board had arrived at the house early and prepared the dining room to seat and feed the family. The usher board kept the line of visitors moving through the kitchen and filtered them to other parts of the house.

Sherri didn't see Anisha at the family table and couldn't find her milling around outside. She slipped down the hall and noticed Grans' bedroom door closed. If she knew her friend, she had retreated from the crowd to find solace alone. Sherri tapped on the door.

"Who is it?" Anisha asked.

"Sherri. Can I come in?"

"Are you alone?"

"For now. But I won't be if people see me having a conversation with this door."

"Come in."

Sherri eased the door open and squeezed through a small opening. "Are you all right?"

"I had to get away for a minute," Anisha said, getting up and walking over to her grandmother's cherry wood dresser. She picked up a brooch from a jewelry box and ran her fingers along its jagged edge.

Sherri listened as Anisha told her about her last minutes with Grans. She'd slipped into a coma soon after the rest of the family rushed to her bedside and never regained consciousness.

"Stand on faith," Anisha recalled. "That's all I have left to do during times like these. I've got to keep reminding myself that God is in control."

Anisha fastened one of Grans' gold bracelets around her wrist and sat on the bed beside Sherri.

"And remind me," Sherri said.

A dam of tears burst from Sherri's eyes, and she collapsed onto Anisha's lap.

Anisha was struck with confusion and panic at the same time. "Oh, Sherri, what is it?"

Anisha returned to the guest room at her mother's house and handed Sherri a glass of water. She didn't think she'd ever seen her friend cry so much in one day. By the time the interment was over and the last guests had been herded out of Grans' house, it was well past eight o'clock before they went back to the Blake household.

"All of this is a mess. A big junky mess," Sherri cried. She took a sip of water and set the glass on the nightstand. "Some days I feel like my life is over, but I know it's just the Enemy trying to play with my mind."

Anisha searched Sherri's face for an explanation. "Why didn't you even tell me when you found out you were pregnant? You don't have to go through this alone, Sherri. You know I'll help any way I can." Anisha picked up her sobbing friend's hand and rubbed it between her own. "Don't ever think you can't come to me with something. Never, and I mean that."

Sherri sniffed. "I thought I could handle this by myself. I was too ashamed to tell that I'd had sex in the first place."

"Believe me. Everybody's got their own issue."

Sherri guzzled the rest of the water and put the empty glass down by the bed.

"But I was always warning you about Tyson, and I basically talked trash to and about Veronica. Now look who fell."

Anisha pictured Xavier. He was a wolf in sheep's clothing who had pounced on her friend at a time of vulnerability. Fury bullied its way into Anisha's emotions and kicked out forgiveness.

"I can't believe he has three other kids. What a jerk," Anisha hissed. "I never should've tried to hook you two up."

"Don't start, Anisha. There were certainly signs that I chose to ignore. I'm an adult who makes her own decisions. I lay on that bed. I'm the one that compromised. Xavier never claimed to be a man of God. But I do want to be free from the guilt, Anisha. I know it's going to take some time, but I can't live in bondage for the rest of my life."

"And you won't. All this stuff—Xavier, Tyson, the baby, Grans, jobs—all of this is going to make us stronger. God said all things work together, not just the good stuff. We've got to believe it will." Anisha corrected herself. "No. We believe it's already worked out. We've got to walk through what God has already done."

Anisha refilled Sherri's glass of water so she could take another sip. She looked drained.

Enough was enough. Things needed to change. It was time to believe and walk in all God had promised. And even if she had to drag Sherri down destiny's path, she was going with her.

35

"hank You, Lord," Anisha screamed. "Thank You, thank You, thank You." She danced around the couch, gyrating her hips and bouncing her shoulders to the rhythm in her head. Anisha put her Vickie Winans CD on and pumped the tunes throughout the apartment.

Anisha crooned into the end of her television remote control and jumped onto the couch. "I hear the music in the air, I feel like praisin', I feel like dancin'."

Anisha leaped from the couch to the love seat, landing close enough to reach the phone on the kitchen counter. She dialed Sherri's number.

"Hello?"

"Sherri girl, Sherri girl. Faith speaks what it believes."

"What, Anisha? I can barely hear you. Can you turn your music down, please?"

Anisha jumped off the couch and paused the CD player. "Eye Spy Editorial Services called me about my proposal," she said, breathless. "They want to talk to me tomorrow about hiring me as a consultant. I'm about to get my first official client."

"Anisha, that's great," Sherri said. "Can a sista get on the payroll?"

"Can a sista get a check first?"

"I guess I can give you some time. I would come help you celebrate if I didn't have class tonight."

"Don't worry about it. I can enjoy a double scoop of mint chocolate chip ice cream in a waffle bowl by myself."

"Must you rub it in?"

"If you hurry up and finish these classes, then you'll have your own clients to brag about," Anisha said. "Then instead of going out for ice cream, we'll summon the cabana boy to bring two virgin piña coladas with cute little umbrellas out to our lounge chairs on the white sands of Paradise Island, Bahamas."

"You've given me the drive I needed to go to class tonight," Sherri said.

"How's the baby?" Anisha asked.

"We're fine. I haven't felt sick in a few days, and I can get used to that. I'm just more tired than usual. Sometimes it can be hard keeping up with my assignments for class."

Anisha ran a brush through her hair and pinned it out of her face with a clip. "I hope you're not doing too much. Just promise me that you'll take care of yourself and the baby."

"You know I will, Anisha. I won't do anything that will jeopardize my health or the baby's. Even if it means postponing school."

Sherri had decided to stay in school through the end of the semester and then play things by ear. Anisha encouraged her to stay focused on the ultimate goal, not the temporary obstacles.

"Stop by my job when you're done with your meeting tomorrow, and I'll treat you to lunch," Sherri said.

"That's a deal," Anisha promised. "I'll call you when I'm on the way. Talk to you then."

Anisha found the windbreaker that matched her pants, slipped on her gym shoes, and ran out the door. Since Sherri couldn't join her, she'd enjoy an ice cream date with God. She never knew their growing relationship and His love would give her life so much brand-new meaning.

Her taste buds danced in anticipation until the first drop of ice cream fell on her tongue. She sat down under an orange-and-yellow striped umbrella that stood over one of the picnic tables outside. She pulled out the prayer journal she'd stuffed into her bag and turned to where she'd written her daily meditation Scripture. The verse was penned in purple ink across the journal's pages. *But I want you to be without care. He who is unmarried cares for the things of the Lord—how he may please the Lord. But he who is married cares about the things of the world—how he may please his wife. There is a difference between a wife and a virgin. The unmarried woman cares about the things of the Lord, that she may be holy both in body and in spirit.*

Spending her personal time with God and reading the Bible daily had become as important to her as food. She found that the meditation and time in God's Word kept her focused on God's promises.

It also kept Tyson off her mind. Not that she necessarily wanted it that way, but evidently he'd moved on with his life, and she wasn't about to chase him down. She was still recovering from the unexpected blow of their breakup.

Anisha put a pen in the journal to hold her space and went back to enjoying her celebratory treat. The signs of spring welcomed a new season and presented Anisha with a fresh outlook on life. A bird sang a song in a nearby tree. It reminded her of the conversation she'd had with Grans when she'd first got laid off. She bowed her head and offered a silent prayer. *God, thank You for caring for me. Thank You for loving me before I even loved myself. I know You have the perfect plan for my life. Help me to see You in every circumstance in my life, and remind me that You have everything under control.*

A slight breeze blew through and left Anisha with a comforting chill. It wrapped around her body, and Anisha felt God's arms surround her. Lately, she'd been aware that His manifest presence was in everything. Lost in thought, Anisha swirled the ice cream around the waffle bowl.

"Excuse me."

Anisha looked up and saw the face of a handsome man with chiseled features. He looked like a model who had stepped out of a magazine's pages. At first impression, he had a corporate businessman demeanor with a half teaspoon of street to make him interesting.

He flashed a crooked-lipped smile at Anisha. "I couldn't help noticing how bright your face looks. Did you know you have a natural glow?"

Anisha felt her face flush. "Oh, thank you," she said, tucking a strand of hair behind her ear.

"Can I ask you a personal question?" He sat down on the edge of the bench across from Anisha.

"Depends on what it is."

"Don't worry—it's not your social security or bank account number," he said.

Anisha thought the way one side of his lip lifted when he smiled was cute. *Why not entertain the brother for a second? This could prove to be interesting.* "Well, shoot then."

"Are you dating anybody?"

"You could say that."

"Too bad for me," he said. "You're a beautiful woman. Make sure he's good to you."

"All the time," Anisha said. *God is good all the time,* she thought.

"Can you do me a favor?" he asked, standing up and reaching into his pocket.

"Depends on what it is."

"You like playing with me, don't you?" he said, handing her a business card. "If he ever starts acting up, give me a call."

Anisha looked at the card and mused to herself. BRYCE COLEMAN. EYE SPY EDITORIAL SERVICES. PUBLISHING DIVISION. He'd find out soon enough. She tucked the card inside the front pocket of her purse.

"Have a nice day, sweet lady."

"Thanks. You do the same." Anisha watched him walk away. His confident stride reminded her of Tyson. She turned her head abruptly when he suddenly looked back and waved at her. *Caught.* Anisha tried to cover her embarrassment and reached in her purse for her cell phone. In all the excitement, she'd forgotten to call her mother and share the good news.

"Ma, guess what."

"This isn't your mother," Nikki said.

"You shouldn't sound so old. Where's Ma? Tell her to pick up the phone."

"Mother! Your daughter said to tell my old mother to pick up the phone," Nikki yelled from the other end before speaking back to Anisha. "She's coming. How are you down in the ATL?"

"I'm doing as good as can be expected. How about you?"

"I think about Grans all the time. Every time we go up to her house and pack up stuff, I keep expecting her to walk in the door. It's like she's gone on vacation or something."

"I know. I think about her, too, but I keep moving forward because I know she wouldn't want us moping around forever. I'm trying to get back into my routine after being out of town for so long. But at least I was welcomed back with some good news."

"What good news? I need info."

"As soon as your mother comes to the phone I'll tell both of you. What's she doing, anyway?"

"She's on the throne. Give the lady some time."

"More information than I needed to know."

"You asked."

Anisha caught up on the latest family news from her sister until her mother picked up the phone.

"Ma, guess what. I got my first client. Well, they haven't made me an official offer yet, but I know I've got the job in the bag. I'm meeting with them tomorrow."

"Anisha, I am so proud of you. Prayer and persistence pays off doesn't it?"

"I wish Grans had the chance to see this happen," Anisha said. She fingered the cross around her neck that had been one of Grans' favorite necklaces.

"She knows all about it, 'Nish," Nikki cut in. "You know Grans. She's probably trying to tell God how to do His job." Nikki mocked her grandmother's voice. "Now Lord, here's what You need to do if You want Your children to listen."

"Hang up the phone, Nikki," Mrs. Blake said, laughing.

"For what?"

"I need to talk to Anisha."

"I thought I was past the stage when I had to leave the room for adult conversation."

"Hang up the phone, girl," Anisha told Nikki. "I'll call you back later."

Anisha wondered why her mother didn't want to talk in front of her sister.

"What's up, Ma?"

"I wanted to see how you're doing since you got back. I didn't know if Tyson had called or anything."

"No, he hasn't called, but I didn't expect him to. It's okay, Ma. I can't lie and say I don't think about him, but this isn't my first heartbreak. I got through those others, and I'll get through this one too. Hopefully, this will be the last."

"I thought Tyson was different from those other ones."

"He was and he is. Maybe it wasn't meant, Ma. I don't know. I'm trying to keep my mind focused on other things right now."

"Okay, I was just asking. You know you can call me."

"I know, Ma. Love you."

"Love you too. Call me after your meeting tomorrow."

"I will. Bye."

Anisha finished her ice cream, then savored the sweet taste of the waffle bowl. She decided to make a trip to an office supply store to buy a few items for what she was sure would be the first of many freelance projects.

As she strolled through the parking lot, a black car with tinted windows came to a slow crawl beside her and kept pace with her long stride. The driver's window rolled down, and a man much too old for Anisha leaned his head out of the window.

"You sho' looking good today, girl. If I was yo' man, I wouldn't let you out the house alone."

Anisha wasn't the least bit attracted to him, but she welcomed his compliment. It was good to know she hadn't lost it.

"Thank you," she said, adding an extra sway to her step.

"Anytime, cutie. Anytime," he said and pulled off.

❧

Anisha had planned to set up an office space in her living room. She'd already envisioned the items she wanted for the quaint corner and had placed a mental limit on how much she would allow herself to put on her credit card.

The Office Outlet was clearing items for new inventory, and Anisha bought a floor model computer desk with a matching bookshelf and a one-drawer file cabinet at a 75 percent discount. She ended up with more than she'd expected and still came in under budget.

She arranged for delivery of the large items over the weekend, designed and ordered a set of business cards, and walked out with a bag of items to start her office supply inventory.

The roads were free from rush hour traffic, and Anisha was glad she'd made the decision to let the traffic dissipate before attempting to tackle the unpredictable stretch of highway on I-285. She flew along the highway until she saw cars at a dead halt in front of her.

"I don't believe this," Anisha complained, slowing to a stop. From what she could see, a chain reaction had scattered cars across three lanes of I-285. A team of police was trying to route the drivers through the one remaining open lane. Rescue crews on the scene drew the attention of rubberneck drivers in both directions, slowing the recovery process even more.

Anisha reached into her office supply bag and pulled out a book she'd bought on business contracts. From the look of her lane, she wouldn't be moving anytime soon. Anisha flipped through the index and found a topic of interest, determined to make use of her time. She was engrossed in the book until a blaring horn shocked her. She threw the book in the passenger's seat and caught herself before ramming into the car in front of her. Her lane hadn't budged.

The horn blared again, and Anisha found its owner two lanes over, laying on the horn as if his impatience would make the lanes move any faster or urge the policemen to clear a lane especially for him.

"Stupid idiot." Anisha rolled her eyes and picked up her book to find the page she'd lost. *God, help me control my mouth,* she thought as her lane began to inch forward. She put the book on the steering wheel and tried to watch the traffic with one eye on the road and the other on the book. Erring on the side of safety, she finally tossed the book back in the passenger's seat and inched her car's nose between two cars to claim a space in the next lane.

She spotted an SUV two cars in front of her that was identical to Tyson's. The Clark Atlanta University sticker in the window confirmed her suspicions. It had to be him. She rolled down her window to get a clearer view. She saw the small dent on the bottom right of his bumper from where one of the boys at the center had crashed his bike. It had to be him. Anisha inched farther into the lane, ignoring the lady in front of her who was trying to do the same. She'd make up for it and extend courtesy to another driver later.

Anisha pulled forward until her car was nearly perpendicular to Tyson's. She couldn't see directly to the front seat yet, but she didn't have to. The beam on her face barely had time to take residence before it was evicted by a look of disbelief. The little girl with the big eyes sitting in the backseat told the whole story. As Tyson turned around to the backseat, and handed something to the small child, their eyes met for a split second, but she knew it was long enough for him to register what had just happened. She couldn't believe he was going to act like she was invisible.

Anisha's eyes shot to Brandy in the front seat, then back to the road. Her bottom lip trembled, and her eyes glazed over. *Hold it together. You can't break. Not now.* She determined not to drop a single, solitary tear.

Anisha's emotions leaped from hurt to fury and back again. Emotions crashed around in her heart, each one determined to wrestle its way to the surface before the other. *Not now. Not now.*

✾

Anisha ran into her apartment. Her chest felt tight. The pressure was stealing her breath. She concentrated on each slow inhale and exhale until her breathing regulated and she no longer felt light-headed. Her eyes were so clouded with tears she could barely see the wicks on the candles she was attempting to light. She turned off the lights in the apartment until only the flickering flames illuminated it.

"God, I need You so much." Anisha paced around the living room, hands lifted. "I can't do this by myself. If You don't touch me, I can't be touched. If You don't heal me, I can't be healed. All I want is a deeper relationship with You. Nothing else matters. This is painful, and the fire in my life seems like it gets turned up with every bend and turn. But I'm not giving up. I'm not getting out until I'm who You want me to be."

Anisha lost control of her muscles and dropped to the floor. She knew it was wrong, but she wished the worst on Tyson. He'd lied to her. He knew the real reason he wanted to break up. *He hurt Your daughter, God, and I want You to get him good,* Anisha thought. Her body shuddered with heavy sobs. She tried to wipe away the flow, but it was useless.

Anisha looked at the clock. It was ten o'clock. Evidently she'd cried herself to sleep for over two hours.

Sister Davenport.

Sister Davenport? The name that popped into her head didn't make sense at a time like this. Anisha hadn't really talked to her since the gala in December. Before she hadn't made the time, and considering her and Tyson's breakup, it was far too awkward now. Had Sister Davenport been on her subconscious mind for some reason? She didn't want to be rude by calling the Davenports' house at this hour on a weekday, but she couldn't shake the feeling urging her to pick up the phone.

Did they know what was going on? Had Tyson taken Brandy to their house for dinner? The thought of the different scenarios Anisha could concoct in her mind rose again. She dialed the number before she had time to change her mind and hoped she wasn't waking them. She was relieved Sister Davenport answered the phone instead of her husband.

The sound of Sister Davenport's voice opened Anisha's vault of tears again. She summarized the story as quickly as she could. The pain grew deeper with each moment she relived, from the first time she saw Brandy, to seeing Brandy at the Labor Day cookout, to that night.

Sister Davenport had been clueless. According to her, Tyson's visits to her house had been rare since the beginning of the year. Her husband had told her that Tyson hadn't been to church as much, and at times he seemed to even shirk their friendship and bonding time together with the deacon.

"Can you get yourself together enough to come over?" Sister Davenport asked.

"Now?" Anisha asked, puzzled.

"Yes," Sister Davenport answered. Her voice was more serious than Anisha had ever heard.

Anisha agreed and went into the bathroom to wash her face. Somehow her hair was wet from tears and had fallen out of the clip she'd pinned it up with earlier. She pushed it back with a headband and headed for the door. She could barely see in the dark and tripped over her office supply bag in the middle of the floor.

This blow won't take me down for the count, Anisha promised herself.

Life in her own eyes was crumbling around her, but she was determined to stand. Stand on faith. God gave her a timeless word before Grans' death. In her weakness, Anisha knew she could rely on God's strength.

Anisha pulled into the Davenports' driveway and knew her decision to call Sister Davenport must have been led by the Holy Spirit. The presence of the Lord welcomed her there, and she already felt revived. She stepped out of the car, and the motion light on the side of the house illuminated the walkway up to the front door. Anisha heard a noise and turned to see the garage door slowly lifting. She walked back into the garage and saw Sister Davenport peeking from the door that led inside the house.

"Come in this way," Sister Davenport said.

Sister Davenport was always so elegant that Anisha never imagined she'd ever look less than perfect. The late-night-at-home Sister Davenport had a face scrubbed free of makeup and a scarf wrapped around her head to preserve her style between weekly salon visits. Her light blue silk robe fell to her toes and danced across the floor as she led Anisha into the living room.

"I'm glad you came," she said, hugging Anisha and directing her to sit on the couch. Sister Davenport sat down beside her and took

Anisha's hand. "You made the call, but I know it was God who sent you here tonight."

"Me too. I was thinking the same thing on the way over." She wiped a tear that escaped her eye. "I'm sorry. I thought I was all cried out."

"There's a verse in the Bible—in Psalms I believe—where David had cried so hard that he told God to put his tears in a bottle, because he knows God keeps count of them," Sister Davenport said.

"Well, God must be working overtime with me tonight," Anisha said, accepting a tissue from Sister Davenport. "I thought what I was going through was enough."

"God has given me a powerful testimony on forgiveness, Anisha, and this test you're going through will give you a testimony too. But our experiences are not just to perfect us, even though they do. They're to strengthen others too."

Anisha nestled into the couch, wondering what Sister Davenport could possibly have to disclose that was so important that she needed to summon Anisha over to her house.

"The first time you came to dinner with Tyson, you were admiring the pictures in the family room of my girls."

Anisha nodded her head, pulling the day from her memory bank. "I remember."

"Yolanda and Raquel are my pride and joy, but it hasn't always been that way."

Anisha was stunned but tried to prevent her face from showing it.

Sister Davenport continued, looking Anisha straight in the eyes. "I've accepted them both as my daughters now, but Yolanda isn't my and Russell's biological daughter together. He cheated on me a year into our marriage and got another woman pregnant. A married woman, working in his office at the time."

Anisha shifted in her seat. At first she was uncomfortable with the confession, but Sister Davenport didn't seem to mind that she was baring her heart and soul.

"A month after Raquel was born, Russell dropped the bomb on me about Marcelle—that was her name—having his baby. It's the worst thing I've endured in my life, and I wouldn't wish it on my worst enemy. I spent years questioning my marriage and my self-esteem."

Sister Davenport peeled off another layer of her life.

"Russell and I didn't have a relationship with God when all this happened. We only went to church like it was an obligation or when it was convenient. I didn't know much about God and His Word at the time, but I'd picked up enough over the years to know only God could save our marriage. Every time I looked at my husband, I saw a lie. He would crawl into bed at night, and I'd envision him with Marcelle. The picture was vivid since I knew who the other woman was. I didn't have to create an image of what the woman looked like in my mind, because I already knew. She and her husband had sat at my table."

Anisha listened intently as the layers kept falling off.

"To make a very long story short, our counseling sessions became the crust that held our marriage together. Our counseling minister helped us work out child support and visitation, and I thought we'd made it over the last hump, until . . ."

Until? Anisha's mind raced, but she couldn't fathom a scenario any worse than the one unfolding.

". . . Marcelle called us and said she needed to talk to us. She came over that night and had Yolanda dressed in yellow pajamas. I'll never forget how much she looked like Raquel. They were both the spitting image of Russell."

Sister Davenport sat back on the sofa and readjusted the belt on her robe.

"Her husband couldn't stand the sight of Yolanda. He said he re-lived the infidelity every time he looked at her face. He made Marcelle choose between the baby and their marriage. Her choice was clear, because Yolanda's clothes were already packed in Marcelle's trunk. And as much as I hated to do it, I couldn't bring myself to abandon an innocent child."

Anisha shook her head. Her heart ached for the suffering Sister Davenport had endured. It had to be God who'd allowed her to share her story without breaking down. Looking at the virtuous woman across from her, she'd never imagined Sister Davenport's life had once been so complicated and full of drama. She couldn't imagine Deacon Davenport tipping out on his wife. Not the man Anisha knew now.

"Do you know how I was able to let God work in my life and in my marriage?" Sister Davenport asked. "Forgiveness. Despite what you feel about Tyson and how he's hurt you, you've got to forgive and pray for him."

Now that's going a little too far, Anisha thought. "I can work to forgive Tyson, but somebody else can pray for him. If he needs prayer, let Brandy do it. She's the one he wants to be with. I don't think I should be expected to pray for him."

"Is it about what you want or what God commands? I prayed for Russell, and God humbled me to the point that I prayed for Marcelle and her family too."

"That's different. You were married to Deac so you didn't have a choice."

"I had a choice. I could've taken Raquel and walked away to start another life without him. Collected my child support check and been done with it."

The force to Anisha's chest felt like the hind legs of a stallion had kicked her.

"Do you know how much I've been through over the last few months?" Anisha wanted to scream, but she kept her calm. The words choked her throat on the way out, and she had to stop to catch her breath. "I did what I thought I heard God say to do, and Tyson walked out of my life. I've lost my job and my grandmother. And this whole time, I keep praying and telling God I'm not going to quit. How many blows am I going to have to take? What did I do to deserve this punishment?"

Sister Davenport handed Anisha another tissue. "Do you think the Enemy would be on your back if he didn't consider you a threat to his plans? If you weren't getting so close to your destiny, he wouldn't be concerned. Think about Job. God was so confident about Job that He *told* the devil to take a stab at him. I mean God literally gave permission for the Enemy to test Job, because He knew regardless of what Satan threw at him, Job would never falter in his belief. He'd never denounce God and turn away. And when Job had been struck with every possible thing imaginable and withstood the test, God gave him twice as much as he had before."

Sister Davenport reached inside the coffee table drawer and pulled out the large family Bible. "Let me share a verse with you I kept hidden in my heart when I was going through affliction with my husband," she said, flipping the large, yellowed pages to Romans 8:18.

"For I consider that the sufferings of this present time are not worthy to be compared with the glory which shall be revealed in us."

Sister Davenport pulled Anisha into a tight embrace.

Anisha wanted to draw herself up into a ball. She laid her head on Sister Davenport's lap and felt the woman God had called to minister to her put her hands on her head.

Sister Davenport called out a mighty prayer over Anisha's life before they prayed together for Tyson. Even if they weren't together as a couple, Anisha realized the responsibility she had to cover him in prayer as a brother in Christ. She'd learned from Sherri's experience that you never knew what a person was going through.

*T*yson added another twenty pounds to his exercise bar and slid onto the weight bench. The weight of stress in his life made the bar heavier than he remembered.

Time had moved in slow motion since that evening. It seemed the hour should be nearing at least three in the morning, but it was just nearing eleven o'clock that night.

Seeing Anisha brought back the feelings he'd tried to ignore. Anisha was all the woman he'd ever needed, and he'd let his selfishness overrule what God had spoken to him. Anisha was not Brandy. She hadn't chosen another man over him. She'd chosen God. If she was guilty of anything, it was for following the leading of God's voice when He needed her to find her identity in Him. How could he blame her when he'd had to do it himself for an entire year?

His actions could very well end up costing him the love of his life. Now he'd thrust himself into another woman's life whose heart he'd end up breaking. Not to mention the fact that Ayana had already grown attached to him.

He was ashamed he hadn't had the guts to acknowledge Anisha.

Not a wave. Not a smile. Another mistake. Only God Himself could persuade Anisha to forgive him, and he prayed God would grant him that favor.

Tyson abandoned his weights and surfed through the sports and news channels on television, but nothing caught his interest.

"Man, this situation is so jacked up. What was I thinking?"

Anisha brought balance to his life. She challenged his spiritual growth and encouraged him to be a better man. A godly man. She'd believed in his vision and never questioned his ideas when the odds seemed impossible. She saw him through the eyes of faith.

Brandy hadn't even mentioned anything about church so far. The only time they prayed together was before meals. She never asked why he hadn't been to church lately and hadn't even bothered to go herself. She rarely asked about his day at the center. She wasn't concerned about the lives of any of the boys and could care less whether Jerome was in or out of the detention center. She wasn't the one. She was nice, and Tyson was sure she cared about him as a person, but it didn't change the fact that she wasn't Anisha. If he kept things up at this rate, it would only lead him to a path of misery.

He knew Brandy had sensed his reserve. She'd tried to force conversation out of him for the rest of the night, but he wasn't in the mood to talk. Unless it was to Anisha.

Sherri had left him a message about Anisha's grandmother, but he'd been too caught up to respond. When Anisha needed him, he wasn't there. Anisha was a strong woman who knew what she wanted in a man. After the way he'd treated her and all he'd done, it probably wasn't him.

Tyson picked up the phone and called Brandy to see if he could stop by. Maybe to make up for the way he'd dumped Anisha over the phone. His father had taught him a man was accountable for every woman's feelings he encountered. Going to Brandy's house was going to be the responsible, though difficult, thing to do.

Brandy tried to slide into Tyson's arms when she opened the door. She looked at him with confusion in her eyes when he patted her back as if she was one of his clients.

"I could tell something was on your mind tonight," she said, sitting on the couch and sliding over so Tyson could have space. "Is there something I can do?"

"Understand."

"Understand what?

Tyson didn't want to sit down. He stood up and looked down at Brandy. He wanted to be out of swinging range in case she decided to unleash one in his direction. Hurt could drive a woman to act out of character.

"When you walked into the center that day, it was the last thing I expected. I was vulnerable at the time and feeling rejected."

"You don't think it was meant for us to see each other again? Look how many times we'd run into each other before."

"I don't think it was a coincidence that we ran into each other after all this time. But now I can look back and see it wasn't in order for us to get back together. It was to close some doors in our lives so we could heal and move on. So I could move on."

Brandy stood up and tried to hug Tyson. He pulled away and gently sat her back down on the couch. "I think I saw this as a chance to prove to you that I'm the man now that I wasn't six years ago. I walked into your life when I shouldn't have, and I'm sorry."

"I loved Anisha," Tyson said, then corrected himself. "I *love* Anisha. And when I saw her tonight—"

"You saw her tonight? You went to try and fix things with her before you came over here?" Brandy walked down the hall to close her bedroom door where Ayana was sleeping. Tyson took it as a sign that things were about to escalate. Maybe he should've called her on the phone after all.

"It wasn't like that. We passed by her on the highway earlier tonight," Tyson explained. "She looked me straight in my face, and I turned away like I didn't know her. It's been killing me all this time. That's why I didn't have much to say earlier. I can't get her off of my mind."

Brandy got up again and walked toward the kitchen. Tyson didn't know if he should step closer to the door in case she came back with a knife. He didn't remember her being crazy, but there was a thin line between love and hate. And it looked like hate was brewing in her eyes.

Brandy pulled a paper towel off the roll and ran it under the faucet. She pressed the wet towel to her face, and when she turned around, Tyson saw she was crying. Maybe it wasn't hate he'd seen in her eyes but dejection.

"I know this is hard for you to hear, but it's better I come to you now instead of dragging out something that's not there."

Tyson put his hand on the doorknob and knew that when he was on the other side of the door, it would be forever.

Brandy threw her soggy paper towel in the trash and walked over closer to him.

"Don't you think God wanted us back together? After all this time—"

Tyson held his hand up and stopped her in midsentence. "Don't try to bring up God's name now. This is the first time you've mentioned Him all this time, and I'm not falling for the manipulation. Not anymore."

Brandy tried again to nuzzle herself into his arms again. "So you'd rather love someone who might not even take you back?"

Tyson forcefully, but gently, pushed her away. He turned the knob and opened the door. "It's a chance I'll have to take."

Tyson closed the door behind him, an act he should have done years before.

Sherri was grateful for a friend like Anisha. They needed a strong sisterhood and each other's shoulder to lean on, especially during times like these. She couldn't imagine how Anisha felt seeing Tyson with Brandy. She was sorry Anisha had to endure attack after attack, but Sherri knew God would pull her through.

From what Sherri knew about Tyson, all of his actions lately seemed to be out of character. If he was a player and hadn't really cared about Anisha, he'd pulled the wool over everybody's eyes. But Sherri couldn't believe Tyson was doing these things on purpose. The Sherri-from-back-in-the-day would've called him and told him what he could do, but the right-now Sherri knew God would set Tyson straight. She wanted God's will for his life and prayed for God's perfect will in his and Anisha's lives together.

Despite her disgust with Tyson's actions, Sherri couldn't find peace in saying things were over between him and her best friend. Something inside of her told her differently. If she was right, God would confirm it to Anisha.

Sherri opened her Bible to the Scripture Sister Davenport had shared with Anisha the night before. She and Anisha had started memorizing Scriptures together. Their minds were full of ammunition to fire whenever the Enemy tried to discourage their souls. And they determined not to go down without a fight.

Sherri reviewed Romans 8:18, then settled onto the living room couch for a power nap. It was another twenty minutes before she had to leave for class. The baby was draining every ounce of strength she had, not to mention the mental toll taken on her body from always thinking about how she was going to talk to her roommates. She wasn't at the stage where she was starting to show, so she had a little time before her body began to spill her secrets. When it was all said and done, it probably wouldn't be as bad as she expected. Her conversation with her mother was nothing like she'd thought.

Veronica approached Sherri in the living room.

"There's something you should know," Veronica said.

"What? I want to take a quick nap before I have to leave for class. Can it wait?"

"I borrowed your purse. The one with all the pockets and zippers inside."

"When?" Sherri said.

"While you were gone to Anisha's grandmother's funeral."

"Okay. Throw it on the bed. I'll get it later."

"No, you don't understand," Veronica said. "It wasn't empty. I found these."

Sherri jolted up so she could get a look at what was so pressing. Veronica tossed the brochures Dr. McIntire had given Sherri on the coffee table.

"I know everything. I know you're pregnant."

Sherri stared at the carpet, and her breathing grew rapid. Her sin had been exposed to the one person she wished she could have kept it hidden from until she was ready to disclose it herself. She couldn't look Veronica in the eye. She'd talked so much trash about her laying up with men, and the evidence of her own fall was scattered across the table.

"The week of throwing up," Veronica said. "The crying."

Sherri's humiliation disguised itself as rage. "Okay, I did it. I slept with Xavier, and I got pregnant. He got me pregnant and didn't want to deal with me. Are you satisfied? Is that what you want to hear? You have your gossip for today, so laugh your butt off and get out of my face."

Veronica stared emptily while Sherri went on with her tirade.

Sherri flung her blanket on the floor and started to storm into her room. She turned around and picked up the blanket.

"And oh, by the way, I'm keeping the baby," she said, her voice rising with every word. "I went against everything I preach and everything I know to be right, and I got caught. My façade for you as Ms. Perfect Little Christian has been ripped off. But nothing you say to me can hurt me more than I already feel. No one who's never been through this can understand."

Veronica approached Sherri toe-to-toe and added a voice to the shouting match.

"Don't tell me I don't understand. You don't even know me anymore, and you haven't tried to know me for years. I know about getting pregnant. In fact, I know about it two times over, Sherri. I've had two miscarriages, and I was going to have an abortion with the second one. I was on my way to the clinic, but I miscarried on the way. Do you understand how it feels not to be able to have children?"

The shock knocked the steam from Sherri's fury. Tears poured down her face. "I'm sorry, Veronica," was all she could manage to say.

Veronica crumpled on the couch and released years of pent-up frustration, regret, and weight from carrying secrets.

A key turned in the lock, and Tamara opened the door.

"What happened?" Tamara said, eyeing the brochures on the coffee table. She picked them up and looked at her roommates. "Somebody tell me what's going on."

After they filled Tamara in on the afternoon's drama, they sat on the floor staring at each another.

Tamara was the first to speak after minutes of silence. "Granted, our friendship hasn't been as close as it could be, but I still love you guys more than you know. We've all grown and changed, but my love hasn't changed for you. This won't change my love for you. I can't claim to know what you're feeling, because it's something that's never happened to me."

Veronica's mascara coated her face and left black tracks down her cheeks. "Can we pray?" she asked.

"Yes," Tamara said, holding out her hands to Veronica.

Sherri had thought she'd be the one expected to pray, but it was a nice relief to see Tamara step up to the plate. The change God had made in her life was apparent. She was getting up and going to the early service every Sunday on her own.

"I have one more thing I want to share," Veronica said, getting up and walking back to her room after Tamara prayed. She returned with a pamphlet in her hand.

"Not another brochure." Sherri giggled to break the tension. "Those things have caused a lot of trouble for me today."

"Not this one," Veronica said, handing it to her. "A counselor at one of the abortion clinics gave it to me years ago and I always kept it. It's some place called Angel's Haven, up in the mountains. It's a retreat center for women who've had abortions, single expectant mothers, rape victims, and women who've experienced miscarriages. I've never had the guts to go."

Sherri opened the glossy pages of the brochure while Veronica told her about the center.

"They talk about healing the complete person and seeing yourself through God's eyes. That kind of thing. I'm not sure if I'm ready for all that deep stuff, but you'd probably like it."

"Why don't we go together?" Sherri asked optimistically.

"How about you go first and let me know how it is?" Veronica suggested.

"I might do that."

Tamara stood up and held open her arms. "Group hug?"

"Leave it up to you to be cheesy at a time like this," Veronica said, joining the embrace of her friends.

Tamara's eyes lit up. "Why don't we all go to the women's service tomorrow night at church?"

Veronica shook her head and broke away from the group. "And watch lightning strike the church when I walk in? I don't think so."

"Come on," Sherri pleaded. "Why not? You'll enjoy yourself."

"Don't you have class?"

"Bump class tomorrow. I'll go early and turn in my assignment. This is much more important to me."

Sherri made plans to meet Veronica and Tamara at the church the next night. In one day, the years of rift in their friendship had been restored. Her meditation Scripture for the day popped back into her head. *God's glory has definitely been revealed today.*

*T*he main floor of the sanctuary was packed with women hungry for the presence of God. First Lady Armstrong never had to worry about a scarce attendance when she called a special worship service for the women. It was a time when the women could leave their husbands, children, and jobs behind and lie undisturbed at the Father's feet.

The Grace Worship Women's Choir wore their white robes with the gold accents for the service. When they lifted and swayed their hands in praise, Anisha noticed how the sleeves of the robes looked like fluttering wings on a dove. The women singing in unison and the congregation in one accord lifted Anisha's spirits. There was nothing like worshiping with her sisters.

She looked at the end of the row, still amazed that Veronica was sitting on the other side of Sherri. She may not have believed it if she hadn't seen it with her own eyes. But then again, God was still in the miracle-working business.

Veronica didn't know the words to the songs, but Anisha could tell she was still enjoying praise and worship. She rocked with enthusiasm and picked up the words to the chorus every now and then.

After praise and worship and offering, First Lady Armstrong approached the podium. She wasn't as loud and aggressive as her husband, but her meek and humble spirit demanded the same level of respect. The ladies greeted her with a standing ovation and cheered with an even louder roar of applause when she announced that a committee was planning for the Women's Retreat to be in Paradise Island, Bahamas, the next year.

Anisha glanced down at the end of the row at Sherri and smiled. They'd already envisioned themselves there. It was only a matter of time until their travels around the world would be a regular occurrence. There was so much more the world had to offer besides the East Coast life. Africa, Spain, Australia. They planned to see it all.

As the first lady finished the announcements, Pastor Armstrong walked through the side door and to the pulpit. It was evident by the look on his wife's face that his appearance was unexpected. He gave her a kiss on the cheek, and she handed him the microphone.

"I know you all weren't expecting me here," he said. "I saw the 'No Men Allowed' signs somebody put on the front doors."

Laughter rolled through the sanctuary.

"But I couldn't help myself, because the Lord gave me a quick word to say to the women tonight. For months, I've been carrying such a heavy burden for the women, and God has been showing me some of the things you all have been going through." Pastor Armstrong took the cordless mike and walked from the pulpit down to the floor.

"God has placed so much power in women, but there are so many women getting lost in emotional pain. Ladies, it's time to step out of your pain and go and pull others out of theirs."

Anisha waved her hand in the air and joined in the chorus of "Amens" and "Say it, Pastor." She wished Sherri was sitting closer to her. Pastor was saying exactly what they'd been talking about earlier that morning. Sherri must have felt the same way, because when Anisha looked down the row at her, Sherri gave her a thumbs-up sign.

Anisha looked beside Sherri at Veronica. Her eyes darted around the sanctuary as Pastor Armstrong walked down the aisle and stopped beside her pew. He placed his hand on Veronica's shoulder as he addressed the women.

Before Pastor Armstrong continued, he paused and looked into Veronica's eyes. He rested his hand on her shoulder and mumbled an inaudible prayer before walking away and going back to the pulpit. Veronica slouched down in the pew and covered her face. Anisha dug in her purse for a tissue and passed it down to the end of the row.

"When you travail in prayer, God will sensitize you to His thoughts and His heart." Pastor Armstrong dropped his tone and carried softness on his voice, as if he felt the pain of the women in his congregation. "But like I've been preaching for months, remember, it's not about you; it's about God and His divine purpose through your life. So instead of crying, rejoice. God has a great plan for your life, so don't get paralyzed in your situations. All things work together for your good," Pastor Armstrong said to the shouts of praise in the sanctuary. "And your situation can turn around," he said, snapping his fingers, "suddenly."

The guest speaker accepted the microphone from Pastor Armstrong and said to the ladies, "I think we can go ahead and hold the call for salvation and benediction now, can't we? What a blessing it is to have a true man of God in the house," she said, opening her Bible and reciting the Scriptures she would use during her lesson for the women.

By the time the service was dismissed, Anisha felt revived all over again. Her intimate relationship with God had catapulted to another level over the past three months. She had and would continue to endure the fire that was sealing God's purpose in her life. Her meditation Scripture for the day pushed to the forefront of her mind. *But now, O Lord, You are our Father; we are the clay, and You our potter; and all we are the work of Your hand.*

Anisha signaled to her crew that she would meet them in the vestibule because she needed to find Sister Davenport. Sister Davenport wanted to share a book with her about the power of prayer.

She walked over to where Sister Davenport was chatting with a group of the other deacons' wives. Sister Davenport excused herself from the conversation when she spotted Anisha.

"As soon as I saw you, I realized I forgot the book I promised to bring you. Can you swing by tomorrow and pick it up?"

"Sure," Anisha said, admiring the diamond tennis bracelet on Sister Davenport's arm and feeling her own empty wrist. It reminded her of the bracelet Tyson had bought for her. *Because we're not together doesn't mean I shouldn't wear it.*

"Another company called me today for an interview, so I'm meeting them tomorrow. Things are happening so fast, but I'm more than ready."

"I know you are. And you deserve it. You've been faithful, and God honors that."

Sister Davenport wrapped her arm around Anisha's waist and guided her up the aisle and farther away from the crowd. "Have you been praying for Tyson? I really believe that's a key to another breakthrough in your life."

"It was hard at first. But the more I pray, the easier it becomes." Anisha hesitated before asking, "Have you seen him?"

"No, I haven't seen him, but he actually called Russell not too long after you left the other night. Russell left the room, so I have no idea what was going on."

"I know it's wrong for me to say this, but I don't want Brandy to take my place with you."

"Nobody can take your place," Sister Davenport said. "I think this Brandy thing is a phase. Tyson's eyes will be open soon enough. You know how hard we prayed for him the other day. Prayer changes things."

Anisha had thrown the situation with Tyson as far to the back of her mind as possible. Probably as a coping mechanism, she'd decided. But as her prayers for him increased, she realized how much she really cared for him. Brandy or no Brandy, as a woman of God, it was her duty to pray for her brothers.

"I'll definitely be by to pick up that book," Anisha said. "See you tomorrow."

⊰※⊱

Jerome was at it again, and Tyson needed to call Deacon Davenport to postpone his visit. He had a lot to get off his chest. About skipping out on church. To apologize for shirking his father figure. About Anisha. He brought Jerome into his office, and the defiant youth plopped down into a chair while Tyson called the deacon.

"What's up, Deac?" Tyson signaled for Jerome to get his feet off of the table in front of him and to sit up straight.

"Nothing much," Deacon Davenport answered. "You on your way?"

"Not now. I've got a situation to handle at the center," Tyson said, his eyes piercing through Jerome's attitude. "Can we hook up tomorrow?"

"That'll work."

"Tell your wife I said hello."

"Will do. She's at the church for some kind of woman's program tonight, so I had a chance to watch my Westerns in peace. A man can't get a night of peace without the wifey wanting to change the channel to some romance movie or makeover show."

"You're too much, Deac."

"I pick on my wife, man, but I wouldn't trade her for the world. If you can find a woman like her, I wouldn't let her go."

Tyson flinched at Deacon Davenport's words. He'd found a woman like that and foolishly let her go. But he was going to do whatever it took, for however long it took, to get her back.

"See you tomorrow, Deac."

"Okay," Deacon Davenport said. "And, oh yeah, speaking of good women, I think Anisha stopped by here last night."

"She did?" Tyson said, hoping the deacon would volunteer more information.

"It sounded like her voice, but I didn't see who it was because I was upstairs."

"If you see her anytime soon, tell her I said hello," Tyson said.

"Why don't you call and check on her yourself?"

"I don't know how she'll react. I've put her through so much," Tyson admitted. "I've been praying that God would let our paths cross when it's time." *And I hope it'll be soon.*

With two contracts under her belt now, Anisha felt anything was possible. She believed she could probably fly if she set her mind to it. First, Eye Spy Editorial Services, and now the Caring Hands Foundation. At this rate, her clientele list would grow by leaps and bounds by the end of the year. She'd be able to call her former colleague Katherine after all. On the same day she ended up being laid off, Anisha had spoken about owning her own business. She was now doing what she believed God designed for her life.

Anisha pumped the tunes of the gospel station throughout the car. *Heck, why not share it with the world?* she thought, rolling down her windows, heading down the stretch of Interstate 20 on her way to the Davenports' house. Her oldies but goodies station was all right every now and then, but she dare not pass up the chance to give God praise.

The ride to the Davenports' was prolonged by yet another traffic jam, but Anisha wasn't fazed by it. She wouldn't have to endure the early morning traffic on a regular basis, because she'd be working from the comfort of her own home. Anisha rolled slowly through the Cascade Heights subdivision, admiring the houses. She was prepared for whatever the world could throw at her—except Tyson's car sitting in the Davenports' driveway.

Had this been a deliberate setup? There was no way, no how, she was going inside the Davenports' to face Tyson and anyone he may have brought with him. Anisha rummaged through her attaché for her cell phone, then called Sister Davenport from the driveway. If she wanted her to have the book, she'd have to bring it outside.

"Anisha?" Sister Davenport must have recognized her cell phone number on the caller ID.

"Yes?"

"I know what you're thinking, and this was not planned. Tyson showed up to see Russell, and I had no idea he was going to be here."

"I don't want to come inside, so can you run the book out to me?"

"Are you sure you don't want to come in and at least say hi? He's here alone."

"I'm sure. It's best this way. I don't want to make him uncomfortable, and I certainly don't want to deal with the aftermath of any feelings on my part."

"Okay. Well, let me—" Sister Davenport dropped the conversation and seemed to be distracted. "You too, baby. It was good seeing you. Don't be a stranger." She rushed to get her words together, but her warning didn't beat what was about to take place.

"Anisha, Tyson is—"

"—coming out the front door," Anisha finished.

Anisha didn't know whether she should stay in the car and ignore him until he drove away or get out of the car and confront him.

It wasn't her choice to make. Tyson left Deacon Davenport's side and practically tripped over his own feet making his way to Anisha. He stopped and stood in front of her car, as if his presence there would deter her from leaving. All she had to do was throw the car in reverse and be gone.

Anisha looked at Tyson, to Deacon Davenport's astonished face in the driveway, and to Sister Davenport who'd made her way to the front porch and was standing with a book in hand. She put the car in park and turned it off. She wasn't sure how long she would've been frozen there if Tyson hadn't taken the first cautious steps toward her door and opened it. She let him.

It's okay.

Tyson spoke low and soft as if a sudden movement would make Anisha bolt away from him forever.

"Can we talk?" His eyes pleaded for her to say yes. "For a minute. Please."

Anisha couldn't make her lips respond in order to say what she was thinking. Her emotions converged, and she wanted to smack him, yell, cry, and fall into his arms, all at the same time.

She followed Tyson into the house and walked into the family room. Sister Davenport stood at the door until Anisha nodded her head and motioned that things were fine. Deacon Davenport put his arm around his wife's waist and led her from her watchful guard.

Anisha wanted to look past Tyson's soft brown eyes and find a man she didn't care for. She wanted to uncover the scheme of a man who'd intentionally deceived her. But she couldn't. He sat before her as a godly man who'd made a mistake and come seeking forgiveness. The prayers she'd prayed for him over the last couple of days covered him in grace and mercy.

"I'm sorry." Tyson barely spoke above a whisper.

The words broke Anisha's thick-skinned attempt to act nonchalant. She nervously twirled the diamond tennis bracelet around her wrist. Of all days, she'd decided to start wearing it again today. It was like the bracelet had sent out a beacon signal and led him to her.

Tyson shifted in his seat and leaned forward as if he wanted to reach for her. Anisha balled her hands up in her lap. If she felt his touch, it would melt away the rest of her indifference.

"I'm sorry for my selfishness; I'm sorry for treating you the way I did; I'm sorry for not understanding you needed your space; I'm sorry for not being there for Grans' funeral. I'm sorry for everything." Tyson took his finger and raised Anisha's lowered chin. "Everything."

"I don't know what you're looking for me to say. Of all the times

I've rehearsed a speech in my mind for if I ever got a chance to tell you off, I can't put the words together now," Anisha said, finally finding the courage to stare Tyson in the eyes. "You hurt me. Point-blank. Maybe I trusted you with my feelings too much. And too soon."

"I don't want you to feel that way."

"Well, you should've thought about that beforehand." A single tear trickled down her cheek.

Tyson sighed deeply. Anisha knew he wasn't used to her being cold toward him. It took him a second to accept the chill of her words.

"I came by here to talk to Deacon Davenport about how bad I'd messed everything up. I tried to pretend everything was fine, but when I saw you the other day—even for that brief moment—I realized my future was driving away. And I was riding in the car entertaining my past."

"How did you look me straight in the face and pretend I didn't exist?" She held her hand up before he could answer. "It doesn't matter. There's no excuse you can give me. None."

"What do I have to do to get you to forgive me?"

"I've forgiven you already, but you've got to earn your trust back from me."

"I'll do whatever it takes."

"I can't say how long that will take. I can't even say it will ever happen."

"I can accept that." Tyson slid to one knee in front of the couch and held out his hand. "Can friends pray together?"

He knows how to work it, doesn't he, Lord? I'll put this in Your hands.

Pray with him.

Anisha adjusted her skirt, and Tyson helped her kneel down in front of the couch. She prayed silently to herself as Tyson led her to the throne of the King.

She wished these episodes between them hadn't happened. She wished they were praying under different circumstances. But God was sovereign, and He knew what needed to happen to mold both her and

Tyson into whom He'd destined for them to be. Their individual lives and their future together—if there was one—were in His hands.

Sister Davenport must've been close by, because as soon as the word "Amen" left Tyson and Anisha's lips, she was standing at the door of the family room with tears in her eyes. Anisha was grateful God had sent her an angel on earth in the form of Sister Davenport. She'd shown her how to release the bitterness she'd harbored toward Tyson before it paralyzed her life.

Tyson stood up and held out his hand to help Anisha. She heard the Holy Spirit speak within her.

Trust Me.

She put her hand in Tyson's. *God, what other option do I have?* she thought.

*A*ngel's Haven was everything Sherri had pictured it would be. Cobblestone paths circled their way down through wooded areas leading to small lakes with piers jutting out into the water's edges. Cabanas sat in the middle of expansive green fields that were decorated only by nature's hands with daffodils, orchids, and other colorful flowers.

With a yogurt cup, apple, and bottled water in hand, Sherri walked to the middle of the pier and spread out a blanket. Four months in pregnancy had inflated her stomach to the size of a small cantaloupe, and she had grown accustomed to watching the growing bulge spread.

The slight fog drifted over the water like baby clouds taking their first cautious steps. Sherri stared at the rippling water. Even at seven thirty in the morning, the sky was a brilliant blue and hinted at the coming of a pleasant day. Sherri soaked in the feeling she was experiencing of God's presence and could sense Him smiling down on her.

Sherri had committed herself to the entire healing process and had left work early on Thursday to prepare for the weekend. Fortunately, she was between terms at school and didn't have to worry about any sewing assignments.

The itinerary waiting for her on the bed when she arrived the night before had scheduled times for solitude and quiet reflection during the day, but Sherri had set her clock to greet Friday morning at sunrise. She needed time alone before their first group setting at eight thirty in the Cherubim Lodge.

Sherri knew they were expected to disclose the details leading to their circumstances as part of the healing process. Sharing her secret with Anisha was hard enough, and she wasn't sure how she would react with sharing it with a group of strangers.

"God, give me strength," Sherri whispered.

Sherri was glad she'd made Anisha ride with her to the retreat center in the Georgia mountains. Their descent to a higher altitude was not only a physical act but a spiritual one as well. Before Anisha left to check in at the Waverly Bed and Breakfast, she'd left her friend with a basket of sealed notes of encouragement to be opened each morning during her prayer time.

Sherri ran her finger along the flap of the envelope and eased out the delicate note card.

Today is the first day of the rest of your life. God has promised that He would never leave or forsake you. Read Matthew 21:22. I'm proud of you and baby Faith. Tell her Auntie 'Nish says hi. Love ya.

Sherri flipped her Bible pages to the passage and read the words out loud. "'Whatever things you ask in prayer, believing, you will receive it.'"

Sherri eased back on her elbows. "That's Your Word, Lord. You're not a man that You should lie."

Sherri spent the next forty-five minutes in prayer and studying her devotional until it was time to start her trek back up the path to the Cherubim Lounge. On the way, she marveled at the size of the evergreens and great oak trees. A squirrel scurried across the path in front of her, busy transporting a pile of acorns. The beauty of nature brought a Scripture to Sherri's mind:

Blessed is the man who does not walk in the counsel of the wicked or stand in the way of sinners or sit in the seat of mockers. But his delight is in the law of the LORD, and on his law he mediates day and night. He is like a tree planted by streams of water, which yields its fruit in season and whose leaf does not wither. Whatever he does prospers.

Sherri stooped down to pick up an acorn and stuffed it in her pocket.

⁂

Sherri expected to walk into a room set up with a circle of hard, gray folding chairs in the middle. Instead the Cherubim Lounge was decorated with a cluster of chaises, love seats, and small sofas set up close enough to have intimate conversations.

Three other ladies were already in the room, making a futile attempt to engage in casual conversation. Sherri chose a love seat along the outer section of the group of chairs. "Hi," she said, without making prolonged eye contact. No one seemed ready to address the reason for their visit until the counselor spurred them into conversation.

Sherri pulled out the journal the counselor had asked the participants to bring. She'd chosen her special prayer journal that she'd bought with Anisha last year. So many of her answered prayers were already penned across the pages, and she wanted to add her prayers and thoughts from the weekend to the number.

Eileen, the program director, floated into the room. Eileen had called Sherri and had a minicounseling session with her when she was deciding if she wanted to attend the retreat weekend. When Sherri had arrived last night, she'd immediately recognized Eileen by her voice. It was soothing, like an aloe vera balm on sun-scorched skin.

"Welcome to Angel's Haven, ladies." She nodded her head toward the only man in the room. "And gentleman. Whether you realize it or not, you've already begun your healing journey just by showing up. For some, it may have taken twenty years, eight years, or two months to make the first step. But no matter how long, you've done it now."

Sherri's eyes scanned the room and tried to size up the rest of the ladies and one man. Everyday people on the street, at her job, in church, wherever she visited, could be carrying a secret. No one was exempt from painful experiences.

Eileen sat on a yellow ottoman in the middle of the cluster of chairs. "This weekend will give you the opportunity as mothers to accept the maternal bond you felt or feel with your child, even if you were a mother for only a few weeks. For women who've had abortions, this is your time to freely enter the grieving process and dedicate your baby back to God. Angel's Haven is not here to tell you how to grieve. Tears are not new to us. Groaning and wailing, even silence, is not foreign to our ears. We're here to help you allow God to transform and liberate your life."

Amen to that, Sherri thought.

"At the end of the weekend, we'll have a special dedication service, giving our lives and bodies back to God," Eileen said.

Eileen moved to a chaise where she could see the whole group at one time. She tucked her legs under her and looked around the circle at her participants.

"Our first session this morning is going to deal with the paralyzing nature of secrets," she said. "Secrets are sometimes a way for us to erase our past. To somehow move on and forget a time of shame, pain, or fear."

Eileen adjusted a pillow behind her back. Her demeanor was unthreatening, Sherri noticed.

"Have you ever thought about the things that can grow in the dark?" Eileen asked. "Mold, fungus. Fear. Loneliness. Isolation."

Sherri nodded and noticed the other women were agreeing, too, as Eileen continued.

"Secrets imprison the mind and restrict our abilities to be truly transparent and vulnerable with other people for fear of being found out. I've lived in a cell before, until God's loving kindness liberated me.

"God's Word tells us we should think on things that are true, honest, just, and pure. But sometimes it can be hard to do those things when your mind is imprisoned."

This woman is really hitting on some stuff, Sherri thought.

"Your mind is a battlefield, and Satan is your worst adversary. But today we're going to start unleashing the warfare on his behind, because we already know the Enemy is defeated."

Sherri wanted to wave her hand and shout a resounding "Amen," but everyone else seemed so reserved. She silently agreed and hoped that by the end of the weekend, everyone would allow the Lord to minister to their spirits as God saw fit.

"So I'd like to share with you a secret I harbored for seven years until the Lord delivered me in 1996."

Sherri listened awestruck while Eileen shared her story of pain and renewal. She'd gotten pregnant at sixteen, then started wearing baggy clothes when her body first began to show the signs of motherhood. She was too frightened to tell her mother, for fear she would disown her. As a mother's instinct would have it, she soon noticed her daughter's changing body and one evening after dinner followed Eileen to her bedroom and forced her to strip down naked. She walked out of the room without saying a word but the next morning informed her she wouldn't be going to school. Instead, she made her dress and took her to an abortion clinic.

"I didn't even know what was going on until we talked to the doctor," Eileen said. "My mother sat in the room with me while they aborted my baby. We never talked about it, and we never told my father. I went on with my life and shut the door to the memory. I went to college, met the man of my life, and got married right after graduation."

"All was fine, or at least I thought, until Jake and I started trying to have kids. It opened the door to that memory, and the devil tried to convince me I'd wrecked my only chance at having children. One day when I was walking our dog through my subdivision on garbage day, I started hearing babies crying from the garbage can. I had to keep telling myself to just make it home and I would be all right. It was all I could do to make it home without having a mental breakdown in my neighbors' yards.

"My husband and I sought help from a counselor at our church, who walked us through the grieving process. During that time, I gave my baby a name. Angel. It became my life's calling to help other hurting men and women who'd been wounded by situations surrounding birth.

Abortion, miscarriage, adoption, abandonment," Eileen explained. "Things of that nature."

The tears around the room had started to pour. Sobs grew heavier as women began to relive their own experiences. Eileen's story of redemption was inspiring and gave Sherri even more hope that her peace would be fully restored.

"One of the hardest things you'll do during this retreat is share your story. But confession is where true healing begins. There's no format to this sharing period, no order for disclosure. When you're ready, begin. If we have to sit here all night until everyone's had their chance, we'll do it."

"I'll go first," a woman with sad eyes said abruptly. She looked to be in her late forties and had a permanent frown etched across her brow. "My name is Gladys." She looked down at her hands and began to pick at her peeling cuticles. "I have no self-esteem or self-worth. For the past twelve years I haven't been able to look people in the eye for fear they might see my secret. I live my life through my children to the point that they're complaining I'm smothering them. I see now that I've been trying to make up lost time with Timothy. That's what his name would've been."

Minute by minute, shackles from years of bondage began to fall off.

"I would have recurring nightmares that he was lost and I couldn't find him," said a Chinese woman who looked to Sherri to be in her early thirties. Her name was Sue.

"When I stretched my hands out to hold him, he'd disappear," Sue said. "At the time, my husband and I were pregnant with *our* first child, but he didn't know I was actually pregnant with *my* second."

The small group of women grew more eager to share their stories. They felt the years of weight fall from their shoulders.

Sherri listened intently to the story of Joyce, who shared that she was a high-powered attorney from Washington, D.C. Sherri could imagine her in a tailored navy blue or black business suit. But today she was wearing a plain, light pink jogging pants set. Instead of the two-inch pumps Sherri imagined she wore on a daily basis, her feet breathed a sigh of relief at the opportunity to enjoy the air in a pair of flip-flops.

"I haven't talked about my stillborn child for twenty-three years. I had left the corporate world to go back to school to get my law degree when I got pregnant. I wasn't ready to have a baby. I never told anyone at first, not even the baby's father. It so happened that I decided to keep the baby because I had grown so attached to it. Then one day I ran across this street and felt this strange feeling, but I couldn't explain it. To make a long story short, when I was eight months pregnant I went to my doctor to have some tests done. The doctor came into the exam room after the ultrasound and told me that the fetus had expired. Suffice it to say, my world was turned upside down, and I thought I would lose my mind. After that, the crying I'd hear in the rooms got so bad that at one point I ended up selling my house."

The women's stories astounded Sherri.

Janet had had three abortions, she said, using them as her own form of birth control. Though she'd said she was only thirty-two, her face wore years beyond her true age.

Barbara's face was dispirited. "I never accepted the two children I had as mine because they were products of incest, so I gave them up for adoption. Depression has been my constant companion for the last sixteen years. "

Shirley was a doctor who had counseled many women who had lost a baby before, but wound up being in the same position after her miscarriage. Around the time when her child would've had a birthday, she'd go into periods of depression. "A weight of intense grief consumes my body. In September she would have been eight.

"My experience has made me more compassionate for my patients. You never know what emotional problems have helped cause their physical infirmities. It's possible you know," Shirley said, looking around at the group. "Worry can cause disease in your body."

Diana stood with her husband, who seemed to be uncomfortable as the only man in the circle. "I'm here because I gave my baby up for adoption due to an abusive boyfriend. He said he would leave me if I didn't give the baby away, because he thought it was someone else's and at the time I would do anything to keep him. Needless to say, years later he left anyway. After I was healed from the pain of the relationship, God blessed me with a wonderful husband in Michael." She grabbed his hand and looked into his gray eyes.

Sherri could tell he wanted to help. To somehow ease his wife's pain.

"We've been trying to have a child for over two years and haven't been able to have one," Diana said. "I feel like God is punishing me."

Sherri wanted the weight off too. When she started to speak, she felt as if she should stand up like they did at AA meetings.

"Despite all I know about God and what He expects of me, I still got pregnant out of wedlock. It went against everything I was raised to believe. The child's father has cut all communication with me. At first I tried to convince myself that I was okay with it, since he's not the kind of father I'd want my child to have, but it still hurts. Every day."

Sherri bit her lip but knew she couldn't stop the swell of tears.

"I'm four months now." She managed a smile and rubbed her tummy. "My baby's name is Faith, because that's what I'm standing on."

Tonya was so petite that the chair she was sitting in nearly swallowed her body. All eyes fell on her because she was the only person left.

"A lot of you all have mentioned you believe God can forgive you and so forth. I don't know about God. I know this is a Christian facility, but I'm not even a Christian. I've never been raised around people who attended church or anything. I'm here because I need help, and when I read about the program, I felt this was a place where I could get in touch with my feelings without being judged. I'm very bitter toward men, and I know that I can't continue to live my life consumed with bitterness. I gave my daughter to my mother, and she'll be raised to think I'm her aunt."

Sherri was blown away at the stories the group shared. Somehow the cross chosen for her to bear seemed a little lighter. She prayed that by the time everyone left, they would allow God to heal and restore them.

At the end of the disclosure session, Eileen had them pull out their journals and write about how they were feeling at that exact moment. She shared how washing their minds with God's Word was critical to their healing. She first led them through select Scriptures about forgiveness and then left the floor open for more discussion until it was time to break for lunch.

"Even after leaving this retreat, your feelings may fluctuate," Eileen said. "You may not feel like you're forgiven, but forgiveness is not a feeling. It's a conscious act of your will. That's why it's important to meditate on God's Word. Your feelings may change, but God's Word doesn't. Now if you would please write down 1 John 3:19–20; Psalm 34:18; Psalm 103:8–12; and Hebrews 4:15–16 to study during your times of solitude."

Sherri was disappointed that for the last time she was walking out to what had become her favorite pier over the past three days. She knew God could meet her anywhere, but it was like this spot had become her secret place. She flipped to the last page of her prayer journal and penned the words marking the end of her old life and the beginning of her new one.

After she left the pier, Sherri took one last stroll to the side of Seraphim Lake where the baby dedication and memorial service was held earlier. Anisha had attended the ceremony with her as she made a special tribute and honored her unborn child, Faith.

Sherri saw Anisha's car pull up and waved her over to the drive-around loading area.

Anisha hopped out of the car. "You ready to live life?" Anisha asked, grabbing Sherri's suitcase and loading it into the trunk.

Sherri smiled from ear to ear. "I've already started," she said, then noticed the bouquet of flowers in the back behind the passenger's seat. "Are those for me?"

"You wish. They were waiting in my room on Friday," Anisha said, slamming the trunk closed and sliding into the driver's seat. "Tyson."

Sherri's eyes popped open. "Ol' boy is on bended knee, ain't he?"

Anisha pulled her shades over her eyes and started down the unpaved trail to the main road. "How hard do you think I should make him work for it?"

"Work? Girl, please. Your nose is wide open."

Anisha's face was aglow. She was receiving so much revelation during her consecration period. She and Tyson were still able to spend time together a couple of times a week, but it never took precedence over her time with God. The quality of their time was more important than the quantity of it, and God was still growing and strengthening their relationship more than she'd expected. She'd learned to go with the flow and rest in God's plan. It was all in God's plan and timing.

Anisha had stood by Tyson while he endured Brandy's short-term stalking episodes. Brandy's unannounced appearances at the Center and endless phone call attempts had finally subsided after two months when she finally realized Tyson's mind wasn't going to change.

Sherri flipped through Anisha's CD case and prepared for the three-hour drive back to the city.

"Considering he's got competition with Bryce in your face every time you go into his office, Tyson is going to have to stay on his toes."

"Bryce is fine and all, but his head is not in the right place," Anisha said. "Talk about unequally yoked."

Sherri threw her hands in the air. "Leave him alone! Leave him alone! Listen to somebody who knows. I'll put my vote in for Tyson anyday if it'll keep you out of Bryce's claws."

"Bryce doesn't have a chance. Tyson is the man. My man," Anisha said, raising her hand like she was taking an oath. "I'd like to propose a new dating commandment, please."

"The floor is open," Sherri pronounced with an air of authority. "Please proceed."

"I propose we adopt a new commandment: 'Thou shalt never ever enter a relationship unless God is at the head, the middle, and at the end of it.'"

"All those in favor say 'Aye,'" Sherri said, then answered her own command. "The ayes have it, and the commandment will take effect immediately."

*T*he entire building of Mount Zion could fit inside the sanctuary of Grace Worship. The choir was outfitted in modest robes that had seen better days, and the lone organist and amateur drummer provided the only musical accompaniment for the choir.

It didn't matter to Brandy. She'd awakened earlier than usual for a Sunday morning—around seven—and couldn't convince her body to take more sleep than it already had. It was the first time she'd slept through the night in over a month, and she wanted to catch all the z's she could before they eluded her again.

Now, as she followed the white-gloved usher to the third pew from the front, she wondered what had compelled her to visit the church she passed every day on the way to work. The small brick church with the tilted white steeple looked misplaced on a city street corner. It would've fared better on a carpet of green grass at the end of a long gravel driveway in the country.

Nevertheless, she was glad she'd made the effort to dress herself and Ayana in coordinating outfits. Everyone knew they were visitors. It wasn't hard considering the oversized white and red VISITOR name badge the usher had given her.

The man who Brandy guessed was the pastor gave her a cordial smile as she settled in the pew. She noticed the small, circular patch of gray hair on one side of his head and concluded it was a birthmark and not necessarily a sign of old age.

When the pastor called all the children around the altar during devotion time to share with them a story about the Good Samaritan, Ayana wasn't her usual shy self. She eagerly joined the group of girls with puffy-sleeved dresses and hyperactive boys who'd already earned warning stares from their mothers.

Although Ayana spent the majority of the time tugging at a loose string on her lace socks instead of listening to the pastor, she'd cry out in unison with the other squeaky voices whenever the pastor gave them a Scripture to repeat.

Brandy was glad she'd decided to follow her inner voice. There were no distractions for her. She wasn't worried about scanning the congregation for a glimpse of Tyson, or any other man for that matter. Along with Minister Calvin Wright, the young guest minister the pastor had introduced, most of the people in the church were her own age. There were a few elderly mothers of the church and old men who looked to have two steps left before crossing the chilly Jordan.

Minister Wright turned out to be a powerful minister. He delivered God's Word with authority and conviction. "You see, church," he bellowed, "I've got confidence. I might not be as easy on the eyes as some of these other ministers in the city, but I know what God has called me to do." He ran a white handkerchief across his forehead, then yelled into the mike. "I know that what God has for me, is for me."

Brandy clapped her hands in suit with the rest of the congregation because it seemed the right thing to do at the time, not because she could wholeheartedly agree. She'd thought Chris was for her. She'd thought Tyson was for her. But evidently, they weren't. When she thought about it, she didn't have the slightest clue what was for her.

She'd heard Mrs. Jamison, Tyson, and some of her other clients talk about having a "personal relationship" with Jesus. She hadn't done so well in the "personal relationship" department so far.

The organist keyed up a hymn at the closing of Minister Wright's sermon.

"There may be someone who doesn't know Jesus. You've never confessed Him as your personal Savior. He's waiting for you. Won't you come?"

Brandy's heartbeats intensified when she looked at the empty altar.

"It doesn't matter who's watching. They don't know what you've been through," Minister Wright said. "There will be lots of people watching you march to heaven or hell, so you might as well get used to it."

The choir director led the congregation in a unified rendition of "Come to Jesus," and the tears began to roll from Brandy's eyes. She was only three pews away from the altar. *It's not a long walk,* she told herself.

"If you have the faith to take that first step, the rest of the way won't be so hard," Minister Wright urged. "Will there be one?"

Her inner voice coaxed her to go. Brandy took Ayana's hand and stepped out of the pew and into the aisle. Today, she would be the one.

Epilogue
Months Later

$\mathcal{A}$nisha ran the duster along the windowsill one last time for good measure, although not a speck of dust could be found in any of the rooms. The guests for her housewarming would be arriving at any minute, and Anisha's tendency to be a perfectionist was wrecking her nerves and Sherri's.

"Anisha, can you please sit down?" Sherri walked into the living room from where she'd been making last-minute preparations in the kitchen. "There's nothing left for you to do except get ready to enjoy yourself."

"Okay, okay, I'm sitting," Anisha said, but instead she walked over to adjust the twinkling white lights on the Christmas tree. "Maybe I shouldn't have had a housewarming so close to Christmas. People have too much to do."

"Give me a break," Sherri said, untying the apron around her waist and rearranging the candles on the fireplace mantle. "They got off easy. This way they don't have to worry about buying you a Christmas *and* a housewarming gift."

"Only you would look at it that way," Anisha said.

"Besides," Sherri said, walking around to light the cinnamon-scented candles dispersed around the room. "It's good to do something different every now and then."

Anisha finally plopped down on the couch. "What's my mother doing?"

"She's upstairs in the guest room getting Faith ready."

"You mean upstairs in *your* room?" Anisha clapped her hands. "It's going to be so good having you here. It'll be like living with a sister."

Sherri came and sat down beside Anisha. "I can't thank you enough for letting me and Faith move in, Anisha. I promise we won't be here long. It'll be a big help for us, since I'll only have to work part-time. This way I'll finish my classes in no time."

"God blesses all of us so we can be a blessing to others. Just throw me a few tailored suits every now and then, and I'll be straight." Anisha looked around her new home. She was amazed at how God was blessing her. It was as if He'd poured out double for her trouble.

"Girl, we have been through so much over the last year," she said to Sherri.

"I know," Sherri said, "but look how it's changed us. For the better, I might add."

Anisha nodded her head. "I'd prayed for a deeper relationship with God, but I didn't know this was how I was going to get it. I depend on Him like never before. Girl, we could've gone crazy from everything that was happening."

"I was right on the edge of crazy," Sherri said. "Xavier brought out the worst in me."

"Good thing he went MIA or there's no telling what you would've done to the brotha. Tyson didn't even know where he disappeared to."

"God's Word pulled me through," Sherri said. "We kept meditating on it over and over. It's like God spoke to us directly through the Scripture, and I personally found out there's no problem His Word can't solve. He renewed our minds so we'd think like Him."

"Whew, girl. We can't even try to think the same," Anisha said. "If you only knew some of the thoughts that used to run through my head."

"I can only imagine. I know how busy my imagination was too," Sherri said. "And I could pull a sermon out for everybody else, but when it came to my own mess, I couldn't even stand on what I was preaching. My motto for the new year is 'Teach what you've been tested on, or be tested on what you teach.'"

The doorbell rang, and Sherri jumped up before Anisha could make a move. "Sit down; I'll get it." Sherri looked out the window before opening the door.

"Well, we should've known Mr. Randall would be the first to arrive."

Anisha walked over to the door. "I'll get that," she said, trying to contain her excitement. When she opened the door, Tyson was standing on the porch with a bouquet of roses in a crystal vase.

"For the lady of the house," he said, walking in and setting the roses on the kitchen counter. He turned and hugged Anisha. "There are eight roses in the vase. One for each month since you graciously let me back into your life. Eight is the number for new beginnings."

Anisha wrapped her arms around his neck. If she could live her life attached to that very spot, she would.

Sherri cleared her throat. "Ummm . . . this looks like a private moment. Can y'all save the lovey-dovey stuff for later or pick it up tomorrow?"

Tyson didn't break into a smile or come back with a joke like he'd usually do after one of Sherri's remarks.

From the kitchen, Tyson looked into the den and motioned for Nikki and Travis. Just as Anisha's younger sister and brother entered the kitchen, Mrs. Blake appeared cradling Sherri's newborn daughter, Faith.

"I had it all planned out to wait till after dinner, but when I saw your face, I realized I couldn't wait another minute." Tyson reached in his pocket and knelt down on one knee.

The small black box was enough for Anisha to know that her king had arrived.

"If you would do me the honor of becoming Mrs. Randall, I promise your life will be the closest thing to heaven on earth," Tyson said, sliding the pear-shaped diamond ring on her shaking finger.

"Yes, I will, Tyson. Yes, I will," she said, screaming at the top of her lungs.

Anisha held up her hand to reveal the rock sitting on her finger. Tyson swooped Anisha up and walked her under the mistletoe hanging over the entrance to the den.

"This is God's will, Mama," Anisha declared. "God's will."

Discussion Questions

Chapter 1

Tyson's visit to Anisha's house lasted until two o'clock in the morning. Although their time together was innocent, could it have given off the wrong impression? Why? Read 1 Thessalonians 5:22. Do you think it's better for acquaintances getting to know each other to meet in groups? Why?

Anisha was supposed to spend some intimate time with God when she returned from work but ended up getting engulfed in a movie and later accepting a visit from Tyson. Has time with God ever taken a backseat in your life when something or someone else changed your plans? Read Matthew 6:33.

Chapter 2

Was it Sherri's place to hold Anisha accountable for Tyson's late-night visit? Do you have friends that hold you accountable? Do you keep information from them that you know is questionable, or are you always open and honest?

At Sherri's apartment, Anisha was approached by a man whom she obviously didn't have much interest in. What do you do in these situations? Are your actions always representative of being a child of God?

Chapter 3

Anisha seemed to feel a bit insecure when she noticed the lady that approached Tyson in the restaurant when they were leaving. Do you deal with any feelings of insecurity? What things cause you to feel insecure, whether in relationships, on your job, about your body, etc.? Read Psalm 139:14.

Chapter 5

Do you give 110 percent at your place of employment, or do you do just enough to get by? Has God called you to be in leadership, and you've settled for less? Read Deuteronomy 28:13.

Chapter 7

After a successful presentation at work, Anisha felt refreshed and renewed about her skills and abilities. Have you ever experienced that? We are all accountable for the gifts that God has given us—whether it be singing, organization, leadership, financial management, etc. How are you using your gifts? Read Romans 12:3–8; 2 Timothy 1:6–7.

Chapter 10

Anisha was beginning to break more of her Sunday lunch "dates" with Sherri so she could spend more time with Tyson. Have you ever experienced being the one put on the back burner when a friend was involved in a relationship? How did it make you feel? Was Sherri being selfish by wanting to keep her relationship with Anisha the same? If so, what are some ways Sherri showed her selfishness, or what others may consider jealousy?

Read Romans 9:21. How has that Scripture been applied to your life? In what ways have you felt the pressure of God's hand in molding you? Was it always a pleasant experience? Be transparent enough to share. Read Romans 8:28.

Chapter 11

Anisha noticed how God spoke through Sister Davenport to remind her not to take her gifts and talents for granted. Does God use people as "messengers" of His Word and instruction? Are these people just limited to ministers?

What are your feelings about Tamara and Veronica? Of the two, which had the most influence over the other? What are your feelings about manipulative relationships?

Like other people, Tamara was hesitant to go to church until she "got herself together." Believers sometimes feel the same way when they have fallen into sin or unfortunate situations. Read Hebrews 10:24–25.

Chapter 13

Sherri was initially hesitant about giving Calvin the time of day because she made her first assessment about him based on his looks. Have you ever disregarded someone because they weren't your "type"? Read 1 Samuel 16:7.

Chapter 17

Sherri's natural talent had been right in front of her eyes for years. Do you have a natural talent that you've overlooked? Ask your friends what they consider your strengths to be.

Chapter 18

At first Sherri clearly realized that she would be "unequally yoked" with Xavier. Why do you think she ignored her instinct? Have you ever done the same? How would you counsel/advise a friend who is in that situation? Read Proverbs 13:20; 2 Corinthians 6:14.

Chapter 21

While spending the Christmas holiday in North Carolina, Anisha began to feel a strong tugging/urging from God to choose between following her own will or God's will. Why would God take away something in your life that you think is good? Is every good thing a God thing? Consider Romans 8:28. Also read Ecclesiastes 3:1–8; Jeremiah 29:11.

Chapter 23

Even though Anisha was obedient in taking some time away from Tyson so she could commune with God, she still lost her job. Have there been times when you felt as if you were obedient but were still being "punished"? Read the parable of the talents in Matthew 25:14–30.

How would you have handled being laid off without notice? Are your finances prepared for unpredictable situations? In what ways can you be a better steward of your finances? Of your time?

Chapter 24

Sherri felt she had dishonored her body after sleeping with Xavier. What does the Bible say in regard to fornication? Read 1 Corinthians 6:13, 18–20. If you are single, you should be living a celibate life. In what ways can you avoid the temptation to fall into fornication?

Chapter 25

Based on his actions and some of his comments, do you think Tyson was being selfish when it came to Anisha's taking time out to spend with God? Why do you think he felt that way?

Chapter 30

Sherri and Anisha had begun to memorize Scriptures that would help them through their situations. Take the time to find Scriptures in the Bible that will help you through situations. Read Psalm 1:1–3; 2 Timothy 2:15.

Even though they were best friends, Sherri didn't confide in Anisha about her situation with Xavier. Why do you think she chose to keep it to herself? Read Ephesians 5:11–16.

Xavier was not willing to step up to his responsibilities as the father of Sherri's child. What does the Bible say about a man who doesn't take care of his children? Read 1 Timothy 5:8. What kinds of responsibilities do parents have in raising children? Read Ephesians 6:4; Titus 2:4; Proverbs 13:24; 17:6; 23:24; and 29:17.

Chapters 32–34

Anisha's life seemed to crumble right before her eyes with Tyson ending their relationship and then the tragic death of her grandmother. Have the rains of tragedy and disappointment ever poured in your life? During trying times, hide Scriptures such as 2 Corinthians 12:9; Philippians 4:6–8; and Proverbs 18:10 in your heart.

Chapter 36

Sister Davenport was able to minister to Anisha about the power of forgiveness. Are you holding a grudge against anyone? Read what God says about forgiveness in Matthew 6:14; 18:21–35; and Mark 11:25.

Chapter 38

Sherri was confronted about her pregnancy by Veronica, the roommate she had criticized about her actions with men. How do you think it made Sherri feel? Read 1 Corinthians 10:12.

Anisha

Anisha constantly made promises to God that she would stay on track and complete some things He had given her to do. Instead, her relationship with Tyson and her desire to help him with his mentoring program often took precedence over God's voice. Have you ever experienced that? Are you ready to commit uninterrupted time with God? In what ways can a person draw closer in a more intimate relationship with Him?

Tyson

Even though Tyson was truly in love with Anisha, he found himself manipulated by a woman from the past. Is it possible to be in love but still fall into temptation? To pray against temptation, arm yourself with Scriptures like 1 Corinthians 10:13; Romans 12:9; 13:13–14; and Psalm 101:3.

Brandy

In what ways did Brandy try to manipulate Tyson into being with her? How could her relationship with Chris have played a role in how she dealt with men?

Sherri

Sherri reached a point when she settled for Mr. Right Now instead of Mr. Right. What "red flags" did she overlook?

If ever there was such a thing as a perfect marriage, Bryan and Nicole Walker had it. Even without the child they desire after five years of marriage, their love for one another is solid. But then, without warning, the very thing they wanted threatens to tear them apart. A marriage that was once unshakeable is put to the ultimate test.

A Love So Strong
by Kendra Norman-Bellamy
ISBN: 0-8024-6834-9
EAN/ISBN-13: 978-0-8024-6834-5

After seven years of marriage, John and Valerie have drifted apart. As God begins to heal Valerie's heart, her husband is taken in a direction she doesn't expect.

The Allure
by Jackie Scott-King
ISBN: 0-8024-1562-8
EAN/ISBN-13: 978-0-8024-1562-2

The Negro National Anthem

Lift every voice and sing
Till earth and heaven ring,
Ring with the harmonies of Liberty;
Let our rejoicing rise
High as the listening skies,
Let it resound loud as the rolling sea.
Sing a song full of the faith that the dark past has taught us,
Sing a song full of the hope that the present has brought us,
Facing the rising sun of our new day begun
Let us march on till victory is won.

LIFT EVERY VOICE

So begins the Black National Anthem, written by James Weldon Johnson in 1900. Lift Every Voice is the name of the joint imprint of The Institute for Black Family Development and Moody Publishers. Our vision is to advance the cause of Christ through publishing African-American Christians who educate, edify, and disciple Christians in the church community through quality books written for African Americans.

Since 1988, the Institute for Black Family Development, a 501(c)(3) nonprofit Christian organization, has been providing training and technical assistance for churches and Christian organizations. The Institute for Black Family Development's goal is to become a premier trainer in leadership development, management, and strategic planning for pastors, ministers, volunteers, executives, and key staff members of churches and Christian organizations. To learn more about The Institute for Black Family Development, write us at:

15151 Faust
Detroit, Michigan 48223

Since 1894, *Moody Publishers* has been dedicated to equip and motivate people to advance the cause of Christ by publishing evangelical Christian literature and other media for all ages, around the world. Because we are a ministry of the Moody Bible Institute of Chicago, a portion of the proceeds from the sale of this book go to train the next generation of Christian leaders. If we may serve you in any way in your spiritual journey toward understanding Christ and the Christian life, please contact us at:

820 N. LaSalle Blvd.
Chicago, Illinois 60610
www.moodypublishers.com

A HEART OF DEVOTION TEAM

ACQUIRING EDITOR
Cynthia Ballenger

BACK COVER COPY
Elizabeth Cody Newenhuyse

COPY EDITOR
Tanya Harper

COVER DESIGN
Lydell Jackson, JaXon Communications

COVER PHOTO
Getty Images

INTERIOR DESIGN
Ragont Design

PRINTING AND BINDING
Bethany Press International

The typeface for the text of this book is
AGaramond